Above the Fray

A Novel of
The Union Balloon·Corps

---

by Kris Jackson

Part Two

for Mom and Dad

Part Two:
Descent

Chapter Nine: Heroes, Whores and Bums

"Why do their eyes stay open?"

"Because they're dead."

"But all the pictures I've seen of dead folk, their eyes were closed."

"That's just the artist's fancy. When a man's dead his eyes stay sort of half open, half closed. Like that fellow."

"Sure enough?"

"Sure. Ain't you never shot a deer?"

"Nope. Birds but no deer."

"Well, birds do shut their eyes when they die. Not deer, though. If'n you shoots a deer and his eyes are closed, he's alive. Every time. I lost a deer one time, thought he was dead and up he pops and jumps away. His eyes was closed and then they open."

Nathaniel's eyes opened. It was pitch dark. Not even a sentry fire flickered on the side of the tent. He could tell he would not sleep again before morning.

He could see the face of Silas Parker before him as he lay in the fallen corn. His neck was at an unnatural angle, lending no support to his head. He was not breathing and his eyes were closed.

The scene was burned onto his brain like a photograph on a plate of glass. He could see Parker's face and the eyes were surely closed.

But they were open. They fixed upon Nathaniel and he gave a cry. Parker gave a cry although he made not a sound, and he sprang to his feet. Nathaniel could not move a muscle in his body, nor did he deserve to, so he stood still as Parker –

He sat bolt upright in his cot, shouting. It was cold enough this day to see his breath and it was morning.

Beside him Solomon Vogler and the Allen brothers stirred, then rose.

Ezra Allen bent over his shoe. "The crow of the God-damned cock," he said.

"You do it too, Ez. At least I waited until morning."

"I suspect we all do it. I hope we can stop when this…" Vapor trailed silently from his lips as he did up the laces.

The morning was clear and quite cold. They huddled around a smoky fire of pine knots and twigs. Breakfast consisted of nigger peas (now called chickpeas), goober peas (alias peanuts) and a slimy strip of fat that purported to be bacon.

James Allen poured everyone a cup of coffee. He said, "Solly, I thought you never ate pork."

"I never did until lately."

"Isn't it forbidden by the Mosaic Law?"

"Yes. I no longer believe in that law but I still observe the stricture on pork. Until lately, at any rate."

"Hunger changed your mind?"

"Yes. And I've done far worse things to men than have ever been done to this hog."

Ezra spoke up: "Aren't you afraid of going to Hell?"

"Not very," he replied. "I've lived there for a year now."

It was an old joke, older in fact than any of them knew.

The Union Army was again operating in Virginia though there had been little fighting of late. The Balloon Corps ascended from time to time and made reports that were for the most part ignored.

General Ambrose Burnside, who had made a great name for himself at Antietam by crossing a bridge, was now Commander in Chief of the Army of the Potomac. He was presently feeling his way toward Richmond. The Army had pushed forward again, had come to a halt outside of Fredericksburg and was reconnoitering.

As part of this effort, Burnside met with the Balloon Corps in his tent. After expressing gratitude for the Corps' efforts and appreciation of its accomplishments the general concluded with, "I can but confide, Professor Lowe, that during the coming attack you and your men will again acquit yourselves with honor."

"Might I ask, sir, what the plan of attack will be?" Lowe asked.

"Well, I don't see how that would be a problem, Professor." Burnside glanced around at his officers to see if there was any dissent. A few of the men looked discomfited or cleared their throats, but Burnside hurried on. "No, it won't do any harm to tell you. I intend to cross the Rappahannock in force, advance to Marye's Heights and Prospect Hill and capture them. The whole enterprise waits only on the construction of pontoon bridges across the river."

This last exchange surprised Nathaniel for several reasons. There was no need for the aeronauts to know this so they should not have been told. Moreover, while Thaddeus Lowe was by this time a well-known figure within the military command structure, the other aeronauts were not, and he, Nathaniel, was likely still an object of suspicion. Yet Burnside hesitated but a second in telling them all his strategy for the coming battle.

The battle plan itself seemed simple to the point of folly. The enemy was dug in on the heights above the city and controlled the surrounding hillside with artillery and muskets. The town itself overlooked the river he intended to cross with his pontoon bridges, and it could only be anticipated that sharpshooters filled the buildings facing upon the water.

Burnside would certainly find crossing that river a harder task than crossing the bridge at Antietam that would forever bear his name, but he approached the task with relish. Nathaniel thought him a fool. As they left the general's tent he felt like throwing up.

As the Army settled into the area around Fredericksburg the Balloon Corps made more flights. Like his comrades, Nathaniel carried officers aloft when he made his observations. Sometimes the results were not happy. One man, a lieutenant who seemed barely older than Nathaniel himself, sat in the bottom of the car and refused to stir. When they reached altitude, Nathaniel scanned the city, made a brief report by telegraph, and then turned to his passenger.

"Won't you get up, Lieutenant Custer?"

"Is this thing safe?" the man answered. He sounded perfectly miserable. Nathaniel tried to reassure him by jumping up and down in the car but the officer protested so loudly that he stopped.

"It's perfectly safe, sir."

"Oh, God. Why did I ever do this?"

"What sort of work do you do, sir?"

"What?"

"What's your job in the Army?"

"Oh. I'm a cavalryman."

"So you run around the battlefield on a horse?"

"Yes. And I wish I was there right now."

"This is a lot safer, sir, and a whole lot prettier. You should have a look."

Custer slowly pulled himself up and peered over the side of the basket. "Oh, you're right, this is quite lovely," he said at last. He stood up and gripped the shoulder-ring. "Look, there's the city. Why, I swear you can see all the way to Richmond."

"If it was clear enough, you could, sir. I think I saw the lights of the city the other night."

"And look at the land. It's like a velvety green blanket tossed on a bed. The farms all look so … you should bring a poet up here. Or an artist."

"Yes, sir."

"How does it look through that telescope?"

"Have a look, sir."

"That's all right. I would have to let go with one hand and I'd probably drop it over the side anyway."

"Are you starting to like this, sir?"

"No, and I never shall. But I'm starting to tolerate it."

Custer was as good as his word. He made a number of flights and became a skilled aerial observer but he never liked flying.

Nathaniel awoke with a cry. Beside him Solomon Vogler awoke. They stared at each other for a moment, then Nathaniel asked, "What time is it, Solly?"

Vogler pulled out his watch. "Quarter of seven. We may as well get up."

As they dressed, Vogler asked, "What was it this time?"

"It was him. His funeral."

Vogler nodded.

Wendell Smith had been given a Christian burial. This hardly seemed proper, but as Vogler pointed out, there was no such thing as an atheistic burial, adding, "He would have liked it this way, I think."

"You really think so?"

"Yes. It would have confirmed his views as to the folly of human nature."

Vogler himself wore a strange little cap for the occasion. It was round and black and covered only the back of his head. When the chaplain saw it he looked angry but said nothing.

The funeral service gave Nathaniel no comfort; every word, in fact, seared. If the Devil Himself had delivered the eulogy, uttering words of bitter sarcasm and mockery, He could not have done better than the solemn and earnest old chaplain.

Jesus said, Whosoever believeth in Me, though he were
dead, yet shall he live.

Nathaniel had been to funerals before this. Though sad occasions, they at least provided the comforting hope that the deceased was going to his reward. But Wendell Smith was either burning in the flames of Hell or was himself a flame that had been blown out. And who could say which was worse?

O Death, where is thy sting? O Grave, where is thy victory?

The best that Nathaniel could hope for was that Smith was indeed in Hell, as Vogler would be in his turn. This dreadful fate for his two best friends was his only path to Paradise.

O Lord, I believe, I believe. Forgive me my unbelief.

"Can I help you?"

The aeronauts, seated at breakfast, looked up to see whom Lowe was addressing. To their surprise it was the hooker known as Red Sally. Lowe had greeted her with stiff courtesy, that due a woman but nothing more. The rest of the Corps didn't bother to rise.

"Yes, Professor. I have business with one of your men."

"Which one?" Lowe said, but Nathaniel had already risen. "May we use your tent, sir?" he asked. Lowe, with equal parts disdain and curiosity, gave his consent with a gesture.

Nathaniel sat behind the table. Sally drew the tent flaps closed and took the seat opposite him. She was dressed in a blue crinoline. It was not as conservative in appearance as the clothing the nurses and *vivendieres* wore, although it was in no sense lurid. She carried a small bag and a parasol.

"How do you do, ma'am?"

"Quite well, thank you."

"Excuse me, but I don't know what to call you."

She smiled. "You don't want your ball-bag banged again, you mean?"

"Not hardly," he mumbled.

"When we're over here, Sally will do fine. I have a favor to ask of you." She took an envelope from her bag. "Perhaps you can help us to understand this letter. It was taken from a Confederate spy. We suspect that it contains a message but we've been unable to decipher it."

Nathaniel took the envelope and removed the letter. It was a single sheet of paper, filled on both sides with what seemed to be a woman's script. He read the letter through but it seemed utterly banal, merely a letter from a woman to her female cousin. It discussed the crops on the family farm and the weather of the year just finished.

"Why do you think I might be able to figure it out?"

She shrugged. "You're a clever lad. And you bring fresh eyes to the problem."

"This smells like it's been scorched."

"Yes, it was heated. Sometimes that brings out hidden messages."

"Not this time, though."

"No."

"Well, I can't make anything out of it." He rose, went to the door of the tent and held the letter in the narrow beam of sunlight coming through the flap. "What's this?"

"What?"

"There are lines or scratches on the paper. Like someone was writing with a pen with no ink."

"Yes, we had seen those. They don't seem to mean anything, though. They don't make letters."

Nathaniel held the page at an angle to the sun. "No they don't. Wait a minute, I do see something."

"You do?"

Nathaniel returned to the table and picked up a pencil. He held this at a shallow angle to the paper and lightly brushed it on the surface.

"Hey! What are you doing?"

"I thought so. Look at this."

He gave her the paper. The pencil had darkened the paper, leaving the scratches light. Red Sally scrutinized the result. "What am I supposed to see?"

"You see how there's a group of four small scratches, then a small one and a larger one? Then there are three small ones and a large one, then a little one by itself."

"Well, yes, I suppose so. What does that mean?"

"It's the word 'have' in Morse."

"Really? It just looks like random scratches to me. What is 'Morse'?"

"It's the telegraphic code. Why don't you let me see what else I can get out of this?"

"Well, very well. No, just try the first few lines. If you're wrong it would ruin the note for us."

Nathaniel rubbed the pencil on the top two inches of the paper. He carefully inspected the result, then took a message blank and wrote *JEREMIAH WILL LEAVE TOMORROW AS PART OF*. Sally gasped when she saw this, then gathered up both the letter and Nathaniel's transcript. "We'll carry on from here," she said.

Nathaniel stood as she rose and held the tent flap for her. "So was this a help?"

"Yes, it was."

"What's this about?"

She paused in the doorway. "You're new to all this. If you were a proper spy you'd wish to know nothing but what you needed to know. Curiosity to no good end will kill you."

"Oh. All right."

"I'll tell you this much, though: today you've saved the life of one man and cost another man his."

"Really?"

She turned to him and he let the flap fall. "You ought to consider joining us when your present situation ends."

"Who says it's going to end? I plan to stay with the Balloon Corps until the end of the war."

She shook her head. "The decision has already been made. You'll be looking for a job soon enough, unless you really have a hankering to tote a musket. Consider being a spy. You come around Hooker's headquarters and we'll take you under our wing."

"Sorry, that's not for me."

"You have what it takes."

"No, I don't. I hate that business. Look a man in the eye, call him your friend and then shoot him. Spend every day expecting the people around you to turn on you and kill you. It's not for me."

She searched his face for a moment, then turned away.

"The man who's going to die – do I know him?"

She turned back. "Are you thinking of someone in particular, Nathaniel?"

"Yeah."

Sally looked wistful. "No, it's not him," she said softly, "though I wouldn't miss him."

"I think he killed David Miller."

She nodded, closing her eyes. "It was either him or you."

It wasn't an accusation, just a statement of fact, and he couldn't begrudge her. Nathaniel realized that she was in love with Miller and felt a fool for not seeing it sooner.

"He might not be dead. He might have been captured."

She shook her head. "He could get out of any prison camp. I think he could get out of anything but the grave."

He raised the flap again. "Give my regards to the man who's going to live," he said.

She put the papers in her bag and stepped out into the sunlight. She looked over her shoulder at him. The sun behind her made her hair glow and he thought suddenly of Amanda. But while Amanda's hair with the sun coming through it was gold, Sally's looked like fire. "You are that man," she said softly.

As she left the camp all eyes were on him, not her. He sat down at the table and resumed his breakfast.

How could she think that he had killed Miller? He remembered the way Miller had killed that soldier. He was far too deadly a fellow for him to take on.

On the other hand he, too, had learned a lot about killing in the last few years.

What sense did it make that she was in love with Miller? She was a fellow spy, yes, but she was a prostitute, a woman who had sold her body to countless men. What man would marry such a person?

How could a woman live such a debased existence and then fall in love with a man? Compared to this, even the notion of him killing Miller seemed plausible.

He sighed as he reached for a piece of bread to soak up the bacon fat. The only thing that was good in all of this was that his comrades would not ask him what was going on.

Later that day a lieutenant came to the camp with written orders from Burnside. Lowe assembled the Balloon Corps for the officer to address them. He required that they stand at attention while he paced before them.

"I'm Lieutenant Comstock," he said. "I have been assigned the task of supervising this organization and assessing its utility. As such I am to have access to all of the Corps' records and accounts. I believe that no accounting of the activities of this unit has been conducted to date."

"We shall be happy to comply," Lowe said.

Comstock stopped in mid-stride as if discomfited that Lowe had addressed him. "I shall go aloft at the next opportunity to conduct my own assessment of the utility of your enterprise," he went on. "I don't mind telling you, however, that I requested this assignment. I have suspected from the outset that your little balloons were a humbug and a waste of Union resources."

Lowe made a sound as if he were swallowing air.

"Nonetheless, I consider myself a fair man. A proper regard will be given to the accomplishments of this organization, if I determine that such accomplishments exist."

Less than an hour later Comstock made his first balloon ascent. Lowe brought him up to look at the Confederate defenses on the heights across the river. Nathaniel Curry and Solomon Vogler supervised their ascent, then waited for them to signal they wished to descend.

From the heights above Fredericksburg they heard light artillery open up.

"Hear that, Solly?"

"Yes, it sounds like our friends across the way don't have the same opinion of our little balloons as Lieutenant Comstock."

"They're pretty far away."

"I don't think they have much hope of hitting their target. More's the pity."

"I know. I wish they'd strike us and get this whole thing over with."

Shells started to land on the broad swath of green between the heights and the river, splashing the black soil around like rocks in a pond.

"That'll make it a bit harder to get across there when the pontoon bridges are finished," Nathaniel said.

"It will give the boys a bit of cover from the defenders, though."

"Yes, but they won't be wanting cover. They'll just want to keep moving."

"Can you imagine how the professor must feel along about now?"

"I know, after pouring heart and soul into this for the better part of two years."

Vogler turned to him, his eyes dark and sleepy behind their spectacles. "Maybe this Comstock will be convinced by what he sees up there."

"I doubt it. He sounds like a man whose mind is already made up."

"I suppose you're right." From above came the signal flag for descent.

Comstock spent the rest of the day holed up in Lowe's tent, going over the accounting books. The aeronauts knew that when the virtues of Thaddeus Lowe were enumerated, care in the accounting of finances would not be amongst them. Comstock left without a word as evening approached.

As darkness fell a common soldier arrived with a message: representatives of the Corps were requested to visit one Captain Thomas in the headquarters of General Joseph Hooker. Lowe, feeling ill at ease, asked James Allen to represent him. Allen in turn asked Nathaniel Curry to accompany him.

Hooker's army was as always a scene of debauchery. Private soldiers and their sergeants mixed freely, the social strata lubricated by various distilled substances. Women of negotiable virtue plied their wares among them. The presence of two fresh faces in civilian garb drew their attention, but this waned as the aeronauts protested their abject poverty.

The general's headquarters was a compound of tents within the camp. The revelry only increased in pitch within this compound. There seemed to be no chain of command, no organization whatsoever.

Allen spotted a soldier sitting by himself on a broken chair beside an open latrine. He had about three days' growth of beard that was liberally stained with tobacco juice. His close-cropped hair was tousled and unkempt.

Despite the cool evening he wore no shirt. The man was so intoxicated that he could scarcely keep from falling into the latrine, yet he manfully continued to pull at the bottle in his hand.

"My good man," Allen began, but he was interrupted.

"I ain't your good man." The soldier leaned dangerously over and spat in the pit. Nathaniel noticed, to his surprise, that the man's trousers had the red piping of an officer.

"Can you direct me to Captain Thomas?"

"Who?"

"Captain Thomas."

"Captain who Thomas?"

"I don't know."

The drunk endeavored to look Allen in the eye, succeeding upon the third attempt. "Who the Hell are you?"

"I'm Mr. Allen of the Balloon Corps. If you would be so good as to --"

"*Kelly!*" The aeronauts stepped back, repelled by the sharpness of his shout and the reek of his breath.

"Yeah?" came the reply from within a nearby tent.

"We got a Captain Thomas around here?"

"No…Wait a minute. Isn't that one of them whore spies?"

The drunk squinted at them. "You boys looking for a whore?" He pronounced it "ho-ah."

"No," Allen replied, but Nathaniel interrupted him: "If one of those whores goes by the name of Captain Thomas, we want to talk to her."

"Kelly, get your ass out here!"

"All right, all right." There was a prolonged rustling from within the tent, interspersed with the soft protestations of a female voice. Then there was a crash like a tree falling. At last Kelly appeared, naked but for an American flag around his waist. "See that tent? The one that's all lit up?"

"Yes?"

"Okay. The wench you want is in there, or like as not they'll know where she is."

"Kelly," the drunk said, "get that woman the Hell out of my tent. I need to sleep tonight."

Kelly turned back to the tent. "General, this isn't your God-damned tent."

Allen and Nathaniel proceeded to the indicated tent. Allen seemed convinced that they were on a fool's errand. "There is no female Captain Thomas in the United States Army," he declared. "If there was one, she surely would not be a prostitute. Those men were making sport with us." Nonetheless he leaned over the door of the tent and said, "Hello?"

"Yes, who's there?" came the reply in a female voice.

"Allen and Curry of the Balloon Corps."

"Oh, good. Please come in."

Nathaniel expected to be greeted by Red Sally. A different woman, however, appeared at the entrance of the tent. She had black hair and dark eyes. She wore a high-buttoned black dress that made her look like a parson's wife. Her manner was quite refined. Both men removed their caps.

"We were looking for a Captain Thomas."

"It was I that summoned you. Thank you for coming."

"Forgive me, madam, but how shall I address you?"

"You may as well call me Captain Thomas for now. Do sit on that cot. Don't mind the blanket, but please hand me those papers."

"Thank you."

She sat on a campstool opposite them. "Mister Allen. Is it James or Ezra?"

"James, ma'am. You've heard of me?"

"You were the first man to fly for the Army. And Nathaniel, I know well your exploits."

"I've done little but stay alive, ma'am."

"Well, even that is an accomplishment, especially these days. We've seen our ranks thin considerably around here lately."

"If this is about David Miller," he said evenly, "I think you'd best look closer to home."

She considered this, then said, "Well! On to business. You have a balloon charged and at the ready, do you not?"

"Well, yes," Allen replied.

"Can you make an ascent in two hours?"

"What, in the middle of the night?"

"Yes."

"Excuse me, but to what purpose?"

"In brief, we need to view a signal from an agent who is in enemy territory. This signal will be in the form of a rocket. We had hoped to have opportunity to observe this from the heights on the other side of the river, but such is not our lot. We think, however, that it could be seen from this side if one were in a balloon."

"I see."

"Does the balloon have a full charge?"

"It received one two days ago. It could make five hundred feet."

"With two people?"

"Then three hundred."

"Three hundred should do it. What about a ground crew?"

Allen smiled. "You know a lot about aviation."

She returned a brief smile. "We can provide hands as needed."

Nathaniel was quite taken with the sound of her voice. It had a cultured and intelligent quality like that of a schoolteacher. In fact, he imagined that the teachers at Amanda Swanson's fancy school must sound very much like "Captain Thomas."

Two hours later Nathaniel found himself helping the lady into the car of the *Constitution*. James Allen supervised a ground crew of six Negroes that had appeared like magic at the lady's summons. They used no lights and spoke in low voices. Unlike the Negroes he was accustomed to, these men sprang eagerly to their task, working quickly and efficiently. Nathaniel wished that the soldiers who served as his ground crews were this good. As was his custom, Allen used a single guy line between the balloon and the ground. Nathaniel was going up as he was lighter.

Mrs. Thomas addressed one of the Negroes: "I'll drop stones when I see the rocket. One stone will mean it was red and two will mean green. You set off the answering signal. Then fly back and tell Major Christian red or green. The rest of you then haul us back down."

"All right," the man said. "One if by red and two if by green." He smiled at his own jest. He spoke with a cultivated Northern accent; if Nathaniel had not seen his face he would have thought him a white man.

Without another word they flew into the chill night air. Nathaniel doubted that the woman had ever flown before but she seemed quite unperturbed by the experience. She held the shoulder ring calmly and didn't even remark when the balloon reached altitude and fetched up against the drag line.

They looked out into the night. The moon was waning and provided little light to the scene. Before them curled the Rappahannock; beyond that the city of Fredericksburg awaited its fate. To the left of the city was the long low hill of Marye's Heights upon which was situated most of the Army of Northern Virginia. Beside that was Prospect Hill which held most of the remainder.

There was an assortment of buildings in view: factories, churches, residences large and small. Every one was dark. Nathaniel found this an eerie sight: an entire city with no one in it.

But he realized that this was not true. Although the civilian population had been evacuated, the city was surely full of soldiers lying in wait. He wondered if anyone saw the dark balloon in the dark sky.

From far beyond the city a thin green line flew into the night. Captain Thomas threw one, then a second stone out of the basket. It was so quiet that he heard them strike the ground.

From below there came a sudden *whoosh*, then a yellow rocket flew past them. Because it had been launched from directly beneath them Nathaniel did not see it until it flew past. The loud hiss and the brilliant sparks of the missile startled and quite frightened him. "God damn it! Excuse me, ma'am," he said as he reeled back in the car. She hardly seemed to notice.

Fifteen minutes later they were on the ground. As he helped Captain Thomas from the car, he said, "Any chance of us hearing what this was about?"

"None whatsoever," she replied. Her black dress and her black companions vanished in the murk.

If his dreams were bad, at least they evaporated as soon as he woke up. Far worse than his nightmares were the thoughts that came into his head as he lay awake at night.

Once more he was riding through that cornfield. He imagined himself pointing his gun at Parker and ordering him to fire his gun into the air. Then he would make him hand over those orders, then he would shoot Parker's horse. By the time Parker had reloaded he would have been way out of range.

Why had he not done such a thing? It all seemed so obvious now. Parker, while a fool, hadn't deserved to die.

The answer came unbidden into his mind. If he had done this, Parker would have denounced him as a Yankee spy as soon as he got back home.

And what was wrong with that? Nathaniel had learned his lesson, the oldest bit of wisdom among soldiers since before the invention of the wooden club: never volunteer for anything. Never again would he go amongst the Rebs.

The nagging thought remained in his mind: wouldn't he? Maybe he was a pretty good spy after all. He kept going over there and making it back alive. This time he even did a right smart job of it.

All right, maybe he did all right as a spy. But he didn't like it.

Didn't he? It was fun to get away with things.

But it wasn't fun to kill people.

From some dark corner of his mind the wicked thought came: Wasn't it?

He threw himself over in his cot and jammed the pillow over his head. He tried to think of something else. He tried to think of Amanda.

Whatever advantages Burnside had at Fredericksburg did not include the element of surprise. It took nearly a month for his army to assemble and the pontoon bridges to arrive.

When the five bridges arrived they were laid across the river under the guns of the enemy. Nathaniel watched this from the shore. It was one of the most heroic actions he had ever witnessed. The engineers labored mightily to set the bridges up, stolidly ignoring the rifle fire from the city and the high ground beyond it. If a man fell, his fellows closed ranks and kept working.

A row of trees stood on the northern shore of the Rappahannock and Nathaniel used one of these for cover. He was actually in view of the enemy but must not have presented a worthwhile target. He watched from behind the tree for an hour without drawing a shot.

"How do you like the show?"

Red Sally had come up behind him and he started at her voice. He turned around sheepishly. "Pretty good. Them boys are having a tough time."

"No tougher than the Army'll have tomorrow, I think."

"I'm afraid you're right."

Sally was seized with a fit of coughing. It was a wet, rattling cough, and at the end of it she turned and spat on the ground.

"We could use a Southern boy this evening," she said.

"Yeah? For what?"

"A little excursion south of the city."

He shook his head. "I done told you already, I'm not cut out for that kind of work. I don't like it and I'll not do it."

"What makes you better – how can you think that –"

Nathaniel turned his back and she left.

By chance, he saw Sally again that evening. He had run a message to Burnside's headquarters and was leaving when he saw two women, their arms linked, speaking to an officer. One of the women was in full mourning, in a black dress with a black veil that covered nearly her entire body. Her companion was in half-mourning, wearing somber gray clothing and a dark bonnet with a deep brim. They were a queer sight in the camp and Nathaniel could not help but stare. The woman in half-mourning turned and caught his eye and he recognized her as Sally. He realized then that they were in disguise and were about to leave for enemy territory. He turned away, suddenly ashamed.

The next day the Army of the Potomac crossed the river and formed up on the farther shore. They, too, received a warm welcome, but they dug in and settled down as well as they could.

The Balloon Corps swung into action. The Confederate gun emplacements were located over a mile away, far enough that they had little hope of hitting the aeronauts, but that didn't stop them from trying. More than once a flier heard the hum of a shell passing near his car, followed by a report far in the rear.

That evening the Balloon Corps took an early supper and an early bed. They were awake and aloft well before daylight. They made ascents throughout the day, usually bringing officers with them. They stayed low enough that they were able to make reports by voice.

As dawn broke the advance began. The various corps emerged from their dugouts and formed up. With colors flying and music playing they began the long march to the two enemy strongholds, Prospect Hill and Marye's Heights.

Nathaniel was up and watching as the first advance began. Beside him in the car was a Major Penrose. Neither attempted to communicate with the ground, transfixed as they were by the spectacle.

Despite the martial grandeur it seemed to Nathaniel that the legions hesitated before they set out. Well might they hesitate at the task before them: they had to cross a lot of very muddy ground toward an entrenched foe and it was uphill all the way. No sooner had they set out than men started falling. Their fellows stepped around them and carried on.

"They'll never make it," he murmured, unmindful of the man beside him.

"They'll be fine," the officer replied. "The only thing that victory depends upon is courage and strict adherence to duty."

No, that's wrong, and you're a fool, Nathaniel thought but did not say.

The color bearer of the leading company fell, spilling the company colors onto the ground. A soldier broke out of formation, pulled the flag from the dead man's grasp and held it high. Nathaniel trained his glass on the scene but could not find the man. Maybe he was looking in the wrong place, or maybe the new color bearer had already fallen.

Men on the right side of the lead regiment began to fall. Nathaniel found this interesting, as they were principally receiving fire from ahead of them. He scanned the left side of the town and saw puffs of smoke coming from some of the windows.

He leaned over the side. "Hey!"

A soldier on the ground looked up. "Yeah?"

"They're getting enfilading fire from the town."

"They are?"

The soldier, a lad younger than himself, stood looking stupidly up at him. "Don't you think you ought to report that?" Nathaniel asked.

"I guess so. What are they getting, again?"

"Enfilading fire. Men in the town are firing into their flanks."

"Okay."

"Go and report that!"

"Oh. All right." The soldier walked away. He looked like he had no idea where he was going or what he had to say. Nathaniel shook his head and returned to his observations.

The boy was a fool. The man beside him was a fool. The general who had ordered this line of attack was a fool.

And what of the soldiers themselves? Were they not fools as well for giving up their lives in this folly?

As the troops approached the summits of the two hills the fire became more intense and much more accurate. The men melted into the ground like spring snow. At last the remnants, with no hope of overcoming their foe, turned back for the river.

More men took up the task of their fallen comrades, marching up that long hill in the face of enemy fire. They, too, were blasted by the entrenched Confederates, only turning back when there were too few men to carry on.

Unit after unit suffered this fate. Nathaniel, who felt he had become inured to the horrors of war, found that he was wrong. This ghastly slaughter appalled him.

What made it even worse was that it was so predictable. Would the Union never find a competent commander?

Another assault was under way. The tactic at this point seemed to be to send so many men up the hill at one time that the enemy would not have time to reload and kill all of them. As stupid as this approach sounded, it actually seemed to be working.

Nathaniel was watching through his glasses. "I don't believe it," he said. "They've broken through."

"What?" Penrose asked. "Where?"

He pointed, then continued to watch. "And it's Jackson. They broke through Stonewall Jackson's line!"

"Who did it? Who?" Penrose raised his field glasses but could not find the indicated area.

"Just a minute…I've seen that standard before. Yes, that's Meade."

"That's *General* Meade, you mean."

"Very well, General Meade, then."

The officer looked at him sternly. "And you may address me as 'sir,' young man."

"Yes, sir. Look, Stonewall is counterattacking, he's driving—"

"And he's not 'Stonewall' to you, he's General Jackson."

"I have to respect the enemy, too, sir?"

"Listen to me, soldier! I will brook no insubordination, particularly in the field."

"Major, sir, I'm not a soldier."

"You're not?"

"No, sir, the Balloon Corps is a civilian agency."

"So! And what is your excuse for not enlisting?"

"Sir, I'm doing my part."

"What, by floating around in a balloon?"

"Yes. Sir."

"You're accomplishing nothing at all by doing this, do you hear me?" The man was shouting in his face from mere inches away. "And you're demeaning these noble dead by comparing your actions to their honorable service."

Nathaniel, his blood boiling, resisted answering. He feared that if he spoke he would not be able to control his tongue. Instead, his ears burning, he trained his glass on Jackson's army. Jackson's counterattack had by this time closed his own line and sent Meade's corps back down the hill.

The major wasn't finished with him. "Do you think yourself so far above the fray that you can bob around up here while better men die beneath you?"

Nathaniel wheeled on him and shouted, "Well, what good would it do to die like those men?" He gestured at the battlefield. "This attack is an act of lunacy. All they're accomplishing is they're using up some of Lee's ammunition."

"That's more than you're accomplishing," Penrose answered quietly. "And it is only by such sacrifice as these men are making that the Union will prevail. What is your name?"

"Nathaniel Curry, *sir*."

"And who is your commander?"

"It's Professor Thaddeus Lowe."

"I need the name of someone in the military structure."

"We serve at the pleasure of the commander in chief," Nathaniel replied, "so that would be Burnside. General Ambrose Burnside. And the Balloon Corps was established by President Abraham Lincoln, so you could talk to him as well."

"Does your organization have a liaison to the commander in chief?"

"Yes, sir," Nathaniel answered, his heart sinking. "It's Lieutenant Comstock."

"Well, I'll be sure to speak to him."

"Yes, sir."

From below came a muffled explosion; it sounded like a large stone being thrown into mud. An instant later there came a chorus of men's voices, all crying the identical word: "Shi-i-i-it!" Nathaniel and Penrose looked down but neither could understand what had just happened.

A man straggled into view. His front side was covered in brown from head to foot. Nathaniel called down, "Hey! What happened to you?"

The man wiped his face and looked up. The flesh around his eyes and his mouth was now the only part of him that was its natural color; the effect made him look like Jim Crow in a minstrel show. "What?"

"What's going on down there? What just happened?"

"A shell landed in a latrine!" the man shouted. "I got covered. Everyone got covered!"

"Oh!"

"I got covered in shit!"

"I can see that!"

"That shell was meant for you, God damn you!"

Nathaniel choked back a laugh, then said, "I know that. Sorry!"

"Sorry? I'm sorry too! I'm sorry the God-damned shell didn't hit you!"

Nathaniel stole a glance at Penrose and for an instant he saw him smile. Then he was all business again.

Both men turned their attention back to the battlefield. A new assault on Marye's Heights was beginning. As the fresh troops moved up the hill, dying men on the ground clutched at them, begging for help. The advancing troops shook them off and kept going.

Nathaniel looked more closely. He had been wrong: the men on the ground were not asking the advancing men for help. They were begging them to turn back, to break off the hopeless assault. But no one would do it.

The Balloon Corps stood down at sunset. Nathaniel sat at the camp's table, too sick at heart to eat or even to talk with his fellows.

Only once did he speak. The Allen brothers were discussing the casualties when James asked, "What about officers? Did anyone of note die today?"

"Yes," Ezra replied. "I heard that General Jackson and General Bayard were both killed."

Nathaniel stirred from his funk. "Jackson?" he asked. "Did Stonewall Jackson get killed today?"

"No," came the reply. "Feger Jackson. He was our Jackson. He was Union."

"Oh."

Nathaniel returned to his dour reveries. He found it odd that he had been saddened by the thought of an enemy general dying. Jackson was a particularly dangerous figure to him; if ever the man laid eyes on him again, he would likely recall him as the bearer of the orders that had ended up in McClellan's hand. Yet he had to admit that he respected and even liked this singular character.

His mind began to play tricks on him again. His vision and hearing were both distorted. His hands looked like they were a hundred feet away. He looked down on his hands and the table they rested upon as if he was still in the car of the balloon, looking at a man far below him. The voices of the men around him came to him as if from another world:

"Did you hear what Hooker had to say today?"

"No, what?"

"'Having lost as many men as was required in the fulfillment of my orders, I am withdrawing.'"

"That's rich. And it's perfectly apt. They should put him in charge. Fighting Joe."

Nathaniel tore his gaze away from his hands and looked around the camp. He shook his head until his vision cleared.

The voices of the men around him were still distant and unreal:

"They couldn't put Hooker in charge."

"No?"

"No."

"Too dissipated?"

"It's not that. There are plenty of profligate officers. But he's insubordinate. That's a quality that can be overlooked in a common soldier but not in a commander."

"Oh."

"Besides, he testified against Winfield Scott at a court of inquiry."

"So what's wrong with that?"

"He told the truth."

"The truth? Really?"

"I'm afraid so."

"Well, we can never have that."

The words echoed in his mind: *we can never have that, we can never have that*...The echoes piled atop each other and he had an attack of vertigo though his feet were on the ground.

What did all of this mean? Was he losing his mind? But if so, why should he lose it in such a singular manner? Didn't crazy people usually think they were Jesus or Napoleon or something?

Out of the gloom strode a tall dark figure in a stovepipe hat. Nathaniel looked up at him, confused. For a moment he thought it was Lincoln, but it was not. Then he thought it was John Wise, but it was not. The man was gaunt and had a grim face like these two men but his chin was clean-shaven and he had white side-whiskers.

"Is this the camp of the Balloon Corps?" he asked in a high, quavering voice.

"Yes, it is," said Ezra Allen.

"Who is Nathaniel Curry?"

"I am, sir."

The man reached into his waistcoat and took out a folded piece of paper. He stepped forward and tapped Nathaniel on the arm with it, saying, "I serve you, sir." The others reacted with surprise, although they seemed to understand what had just happened. Nathaniel, however, had no idea.

Nathaniel was afraid, more afraid than he had ever been in his life. He found himself wishing that he were off on some battlefield somewhere instead of seated in this straight-backed chair.

He was sitting in a finely-appointed room hung with gold-framed paintings depicting great battles on land and sea. He was freshly scrubbed and wore new clothes. Around him officers in full-dress uniform read newspapers or chatted in small groups. None seemed interested in conversation with a seventeen-year-old civilian, so he sat quietly and worried.

From time to time the door at the end of the room opened and a sergeant would appear. The room always fell silent and all eyes would turn to the enlisted man as he came to attention and spoke a name. The man whose name was called would instantly leave with the sergeant.

Nathaniel had arrived at seven o'clock in the morning. At a quarter past one in the afternoon, there having been no midday meal, the sergeant appeared at the door and said, "Nathaniel Curry!"

Nathaniel neither spoke nor rose, but gave such a violent start as to clearly acknowledge his presence. He scrambled to his feet and headed for the door, then turned back. A brigadier general handed him his cap.

The sergeant led him down the hall to a large courtroom. They entered the room through the double doors at the end and walked the length of the room. Nathaniel felt increasingly anxious; there was not a soul in the room whom he recognized.

No: there was one person. As he took his seat in the witness section he saw, seated at the defendant's table, General Fitz-John Porter. He too was in dress uniform and his hair and beard were neatly trimmed.

Nathaniel was surprised that a woman was in the witness section, in fact seated right beside him. She was in full mourning, veil and all.

No sooner was he seated than the bailiff came to attention and said, "Nathaniel Curry!" Nathaniel got up and went to the witness chair. This was a heavy wooden chair on a low dais in the front of the room, surrounded by empty space. The bailiff swore him in, then told him to state his name and be seated.

Everyone in the room, and there seemed to be thousands, was looking at him. From the defendant's table Porter nodded and smiled at him. On Nathaniel's right was a table at which were seated the president of the court and his staff.

Porter's advocate, one Reverdy Johnson, approached. Nathaniel relaxed a bit at this; he had met the man before to discuss the testimony he was about to give. Johnson was in his middle sixties. He was tall, over six feet, and portly. He had a shock of white hair on top, ample jowls and sad-looking eyes.

"Master Curry, do you hold a position within the military structure of the United States?"

"Sir, I am an aeronaut of the Balloon Corps, attached to the United States Army."

"You are yourself a civilian, are you not?"

"Yes, sir."

"Describe to the court, if you will, your whereabouts on the afternoon of Friday, the twenty-ninth of August, 1862."

"Sir, I was at Manassas, Virginia."

"In what capacity?"

"Sir, I was with the army of General Pete Longstreet."

A murmur swept the room; the president of the court suppressed it with a glance.

Johnson said, "Let the record show that the witness is referring to Major General James Longstreet of the Army of Northern Virginia."

"Oh! Yes, sir. But they call him 'Pete.'"

"That is indeed his *nom de guerre*," the lawyer said gently. "Can you describe to the court why you were in the ranks of the enemy?"

"Sir, I had gone on a scouting expedition with a Yankee spy, I mean a Union agent, sir..." Nathaniel gave the advocate a beseeching look as several present quietly laughed. "We met up with General Longstreet's forces, and he took my horse for one of his officers and made me fall into the ranks."

"You were, I take it, in Confederate uniform?"

"Yes, sir, of Lee's army."

"Mr. President, at a future time, the defense will present further evidence that Master Curry here present did indeed take part, as a volunteer, in a scouting expedition, operating under legal orders, and that he did so in the uniform of the enemy. Master Curry, returning now to the afternoon of the twenty-ninth of August last, were you in a position to see the battlefield?"

"Yes, sir."

"And what did you see?"

"Sir, we were in the woods, I think they were on the south side of the battlefield. The armies were about half a mile away. Stonewall Jackson was on our left, behind a railroad embankment. Pope's army was advancing on them, but old Stonewall was pushing them back with musket fire."

"Did you see the army of General Fitz-John Porter?"

"Objection," the Judge-Advocate said. "The witness was too far away to distinguish one army from another."

Johnson turned to the president's table. "I pray the indulgence of the court," he said. He turned back to Nathaniel and asked, "Could you distinguish the different armies at that distance?"

"Yes, sir. I was carrying a pocket telescope."

"And do you have said telescope upon your person today?"

"Yes, sir."

"Let's have a look at it."

Johnson presented the telescope to the bailiff, who in turn gave it to the president. The president peered through it, as did several of his staff. They conferred for a moment, then the president said, "The objection is overruled. Proceed."

"Again, Master Curry, did you see the army of General Porter?"

"Yes, sir, I did."

"And what did this army do?"

"Well, sir, at first they held back on Pope's left, but then they flanked Pope and moved in on Jackson."

"Do you mean to say that the army of General Porter advanced, under fire, upon the position held by General Jackson?"

"Yes, sir. Or they tried, at least."

"What do you mean, they tried?"

"Well sir, Pope was advancing too, so Porter had to swing around him as he went. He started out behind him, behind General Pope that is, and swung around his left side, so his troops really had to keep moving."

"What resistance was Jackson giving to this advance?"

"Well, sir, he gave him musket fire, and when he got a little closer, he gave him cannon shot and canister."

"How well could you see this from your position?"

"Quite well, sir."

"Were there any other Union forces that could see this advance?"

"Objection!" the Judge-Advocate said. "The witness could not know of the position of other Union forces. Or, I should say, of any Union forces, as the witness himself was—"

"Sustained," the president said.

Porter's advocate said, "Continue, if you please. General Porter's army advanced upon Jackson. Did he complete this advance?"

"No, sir. We charged him."

"You mean that General Longstreet's army charged the army of General Porter?"

"Yes, sir."

"How did Longstreet charge him?"

"From the side, sir. From straight out of the woods."

"And what was the response of General Porter's troops?"

"They skedaddled, sir. I mean they broke and run, sir."

"But General Porter's army was larger than that of Longstreet. How could a smaller force overcome a larger one that way?"

Nathaniel shrugged. "I reckon we took 'em by surprise."

"Do you mean that General Porter's forces did not see Longstreet's army?"

"I reckon they didn't."

"We're talking about an entire army on a battlefield. Do you suppose they were overlooked?"

"Mister President, I object!" The Judge-Advocate sounded quite offended. "The level of supposition required—"

"I withdraw the question," Johnson said evenly. "Master Curry, how close were you to Porter's army when it turned and began its retreat?"

"I was about a hundred yards away when I could see they were going to break."

The advocate raised his finger and spoke with great precision: "Master Curry, did General Porter's army receive orders to retreat, or did the soldiers do it on their own?"

"*Ob-jection!*" gasped the Judge-Advocate.

Porter's advocate turned to the president's table. "Sir, the witness was uniquely qualified by virtue of his vantage point outside of but yet near to General Porter's army to observe whether any communication was made by the officer corps to the enlisted men at this moment."

The president said, "Is the witness familiar with the methods of communication within General Porter's corps?"

All eyes turned to Nathaniel so he spoke up. "Yes, sir. When the Balloon Corps began to follow Porter's army, we learned their signals to make it easier to communicate with them. They used drums at first but it was too hard to make out over the firing. They mostly use bugles now. And sometimes—"

"The objection is overruled," the president intoned. "The witness will answer the question."

"No, sir. I saw no communication to the men that they should retreat. They just all skipped at once."

"Your witness."

The Judge-Advocate, Colonel Joseph Holt by name, approached the witness chair. Nathaniel had not seen him before and he didn't much like what he saw now. Holt was a heavy-set man in his fifties with blond hair and piercing eyes. He looked like an especially difficult schoolteacher, or perhaps one of those parsons who is always telling people they are going to Hell. He regarded Nathaniel with hostility and suspicion. "How old are you, my boy?"

"Seventeen, sir. Eighteen in two—"

"Let the record show that the witness has not achieved the age of majority. I again note the prosecution's objection to the acceptance of this witness on these grounds. Now, then, Master Curry, where is your home?"

"It's Richmond, Virginia."

"So you are a Southerner, are you not?"

"Yes, sir."

"Why, then, do you profess loyalty to the Union?"

"Objection!" Porter's advocate said.

"On what grounds?" the president asked.

"It is a perfectly natural thing for a person to be loyal to his country."

The president conferred with his staff. "There are after all many Southerners presently serving in the Union army," he said at last. "The objection is sustained."

Nathaniel didn't understand. "Do I still have to answer the question?" he asked.

"Only before God," the Judge-Advocate replied.

"Oh, good."

"Now, then, my boy, tell the court again how you came to be in the service of General Longstreet."

"Sir, I was on a scouting expedition."

"What officer sanctioned this mission?"

"Objection!"

Holt waved his hand. "Tell us, then, if any officer was present when you were assigned to this mission."

"There were at least two," Nathaniel said. "One of them was General Porter."

"The same General Fitz-John Porter who is on trial here today?"

"Yes, sir."

"I will decline to ask him to confirm this. Who was the other one?"

"I don't know his name, sir, but he's a big fellow with one eye."

Holt turned to the president. "Mister President, the officer to whom the witness is referring is in an extremely sensitive position. The Army prays this honorable court that his mention be stricken from this record."

"So ordered." The president peered over his glasses at the recorder as he drew a line through the transcript.

Holt turned back to his witness. "Who was the agent to whom you were assigned?"

"He's a civilian name of David Miller."

"And what became of him?"

"Sir, after Pete, after General Longstreet took my horse, Miller rode back the way we had come."

"But the agent Miller never returned to our forces."

"I know nothing of that, sir."

"Sure you don't. The truth of the matter, though, is that you yourself killed this agent David Miller, is it not?"

"I did nothing of the kind, sir."

"What, then? Did you denounce him to the enemy? The very enemy you in fact serve?"

Nathaniel felt the hairs rise on the back of his neck. It was a most singular sensation: the hair on his neck was literally standing on end and pressing his collar away from his neck. "I serve the Union and only the Union."

"Except when you serve the enemy."

"No, sir."

"Master Curry, this…sojourn with General Longstreet's corps, was this the only occasion on which you served the Confederacy?"

"Yes, sir."

"During your service with the United States Army, did you ever quit your post without proper leave?"

Nathaniel hesitated. Porter and his advocate had told him to tell the truth, even if it seemed to serve the prosecution. "Sir, during the Peninsula Campaign I visited my family in Richmond—"

"Just like that?" Holt asked rapidly. "Did you have leave?"

"No, sir, but I'm a civilian so I—"

"—can cross the enemy lines at will."

"Objection," Johnson said wearily. "The Judge-Advocate is badgering the witness."

Holt coolly regarded his opponent. "This witness is lucky to have not been executed several times already."

"Mister President!"

"Counsel will restrict himself to cross-examination," the president said.

"My apologies, sir. Master Curry, leaving aside the question of David Miller, have you ever denounced a Union agent to the enemy?"

"No, sir. Of course not."

"No further questions at this time, Mister President. We will, however, ask Master Curry to remain in the witness section pending further questions."

Nathaniel returned to his seat. The Judge-Advocate said, "Mister President, the prosecution calls Mrs. Herbert Pettijohn to the stand."

The president peered over his glasses at Holt. "Isn't it still the defense's turn?"

"It is material to the testimony of the last witness."

"Call Mrs. Pettijohn," the president said.

"Mrs. Herbert Pettijohn," the bailiff barked, and the woman in black seated beside Nathaniel rose. Nathaniel rose to let her pass, and as she did he saw, beneath her hat, her red hair.

After the witness was sworn in the Judge-Advocate addressed the court: "Mrs. Pettijohn here present is appearing incognito, as she functions as an agent of the Union." He turned to Nathaniel. "Master Curry, please stand."

Nathaniel felt himself flush bright red but there was nothing he could do to stop it nor to prevent what would now transpire.

"Mrs. Pettijohn, have you ever seen this youth before today?"

"Yes, sir, I have." Her voice was sweet and clear and her accents refined. She was nothing like the raucous being Nathaniel had first encountered in the camp of General Hooker.

"And where did you see him?"

"While serving the cause of the Union in the camp of General Robert E. Lee."

"And what transpired upon that occasion?"

"That young man said, in the presence of a number of Confederate officers and soldiers, that he had seen me in the Union camp, and in particular in the camp of General Joseph Hooker."

A stir went around the room and the president suppressed it.

"Mister President," the Judge-Advocate said, "the prosecution begs this court to strike the testimony of Nathaniel Curry. The prosecution also begs the court to strike the testimony of Mrs. Herbert Pettijohn here present, to preserve her anonymity."

"So ordered, in both instances," the president said. He turned to the recorder. "Cross this out as well, and this over here." He looked up. "The witness is excused, with thanks for her testimony and for her service to her country." He turned to Nathaniel. "I don't know that you are a Confederate agent, young man, but I don't know that you aren't. In any event, that is not the issue before this court. You, too, are excused." He handed Nathaniel's telescope to the bailiff.

Nathaniel stood his ground. He was shaken and felt on the edge of tears. "General Porter is no coward, and he's a good soldier," he said, but the banging of the president's gavel drowned him out.

Nathaniel had found the court-martial a humiliating experience; he found the train journey back to northern Virginia even worse.

Getting to Washington had been easy. He had the summons and he had military orders. The orders required all that beheld them to "speed" him, and speed him they did. It had taken less than a day to complete the journey.

Now, however, he was on his own. First he tried to board a military transport. He found a railroad train in Washington that included cattle cars full of soldiers. He attempted to clamber aboard a car.

"Hey! You a soldier?" a young man demanded.

"No, I'm a civilian attached to the Army," he replied.

"What, a sutler?" another man asked.

"No, I'm with the Balloon Corps."

"The what?"

"The Balloon Corps. Professor Lowe's Balloon Corps."

"Aw, get the Hell away from our train! This is only for soldiers. Not for little boys and their balloons."

It may have just been youthful exuberance combined with *esprit de corps*, or perhaps the soldiers bore real antipathy toward the aeronauts. At any event, every man Jack began to jeer him:

"Give the child his balloon!"

"Go fly away somewhere else!"

"Why do you want to ride with the likes of us?"

"You want a ride? Go on the bum!"

"Why don't you get a gun and really fight? We can teach you how."

In the end, he bought a third-class ticket and boarded a car with no glass in its windows far in the rear of the train. He was the only white person in the car.

Washington to Fredericksburg was only about sixty miles as the crow flies, but he was not flying. The train route went west through Maryland, then south through the portions of Virginia then under Union control.

The second day of his journey found him in Warrington. His route had brought him only a few miles closer in actual distance to his objective. Worst of all, he no longer had enough money for even a third-class ticket. He had eighty cents to his name, he had not eaten since the night before and it was evening. He squandered forty cents on a meal, then went in search of a place to sleep.

He was scouting the alleys of Warrington when a youth of about fifteen accosted him: "You're looking for a place to sleep, then?"

By his speech Nathaniel could tell that he was Irish, though his hair was jet black. Nathaniel smiled in response. "Yeah."

"Sure and there's places aplenty. You're a bummer, are ye?"

"I – don't know what that means."

"Ah, don't you, now? It means you're traveling with no money."

"Yes, that I am. I'm down to my last few pennies."

"Well, lack-a-day, me boy. Let Johnny help you out. There's an alley I know, cozy as your little trundle bed. Come have a look."

Johnny put his arm around Nathaniel's shoulder and led him away before he had time to consider the notion. "Where be you a-going?"

"Fredericksburg."

"Sure and there's a big fight there! Many an Irish lad in it too, I hear."

"Yes, there's an Irish regiment." He stopped. "Is this the alley?"

"Yes, right here it is."

The alley was dark and Nathaniel hesitated to go into it. Then he mastered his fear and stepped in. As his eyes adjusted to the light he could see that there were several barrels lying on their sides. They had blankets and other sorts of cloth in them and apparently were serving as beds.

There were also several other boys in there. Two of them were smaller than he was, as was Johnny, but one stood a head taller than him. This one spoke: "What's this, then, John?"

"Just a lad as needs our help," Johnny said evenly. One of the smaller boys turned and picked something off of the ground.

"Yeah, I don't have any money left," Nathaniel said as cheerily as he could. The taller boy walked right up to him. His cap obscured his eyes but his mouth was set in a grim expression.

"I thought I might—" he began, then leapt at the boy, swinging with both fists for his face. He must have struck his eye, for the youth turned away with a cry of pain. The others hesitated and Nathaniel made use of this moment to turn and flee.

The Irish boys followed close on his heels, jabbering incomprehensibly. Nathaniel dug his few remaining coins from his pocket and threw them over his shoulder. When he looked back a few seconds later he was alone.

He returned to the military train where he had been rejected before. He considered asking the officers if he could ride with them. But the officers might not merely refuse him, they might have him arrested or something. He turned to the rear of the train.

He found a cattle car whose door was ajar. He looked around to see if anyone was watching, then climbed aboard.

He found himself in the company of horses. They were tied by their halters to the sides of the car. Several of them turned to see who had joined them, but they made no objection to his presence. Nathaniel slid the door closed.

He lay down in the space at the center of the car, the only spot not occupied by horses. All around him were horse hindquarters, the most unsanitary and the most dangerous part of a horse. He had little choice in the matter, though. He scratched some hay together and fell asleep.

There presently came the jolt of the train starting. As it picked up speed the wind came through the sides of the car, improving the odor but lowering the temperature. He pulled more hay over himself and went back to sleep. This was, after all, not the worst place he had been.

He was awakened by the door opening and sunlight streaming in. He could scarcely believe it was morning; it felt as if he had only been asleep for a moment. He was so cold that he could hardly move.

Soldiers had entered the car and were unhitching the horses. They laughed at the youth on the floor: "Get up, tramp! It looks like you took the wrong train."

"What? Where – where am I?"

"You're in Falmouth. You're at the front."

"Oh, good. This is my stop, then." He clambered stiffly to his feet and exited.

It took him a few minutes to get his bearings but he soon made his way to the camp of the Balloon Corps. His fellows greeted him warmly. He sat down with the Allen brothers and Solomon Vogler, who gave him breakfast and pumped him for news.

"How did the court martial go?" he was asked.

"Pretty poorly. It looks like General Porter is a goner."

"What, don't you know?"

"Know what?"

"They came back with a verdict. He's guilty. The verdict has to be ratified by Lincoln, but that's just a formality."

Nathaniel examined the scrambled eggs before him.

"Nathaniel, there was after all little you could do to save him."

"Yes, but it's still not fair."

"Well, no, it isn't."

"You know, I think I might have done something to save him but I was stabbed in the back by that hooker, Red Sally."

"Red Sally?"

"Yes. She's a God-damned filthy whore, and she's consumptive, and I'll be glad when she's dead." Everything he had gone through the last ten days was summed up in his feelings for Sally, and he let them pour out. "She had no reason to do what she did on the witness stand, the bitch."

"Why, what did she do?"

Briefly Nathaniel described his testimony before the tribunal and Sally's ensuing testimony.

"Why do you suppose she did that?" Vogler asked.

"Because she has it in for me, that's why, because I won't join up with the spies, and because she thinks I killed a fellow she was sweet on."

"And for that she went all the way to Washington? I doubt that."

Nathaniel hesitated. Sally had indeed gone to a lot of trouble to counter his testimony. Was it in fact spite on her part? Or even revenge for Miller's death?

If she had wanted to do him harm she could have done worse right there in camp. She certainly had the means to kill him, directly or indirectly.

He shook his head. "I don't know. I'll have to think about this. How are things going with you all? What's happened since I was here last?"

"We have a new commander-in-chief," James Allen said.

"We do? Who is it this time?"

"Joseph Hooker."

"Hooker? When did that happen?"

"Just yesterday. He's meeting with the heads of all the services tomorrow. And that includes us."

"Us? Or just the professor? Wait, that would be Lieutenant Comstock, wouldn't it?"

"Comstock's a captain now. And the order was for all of us to report."

"Really? What does Comstock think about that?"

"He didn't like it, that much was evident. But there was nothing he could do about it, so we're all going."

"So! Hooker in charge, hey? What do the men think of that?"

"Well," Allen said, "the ones I've spoken to approve. They say he has brains and he has balls."

"Yes," Nathaniel replied, "but it's a shame he's such a God-damned drunk."

"I know."

The Balloon Corps looked appropriately spruce when it reported to Hooker's tent the next morning. Lowe wore a cutaway and top hat; Comstock was in full dress uniform.

Joseph Hooker, as well, was in full dress, with an ornate saber at his side. Hooker was a handsome, strapping man and he looked this day like he was spoiling for a fight. He was nothing like the inebriated creature Nathaniel and Allen had encountered a few weeks earlier; he looked as sober as a Lutheran minister.

He opened the meeting by stepping forward and reading the order appointing him to command. He then handed the order to an aide and said, "I am of course honored and gratified by this appointment and will fulfill my duties to the utmost of my abilities. The corps that is called to serve me is the finest army on this planet. With the help of Providence we shall carry the fight to the enemy and we shall prevail."

Nathaniel was impressed that Hooker knew that he lived on a planet.

"A due regard for the opinions of the men who serve me impels me to say something more. There have been observations made as to my personal conduct. While these observations have not been entirely correct, I wish to remain above reproach in such matters. Therefore, I shall abstain from the consumption of alcohol until such time as I have compelled the surrender of Robert E. Lee."

Nathaniel looked covertly around the room to see if anyone was reacting to this; no one was. He did, however, see three women who had entered the room after the general had begun to speak. He looked away lest one of them catch his eye. He sat seething with anger during the rest of the general's remarks.

As the meeting broke up he told Vogler, "Y'all go on back without me, I'll be along in a piece."

Vogler nodded. "Be careful," he said. "Don't get carried away."

"I won't." He turned and came face to face with Sally.

She smiled. "Good morning, Nathaniel. Were you looking for me?"

He nodded. Her courteous mien threw him off his tack. "Can we go and talk somewhere?"

"Yes. Please come to my tent."

The tent was the same one where he and Allen had met "Captain Thomas." She held the flap open for him. "Just a minute," she said, then coughed, then spat on the ground outside. She dabbed at her lips with a handkerchief pulled from her sleeve, then closed the flap and turned to him.

He had been turning over in his mind what to say to her but none of it seemed right. "Look," he said at last, "you had no call to say that about me on the witness stand."

"All I did was tell the truth. That's what I was ordered to do."

"Ordered? Whose orders?"

"This conversation is *sub rosa*. Do you understand?"

"What? No, I don't."

"It means that this is just between us. I was ordered to testify against you. I happen to agree that the order was wise."

"Who ordered you?"

"Ask me something else."

"Listen, you know I ain't no Rebel spy."

"I know no such thing. I doubt you're a Rebel spy, but I don't know. For that matter, you don't know that I'm not one, either."

"No, I don't, or...or...somebody else, either."

"Let's not get into that."

"Well, all right, but all you ended up doing was hurt General Porter. He got convicted, no thanks to you."

"Nathaniel, General Porter had to be convicted. The Union shouldn't have lost Manassas, they had the Rebs outnumbered and surrounded. Someone has to take the blame. It can't be Lincoln or the war is lost. And it can't be that Porter's men were cowards or the war is lost. It has to be Porter. He'll lose his command and his career and his good name but the Union Cause shall go unharmed."

He gaped at her. "You mean it was all planned out like that?" He recalled Wendell Smith saying a similar thing but that was just the sort of thing Smith would say. Sally spoke as if all of this was factual.

"Of course it was. The outcome was known before the court martial ever began."

"Such a thing is monstrous! Why, that a good soldier like Porter should be disgraced like that…Mister Lincoln would never go along with it."

"But he shall. He'll certify the conviction, you wait and see."

Nathaniel looked away. He could see she was right, and that was the worst part of it.

"Nathaniel, what I did up there was for your benefit as well."

"My benefit? You call me a traitor or a Rebel spy, or whatever you…?"

"I called you no such thing. But I did cause your testimony to be stricken. Those minutes will become public record once Lincoln certifies the verdict. You wouldn't want your name to come out in this way, boy. There are no famous living spies."

"God damn it, I ain't no spy nohow!"

"I consider this matter closed," she said, and opened the tent flap.

Unlike McClellan, Hooker was eager to take the war to the enemy; unlike Burnside, he would plan carefully before attacking.

The problem now was a simple one: Richmond lay less than a hundred miles from the Army of the Potomac, and Lee stood between that army and its prize. Lee had to be defeated or evaded.

Hooker's first need was to see where the Confederate forces were and what their intentions were.

Balloons took to the skies near Fredericksburg to descry the enemy positions. It appeared that forces remained on Marye's Heights and Prospect Hill, but these were only token forces. The bulk of the Confederate army had withdrawn to the south and west.

Spies were sent out. The Rebels, they reported, were massed north of their capital. Their message to the new Federal commander was clear: it's your move.

As Hooker took command of his army, so did Captain Comstock take a firmer grip upon the Balloon Corps. He issued stern regulations concerning the operations of the Corps and the activities of its members.

The Corps was mustered one morning in February to report on its recent activities. Nathaniel gave a belated report on the ascent he had made with "Captain Thomas."

"No such ascents are to be made in future without my express consent," Comstock said. "Is that clear?"

"Yes, sir."

"What did you do after you saw the rocket go up?"

"Well, sir, the lady dropped two stones to signal the folks on the ground, then they let off a rocket."

"What?" Lowe said. "They let off a rocket below you?"

"Yes, sir. I thought it was going to hit the balloon for a second."

"Well, it certainly sounds like it might have. Even a near miss might have set the hydrogen alight."

"Yes, sir, but it did not."

"In future, there are other sorts of illuminations that might serve better."

Comstock turned to him. "What do you mean, Professor?"

"Why, I have devised flares and rockets that can be safely released from the balloon itself. Additionally, I have signal balloons that can be used to send colored flares aloft. At night they could be seen twenty miles away or farther."

Comstock nodded, then turned back to Nathaniel.

That evening General Hooker paid a visit to the camp. He and an aide simply walked into their midst, taking them at unawares. Comstock called, "Ten-*hut!*" and the men snapped to like genuine soldiers.

"As you were," the general said. "Captain Comstock, I read your report of this afternoon with great interest. Good evening, Professor Lowe, I don't recall meeting you before."

"We did, but briefly, sir," Lowe said, taking the general's hand.

"You have, I understand, devised illuminations and signals that can be used in conjunction with your balloons?"

"Yes, sir, I have."

"Please describe these to me."

"Gladly, sir." Lowe spoke rapidly, knowing this was his one chance to make a good impression upon the general. "For use in the daytime, banners can be suspended beneath balloons with messages on them which could be descried by distant observers with telescopes. These balloons could either be our current manned balloons, attached as they are with static lines to a fixed point on the earth, or free-flying, unmanned balloons. In this manner messages could be conveyed great distances without the use of telegraph or other agencies.

"In a like manner, when sending signals at night, signal illuminations can be affixed to the car of a balloon, either a static device or a free-flying one. The illuminations can be of different colors, as is commonly done with signal rockets.

"Additionally, a hydrogen-oxygen lamp could be affixed to the bottom of a balloon in such a manner that it can rapidly brighten and dim, and by this means signals of the Morse variety could be sent. If this were done at night it would be particularly effective. The signal could be observed and recorded by an observer at a great distance, perhaps as great as twenty or thirty miles, depending upon the atmospheric conditions."

"Well, that's excellent, Professor. Shall we set up a demonstration?"

Lowe looked perplexed. "A demonstration, sir?"

"Yes, I would like to see a demonstration of these signal balloons."

"Sir...no such balloons exist."

"They don't *exist*?"

"No, General, they do not." Lowe was at a loss; he clearly had not expected this. "These signaling methods have been devised by me but never constructed."

Hooker looked aghast. "It was my understanding that you had constructed these devices. You mean to say you have not?"

"No, sir," Lowe said. "However, I can begin construction at once."

"So how long will it be until...?"

"Six weeks, no longer. The materials required can be procured in Washington, or, if not there, Philadelphia."

"Six weeks? I had hoped to use them in the upcoming campaign."

"The cost should not be in excess of six hundred dollars."

Hooker shot a venomous glance at Comstock, wheeled on his heel and departed. Comstock in turn said to Lowe, "Professor, I need to speak with you alone." The rest of the Balloon Corps rose as one and departed.

"Well, that pretty much settles the matter," Ezra Allen said. "James and I will be back in Providence within the week or I'm an oyster."

The next day Captain Comstock called a meeting of the Corps. "When I assumed command of this agency," he said, "I required that Clovis Lowe leave the employment of the Corps immediately. May I learn why this has not occurred?"

"He serves at the pleasure of General Hooker," Thaddeus Lowe replied. "The general has seen fit to continue to pay for his services, which are of value to the Corps."

Comstock considered this before replying. "As I had anticipated, this experiment is a failure. Unfortunately, I do not have the authority to terminate its activities. I can, however, affect the remuneration this group receives. Professor Lowe, your pay is excessive. I require that it be reduced forthwith to six dollars a day."

"That is quite impossible, sir."

"In what sense is it impossible?"

"When I founded this enterprise, the Army wished to pay me thirty dollars in gold a day. I replied that that amount was excessive, and that I desired neither to enrich myself nor to impoverish the Army, but to be of service to my country and to further the science of aeronautics. I requested that I receive but ten dollars a day, which is not an excessive amount for the work that I do."

"It is still not impossible that you be paid six dollars a day."

"But it is, sir. In order to accept that figure, I would have to be paid that amount for the entire tenure of my service to the Union, from the beginning. This would require that I reimburse the Union four dollars a day for every day I have served. I do not have the funds to do so."

"Let me see if I understand you aright…because you cannot reimburse the Union for your earlier salary, you can not accept a lesser amount now?"

"That is correct, sir."

"Your argument is specious, sir."

"I'm sorry, Captain, but it is not."

"It is specious and absurd."

"Captain, I can not accept six dollars a day. It must be ten dollars a day or nothing."

"Then it shall be nothing," Comstock said. "I shall see to it tomorrow."

"As you will."

"Does this mean that you resign?"

"Nothing of the sort, sir. But I am certain that General Hooker or at least General Butterfield will overrule you."

"We shall see."

Ezra Allen was not an oyster. The incident with Hooker, while not to the advantage of the Balloon Corps, did not actually signal its demise. Lowe's pay was reduced to nothing but the rest of the Corps continued to receive its pay as before and they all continued to fly.

Lowe wrote a letter to General Daniel Butterfield, the Army Chief of Staff, describing the circumstances under which he had been compelled to serve without pay. The letter was returned unread, with the notation that it should be submitted through Captain Comstock. Lowe, seething with resentment, submitted the letter through Comstock. Comstock in turn neither forwarded the letter nor replied to it, letting the matter die. Lowe continued to serve without pay.

Then, only a few weeks into his tenure, Joseph Hooker made a decision that made military history. All armies throughout time had gathered intelligence but it was considered a shameful practice. The conduct of war was supposed to consist of grand strategies and brave men contesting in the field, not spies slinking in the shadows, peeping in windows and eavesdropping.

Hooker did not quail at the loathsome practice of violating the privacy of the enemy. He established the Bureau of Military Information with the mission of coordinating and analyzing all the intelligence that streamed into his command. Reports from spies, from contraband Negroes, from balloon observers, all were compared and studied.

The director of the Bureau, one Colonel George H. Sharpe, paid a visit to the Balloon Corps in early March. Captain Comstock, as ordered, mustered his men for the occasion.

Sharpe was a nondescript man in middle age with a drooping mustache and short hair. After placing the Corps at ease Sharpe asked that copies be made of all reports that the aeronauts had made in the last six months and these copies forward to him. In future, he said, all communications to Headquarters must be copied to him.

Comstock rose to object. "The command structure recognizes that the Balloon Corps is a creature of politics and of no real military value," he said. "Such reports would be superfluous."

"I represent the command structure in this instance, Captain," Sharpe replied, "and I shall determine the value of these reports."

"It would be a waste of everyone's time to comply," Comstock said.

Sharpe regarded him coolly. "Is that to be the reply I bring to General Hooker?"

"Of course not, sir!"

"Thank you." Sharpe departed before the Corps could again be called to attention.

Winter turned to spring. In March Nathaniel Curry turned eighteen, an occasion that caused him to reflect upon his life and to take stock of his present circumstances.

He was slightly under average height and lightly built. His hair was light and he wore it short. His beard was thin and very light in color; from a distance he looked clean-shaven even when he was not.

He tended to be shy and reticent with people he did not know, though his unassuming character masked a quick and agile mind. Although nearsighted, he saw a lot and remembered what he saw.

Nathaniel did not look or feel like a fighting man, and indeed in a head-to-head fight he would have been at a disadvantage. He was, however, intelligent and resourceful, as well as resilient and persistent. Perhaps most importantly, he kept his head in trying circumstances.

He was also by this time firmly committed to a Union victory.

One afternoon found Nathaniel taking a young cavalry officer up. Lieutenant Spencer had light hair and a fair complexion and a fine new pair of field glasses around his neck. His uniform proclaimed him a member of Hooker's corps.

Spencer was very interested in the balloon and politely asked to look it over before flight. Nathaniel walked him around the *Union*, pointing out the various features of the device.

"Why do you have two valves?" Spencer asked.

"Well, sir, it's easiest to fill it from the bottom. And when we're flying we can make fine adjustments to the buoyancy with the bottom valve. But if we want to come down in a hurry we can open the top valve. The gas just pours out of that one."

"Why do you have those sandbags? Doesn't that make it harder for the balloon to rise?"

"Yes, sir, and that's just why we have them. With more lift above and more weight below the balloon flies steadier. And if we're flying free we can drop a bag or two to go up."

"Oh, I see."

"What would you like to observe today, sir?"

"Why do you ask?"

"Well, it matters in how high we need to go. The higher we go, the farther we can see. On the other hand, if you wanted to observe things nearby, you'd want to stay lower."

"Ah. I see. Well, I'd like to see as far south as possible."

"Will you want a telegraph along?"

"No, I'll write a report upon landing."

Nathaniel set the soldiers to knotting some coils of rope together, testing the strength of the knots himself. To save weight he used a single line.

"How much line are you laying on?"

"Three thousand feet."

"Whew! More than half a mile."

"Would you like to go up now?"

"Well, I suppose so."

They climbed aboard and Nathaniel ordered the ground crew to cast them off. As they rose he sneaked a glance at Spencer. Most people making their first flight wore expressions of awe or fear, but Spencer looked calmly around at his surroundings. He was holding the shoulder-ring with both hands, but it wasn't the white-knuckled death grip of most new flyers.

"Is this your first flight, sir?"

"Yes."

"How do you like it?"

"It's most instructive."

They passed eight hundred feet. It was now possible to see over Marye's Heights and Prospect Hill; there were still Confederate forces there. They rose more slowly now, as there was less buoyancy at this altitude and they were lifting more rope with every second.

"May I ask how old you are, sir?"

Spencer glanced at him. "You aren't a soldier so I guess I can be familiar with you. I'm eighteen."

"Why, so am I, just this past month. Isn't that rather young to be an officer?"

"It certainly is," he replied ruefully. "The older men indulge me something awful."

"Well, there are worst fates."

"Of course there are. Still, I hope I can make a name for myself in this conflict. It's a wicked thought, but I sometimes find myself hoping it doesn't get over too soon."

"Or you don't die." Nathaniel instantly regretted these words but Spencer smiled in agreement.

"Yes, or I don't die. Still, one mustn't fear dying too much, either."

"Well, you don't seem to fear flying, and most men do the first time."

"I assure you, I am on the absolute edge of panic," Spencer replied with a laugh.

Nathaniel glanced at the silk strip, the sole legacy of John LaMountain's tenure with the Balloon Corps. They were still rising.

"Tell me, Curry, was that the Jew Ezekiel Vogler I saw in your camp this morning?"

"No, that was Solomon Vogler, his younger brother. Why, is Ezekiel a friend of your'n?"

"My father has had business dealings with him. I wouldn't call him a friend; his family after all can't be received in society. But they're one of the richest families in New York."

"Really?" Nathaniel raised his eyebrows. "I must remember to be nicer to him."

The balloon fetched up against its line. With so much rope below it the jolt wasn't hard, but it still made the balloon bob and roll. The light breeze pushed them to the west, turning the balloon. "End of the line, ladies and gentlemen," Nathaniel said.

Spencer smiled and took up his field glasses. At first he scanned the horizon, but after a few minutes he turned his attention to the city of Fredericksburg. He said, "Can we get any closer to that?"

"Sir?"

"Can the balloon go any closer to the city?"

"Well, sir, we're fixed to the ground by the drag line."

"Yes, of course, but that doesn't answer my question."

"Well, no, sir, it doesn't. The truth of the matter is we could get closer."

"I thought so. Let me see if I have this figured out. The breeze is out of the east so if we released some gas we would settle to the west, over the city. Then, when we were through observing, we could drop some sandbags to rise over the camp again."

"Very good, sir."

"Well, shall we?"

"Well, first off, why do you want to do this? It would be dangerous."

"Not if we stay out of musket range. And I'd like to see if there are sharpshooters in those buildings."

Nathaniel thought it over. They were at three thousand feet and the city was about twenty-five hundred feet away. They could settle right over it.

Should they? It was certainly an unorthodox move, but nothing in the rules forbade it. And it would be good to know if the city was indeed deserted.

He gave a hard pull on the rope attached to the top gas valve. He smiled at Spencer and said, "I hope I live to regret this."

"Bully," Spencer said.

The breeze wasn't very strong. As they released gas the balloon initially dropped straight down, with large loops of rope falling onto the ground. Then the wind moved them westward. The line lifted from the ground again; as it grew taut the balloon was pulled down some more.

Nathaniel looked things over. The line behind them now ran at a forty-five degree angle to the ground. They were above the river now, near the edge of the city, at about two thousand feet. That left them well out of musket range. A rifle cannon could reach them but it would probably not be accurate enough to hit them.

So far no one on either side seemed to have taken note of what they were doing. No: the ground crew must have noticed it. Well, he would have to talk to them when they got down.

Spencer was looking through his glasses again. Nathaniel spoke low: "Can you see anyone?"

"No," Spencer said in the same tone. "Maybe the city really is deserted."

"Only one way to find out. Shall we?"

"By all means. 'Lay on, Macduff, and damn'd be him that first cries, "Hold, enough!"'"

Nathaniel used the lower valve this time. He vented for a few seconds; a few drops of evil-smelling water fell into the car.

The balloon had so little buoyancy that it did not respond at first. Then it dropped several hundred feet. As it settled at its new height it drifted to the west, to the edge of the city.

Nathaniel glanced back at the line. Some of it was now in the river, and he had a sudden fear that the weight of the water in the rope or the river's current would pull them downward. But the line pulled reluctantly from the water. As the line grew taut again the balloon was once more drawn downward.

It was the same pattern as before: the balloon dropped, it drifted to the west, then it dropped again.

Fredericksburg was not as large as it appeared from the other side of the river. The city extended a mile along the waterfront but it did not go back more than a few blocks.

They were over the city now and about seven hundred feet up. Whatever else they did, they could not linger here very long.

"Do you want to go lower, sir?"

Spencer leaned forward, placing a hand on the edge of the basket, a look of wonder on his face. "Do...do we dare?"

Nathaniel gave another pull on the lower valve. A few seconds only he held it open, but that was enough. The balloon dropped to four hundred feet, then crept deeper into the city. City blocks moved slowly beneath them. Then the line grew taut again and the balloon edged downward.

Nathaniel's heart was in his mouth. The buildings were a mere hundred yards below. If the breeze picked up it could drive them right down onto the rooftops. A steeple or a weathervane or, God forbid, a lightning rod could then puncture the gasbag. But the breeze held steady.

"If we get shot at, keep in mind there's an iron plate under our feet."

"Wouldn't we go up like a powder-keg if the gasbag got hit?"

"Probably not. But it would start leaking and we'd have to skedaddle."

Both were whispering.

The densely-packed buildings of the business district were below them, a patchwork of shakes and shingles. Pigeons flew between buildings and perched on the eaves.

The city was laid out in a grid like any modern American city. Some streets ran in sinuous patterns, following some landform or another, but most of them were straight.

It was a prosperous and pretty town. Some of the nicer homes had gardens. Nathaniel saw several churches, a dry-goods store and a slave market, but not a sign of life.

He looked back toward the river. The line was just above the rooftops. What if it caught on something? What if someone reached up and grabbed it?

Then he would drop some ballast.

But what if the line was fouled and they couldn't rise?

Then he would cut the line. He would rise high enough to catch the easterly and ride that back to friendly territory.

"There," Spencer whispered.

"What?"

"Two horses at the back of that building."

Nathaniel squinted at the shadows, then pulled out his pocket telescope. The horses were on the west side of the building where the Union Army couldn't see them. They wore saddles and were tied to a post.

"So that proves—" Nathaniel started, but Spencer whispered, "Ssh. Listen."

The deliberate clop of draft horses drifted up from below. They both searched for the source of the sound and both found it: a wagon, making its way down a narrow side street. The surrounding buildings nearly blocked it from view.

Spencer said, "Is there any way to bring us over more that way?" and waved his arm to the north. Before Nathaniel could answer there came a sharp *crack* from below, followed by the angry hum of a musket ball passing near the car.

Both youths started shouting at once. They sounded like schoolboys caught in a prank by the headmaster. Nathaniel began pulling the knots of the sandbags, dropping them. Spencer began doing the same thing on the other side of the car. Nathaniel shouted, "Stop, that's enough, don't drop any more."

"Are you sure?" As if in answer several more shots were fired beneath them. There were also a couple of deeper booms.

"Look over the side and see."

Union was again taking to the sky. It was swinging up and to the east like the second hand of a titanic clock. They watched the city drop away from them. They were soon at a thousand feet and nearly over the river. There were no more shots but they could hear curses shouted from below.

"What were they firing at us?"

Nathaniel shrugged. "Sounded like muskets."

"Yes, but there was another sound. Was that mortar?"

"Oh, that was our sandbags hitting."

"Oh, heavens!" Spencer laughed. "I hope we didn't damage their roof."

"Well, I suspect we did, sir."

Nathaniel checked the line. They were rising clean, with no fouling. They were well over the Rappahannock now and above two thousand feet.

"Well!" Spencer exclaimed. "That's the closest I've come yet."

"Really?" Nathaniel said.

"What, you've come closer? I thought you fellows were above it all in these things."

"Well, not entirely."

The balloon didn't reach its full height; the second hand drifted to a stop about five seconds short of the twelve. Nathaniel could see no holes in the gasbag or in either of them.

"What shall we do now?" Spencer asked.

"Well, we're at altitude again. Do you want to look around the horizon some more?"

"Yes, I do, thank you." He raised his glasses.

"There's something else we can do, sir."

"Yes?"

"Well, that is, I don't think anyone needs to know about this."

"I heartily agree."

Chapter Ten: Bones

The Army of the Potomac was advancing along the Rappahannock River, attempting to flank the Army of Northern Virginia. The Balloon Corps accompanied the Army and made ascents at every stop. Officers often went up with the aeronauts.

A letter arrived for Lowe from the Assistant Secretary of War. It requested that Lowe name an aeronaut to be sent with a balloon to either Charleston or Baton Rouge. The letter also inquired as to what would be necessary to support said balloon and aeronaut. Lowe replied that James Allen would be the best man for this job and detailed what he would need in the way of remuneration and supplies.

The letter was returned to Lowe with the notation that it should be forwarded through Captain Comstock. Comstock met with Lowe, quite upset that Lowe was again flouting the chain of command in this manner.

"I assure you, Captain," Lowe told him, "I had no intention of disrespect in this matter. Since I had received this communication from the Assistant Secretary directly, I felt I should respond directly to him."

The other members of the Corps lingered outside Lowe's tent, listening to this conversation. All made sure to make no sound nor to allow any shadow to fall upon the tent.

"I would have anticipated that you would have known better by this point, Professor."

"The mistake was inadvertent and I apologize for it."

"Very well."

"Shall you forward the letter to the Assistant Secretary, sir?"

"Only upon due consideration. Are you certain that Allen is the best man for this position? What about Curry or Vogler?"

"Curry might fall under suspicion by the Federal forces in the South due to his southern origins. Vogler in turn might be suspect because he is a Jew. In any event, James Allen has the greatest aeronautical experience of anyone in the Corps, myself excepted."

"All right. I'll take that under advisement."

"I believe the Assistant Secretary was expecting a reply forthwith, sir."

"That is not your concern, sir."

Lieutenant Spencer requested that Nathaniel Curry take him up for an observation and that telegraphic communication be made to Headquarters. They went up to six hundred feet. As Spencer began his observations, Nathaniel slyly inquired, "Would you like to descend over the enemy, sir?"

Spencer did not lower his glasses, but he smiled and said, "That won't be necessary today, Curry, thank you."

"Very good, sir."

"Please transmit this: enemy forces still holding heights around Fredericksburg. Signs of new massing of forces west of these positions."

"Yes, sir. Message is sent, sir." Lowe had already communicated this, but it didn't hurt to repeat the observation.

Spencer lowered the glasses. "It may interest you to know that I reported sharpshooters in Fredericksburg. The report was quite a fillip for me, I think."

"That's very good, sir. Ah, how much detail did you report?"

"Not very much, I assure you."

"That's good."

Spencer and Nathaniel became friends, making frequent ascents together. Their rapport was initially founded upon the shared secret of their descent upon Fredericksburg, but grew into a more sincere camaraderie after that.

Spencer clearly came from money. His uniform was nicely tailored. His boots were fine leather, quite unlike the "Shoddy and Company" footwear most soldiers wore. His binoculars were German and even better than Professor Lowe's.

Once he showed Nathaniel his nametag. It was pewter, with his name and address nicely engraved upon it. "I hope this never goes home to my mother," he said. "It would break her heart."

The Confederate forces completed their withdrawal from their positions above Fredericksburg, leaving only token forces upon Marye's Heights and Prospect Hill. From the balloons, it could be seen that the troops were cooking rations in preparation for a march. Still, the enemy's intentions were unknown.

These movements were most inconvenient for Hooker. He desired nothing more than to swing around Lee and his army and march upon Richmond.

A written request for an observation flight arrived from Hooker's own corps. The note specifically asked that Nathaniel Curry be the pilot; there was no signature. Nathaniel prepared the *Intrepid* and awaited his passenger. He anticipated that it would be Lieutenant Spencer. To his surprise it was the one-eyed man. "Good morning, sir," he said, snapping to attention. The man nodded in reply. "What would you like to observe today, sir?"

"What?"

"I need to know what you'd like to look at so I know how high to go."

"Oh. The city."

"And will you want a telegraph line?"

"No."

Nathaniel set two drag lines at eight hundred feet, spoke with the ground crew and ordered them to cast off. *Intrepid* had a ten-day-old charge in its bag so it rose slowly.

Nathaniel did not use the shoulder ring and the man followed his lead. As they passed two hundred feet the youth walked to the side of the car and looked at the ground, causing the car to rock. He never wavered.

Nathaniel looked up. There was a ceiling of broken cumulus at a thousand feet. The winds were light out of the southwest. It was a perfect day for flying. He held the ring for a second as the balloon reached altitude and fetched up against the guys. The big man's hand reached for the ring, then returned to his side.

"Here we are, sir."

"Very good, Curry. Thank you." He observed the city in silence for a minute, then pulled a telescope from his inside tunic pocket. Nathaniel felt sure this was his first flight but he handled it with utter aplomb.

"Is there anything in particular you'd like to know, sir?"

"No, Curry. Is there anything in particular you'd like to know?"

"I beg your pardon, sir?"

"Let's stop beating around the bush, boy." He lowered the telescope. "You think I killed David Miller, do you?"

"Sir, I don't know what happened to him."

He stepped toward Nathaniel. He was nearly a head taller than the boy and more than twice as heavy; his dark eye looked like the muzzle of a gun. The two regarded each other from about six inches distance. Nathaniel felt a thrill of fear. He wanted to grab the support line behind him. Instead he smiled.

"I see and hear everything," the man said. "Walls have ears. Niggers have ears. Do you understand me?"

"Perfectly, sir. Sir, folks have been saying I done it, too."

"I don't give a shit for what you think of me, or what whores or niggers think of me. I use my men as required and like Grant I don't count my dead. If I killed Miller I did so for a reason. A reason that does not concern you. If I didn't kill Miller it concerns you even less." He stabbed a finger into the youth's chest. "If you have any suspicions about me, any thoughts at all, keep them buried in the deepest parts of your soul where even you can not see them. It will do you no good to do otherwise. Got it?"

"Got it."

"Now take me down."

The Union Army crossed the Rappahannock and moved south. No sooner had the Balloon Corps crossed the river and set up camp than Lieutenant Spencer rode into camp, leading a saddle horse. He dismounted and saluted Captain Comstock. "Good morning, sir. General Hooker has asked me to detail an aeronaut to assist with scouting the location of a new headquarters."

"Why an aeronaut, young man?"

"Because it should be in an area visible to the balloonists when in flight, so that visual signals can be made. It also has to be suitable for telegraphy."

"Very well. Curry, you're the most experienced telegrapher. Do accompany this officer and report back here as soon as you are done."

"Yes, sir."

Nathaniel was soon riding hard beside the young lieutenant. "You're a good rider, sir."

"Thank you."

"Were you a racehorse-jockey before the war?"

"No, but I did take lessons. It was in the English style, but it all helps."

"Mind telling me why you dragged me along on this?"

"Why, you heard what I told your commander."

"Yes, but I don't need to step in shit to tell that it's shit. Sir."

Spencer smiled and leaned back, slowing to a trot. "There's our party up ahead. You led me on an adventure a few weeks back, Curry. I just thought I'd return the favor."

Adventures never seemed to go so well for Nathaniel. "Thank you, sir," he said. Spencer clucked and both horses went back to a gallop.

The party consisted of a captain, a first lieutenant and twenty enlisted men. All rode like the cavalrymen that they were; the guide bore a small regimental flag beneath a large Old Glory with gold fringe. Spencer fell in with the officers, tossing a quick salute to the man beside him.

Nathaniel fell into the ranks. This was done through no agency of his own. The horse knew to fall into formation and somehow realized Nathaniel's place was with the enlisted men.

Nathaniel was becoming a better rider. He stood in the stirrups, holding himself just above the saddle, and gave the animal its head. It was tiring but it meant for a smoother ride for both of them.

The other men gave him no more than a glance, though it was strange for a civilian to ride with soldiers this way.

It was several minutes before he considered his position: he alone was unarmed. If they were attacked he would be defenseless. Well, that was little matter: he was a terrible shot anyway.

But what if he were captured? Since he was not in uniform he would be shot as a spy.

He kept saying he wasn't a spy but circumstances kept saying he was.

Five miles further the road widened and a large mansion house stood before them. The group pulled up. There was a quick reconnoiter to determine that no enemy lay near; then they looked the house over.

The house was in the Classical style, with tall fluted pillars supporting a triangular portico. There was about a half acre of grass yard and flower garden; all the rest of the surrounding land was cotton fields. There were four weather-beaten red slave cabins in the rear.

The captain knocked on the front door, not bothering to remove his hat. The creature who opened the door was ancient and wrinkled, but wore an air of *gravitas* and great dignity. He wore black tails with a snow-white shirtfront and gleaming black shoes. He would surely have been accounted the owner of this house were he not black.

"Is your master at home?"

The servant literally looked down his nose at the officer, so haughty was his air. "He is not, sir."

"Who is in charge in his absence?"

"I am."

"No white people here at all?"

"No, sir."

"Well, damn it all, where are they, then?"

"The white folks all lit out south, sir. They hear tell the Yankees going be a-coming and they not want to stay nohow. Only the niggers be left behind, we gots to mind the bugs, you see, sir."

"Now slow down, you rascal, I can't understand a word you're saying!"

Nathaniel had to suppress a laugh at the officer's discomfiture. He had understood the old man, but he could see why the officer, a Northerner, had not.

The old man spoke like a field hand. The word "going", from his lips, sounded more like *gwah*; "the white folks" he rendered as *dwafo*. To make matters worse, he had not a tooth in his head.

Nathaniel stepped in to serve as translator. He felt like "Mr. Locutor", the white character in a minstrel show who serves as interlocutor between the blackface actors and the white audience. When the captain ordered that all the slaves be summoned the old man hobbled to the back door and rang a large triangle.

They started to drift in from the fields in groups of two or three. About a hundred and fifty colored people soon filled the road before the house, all scraping and bowing before the strange white men. They were filthy and stank and were dressed in rags. They looked afraid, yet hopeful and curious.

"You are all free," the captain said, and an excited jabber arose from the throng. It died away rapidly and everyone looked from one to the other, uncertain of what was now expected of them.

One young man, still clutching his hoe, stood up and said, "Beg pardon, master, but what does you mean?"

"I mean that by order of Abraham Lincoln, President of the United States of America, all of you are no longer slaves and are forever free."

The clamor from the throng increased with every word of this until it was a joyous shout. The slaves – no, the freedmen – rose to their feet, praising Jesus, the President and the strange white man before them. Although nothing like this had ever occurred in their lives they were no longer perplexed. This was a day they had long anticipated.

The same young man quieted the others and asked, "But what we do now, master?"

"Do? Why, do as you like, within the law. One thing you must not do is call me master, nor shall you call anyone but the Lord master ever again. But if it's work you want, the Army will pay you fifty cents a day. Just head north up this road here and they'll pick you up."

The crowd started up the road until the shout of a woman stopped them. They flooded back into their quarters, coming back with their meager possessions. The women had donned their best dresses and carried baskets and bundles on their heads and babies tied to their waists. The men carried washtubs and wooden boxes filled with sacks of flour, sorghum meal and cooking utensils. Everyone, even the smallest child, bore a burden, but all wore smiles. They started up the road, a longer and a harder road than they knew, and they sang as they went.

One man alone did not leave, and that was the old butler. "Why aren't you going?" the captain asked him.

"I too old," came the reply. "I free, but I too old and lame-up to go. And I don't know nothing but this house." He took out an immaculate white handkerchief and wiped his eyes. "You come too late," he continued. "You come too late for Joe. Still, I's glad I seen this day. Please, sir, can I stay?"

"Yes, you can," the captain said, his voice kindly. "You can mind the house for us."

"Yes, sir. What you going do now?"

"This house is our headquarters," the captain said. "It will serve as the residence of the Union commander in chief during the present campaign. Please show me around, and first show me the master's study. You, young man, what's your name?"

"Nathaniel Curry, sir."

"You a telegrapher, then, Curry?"

"Yes, sir."

"Come along, see if you can set up here."

There was a pluck at Nathaniel's sleeve. "If I die tomorrow," Spencer whispered, "I'll know it was all worthwhile."

When Nathaniel returned to camp he was surprised to find General Stoneman there. Several young officers waited on horseback while the general conferred with Captain Comstock and Professor Lowe. Lowe seemed glad of his presence; Comstock did not.

"I am happy to write you that letter, Professor," Stoneman said. "I count your aeronautical experiments a great boon to the art of warfare."

"You are most kind, sir."

"Not in the least. I consider your actions during the Peninsula Campaign to have been of great advantage to my corps. I can but anticipate that General Hooker feels the same. Wouldn't you agree, Captain?"

"Of course, sir," Comstock replied, a bit more stiffly than was required.

The officers saluted and Stoneman left. Comstock turned to Lowe. "Professor," he said, "I must require that you give me that letter."

"To what purpose, sir?"

"It must travel through channels."

"It did. General Stoneman gave me the letter in your presence. It is addressed to me. What purpose would there be in my giving it to you? Would you immediately give it back to me?"

Comstock held out his hand. "Professor Lowe, I *order* you to give me that letter."

"Is that a military order, sir?"

"Yes, it is."

"May I see that order in writing, sir?"

"What?"

"If you are acting in the capacity of my military commander then I have the right to receive orders from you in writing except when in the face of the enemy."

Comstock made no reply to this except to turn purple with rage. He turned and left the camp.

When he was well out of earshot James Allen ventured, "Well, you won that one, sir."

Lowe placed the letter in his pocket. "To quote King Pyhrrus," he said, "'another such victory and I am undone.'"

The Army of the Potomac was now gathered in strength on the south side of the Rappahannock and Hooker had established his headquarters in the manor house at Chancellorsville. Lee's forces were massed west of Fredericksburg, but his intentions were unknown.

Everyone expected Hooker to attack his smaller and weaker foe but he did not. He withdrew into a defensive position. This action was pondered by the military experts of the Balloon Corps.

"Do you think he has something planned?" James Allen asked, reaching for the hardtack.

"It's hard to say," Solomon Vogler replied, pouring himself a cup of coffee. "He seems unsure of what to do next. There's an old military maxim, 'when in doubt, attack.' But he's ignoring that."

"The worst of it is, this gives the initiative to Lee," Allen said.

"Do you think he has something planned?" Nathaniel asked.

"I sure don't know," Allen replied. "Why don't you ask your spy friends? They'd probably know."

"I doubt they'd know," Nathaniel replied. "If they did know, they wouldn't tell me. And they ain't nohow my friends, anyhow."

"If they were," Vogler said with a smile, "would you tell us?"

Nathaniel didn't have a witty rejoinder so he turned back to his breakfast.

"You know what I think?" Ezra Allen asked. All eyes turned to him. "I think Hooker's lost his nerve since he stopped drinking."

All were silent for a spell. His brother spoke at last. "You're not the only one to think this, I'm sure," he said. "But if that's so, we can but hope that he recovers from this unfortunate and ill-timed bout of temperance pretty damned quick."

The armies were separated by no more than a few miles but they might as well have been on opposite sides of the globe. The terrain was hilly and rolling. Some of it was freshly-sown farmland; other parts were forest.

Only the Balloon Corps had a hope of seeing what Lee was up to, and the Corps was called upon to do just that. Even the aeronauts, however, found it difficult to make out what was going on. Thaddeus Lowe ascended daily from the vicinity of Chancellorsville; other members of the Corps ascended from Falmouth, across from Fredericksburg. All could see troops in motion, but it was as through a glass, darkly.

Hooker and many of his officers by this time appreciated what the aeronauts could accomplish at their best. They were, however, weary of playing nursemaid to these troublesome civilians. They were also greatly distracted by the impending battle.

The Assistant Secretary of War had repented of his decision to send a balloon to Charleston or Baton Rouge. This decision may have been influenced by Comstock, who reported that the balloons were extremely expensive to operate and were in any case of very limited utility.

Thus it was that at the very same time that the Balloon Corps was at last being recognized for its contributions to the war effort it was being driven out of existence.

Nathaniel Curry considered these and other matters while he sat at breakfast one morning, alone but for Solomon Vogler. Vogler was reading the *New York Times* and becoming steadily more distracted as he read.

"So what's going on in New York, Solly?"

"Oh, it's bad, Nathaniel. It looks like there's a second civil war set to start there."

"There's a what? You consider this a civil war?"

"Certainly."

"What's civil about it?"

"A civil war is a war within a nation, as distinct from a war between nations. That's what our nation has been undergoing the last few years."

"Oh. And you say there's a second one about to start?"

"Well, you've heard about the conscription, haven't you?"

"Who hasn't?" The Union, running low on soldiers, had ordered the conscription of all healthy white men between the ages of eighteen and forty; the Confederacy would soon follow suit.

"Well, New York is full of gangs, and these gangs are starting to resist the draft. Things could get really ugly there. These boys know how to fight."

"Really? Well, if the Balloon Corps gets dissolved, where do you plan to go?"

Vogler put the paper down. "Oh, New York, of course."

"Really? But you just said…"

"Yes, but this is nothing a New Yorker couldn't handle."

A private came into the camp. "Do you know where the Balloon Corps is?" he asked.

"This is it," Nathaniel said.

"Yeah? Where's your balloons, then?"

"They're both out flying today. What do you want?"

"I have an order for—" he glanced at the paper in his hand "—Nathaniel Curry."

Nathaniel took the paper and looked it over. "I'm supposed to report to General Hooker? To Hooker himself?"

"I don't know. *I* didn't write it."

"Hooker didn't either. Who gave this to you?"

"I don't know," the youth said petulantly. "Do you think I know the name of every brass chicken in the Army?"

"Hooker holed up in that big manor house at Chancellorsville?"

"Last time I looked. He and I ain't close. I don't know where he is. You got any money?"

"What for?"

"I delivered a message to you, didn't I?"

Nathaniel threw the order on the table. "Not one that I wanted," he said. "And let me tell you something from experience."

"Yeah?"

"When you deliver a message, run the last fifty yards or so. Arrive there all out of breath. You might get a penny or something."

The private departed without another word. Nathaniel bade Vogler good morning and set out.

Two miles of walking brought him to the manor house. He presented the order to the sentry, who brought it inside. A captain came out and told Nathaniel to bring the order to the hospital which had been set up in an adjoining dairy barn.

The hospital had a sentry as well and he was anticipating the order. He told Nathaniel to go to the back of the building, where a separate ward had been set up.

Nathaniel was increasingly perplexed by these events. He walked through the barn to the pens at the back. The barn had been swept clean of any evidence of its former function and now looked as much like a hospital as a barn could. Cots were set up every few feet. These were at the moment empty, although this was likely to change.

One of the pens contained a patient and a doctor. The patient, to Nathaniel's dismay, was Red Sally. He almost turned on his heel and left but he did not. He after all had received an order to report there from the commander in chief himself.

Sally did not look at all well. She was flushed with fever and seemed delirious. The doctor was holding a cup of some steaming liquid before her. "But you must drink this, my child. The willow bark will cut the fever."

"But it tastes like shit. Oh, if I must." She took a deep draft, then lay back on the cot.

The doctor looked up and said, "Do not bother my patient, young man. Go on, go back."

"It's all right, doctor," Sally said. "I sent for him."

"What do you want?" Nathaniel asked, quite forgetting his manners.

"I need you to go on a mission," she replied. "They wanted me to go but I took ill."

"I have a job already."

"Yes, but I know you can be spared. Nathaniel, this is very important."

"I don't want to do it. I'm not good at this."

"Oh, please, doctor, send for Herbert. Herbert will know what to do."

"That's all right, my dear," the doctor said. "You know that Herbert is not here."

"Tell Nathaniel…tell Nathaniel what is wrong with me."

"Are you sure you want that?"

She had a spasm of coughing, then weakly nodded her head. The doctor walked into the main part of the barn, signaling with an eyebrow that Nathaniel should follow.

"I know what she has," Nathaniel said as the doctor turned to him. "It's consumption, isn't it?"

"It's consumption," the doctor said, "but not of the sort you're thinking of. That malady is better known in the medical community as *tuberculosis.* No, Mrs. Pettijohn has syphilis."

"Syphilis?"

"It's a disease that's contracted through venery. That is, it's contracted through lying with a person carnally who has the disease."

"Oh. Yes, I've heard of it."

"It's a consequence of the life she's lived, I'm afraid."

"Yes, sir."

"It's treatable, but it's not curable."

"So is she going to die?"

"She may recover from this current bout, but she has no more than a few years left. I just hope this fever breaks soon so she can get some sleep."

"Who was she calling for?"

"Calling for?"

"Herbert."

"Oh. Her husband. She's been calling for her husband and children off and on for hours."

"She has a family?"

"They're all dead."

"Oh."

"Nathaniel." The sound was no more than a whisper, but in the stillness of the empty barn it carried to him.

She was holding a hand out to him. He took it and sat beside her.

The hand was hot and damp. Her face was flushed and her lips were cracked. There were large ugly sores around her mouth. Her red curls were matted to her scalp.

"You have to buy a newspaper."

"A newspaper?"

"Get one of the Richmond papers. You should be able to get one at Spotsylvania Courthouse."

"Why should I do that?"

"Look for something that says what the Confederates are going to do."

"Sally, I think the fever is making you say this."

She shook her head. "No, no, listen, Nathaniel. Listen to me. The reporters, they go to Lee and the others and they ask them what they're going to do. We read the papers and we find out."

"Really?"

She nodded. "Get a paper, read it and see what they're going to do. Then take the Courthouse Road northeast from the courthouse. There's a telegraph line that runs beside the road."

"Okay."

"A cart path comes onto this one from the right, and three telegraph poles later there's a key hidden in the woods."

"A key?"

"A telegraph key."

"There's a telegraph key in the woods?"

"You'll find it. Send a message to Captain Thomas saying what the Rebels are going to do. Then get away fast."

He said nothing. She gripped his hand harder. "Nathaniel, victory might well depend upon this. I promised to go but I cannot."

"You saying you trust me now?"

"Yes. I trust you." A tear glistened in the corner of her eye.

"That big friend of your'n doesn't trust me. He threatened to kill me the other day."

"Don't worry about that. He threatens to kill everyone. Everyone but me."

He sighed. "I'll go," he said.

She released his hand. "Captain Thomas will get you set up. They know where she is at the big house."

"All right."

"Nathaniel...Nathaniel, you didn't do it, did you? Tell me the truth."

"No, Sally, I didn't."

Her eyes were closed. "It was him, then," she murmured.

He was halfway through the barn when he heard her calling him back. When he got back to the pen she opened her eyes for a moment only, then said, "This is the most important thing. You must remember this."

Her voice was no more than a whisper. She seemed to be struggling to express herself. He went to the bed and leaned over her.

"Try to be happy. Try to be happy while you can," she said, then was silent.

At the manor house he told the sentry that he wanted to see Captain Thomas. The man leered back at him. "You want to see a whore, huh?"

"Just tell me where she is."

"Huh! Well, I'd like to tell you more than that. You'd best watch that mouth on you, son. See that nigger over there? The one reading a book?"

"Yeah?"

"Go talk to him. He puts on airs the likes of which I never seen. You two should get along just fine."

Nathaniel recognized him. At Nathaniel's approach he snapped the small book shut and put it in his pocket. "Good day, Nathaniel," he said with a smile. "My name is Carl Morgan. I hear you're going on a little trip for us."

"Yes, I guess I am. I was told to find Captain Thomas."

"Well, I can help you out."

The man was remarkably bold. He didn't shy at all from looking Nathaniel directly in the eye as he spoke and even smiled at him. "You was there when I brung her up in the balloon, right?" Nathaniel asked.

"Right as rain. Come along to the stables here."

"The stables?"

"We have some clothes and a horse."

"What's wrong with the clothes I'm standing up in?"

"Well, they're not proper spy clothes. Don't worry, we've thought all this out. We have you well in hand."

"Well, that's good. Tell me, Carl, do you talk to all white men this way?"

Nathaniel did not look at him as he said this, but out of the corner of his eye he saw Carl glance at him. "No," the Negro replied affably, "most white men I just slit their throats from ear to ear and let it go at that. Ah, here we are."

Several people, "Captain Thomas" among them, waited at the stables. She was dressed as a sutler, in a plain gray dress with a white apron and white hat. "Good day, Nathaniel," she said.

"Good day, ma'am."

"Thank you ever so much for making this trip for us."

"You're welcome."

"Do you know what you have to do?"

"Yes, Sally told me. Ride down to Spotsylvania Courthouse, buy a Richmond paper, see what Bobby is up to. Then I ride northeast up the Courthouse Road that runs to Fredericksburg and find the telegraph key in the woods. Then I send you a message and beat it for home."

"Quite right. Very good."

"Now, Carl here says I should be putting on some different clothes?"

"Yes, I have them right here."

Nathaniel went into the hay-room and changed. He felt ridiculous putting these clothes on. The shirt was homespun linen of the coarsest sort. It was old and worn and was much too large for him. The pants were no better; its belt was a rope and there were no braces. A floppy straw hat of the kind worn by slaves completed the ensemble. He knew enough not to put his shoes back on.

Laughter greeted him as he came back to the front of the stable; even the horses turned to look at the spectacle. "Jesus Christ Almighty!" he said, holding his arms out. "You have me tricked out like a nigger field hand."

"That was the desired effect," Carl said.

"We thought that the best thing for you would be to say that your family has a farm in Fairfax County and you left it when the Yankees moved in," Mrs. Thomas said. "Now you're looking for work out this way."

"Looks like I ain't finding much."

"Well, you're not," Mrs. Thomas said.

"But don't say that unless you have to," Carl said. "Don't say anything unless you have to."

"Am I supposed to buy the paper with my good name?"

"No, here's twenty cents. The paper shouldn't be more than five but it may cost more in such an out-of-the-way place." Carl gave him a dime and ten pennies.

"Do you know the way?" Mrs. Thomas asked.

"Yes, I've studied on the maps of this locality. And I been to Spotsylvania Courthouse once, but I was just a tad."

"All right."

"Am I supposed to walk there?"

"No, we have a horse for you. Lucius?"

An old colored groom stepped up with an old chestnut gelding. Nathaniel took one look at the beast and said, "I'd rather walk."

This produced more laughter from the assembled throng. "This here's Bones," the groom said. "He don't look like much but he'll get you where you wants to go, boss."

"He looks like he's older than I am."

"I reckon he is. I done took care of him for fifteen years myself. I know he was in the war in Mexico. I don't know what he done before that."

"Before that," one of the white men said, "I think he was one of the horses that were shot out from under George Washington at the battle of Valley Forge."

Everyone laughed at this as well. Bones stood with his head hanging down. He turned and looked at Nathaniel. He seemed to be sizing him up as well and he didn't especially like what he saw, either.

"Can this old boy even run?"

"He'll run," Lucius said, "but he won't like it. It would be best to take him at a trot most of the time."

"If it's so all-fired important that I go and do this," Nathaniel said, "couldn't the Union afford a better horse for me?"

"You don't want a better horse," Mrs. Thomas said. "It might get stolen."

"Well, no one will want to steal this thing, that's for sure."

"Bones will be fine for you, boss," Lucius said. "He don't look like much, but he in fine shape. And I love this old boy, I been taking good care of him."

Nathaniel looked the horse over. Although he was old and swaybacked his coat was clean and well groomed. His shoes were fine and his hooves were in good shape. He never seemed to put his ears forward, but an old warhorse was entitled to be cantankerous.

"Won't someone remark on his brand?"

"Lots of horses have Uncle Sam on their ass," Lucius said. "Excuse me, ma'am. Just say you got him at an auction."

"Do I get a saddle, or am I a wild Indian too?"

Lucius pulled a blanket and a saddle off of a barrel and threw them over Bones' back. He started to cinch the saddle, paused, and told the horse, "Now, don't make me do it." Bones did not respond and Lucius drove a knee into his ribs. Bones relented and let his breath out, allowing the groom to tighten the cinch. Lucius gave Nathaniel a glance and raised the stirrups.

Nathaniel mounted up and walked Bones around the yard. The old fellow responded smartly enough, turning with a flick of the reins. "Now, if I just send a message for Captain Thomas, you'll get it?"

"Yes. They'll be looking out for it."

"Can you get a message to the Balloon Corps? Tell them I won't be back for a few hours."

"Whom should we tell?"

"Well, anyone. The captain has been gone for over a week and Professor Lowe is flying, but there should be someone there."

"All right."

He tipped the ridiculous straw hat to her and headed down the road.

It was a nice day in early May. It was late morning by now and it was starting to get warm. He worked out a story in his mind of who he was and what he was doing. Most of it was in fact true: he hied from Fairfax County in the north of Virginia, and he had been a farm boy.

He picked his way south one road at a time. Most of the "roads" were just dirt tracks, branching into each other at intervals of about a mile. Bones did not give a very smooth ride but Nathaniel didn't mind.

He reached the courthouse at about two in the afternoon. Aside from the courthouse itself there were an inn, a church and a few small stores. He entered one of the latter.

It wasn't quite a general store but there were various types of merchandise on display. The shopkeeper was a big burly son of a bitch with long muttonchops. One look at Nathaniel and he knew he was a Yankee spy but he said nothing.

"Got a newspaper, mister?"

"Which one?"

"The *Enquirer*?"

"Yes. Got five cents?"

"Here."

He gave him the dime and took the five cents change – all US currency, though neither objected. "What you want with a newspaper, boy?"

"I'm looking for work."

"Join up."

He took the paper. "Maybe I will."

He sat on the front stoop and read the paper. The story he wanted was on the front page. He read the article on the impending battle, eventually turning to page 2. There he found what he was looking for:

> General Lee, when asked of his intentions in countering the Federal aggression, replied that he planned to meet force with force. "The Army will attack the enemy head to head," he confided. "Our forces will be massed in a single great salient."
>
> This reporter replied that he had heard that Lee would split his

forces and attack on several fronts at once. "This is false," the General replied. "The forces will not be split."

Nathaniel left the paper on the stoop and headed northeast. After half a mile he saw the cart-road that connected with the road that he was on. He stopped at the third telegraph pole after this intersection.

At first he saw nothing remarkable. The shiny copper wire ran to the glass insulator and on to the next pole. A second glance, however, showed something else. A sheathed wire, one covered in tarred cotton, ran around the pole to the back.

He walked around the pole and squinted up into the foliage. The black wire – no, two black wires – ran into the woods. He led Bones into the trees and tied him.

The tarred wire ran to a tree, wrapped around an insulator and went thence to a piece of oilskin nailed to the base of the tree. Under the oilskin he found a telegraph key. It wasn't a linesman's key but a standard "camel-back" one.

He tapped the key; it was live. The screws were not set exactly as he liked them but they were close enough. He transmitted:

TO   CAPTAIN   THOMAS   CHANCELLORSVILLE   FROM NATHANIEL STOP GENERAL LEE WILL MAKE FRONTAL ASSAULT WITH MASSED FORCES STOP HE WILL NOT SPLIT HIS ARMY 73

He hurried out onto the road. First he galloped hard toward Fredericksburg. Then, seeing no one before or behind him, he reined in and turned back toward the courthouse. If anyone came upon him now, he would say he saw a man in a Confederate uniform riding hard toward Fredericksburg.

No one, however, gave chase. He passed through the small crossroads town again and watered his horse at a trough, then headed back north. It appeared that nothing much was happening in that town this day; his newspaper still lay on the stoop of the little store.

It wasn't very difficult to find his way back. The profusion of little roads was confusing but he just turned north whenever possible.

It was late afternoon by this time and the day had gotten quite warm. Everything was in bloom, it seemed, and the myriad perfumes made him feel half-drunk. The sensation brought him back to the evening after the Antietam battle, when he had gotten intoxicated on brandy with Vogler and Smith and the three of them had explored the planets. It was a bittersweet memory; how strange that at his young age there should already be things that were in the irretrievable past.

It was while in the midst of such reveries that he came over a rise and saw a dark blue river moving through the valley before him where no such river should be.

"Whoa up."

Bones stopped and let his head sag to the ground. Nathaniel squinted at the sight before him.

Moving along what he took to be the Furnace Road was an army. He couldn't see it very clearly but he had seen enough armies to be sure. There were men on horseback and there were wagons and field artillery, but mostly there was marching infantry raising clouds of reddish-brown dust. The occasional flashes of sunlight told him that they had their bayonets fixed.

Who the Hell were they? At first he thought they were Union forces, but they were moving from right to left before him. They were not moving away from Chancellorsville, they were moving toward it.

And that told him all he needed to know about these men.

He gave a tug on the reins. Bones turned his head in anticipation of the action, sparing his mouth, and wheeled smartly around. Nathaniel had intended to ride back the way he had come but another look at the army before him inspired him to sit tight.

Half a dozen men on horseback had broken from the flanks of the marching column and were riding hard toward him. Nathaniel knew that Bones could never outrun them so he sat and watched them come.

They got to him in less than two minutes. Nathaniel didn't like what he saw. They were all men in their early twenties. They looked rugged and grim and they looked like they knew how to fight. They all wore carbines over their shoulders and Colt pistols at their sides.

Nathaniel now knew exactly who these men were. It was even likely that he had met some of them before. He slouched in the saddle and looked stupid.

One man rode up and grabbed Bones' reins. Bones looked annoyed but did not resist. The sergeant pointed with his chin at the ridge behind Nathaniel and another man rode up there, looked around and shook his head.

No one had yet spoken a word. Nathaniel took it upon himself to initiate discourse. Partly to play his role as the ignorant civilian and partly to be contrary he said, "You boys Yankees?"

"Fuck you! You think we're *Yankees*?"

"I'll bust a cap on your ass and take this here horse, you call me a Yankee again."

"Why you think we Yankees, boy?" the sergeant asked.

He shrugged. "Yankees wear blue."

"We're with Stonewall Jackson. We'll wear blue 'til the end of time, and thankee."

"What you doing here, boy?"

"Nothing."

"Nothing be damned! Who give you this horse? Was it Farting Joe Hooker?"

"My daddy got him at the auction."

"You a Yankee spy?"

"Hell no! I'm a Virginia boy."

"You a Virginia boy, how come you not in uniform?"

"Yeah, you scared?"

"My maw won't let me join up. I ain't scared."

"Is that so? Well, maybe the conscription will change her mind."

"Yeah, boy, you'll be conscripted or your maw'll pay Jeff Davis six hundred dollars. Your maw got six hundred dollars?"

"No."

In point of fact, Nathaniel was scared. He didn't fear these men but he was beginning to fear what would happen to him upon his return to the Union lines. He was anxious to get away but at the moment he needed to sit still and play the farm boy.

"What you looking for around here, boy?"

"Work."

"Work? Join up with us and we'll give you work. We'll give you God's work."

"Sergeant, what you want to do with him?"

The sergeant made a face. "This boy don't count for nothing."

"What about his horse?"

He looked at Bones' skinny legs and sagging belly. "I don't think we're that hard up yet." Without another word they wheeled back and rejoined the column.

Nathaniel sat and watched the column for a minute, reckoning the size of the force. He concluded that it was an entire corps. Stonewall Jackson himself was down there, probably at the head of the column.

He turned back over the ridge. He stayed at a walk until he was out of sight, then kicked Bones up to a trot. Although Bones could not have outrun those cavalrymen, he could easily run faster than the foot soldiers could walk.

All of the roads seemed designed by the Devil to draw him away from where he wanted to go. More than once he had to head cross-country to find a road that would bring him around Jackson and back to Chancellorsville.

It occurred to him that it might be better to go back to the telegraph key and alert Captain Thomas that way. But it was too late for that: the Union army was a lot closer than that hidden key by now.

Bones, old war-horse that he was, tried to stay at a trot but it was more than he could manage. He fell back to a walk more and more, ignoring Nathaniel's kicks to his flanks. Even if he had had spurs it would have made little difference; the horse had given all he had.

He found himself following barely-visible tracks going through the woods. The sun was approaching the horizon and this made it easier to tell his direction. As long as he kept the sun on his left, he was heading north and toward the Union positions.

He came, unexpectedly, to the top of a low hill. It was clear of trees and he saw, about a quarter mile to his right, Jackson's forces. They were hidden in the trees, massing for an assault. The men in front had stopped and the men coming in crowded in behind them. At the signal, they would break upon the Union right like a wave upon the beach. He saw this for but a second; then he was back in the trees himself.

He finally reached the Union lines and he was sickened by what he saw. The Union right flank was "hanging in the air" – it had no natural or artificial structures to protect it from the coming onslaught. Moreover, they clearly didn't know an attack was coming. Pickets were keeping watch, but it was without any sense of alarm.

They accosted Nathaniel, demanding that he stop and state his business. "I'm a Union agent," he said. "I have to get a message to General Hooker straight away."

The soldiers looked bewildered at this. Nathaniel did not look or sound like a Union agent. They stood looking at him dumbly until a captain came up. The soldiers snapped to attention.

"What's going on here? What do you want here, young man?"

"Captain, General Tom Jackson is coming here with about fifty thousand men."

"Oh? And what do you know about it?"

"I just saw him on the Furnace Road."

"You saw him? Did you stop and talk to him?"

"No, but I done talked to some of his men."

"I doubt that very much."

"Yes, because you think he's coming head-on from the east. But he's swinging around you and will be coming in on this flank. You'd better dig in."

The captain looked at him as if seeing him for the first time. "Wait a minute, what are you talking about? Who told you these things?"

"Like I tried to tell your men, I'm a Union agent. And Stonewall Jackson is going to be jumping on your tail in a few minutes."

Another captain came up, necessitating a full repetition of this intelligence. The two officers didn't like the looks of Nathaniel and certainly didn't like what he had to say, but neither would they dismiss his words out of hand. They decided to send a party out to reconnoiter the Furnace Road.

Artillery fire began; everyone looked off to the south. "Those are Dahlgren guns," one of the captains said, "so they're ours."

"Well, yes," the other one said. "I doubt they could sneak artillery up on us. Not through those woods."

"So what are they firing at? Do you suppose—"

Nathaniel interrupted him: "Do you have a telegraph line to General Hooker's headquarters at the manor house?"

The officers looked annoyed. "What business is that of yours, my boy?"

"I have to get word to one of his officers."

"Which one?"

"Captain Thomas."

"I know of no Captain Thomas on General Hooker's staff."

"She's a hooker."

"What?"

"Never mind. Do you have a line to the manor?"

The officers looked at each other, uncertain how to reply. The artillery fire south of them trailed into silence.

"Look," Nathaniel said, "just let me go and I'll talk to Hooker myself."

The men talked it over, eventually deciding to let Nathaniel pass; General Hooker's sentries could detain Nathaniel if they didn't like him.

"Can you give me a fresh horse?"

"You're pushing your luck, young man."

"Yes, sir."

Nathaniel set out again, riding through the Union forces to the manor house. Everywhere he went men were relaxing, writing letters, reading or playing cards. All expected to go into battle within a day or so and were making the most of their time in the rear. Bones plodded through the camps, his hooves the loudest thing in the clearing.

A bugle rang out about half a mile away, carrying easily through the stillness. There instantly followed the rattle of musket fire and the whoop of the Rebel yell. The soldiers around him stirred and looked toward the sound, not yet realizing what was going on.

Bones was moving at little more than a walk by this time, though his flanks were heaving. The battle was about half a mile behind him but it was very loud. There was no cannon but there was so much musket fire that it made a continuous roar like the sound of the sea.

Was that the echoes or was there gunfire coming from several directions now? He couldn't be sure.

Nathaniel did not look for Mrs. Thomas but went right to the manor house. He leapt to the ground and ran the last fifty yards to the steps. Before the sentry could challenge him, he shouted, "I have an urgent message for General Hooker."

The sentry shook his head. "Official business only," he said.

"This *is* official business."

"What's the password?"

"I don't have time for that! I don't know! General Hooker! Please let me talk to you!"

Hooker came out, drawn perhaps by the sound of the battle, perhaps by Nathaniel's cry. His tunic was off and he stood on the front steps of the mansion in his braces, a sheaf of papers in his hand. "What's all this ruckus?" he demanded.

"General, Stonewall Jackson is coming around your right side."

"What are you talking about? Jackson is with Lee. Who the Hell are you?"

Nathaniel shook his head. "Lee split his forces," he said. "Jackson is coming from the right. I don't know who-all is coming elsewhere, but you best be ready for them."

Hooker looked off to the south, where the musket fire was now joined by the boom of artillery. "No, it couldn't be," he said. "I have it on good authority." He tapped the papers in his hand.

The paper on top looked like a telegram. "General, is that message for Captain Thomas, and it's signed Nathaniel?"

Hooker looked at the telegram, then looked up as another man, an officer on horseback, came riding up, shouting, "General! We've been betrayed! They're attacking from three directions at once!"

Hooker seemed to be at a total loss. For about five seconds, as the firing continued and everyone stood and looked at him, he could but look in the direction of the roaring. Then he gave a start as if waking from a bad dream. The sheaf of papers fell to the ground. He pointed at Nathaniel and said, "This man is a Rebel spy! Take him into custody. Keep him here, I'll want to question him after the battle."

Before Nathaniel could blink two soldiers had grabbed his arms and another came up behind him and threw an arm around his neck. They threw him to the ground and beat him up. A man came from inside with manacles. His arms were bound behind him and he was dragged nearly insensible into the house.

The soldiers deposited him on the floor of a small room. One man was left to watch him.

Despite the beating and the fact that he was bound and under arrest and probably facing execution, it felt good to lie down. It had been a long day.

He was in a small sitting room whose sole window faced out upon the front porch. A small fender-style fireplace was set into the interior wall, with a settee and a straight-backed wooden chair before it.

The sound of battle continued outside. It didn't seem to be getting any closer. He looked over his shoulder at the window. There was less than an hour of daylight left. They generally left off with battle at sundown but there was no telling what Jackson might do.

He looked at his guard. He was a young man, a few years older than himself and about a head taller. He sighed, sat down in the chair and laid his musket across his lap. The shadows were deep enough that Nathaniel could not read his facial expression.

"What's your name, soldier?"

"My name is Shut Up and your name is Dead Soon Enough."

"Sorry. I'll shut up if'n you want."

"Go ahead and talk, Secesh, but don't expect no sympathy from me."

"Listen, I ain't no Rebel spy."

The solider leaned forward. "I hear different."

"Yeah, but who did you hear it from?"

The man made no response.

"It was Joe Hooker."

He sat as stolidly as before, then sat back with a sigh. "Yeah. Yeah, it was."

It grew dark; the soldier lit the lamps on the mantle. As the sound of fighting died away the two of them began to converse.

"So, Curry, if'n you ain't a Rebel spy, what are you? You don't seem the type to be an agent."

"I'm not. I'm supposed to be with the Balloon Corps."

"Really? You go up in them things?"

"Sure."

"And what, you just float around looking at the fighting?"

"I do a little more than that. I report back to the ground by telegraph."

"Shoot! You couldn't get me up in one of them things."

"It's pretty safe most of the time."

"Why do they think you're a Rebel spy, then?"

"Well, they sent me out to spy on the Rebs. I'm not a very good spy, though. I can't do anything right."

"What were you trying to do?"

"Buy a newspaper."

"What? You go out to buy a newspaper and you end up like this?"

"Yeah, I know it. Listen, Daniels, I need to take a piss."

"God damn it, soldier, you don't expect me to be of much help with that, do you?"

"Well, I'm in kind of an awkward position here."

"Well, you can go and wet your pants for all I care to do about it."

"Listen, I think I can get my hands around in front of me."

"How you going to do that?"

"Well, just watch me. Just don't shoot me, okay?"

"Okay." Daniels shifted his weapon around so that it was pointed at Nathaniel but he left it at half-cock. "Just don't try anything clever."

"Don't worry." Nathaniel squirmed around and got his left foot up and over the chain connecting his hands. With a few minutes of effort he got his left leg behind him. The exertion left him panting on the floor.

"Well, damn, boy, it looks like you worse off than when you started."

Nathaniel had to laugh. "I know it," he said.

"Looks like you like yourself, too."

He had to laugh at that as well; the chain ran between his legs, forcing his left hand onto his crotch. "I think the other leg will be harder."

It was, but after ten minutes he had gotten his right leg across the chain and his hands were before him. He sat against the wall and rested, holding his hands up triumphantly before him.

"Good work, Curry."

"Is that a thunder-mug in the corner?"

"Sure is. Help yourself."

As he set the lid on the chamber pot he said, "Sounds like the festivities have ended for the day."

"Jesus, I hope so. I never did take cotton to night fighting."

"Well, one thing I've learned to expect from Lee, and that's not to expect anything."

"Or Jackson."

"Jackson's even worse. There's no telling what Old Jack will do."

"They say he's crazy."

"Yes," Nathaniel said, settling back against the wall. "Crazy like a fox."

"The South got all the good generals."

"You're not the first to say that." He dropped his voice to little more than a whisper. "Do you suppose Hooker is done, now?"

"Well, he might still win this one. The Rebs might make a mistake or Hooker might get lucky."

"Yes," Nathaniel pressed, "but if'n he doesn't win? You suppose he'll get put out to pasture like the others?"

"I have no idea."

The old butler opened the door carrying a candle. "Do you gentlemens want something to eat?"

"Yes, please," both answered in chorus.

He withdrew and returned in ten minutes with plates of food. It was better fare than either had expected. "There not much in the larder," the old man explained, "but the Union Army can have it all. And the hogs can all get slaughtered up, too, and I don't mind."

Daniels was still sitting on the chair; he put the plate on the settee. Nathaniel sat against the wall. As he was handed the plate he said, "Thank you, Joe."

The butler paused at this and studied Nathaniel's face. After a few seconds his eyes lit up and he smiled. Then he looked down at the manacles on Nathaniel's wrists and the smile died. Without another word he went away.

From the master's study they could hear the general staff conferring late into the night. One voice could be distinguished above the others: Joseph Hooker, wailing and quavering like a little girl.

An officer brought Daniels out into the hall and spoke to him. He made no effort to prevent Nathaniel from hearing their conversation: "The general wants him kept here overnight. You stay in the room with him. Don't be afraid to get rough if he needs it, but try not to kill him."

"What's going to happen to him?"

"Soldier, I don't know what's going to happen to any of us. The nation is very near disaster."

"This man is innocent, you know that, don't you?"

"Don't be insubordinate." The officer locked the door behind him.

The two spent a fitful night. Daniels no longer wanted to talk so Nathaniel let him be.

They were awakened by gunfire. Musket fire came from every quarter; there were cannon to the east.

Nathaniel was sore from his ordeal of the day before. He hadn't lost any teeth but he seemed to have a black eye and bruises all over his body. It hurt to breathe so he likely had a few cracked ribs as well.

He got to his feet and looked out the window. A thick fog had come in during the night. Men were running pell-mell through it, shouting to one another. Several shells struck nearby.

"I think they've found the range on this house," Nathaniel said.

"Yes," Daniels said. "I suspect some spy told them where it was."

Nathaniel turned away from the window. "Don't start that again."

"Curry, you know if I get the order, I have to do my duty."

Nathaniel turned and looked him in the eye. "Well, if you do, please get word to the Balloon Corps."

Daniels nodded. He looked like he wanted to say something, but before he could formulate the sentence both of them were dashed to the floor by an explosion.

Nathaniel staggered to his feet, then helped Daniels up. "You okay?"

"I think so. I lost my gun."

"There it is, by the settee."

"What happened?"

"I got glass on me," Nathaniel said. "And it's all over the floor."

"The window blew out. It's all over the place. Am I bleeding?"

"Let me look at you. Not much. You got a little glass on you. Come over to the window."

"Be careful, Curry, there's glass all over the floor."

"I see it."

There wasn't much glass by the window itself. Nathaniel, wishing more than ever that he was wearing shoes, made his way to the window and looked out.

A shell had struck one of the elegant wooden pillars of the mansion, shattering it. The pillar was split top to bottom, with large sections blasted loose. Pieces were still falling out of the air.

Hooker stood before the building, babbling incomprehensibly. Gradually his words made more sense: "We have to fall back to the river. They have us overrun. We need to form a defensive U with our back to the river. Order the men to fall back."

"General, our forces are engaged right now, they can't fall back."

"Order them to break off! We have to get out now or we'll be annihilated."

"Yes, sir."

Although Hooker himself was now a shattered pillar, his staff moved calmly to obey his orders. Junior officers were detailed to remove documents from the study and other rooms that had been used as offices. A major with long red mustaches burst into the room where Nathaniel was being held and said, "Clear out, soldier. Time to go."

"I have a prisoner here, sir."

"Well, time for him to go, too. Time for him to go to Hell." The major vanished.

Daniels turned to him. Nathaniel was hoping to see compassion in his eyes but he saw only steely resolve. "Curry, get against that wall."

"All right." He walked to the wall, heedless of the glass, and turned to look at Daniels.

"Turn around."

"Why?"

"I said so."

From far away his father's words came back to him: His wounds were all in the front. That means something.

"No."

"God damn it, turn away from me!"

He wasn't afraid. He didn't think he was afraid, at any rate, but his knees were trembling. A phrase drifted back from some Sunday morning long ago: the spirit is willing but the flesh is weak. "Just shoot me and be damned, Daniels."

Daniels said something but Nathaniel couldn't understand it and didn't care to. He felt as if he were already half in the next world. The cares of this stupid world and the fools that inhabited it would soon be left behind.

Daniels fumbled with his musket. He brought it back to full cock, raised it, took careful aim and fired.

Within the confines of the small room the report of the musket was as loud as the artillery shell had been. Nathaniel felt a blast of burning powder on his face and neck and a different stinging sensation on his back. His knees buckled and he fell against the wall, then onto the floor.

When he opened his eyes he was alone. His heart was beating more rapidly than he had ever felt it in his life. He moved around; he felt no worse than he had a few seconds ago.

There was now a hole in the wall where none had been before. The ball could not have missed his head by more than an inch. Daniels was either a very good shot or a very poor one.

The Army of the Potomac went away, drawing the sound of battle with it. Silence fell upon the house. Nathaniel lay where he had fallen.

He was awakened by the sound of someone entering the room. It was Joe. His suit was immaculate, as always; it made a strange contrast to the disorder around him.

"Good morning, sir."

"Good morning, Joe. Can you help me up?"

"Sure enough. Come over to the settee. Mind that glass."

"Joe, do you have a pair of shoes I could borrow?"

"Let me look, sir."

He returned in a few minutes with a fine pair of shoes. According to the label they were made in London. The stockings were long and sheer and were probably intended to be worn with knee-garters. He brushed the glass off his feet and put them on.

"They don't suit the rest of my clothes, do they?"

"Not very well, sir."

"Perfect fit, though."

"Yes, indeed."

"These belong to your master?"

"I have no master, sir. I a free man."

Nathaniel went to the window. The morning sun shining through the fog made a dim yellow light. There were several overturned and broken wagons in the rutted road. Beyond the wagons the fog hung like a curtain. The scene looked like the stage for some queer play.

Joe came back into the room and swept up the glass.

"Everyone gone, then?"

"Everyone but you, sir. You and me."

"Well, it won't be for long, I suspect."

He was right. Within a few minutes Confederate cavalrymen brandishing carbines rode onto the stage. They reined in and peered around them silently. They knew they were the first Confederates on the scene and were wary of an ambush.

These were crack troops, Nathaniel knew. They were burly and hard and they knew their business.

The sergeant pointed his rifle one-handed at the window and said, "Come out of there with your hands up."

"We're a-coming," Nathaniel said. "Don't shoot."

He headed for the front hall, Joe tagging behind him. "Let me do the talking, Joe."

"Yessir."

The soldier kept his weapon trained on him as he came onto the front porch; the other soldiers didn't look at them. "Who the Hell are you?"

"The Yankees ketched me and stole my horse."

"Where'd you get that jewelry?"

"The Yankees put it on me."

"Yeah? They say why?"

"They said I was a Rebel spy."

"Yeah? Are you?"

"No. I'm just looking for work."

"Who else is in the house?"

"Nobody. Just me and this old darkie."

"No other slaves?"

"Contraband."

"Where they go, these Yankees?"

"I don't know. They lit out about an hour ago."

"What, they left you behind?"

"They were in an all-fired hurry."

The sergeant pointed his weapon at the sky and fired a single shot. Within minutes the infantry arrived. The officers set the men to securing the perimeter. The men deployed into the murk as far as they could without losing sight of one another. Other men started to clean up. Within a few minutes the area around the house was a Confederate camp.

Nathaniel and Joe sat on the top step and watched the goings-on.

A cry arose from the fog. It wasn't the Rebel yell, it was cheering and clapping. Nathaniel knew what would happen next and got to his feet; Joe followed suit.

The sunlight had done little to dispel the mist but had instead brightened it to a yellow glow. Out of this mist rode a tall figure in a broad hat. Robert E. Lee looked weary, but no more weary than he always looked, and his uniform was as spruce as ever. Every man present cheered and clapped; many waved their hats in the air.

The heavens themselves acknowledged his arrival for the mist began to rise at that very moment. Sunlight broke through and shone on his face like a limelight. Lee rode up to the house and gave the blasted column a glance, then turned to speak to the man who rode behind him.

Still the cheering continued. Every man present gave voice to his adulation. No: as Nathaniel looked around, he realized that it was more than love and gratitude these men were expressing, it was fealty. Lee was at that moment more than their commander, more even than a victor. He was a conqueror and this was his triumph.

Joe leaned over and said, "This mean I a slave again?"

Nathaniel shook his head. "It ain't over yet."

Lee had recovered from his injuries of the previous autumn, for he got down from Traveller without assistance. Nathaniel and Joe stood aside at his approach; Joe glanced at the ground. Lee looked at Nathaniel and asked, "Why is this man in bonds?"

No one could answer this, for the soldier who had initially questioned Nathaniel was gone. Nathaniel had to answer: "Sir, the Yankees caught me. They thought I was a Rebel, excuse me, sir, a Confederate spy."

"Did they abuse you as well?"

"Yessir."

"Don't I know you, young man?"

"Sir, I was a camp boy with you last year."

"Why are you not in uniform?"

"I made a promise to my mother not to join up, sir."

"Where are you from?"

"Fairfax County."

"What are you doing in these parts?"

"Looking for work."

Lee nodded. "We can give you work." He turned to the officer behind him. "Remove his bonds and clean him up. Send him around to me after noon." He glanced at the youth's shoes, then went into the house.

Several enlisted men took charge of Nathaniel. At first they tried to find a key that fit his manacles but none would do the job. At last they brought him to a blacksmith who was traveling with the army. This man was a free Negro, black as coal, with bare arms like the trunks of trees. He gave the manacles a glance, then set Nathaniel's hands on an anvil. He placed a cold chisel on the bonds and with two taps of the hammer he was emancipated.

The soldiers then cleaned his injuries as well as they could and brought him back to the manor house. Several parties had business with the commander and they waited their turn.

As they stepped up to speak to him a captain approached. Lee turned to the man anxiously. It seemed to Nathaniel that the junior officer was older than most men of his rank and did not have a military bearing; he surmised that he worked in a specialized capacity, such as medicine. This turned out to be the case. Nathaniel caught snatches of what the man told Lee: they took the arm...fear of sepsis...holding up but he lost a lot of blood...pneumonia. Lee closed his eyes and nodded; the captain left without saluting.

When Lee opened his eyes he caught sight of Nathaniel and gestured for him to approach. He nodded to the soldiers, dismissing them.

"Your name is High, is it not?"

"Yes, sir."

"You promised your mother not to join up?"

"Yes, sir. I'm all she has left."

"And where is she?"

"She's on the farm."

"Fairfax County is in Union hands."

"Yes, sir, but she won't leave."

"And you wouldn't stay?"

"I don't think I could have brung in a crop on my lonesome, sir. And if I did, the Yankees would have took it."

"Yes. And that is why you're looking for work down here?"

"Yes, sir."

"But they pay you in Confederate money, don't they?"

"Yes, sir. If I can even find the work."

"Confederate money must be worthless in Fairfax County."

"Well, yes, sir." He was making this up as he went along and was wary of making a mistake in the logic of his lies.

"Why don't you seek work in the North?"

"Sir, among the Yankees?"

Lee nodded. "I can pay you a dollar a day in gold."

"Sir, that's very good."

"And you realize that your country is conscripting now. If you were taken in the draft, your mother's objections would not stand. But I could keep you from it."

Nathaniel hesitated. He had no desire to stay among the Confederates any longer than necessary but he could hardly tell Lee that. "Why me, sir?"

"I have soldiers detailed to help me but they always have other duties to attend to. I need a lad who won't be called off on kitchen police or guard duty."

Nathaniel nodded. "I'll help you out, sir."

"Fine. You can start by taking notes for me." He took a piece of board off of a barrel that stood beside him. Upon the board were a sheet of paper and a pencil.

Nathaniel again hesitated. During his previous time with the Army of Northern Virginia, he had intimated that he was illiterate. Would he be compromising himself if he could now read and write? He decided that he would not.

Lee noticed his hesitation and looked at him. Nathaniel said, "Excuse me, sir, but was a friend of your'n wounded?"

Lee nodded, and upon his noble visage Nathaniel now saw a look that he had seen upon countless men in the past year and a half. "General Jackson was wounded. The outlook is grim, I'm afraid."

"General *Stonewall* Jackson?" Nathaniel gasped.

"Yes," Lee said. "He has lost his left arm, but I have lost my right arm."

The stricken look Nathaniel displayed was genuine, despite his sympathy for the Union. He mastered himself a moment later as a major approached Lee. "We have the Union officers here, sir."

"Which ones?"

"The quick and the dead."

"Good. Come along, High."

The fog was gone now and it was turning into a nice day. Nathaniel and Lee followed the major to the side of the house, where eight Federal officers stood. They were of various ranks and wore different uniforms. They came to attention at the general's approach.

Two of the eight were known to Nathaniel, and they in fact looked at him in recognition, though they had the wits to say nothing.

Lee greeted them courteously, offering his hand to a man whom he knew, and made sure that their immediate needs had been looked after. He then said, "Gentlemen, I call you to a sad task. There are several of your comrades whose remains we hold and whose identities my staff were unable to ascertain. It is not right that honorable men should fall and their families not get word. I wish to observe them now, to see if there is any man I know, and I wish your aid in this."

"Sir," the senior man present said, "we shall be happy to assist you."

"Good. Come this way, then, please, gentlemen."

The remains had been laid out behind a stable that was about fifty yards from the house. The bodies lay under several sheets to ward off the flies that had already gathered.

Lee himself named the first man to be exposed and Nathaniel set his name down. The second, a younger man, was known to an officer who first turned to Lee, then, at his nod, to Nathaniel.

The second sheet was removed and there lay Nathaniel's friend

Lieutenant Spencer. He had been killed by a bullet to the head. Behind his face and above his right ear the skull had been neatly removed, as had the portion of brain beneath it. It must have been so sudden that he could have felt no pain. He stared sadly up at Nathaniel and Lee.

Several of the officers expressed sorrow at the sight of this fair youth, but Nathaniel lost control of himself. Tears blinded him and he was racked with loud sobs. Even within his grief, however, he realized the danger he was putting himself in. He struggled in vain to get control of himself.

Lee turned to him, surprised at Nathaniel's reaction to the death of a person he could not have known, and Nathaniel had to turn away from him.

In that moment Nathaniel hated Lee. He saw Lee's gesture in turning to him as meaning, See what I have done, see what I enjoy doing. Lee was the motor for this war; it was because of him that the South had not surrendered as it should have. If he had had a gun he would have slain him on the spot.

It was Lee himself who comforted him. He touched his arm and said, "There, there, my boy. It's sad, but this lad must have died nobly, and he is surely in a better place. Come, now. Come, now."

Nathaniel drew a breath and nodded. This was after all not the first friend he had lost. He took up the board and pencil again and nearly wrote Spencer's name before he caught himself.

He wanted to return to the Union lines but could not see a ready way to do so. The Union Army was presumably only a few miles away, but it was across a river and both sides kept close watch on the shores. He would have to bide his time.

He fell back into the routine of Confederate camp life. Lee spent most of his time closeted with his generals, so he had a lot of free time. At first he did nothing when not with Lee, but then he began to pitch in with the other camp boys.

The camp boys were mostly lads too young to enlist in the Army, or not fit to serve for some reason. The work that they did was invariably the meanest tasks. Their remuneration was usually in Confederate currency, which was increasingly worthless. The Army, however, provided them both sustenance and excitement, so there was no shortage of hands.

A number of free Negroes also did camp work. Nathaniel hoped against hope that he would find Uncle Sammy there, but he did not.

On his second day in the camp, upon being released by Lee, Nathaniel sought out the camp prostitutes. He found this an embarrassing experience, having never done so before. He approached an area on the outskirts of the camp that was the domain of sutlers and other merchants. He encountered a woman in late middle age, luridly painted and quite fleshy. At his approach she gave him a smile that would have benefited from a few more teeth and asked, "Hello, honey, want to have a party?"

"Sure," he said, smiling back. "Is there somewhere we can go?"

When they had sequestered themselves in a tent, she said, "First let me see the color of your money, and it better be yellow. I've had quite enough of this Confederate stuff."

"To tell you the truth, ma'am, I haven't any."

"Do you think I brought you in here to make friends with you?"

"No. I wonder if you know a girl name of Muriel."

"No. Should I?"

"You might know her as Sally or Mrs. Pettijohn."

She gave him a withering look. "What are you playing at?"

"You don't know her at all?"

"You're wasting my time, boy," she said, and threw him out of the tent. Utterly humiliated, he declined to try again.

The next day he was idling with the other camp boys when a youth he knew only as Thompson said, "Hey, look, it's the Dummy!"

Everyone looked up. A young Negro stood in the midst of them, smiling shyly.

"Who is this?" someone asked, and Thompson replied, "Why, this here's the Dummy. He don't never talk. I don't know if he deaf or just stupid, but he never talk. Funniest God-damned nigger you ever seen, though."

"Yeah? What he do?"

"Oh, he just a cutup, that's all. He can dance, too. Dummy, you cut us the pigeon wing, now. C'mon, dance for us, boy!" Thompson got up and pawed at the ground with one foot, flapping his arms like a chicken, and the Dummy responded. He did several dances popular in minstrel shows. He did them well enough to draw laughter and cheers from his watchers, though none offered money.

"So who does this Dummy belong to?" someone asked.

"Don't rightly know," Thompson said. "He might be a stray."

"I wouldn't be surprised," another man replied. "I wouldn't want no nigger couldn't talk. He wouldn't be good for nothing but a field hand."

"So what's the matter with a field hand?"

"Well, I ain't own no cotton fields."

"How come we ain't seen him before?" someone asked.

"Shoot, I don't know," Thompson said. "He come and go. I ain't seen him in months. Yeah, you stop that now, Dummy," he said, picking up a piece of horse dung and throwing it at him. The Dummy stopped dancing and smiled benignly at Thompson.

Nathaniel went to Lee's tent to see if the general had awakened from his nap, but he had not. As he returned to the camp boys he saw the Dummy standing apart from the others as if waiting for him. At Nathaniel's approach he held something up. To Nathaniel's surprise it was his rosewood-handled jackknife.

"Nigger, where you get that—" he began, then caught himself. It couldn't be his knife, he had left it behind in the Union camp.

The Dummy held the knife close to his chest so that only Nathaniel could see it. He gave Nathaniel a look of simple-minded astonishment as if to mock the confusion Nathaniel felt.

Nathaniel struggled to make sense of what was happening. It *was* his knife. He recognized the little brass rose. For some reason the Dummy had it, and he wanted Nathaniel to know he had it. When at last he understood, the Dummy's face lit up in a joyous grin.

"What's he got?" Thompson said, coming up behind the Negro. He took both of the Dummy's hands, but the knife was gone.

"Oh, nothing," Nathaniel said. "I thought he had something in his mouth but it's gone."

"Oh. You got to watch these niggers, they'll rob you blind."

"I know it. Say, I'm going to take him and get some kindling, how's that?"

Thompson shrugged. "I don't care."

Nathaniel tugged the Dummy's sleeve and they both set out for the woods.

It was a beautiful day. Spring had finally come and the trees were leafing out nicely. The foliage cast shimmering shadows on the forest floor and all around them birds were singing. They followed an old Indian path that was barely visible through the fallen leaves.

Nathaniel said, "Your name is Carl, right?"

"Yowsah, Mars' N'than'l."

"You stop that. You ain't nohow no good at it."

"Well, I'm no Booth."

"I can see why you don't talk. You sound just like a God-damned Yankee."

"Well, I am a God-damned Yankee. I'm from Boston. You can't get more Yankee than that without going to New Hampshire." He handed Nathaniel the jackknife and he slipped it into his pocket.

"Did you come here to rescue little old me?"

"I certainly did."

"I didn't do anything worth a tinker's dam."

"Yes, you did. You were willing to go, and that's something."

Nathaniel glanced at him. "I transmitted what was in the paper, you know."

"I know. We got a copy ourselves. Lee either changed his mind or he's learned to lie to the newspaper men."

"Someone better tell Hooker that before he orders me shot again."

Carl made a dismissive gesture. "I don't think General Hooker will be a danger to anyone but himself from now on."

"Oh, he's going the way of the others, then?"

Carl nodded. "He's 'a poor player who struts and frets his hour upon the stage, then is heard no—'"

"Hey! Are you *talking?*"

Both stopped and turned around. Thompson was coming up behind them. He didn't look angry or alarmed, just surprised.

As he approached, Nathaniel had a queer moment in which he saw Thompson as if for the first time, and very clearly. Every detail of his visage was imprinted on his consciousness, and Nathaniel knew that he would never forget it. Thompson's squinting eyes, apple cheeks and broad mouth made him look like he was always smiling. His freckles and tousled hair imparted a childlike quality to his appearance.

Carl turned to Nathaniel, bowing like an English gentleman, and held out his hand. His face was expressionless but there was death in his eyes. Nathaniel bowed in return and surreptitiously handed him back the knife. He was simultaneously amused by their courtly gestures and repelled by what was about to happen.

"Nigger, how come you ain't never talked before?" Thompson said, a broad smile on his face. Carl responded by lunging forward like a fencer and thrusting the knife into his stomach. As Thompson doubled over from the sudden pain, Carl slashed the knife across his throat, then stepped back to avoid the fountain of blood. He accomplished all of this in a single motion, as if it were a dance step.

Thompson was so taken by surprise that he spent his last earthly moments staring at Carl in confusion. As he started to fall, Carl grabbed the seat of his pants and his shirt collar and threw him off the path into the woods. He didn't get up.

Carl and Nathaniel each took an armful of leaves and threw them on top of him. "There you go, Johnny Reb," Carl said, "*Requiescat in Pacem.*"

"That was too bad," Nathaniel said, retrieving his knife from the path. "He really wasn't a bad sort." They turned back down the path.

"He had dedicated his life to making me a slave," Carl said. "I was happy to kill him. I'd like to kill more like him."

"Oh, you sound like Old Jack," Nathaniel muttered.

"Who?"

"Stonewall Jackson. I heard him talk about killing Yankees that way. 'Kill them all, kill them without mercy!' He was hollering."

"Indeed? Well, I'd like to show him the same favor."

"Someone beat you to it. He lies a-dying."

"He does? How sad. What happened?"

"He was shot by his own men."

"Oh, that's rich. That's enough to restore my faith in human nature. Your knife wants sharpening, you know."

"I know it, but I don't have a stone. Say, where are we going?"

"Down the road a piece. You'll see."

"Okay."

An eastern bluebird, heedless of war and all the affairs of men, landed on a branch and cocked its head at them. Nathaniel made a pistol of his thumb and forefinger and shot at it. He missed and it flew away.

"Tell me," Carl said, "where'd you get those shoes?"

Chapter Eleven:
High and Lowe

"Solly," Nathaniel Curry said, "you get more mail than the rest of us put together."

Vogler looked over his glasses at him and smiled.

"What are you reading now? What language is that?"

"It's German. This is the journal of the Royal Society of Prussia."

"Wouldn't they speak Prussian?"

"No. You're thinking of Russia, where they speak Russian."

"Oh. The letters aren't the same as ours."

"Well, they're the same letters, but they form them differently."

"What's it a Royal Society of?"

"It's a scientific organization, modeled after the Royal Society of England."

"So that magazine's like *The Scientific American* in our country?"

"Very much like it, indeed."

"So what's new in science in Prussia?"

"Well, I think all of us might be interested in this story. It concerns aerostatics."

The entire camp bestirred itself. The Allen brothers looked up from their breakfast. Professor Lowe put down the letter from his wife. Only Captain Comstock showed no interest.

"I shall endeavor to translate this as I read it. You'll have to forgive me, but it's not the easiest of tasks." He cleared his throat.

"'A new altitude record has been set by two English balloonists. On July 17 of last year, aerialist Henry Coxwell and scientist James Glaisher made an ascent from Dunstall in the balloon *Mars*. It was a very windy day and the two were on the point of calling off their attempt when the rope securing the *Mars* to the earth sundered. They made the best of the situation and ascended to an altitude of 22,357 feet. They made numerous observations of atmospheric pressure and temperature along the way. The altitude they attained is counted the greatest ever attained by men.'"

"Why, that's almost certainly the case," James Allen interjected. "I believe the old record was about eighteen thousand feet. Twenty-two thousand? That would be higher than any known mountain on Earth."

"But there's more," Vogler said. "'On September the Fifth –' why, this was about the time of the Antietam battle – 'the two made a second ascent. This time the municipal gas with which *Mars* was charged was of a higher quality and provided greater lift. The aerial explorers made a controlled ascent and rose above two miles within nineteen minutes. In short order the four mile and five mile marks were passed.

"'This passage was not made without peril, however. Because the car was unevenly loaded, the gasbag turned within its harness and fouled the release line to the valve.'"

"Now, there's a concern," Ezra Allen said. "I don't see how the loading of the basket could do that, though."

"Well, we haven't seen their arrangement, either," his brother said. "But I find it more likely that the expansion of the bag fouled the line."

"Yes, indeed," Ezra replied. "Atmospheric pressure halves every three miles of altitude. Why, the bag would have expanded four times! One would need to valve to keep from bursting."

"Oh, it's better than that," Vogler said. "'Coxwell clambered into the rigging to free the valve line. Glaisher, for his part, lost his sight, then sensation in his limbs, and then lost all sensibility. This may be attributed to the paucity of oxygen at that altitude as well as to the extreme cold, which was recorded as minus eleven degrees.' Let me see, that would equal about twelve degrees on the Fahrenheit scale. I'm afraid I'm not translating this very well."

"Oh, no, you're doing splendidly," Nathaniel said. "So this fellow went climbing in the rigging at over five miles altitude? What happened next?"

"'Coxwell lost sensation in his hands and felt his eyesight and his consciousness failing, but attempted nonetheless to free the line for the valve. He knew that if the balloon were not brought down, it would either continue to rise and must eventually burst, or would stay at a high altitude until its occupants expired for lack of oxygen.'"

"Well, the gasbag might have burst and formed a parachute," James Allen said. "John Wise ends his exhibitions by doing that very thing."

"Yes," Ezra replied, "but he employs a rip panel so it happens in a controlled fashion."

"But think of the position he was in!" James said. "He was climbing in the rigging, losing eyesight, losing sensation, and he was on the edge of passing out. One slip and it would have been all over. Except that it would have taken four or five minutes to reach Mother Earth."

"'At length, Coxwell freed the line and returned to the car. He vented gas and began the descent. He then endeavored to arouse Glaisher, who remained insensible.

"'They descended into Groton, which is twenty miles distant from Dunstall. Coxwell managed to rouse Glaisher, then went into the town to secure assistance.

"'An examination of their instruments indicates that the *Mars* attained an altitude of 37,000 feet, or approximately eleven kilometers. This makes Coxwell and Glaisher the first men to enter the stratosphere. This is a significant milestone in the exploration of the upper atmosphere. That these men accomplished this feat without the employment of supplemental sources of oxygen and survived is a further achievement.

"'However, it is the opinion of this writer that this experiment shall stand as the ultimate achievement in the exploration of the upper atmosphere. Glaisher's observations demonstrate merely that in the upper atmosphere, atmospheric pressure and temperature both decrease, which is precisely what intuition would tell us.

"'Moreover, it must be recognized that this experiment was dangerous in the extreme. Any attempt to reach a higher altitude in a manned balloon would be folly. It is true that the employment of carbolic acid or other means of generating oxygen could help aeronauts to survive at extreme altitudes, but there would be little utility of risking human life in this manner, particularly when there is so much still undiscovered down here upon the Earth. The flight of the *Mars* almost certainly marks the end of scientific exploration of the upper reaches of the atmosphere.'"

No one spoke for about a minute. Then Lowe turned to Comstock. "Captain, I did not wish to resign my position while a campaign was in progress. I would like to know if it would be convenient if I did so now."

Comstock considered for a few seconds, then replied, "This would be as good a time as any."

Lowe nodded. "I shall write a letter to you to that effect forthwith." He put his wife's letter in his waistcoat pocket and went into his tent.

"Professor, I wonder if there was anything I might do for you."

Lowe turned from the trunk he was packing and nodded to indicate that Nathaniel might enter the tent. The youth dropped the flap and stepped in.

"There is really nothing, Nathaniel, but I sense that that is not what inspired you to visit me."

"Of course it isn't, sir, but I didn't know what else to say."

Lowe smiled. "I know: it's like speaking to one who is in mourning, isn't it? Still, it isn't that bad. We've accomplished something, though not all have the eyes to see it. And with one exception, we've lived through it. Not everyone who has been in this conflict can say that." He placed his field glasses in the trunk and closed the lid.

"What will you do now, sir? Where will you go?"

"Well, I'll go back to New Hampshire to begin with. The first thing I want to do is take a rest. After that, I might resume my aerial exhibitions. The dream of flying the Atlantic remains, of course, as it must for all aerialists, but I must first concentrate on making a living."

"What about the war, sir?"

"Well, I suppose the war will go on. The South will continue to fight valiantly and brilliantly. The North will counter with greater arms and armies and with lesser leaders. Where it will end up no one can now say, but it looks like it could drag on for years."

Nathaniel nodded. He had meant to ask Lowe what he intended to do to support the war effort, but he had his answer.

Lowe turned to him and smiled. "I'm glad we had this moment together, Nathaniel. You were the first to follow me on this fool's errand. The first and the last. Thank you."

Upon Lowe's departure Captain Comstock assembled the Balloon Corps. "I consider this experiment unhappily concluded," he said, "and this organization dissolved."

"If I may, sir," James Allen said, rising, "I do not consider the experiment concluded. I was making observations for the Army before Professor Lowe was, and I intend to continue to do so."

"Do you think anyone will avail themselves of your services?"

"Indeed I do, sir." He held up a military message sheet. "This is a note that was delivered to me a few minutes ago."

"A note? What does it say?"

"General Butterfield inquires as to why Professor Lowe has not gone up today."

"That note should have come to me."

"Do you want it? It would serve as a nice trophy of your victory."

"Don't be impertinent, young man!"

Allen shrugged and sat down.

Comstock was nearly livid with rage. "You people are a disgrace to the Union! You have wasted the treasure of the Army, and you have made it a laughingstock in every theater of war you have entered. Worst of all, you have wasted my time for some months now. You shall not waste another second of it. Farewell!" He stormed out of the camp.

Everyone sat in silence for a few seconds; then James Allen stood and said, "I shall now take charge, if there are no objections." There were none, so he continued, "I can't promise to pay any of you, but we have all made good shift of begging from the Army the last few months. Iron filings and vitriol for charging the balloons are in short supply, but if we're parsimonious, we can keep flying for a couple of months.

"There is a demand for our services and we must meet that demand. In that way, the Army will come to appreciate what we are doing. Then we'll get supplies and our salary.

"We have a difficult time ahead of us, but we must all bear in mind that it is for a greater good. We must also remember that our sacrifices are as nothing compared to what the boys in the field are giving up."

Chapter Twelve: The Prince of Arabee

"Jim, *Eagle* needs a charge."

"We can't do that, Nathaniel."

"When do we get more vitriol?"

"The Army says it's on order and is expected any day now."

"They've been saying that for weeks."

"How bad is *Eagle*?"

"It won't lift over a hundred feet."

"Are there still sandbags on it?"

"Just one."

"All right, drop it."

"It's not going to be steady."

"I know it! You'll just have to live with it."

"Can't I try to charge it?"

"No, you can't. I want to save the charge that's in there for *Intrepid*."

"All right."

"And Nathaniel?"

"Yeah?"

"Call me 'Mister Allen.'"

"Can I tap in here?"

"Who the Hell are you?"

"I'm with the Balloon Corps."

"We don't want you on our line. Stay out."

"But I have to get a line in to the commander-in-chief."

"You got orders?"

"Yes, General Butterfield wrote them. Here."

"Aw, Jesus. All right, I guess. Just no chatter, keep it strictly business, you hear?"

"Yes, Sarge."

"Do you even know code?"

"Sure I do. Look, is this really such a bother?"

"We have enough hands on the line right now. The field commanders are all sending telegrams to each other during the fighting now."

"What I'm doing is important, too."

"Of course it is. And I'm the Prince of Arabee."

TO GEN BUTTERFIELD FROM CURRY BALLOON CORPS FIVE THOUSAND MEN SIX MILES SOUTH OF MY POSITION STOP

THOSE ARE OUR MEN SOLDIER

NO THEY ARE NOT THEY ARE TOO FAR AWAY STOP

YES THEY ARE CHASING JOHNSTON

THANK YOU SOLDIER 73

"How long has *Enterprise* been charging?"

"Six hours now."

"God damn it, and it's still not full?"

"The vitriol's shot to Hell, Jim."

"I told you not to call me by my first name, Nathaniel."

"Well, you can forget about that. Can we get any more juice?"

"No…but there's still a little iron left. Pour some of that in there."

"Okay."

"And call me James if you must. But not Jim. No one's ever called me Jim."

TO GEN BUTTERFIELD FROM CURRY BALLOON CORPS CONFEDERATE FORCES SOUTH OF FBURG MOVING WEST STOP

SHUT UP SHUT UP STAY OFF OF THIS LINE

NO FORWARD THIS TO COMMAND STOP

WHO IS THIS

BALLOON CORPS

REBELS ARE LISTENING ON THIS LINE STAY OFF DAM YOU

SORRY I DID NOT KNOW

PARTY USING IMPROPER LANGUAGE ON THE TELEGRAPH IDENTIFY YOURSELF

SHIT IN YOUR HAT AND PUT IT ON YOUR HEAD

"Are we moving again?"

"They think Lee is forming up south of Fredericksburg now, Ezra."

"Think? No one knows?"

"If anyone knows, they aren't telling me."

"One of us should go up and see if there's any dust around."

"No. We have to pack the wagon now. We don't want to be in the last wagon train out again."

"That's for certain."

"Nathaniel, look what I got."

"Where'd you get ten dollars, boy?"

"My father sent it to me."

"I thought he disapproved of you being here."

"He does, but he doesn't want me to starve."

"Does he know you're eating stuff you shouldn't be a-eating?"

"No, but he isn't here, and neither is my rabbi. Want to go get something to eat?"

"Sure enough."

"Did you hear they're investing Vicksburg?"

"No, I didn't. Where'd you hear it, from the spies?"

"No, I have as little truck with them as I can manage. I heard it at Headquarters."

"Who is doing it?"

"It's Grant."

"Grant the drunk?"

"The very same. He's been tearing up the map out west, they say."

"I hope he isn't another Hooker."

"No. He won't stop drinking, and that's a fact."

"Yeah. And is that good or bad?"

"Well, by their fruits shall you know them, I suppose."

"So he wants Vicksburg, does he?"

"Yeah, and why there, Ezra? Isn't it a little out of the way?"

"No, not really. It's in the middle of the Mississippi, and it would split the Confederacy in twain."

"Well, good luck to him, then."

"Yeah, good luck and good hunting."

"Nathaniel, wake up!"

"Nuh? What is it?"

"You hear them guns?"

"Guns?"

"Yes, there's guns! Are they going out or coming in?"

"Shucks, those are Parrott rifle cannon, Sol. Johnny Reb ain't got none of them."

"You sure?"

"Sure as shooting."

"Could you tell that in your sleep?"

"I reckon. Can I go back to sleep now?"

"Yes, I'm sorry."

Chapter Thirteen: Survival of the Fittest

"How many prisoners are there?"

"Well, I heard about two thousand. That's a pretty good haul on any day."

"Well, I should say so. I thought Johnny Reb was going to fight to the last man."

"Well, they did, and the last man was a Quaker."

"So where-all are they?"

Ezra Allen pointed toward the north. "They're going to march them off to the railroad station, I hear."

Nathaniel looked in the indicated direction. "Maybe I'll go have a look."

"Think you might see someone you know?"

"Well, you never can tell. Also, sometimes I just miss how folks talk."

Allen shrugged. "Fine. We're pretty much on casual status now, you and I. *Eagle* is the only ship with gas in it and James is up in it."

"Ezra, what's going to happen to us? Are we ever going to get our due?"

Allen shook his head. "We'll get our due like every man does, I suppose. The only question is when it happens."

The Rebel soldiers sat in the middle of a clearing. It was a hot day and every man present looked thirsty. Nathaniel turned on his heel and returned a few minutes later with a bucket and ladle.

A company of soldiers surrounded these unfortunates and they were reluctant to let Nathaniel approach the prisoners until a sergeant gave his permission. The desperate soldiers leapt to their feet at his approach. "Give it here, Billy! Give me some of that!"

"Take it easy, fellows, you'll spill this."

"There ain't near enough here for all of us anyhow. Give me another drink, damn you." The soldiers spurned the ladle and dipped water from the bucket with their hands, spilling as much as they drank.

"Don't drink so fast, you'll get the trots," Nathaniel warned.

"Trots? Christ sakes, boy, you need to have food in you to make shit."

"Do you have any food, Billy? If you have anything at all, I'll bless you, and that's a fact."

"No, I don't. You boys are hungry, are you?"

"I ain't et in two days. Some have gone longer."

"Lansbury, don't go telling him things," the man beside him said. This soldier had not risen from the ground and now spoke with his back to Nathaniel. "This man is our enemy, you know."

"Not any more," Nathaniel said, assuming a friendly air. "The war is over for you boys. And it's up to the Army to take care of you now."

"We've heard all about your prison camps," the seated man said.

"Why, what have you heard?" Nathaniel asked.

"That you're better off dying on the field," the man said.

This was the first time Nathaniel had seen Rebels up close in several weeks. He was struck by the change he saw. The men who had cheered Lee's triumph at Chancellorsville were now hungry and dispirited. He knew that he should be cheered by the sight, but he was not. The thin and weary wretches before him, clad in filthy rags, only inspired pity.

He had not thought much about the prison camps. This was principally because he figured he would never be going to one. He might get stood up against a wall and shot, but he wouldn't go to a prison camp.

The soldiers on both sides spoke of the camps with dread, though. To some extent this was merely due to fear of the unknown, but there had to be some truth to the terrible rumors each side heard of the other's camps.

There was only a little water left in the bottom of the bucket now and a man picked it up and poured it into his mouth. The man beside him said, "Where you from, Billy?"

"Who, me? No place special."

"You talk like a Southern boy. Where you hie from?"

The other soldiers were not so friendly now that the water was gone. "Yes, where you from, boy?" another man asked. "You a turncoat?" asked another. Within seconds the entire mass of men rose to denounce him as a traitor.

Nathaniel stepped back, surprised at the sudden change. These men were hungry, thirsty, barefoot and defeated, but they were still defiant.

The bucket and ladle were tossed at his feet. He gathered them up and walked away.

"That's fine work, soldier," the sergeant of the guards said. "We done all we could to settle them down and then you rile them up again. Get the Hell out of here."

Nathaniel complied, reflecting on his way back to the Corps' camp that everything he did, no matter how noble the intention, redounded to his ill.

At the camp he was given a message to report to Captain Thomas immediately. He went to Hooker's headquarters and found her waiting for him. "How do you do, Nathaniel?" she asked, taking his hand. He removed his hat and returned the greeting. "Will you walk with me?"

"Of course, ma'am."

She raised a small black parasol against the afternoon sun. "How are things going in your organization, Nathaniel?"

"Pretty poorly, ma'am, but I suspect you knew that."

"Yes, I did. I suppose you know it's only a matter of time before you are dissolved once and for all."

"I'm afraid so."

"What will you do then?"

"Well, I don't reckon I know."

"Do you have six hundred dollars?"

He smiled. "I don't think I'd buy my way out of this even if I could."

"Then it's the infantry for you unless you find a different line of work."

"I could be an operator."

"Yes, you could, unless we decided otherwise."

He turned to her. "What?"

"Our organization holds considerable sway. The telegraph division listens to our opinions." She said this as calmly as if she was discussing the weather.

"So it's work for you or carry a musket?"

"It would be to your advantage as well."

"My advantage? That's shi—I mean, that's not true."

"Come on, Nathaniel. We've always been your friends."

"All of you have threatened to kill me at one time or another."

She waved her hand dismissively. "Pay that no mind. If someone really wanted to kill you they would have done it."

"Sally Pettijohn still suspects me of killing David Miller."

"No, she does not."

"You sure?"

"She told me that she knows you didn't do it. She said she's very sure of it."

"Well, that's good. She say who did it?"

"No."

"I reckon I know."

Thomas glanced at him. "If he did, I'm sure he had good cause."

"Yes," Nathaniel replied, "but was it the Confederate Cause?"

She turned away, putting her parasol between them.

"Nathaniel," she said a moment later, "even if you don't join us, I'd like to thank you for what you've done already."

"You're welcome, ma'am," he said politely. "Say, did y'all translate that letter Sally showed me? She never said."

"No, we never got anything usable out of that."

"Well, that's too bad."

"Yes." She hesitated, then said, "I'm very sorry our commander said that to you. He cannot apologize but I can do it for him."

"Sally says she's the only one he doesn't threaten to kill," he said.

"Yes," Thomas replied, "I can believe that. She's rather beyond his reach."

"Well, that looks like a good place to be."

"What do you mean?"

"I mean I have no interest in joining up with y'all. You all are so busy trying to kill each other and cover it up I'm surprised you find the time to do anything else."

"Nathaniel, wake up."

"Whu? What time is it?"

"It's late…or early, I don't know. You have to get up."

"James, what is it? Is there an attack?"

"You have to take *Intrepid* up. Something's going to happen."

"What's going to happen?"

"I don't know. They want a balloon up with a telegraph line."

Nathaniel drew his trousers on. "How am I supposed to see anything in the middle of the night?"

"You've flown at night before. Besides, the dawn's a-coming."

"All right."

Within the half-hour he was on a wagon with *Intrepid*, heading west. He had no notion of the time nor of his destination.

Ten soldiers had been detailed to assist him and they were none too pleased to be doing so. To be roused in the middle of the night to do battle was one thing; to be dragged from their bedrolls to mind a balloon was quite another. Nathaniel only made things worse by telling them that they could not smoke. They gave voice to their displeasure, put their pipes away and went back to sleep in the bed of the wagon.

It wasn't merely dark, it was foggy. Nathaniel could just make out the pine trees beside the road. They were but dark vertical lines barely discernible against the surrounding darkness.

He could see nothing of the road. The driver must have been familiar with it, though, because his course was slow but steady. The wagon bumped along while the half-charged balloon bobbed and jiggled overhead.

The wagon crossed the Rappahannock at a ford and continued on a few more miles, then crossed again. At last it stopped where a railroad track crossed the road.

It had to be near dawn for Nathaniel could now see a little. Before them was an open space. A few pines stretched into the murk overhead. On their left the fog flowed like a broad river in its bed. Beneath that river of fog, Nathaniel knew, there flowed the Rappahannock. A railroad trestle spanned the invisible river.

Two infantrymen, their bayonets fixed, silently challenged the wagon, then stared in wonder at *Intrepid*. Another man, a civilian by his manner, stood beside a small table.

Nathaniel squinted at the civilian. He recognized him as a telegraph operator of his acquaintance, a man named Merkin. He leapt to the ground and waved to him. The man nodded in reply. "Mind telling me what we're doing here, Merkin?" he whispered.

"They don't tell me nothing," Merkin replied, "but you're supposed to go up here. I'll help you patch into the line."

"What line?"

Merkin hiked a thumb over his shoulder. "This is a telegraph pole, though you'd scarcely warrant it. I've contacted Headquarters on this line. They want you to report on the battle today."

"I don't think I'll be seeing too much."

"It should lighten up as the day goes on."

Nathaniel looked at the table. There was a telegraph key there, all wired up. There was also a battery, which saved Nathaniel the trouble of charging his. He turned back to Merkin.

"Headquarters requested this?"

Merkin shrugged. "I guess so. You'd never believe who actually gave me the orders, though."

"Who?" Nathaniel thought of Captain Comstock, but he was mistaken.

"It was a whore."

Nathaniel had a flash of anger which he suppressed. "Well, let's get a line into the balloon."

"How much you need?"

"Well, let's see. I'll go up two hundred feet. That will get me well over the trees and let me see anything in this locality."

"So you need two hundred."

"No, I need to run a ground down as well. You got a grounding spike? Or you could run the other end into the river."

Merkin shook his head. "I'm patched in here, I'm not grounded. I'm live in both directions."

"Which way is Headquarters?"

Merkin pointed to his left, downstream. "I think it's that way but I don't rightly know."

"This line was here before the war?"

"Looks like it. Those insulators have been there five years."

"What's at the other end?"

"I don't know."

Both fell silent to listen to a message tapping faintly from the key on the small table. As the message was not for either of them they ignored it.

"This line you have, is it coated?"

Merkin shook his head. "Bare copper."

"Okay, I'll run one wire up one of my drag lines and the other down another so's they don't cross. I'll run those two drag lines from the wagon and two more from trees."

"Fine by me."

"Hey, did you hear that?"

"What?"

"That message ended with '73 CURTIS.' I don't know any operator named Curtis, do you?"

"Well, no."

"He must be a Rebel."

"Could be. That line runs into Fredericksburg, then."

"Break that line."

"I ain't breaking no telegraph line."

"But if you don't, the Rebs'll hear everything I transmit."

"Listen, Curry, that ain't our concern. Now, we both got work to do before the battle. You best get to it. It's going to get real busy around here."

He nodded. "Say, Merkin, what's over there, anyway?"

Merkin nodded over his shoulder at the fog. "That's Culpeper County on the other side of the river."

"I know that, but what part?"

"It's Brandy Station."

"Yeah? Where's the brandy?"

Merkin snorted. "Damned if I know. I'd be happy if I could see the station."

Nathaniel and Merkin laid out wire and connected it while the soldiers attached the drag lines to two wheels of the wagon and two more to nearby trees. The soldiers, fearful of electricity, refused to come near the wires. Nathaniel got into the car of the balloon and tapped CQ HEADQUARTERS. The reply came, HEADQUARTERS BY. He looked up at Merkin and said, "Now, you'll be here, listening on your key, right?"

Merkin shrugged. "I got no better place to be. If it gets hot here, though, I'm lighting out."

"All right." He turned to the soldiers. "All right, boys, I've explained what I need here. I don't have much lift so it should be easy to bring me down. Just wait for the signal."

"What will you use for a signal?"

"The green flag."

"Do you think we'll see it?"

He glanced up at the fog. "This'll burn off in jig time."

"All right."

They paid the line out and *Intrepid* started up. The flaccid bag bounced and jiggled above him like the breast of a fat woman. The basket, with no sandbags to steady it, bobbed and rolled. The ground vanished within seconds.

Nathaniel was surrounded by fog. Looking down he could see only a few feet of his lines.

Above him it started to get light. As he watched, the swirling mists thinned and he broke through into daylight. The fog sank slowly away from him.

The balloon fetched up against the lines. *Intrepid* would not have risen much higher even if not tethered, so it was a very gentle stop. He was about fifty feet above the level of the fog.

There was blue sky overhead but beneath him the world was white. The fog reflected the shape of the land beneath it: he could discern hills and valleys and the winding shape of the river. There wasn't much else to see.

The air was perfectly still. The only sound was the quiet conversation of the birds in the trees below. He sat down, crossed his legs on the side of the car, and looked around. It was like a vision of Heaven, or perhaps a scene from a dream. For a few minutes it was possible to forget about the States War and everything else transpiring on the world that lay hidden beneath him. Then the shooting started.

He transmitted, TO GEN BUTTERFIELD FROM CURRY BALLOON CORPS SMALL ARMS FIRE AT BRANDY STATION. A minute later came the acknowledgement from Headquarters in the form of the telegraphic code 13, "I understand," followed by the question, WHAT CAN YOU SEE.

He replied with the single word NOTHING.

At that moment the sun rose above the fog. Its yellow beam was warm against his face, giving the promise of a hot day ahead. He brought out his telescope, actually the Balloon Corps' telescope. It was a larger and much finer instrument than his own pocket telescope, but there was as yet nothing to see with it but fog.

The firing was coming from the other side of the river, from the east. It did not sound like a typical battle. The firing was all small-arms fire. In fact, it sounded like carbines and pistols. There didn't seem to be any muskets.

Carbines and pistols? That sounded like a cavalry engagement.

Aside from this, however, there was no other sound. He did not hear the boom of artillery nor the shouting and cheering that usually accompanied an infantry attack.

Headquarters asked, WHAT FORCES ENGAGED AT BRANDY

STATION. He replied, I DONT KNOW.

He frowned at the sea of fog beneath him. This seemed to be entirely a cavalry engagement, though it was hard to tell. If so, it would likely not end to the Union's advantage. The South had better horses and better horsemen, and it had them in greater numbers. It was common knowledge that whenever Confederate cavalry were involved, things turned out badly for the United States. If both Confederate and Union cavalry took part in an engagement it was sure to be a disaster for the Union.

The rising sun was starting to burn the fog away and he could soon discern riders. Even through the telescope, though, it was impossible to tell friend from foe. Horses and men were all just dark shadows milling madly about.

There were a lot of these dark shadows. He transmitted, MANY HORSES ENGAGED. The reply came, WHAT FORCES. He didn't reply.

Little by little things started to make sense. A large Confederate force had been attacked by a smaller Union one. The Confederates were encamped directly across the river from him, and the Union forces had come in from the right, from the upriver direction.

There was a Rebel camp on a hill about two miles from him; it seemed to be a corps headquarters. Men had been roused from sleep and were pulling on boots and mounting up with as much speed as they could manage.

He set the telescope on the edge of the basket and focused as carefully as he could. He knelt in the bottom of the car with his left hand bracing the telescope against the side of the basket and his right holding the eyepiece. He held his breath and concentrated on making out every detail of the scene before him.

A man had just mounted and unfurled the regimental colors and for an instant Nathaniel could see the banner with great clarity. He turned to the key and transmitted JEB STUART AT BRANDY STATION.

The reply came, WHAT UNION FORCES. This seemed queer; Headquarters should certainly know who the Union commander was.

Another message came over the instrument. It was a weak signal, much fainter than the one from Headquarters, and he had to look at the key to follow it. He made out CAN NOT CONFIRM THAT IT IS STONEMAN. There was a pause, then came the single word NO.

All right, these had to be Confederates. He could hear a man who could see the battle but he could not hear the Rebel headquarters. The weak signal meant he was either using a weak battery or, more likely, was about ten miles away.

Could the Rebs hear him? Would he be doing more harm than good by telling Headquarters what he could see? He did not know.

It frustrated him that Merkin had refused to break the connection to the Confederate side. He would have only needed to disconnect his instrument on one side and run a line to ground. True, he might not have been able to cut out the Rebels without losing contact with Headquarters, but it would have been worth the trial.

He turned back to the battle. The men at the camp had formed up and were about to set out when a rider came in from their rear, Nathaniel's left, at a full gallop. Whatever he had to say to them caused great consternation, for instead of setting out they held a quick parley on horseback. One man broke off from the group and rode to the top of the hill.

Nathaniel followed him with his glass. On the hilltop was a single cannon, and the rider gave the crew manning the gun quick instructions. The crew swung the gun around and fired it toward Nathaniel's left, away from the gunfire he had heard before.

He looked in that direction. A second Union force was coming from that direction. He still could not see the size of any of the forces involved, although he thought that Stuart's entire cavalry corps must be with him.

The weak signal came over the telegraph again, and he turned from the telescope to watch the key. I DONT KNOW, the Rebel operator said, I CANNOT SEE.

He looked again to the left. The second Union force was holding up, delayed by the single cannon on the hilltop. Stuart and his staff were making the most of the delay to take cover. They were literally heading for the tall timber.

It was by this time full daylight and the fog was gone. Nathaniel raised his glass and looked past this engagement. What he saw surprised him.

About five miles farther to the west hundreds of white specks covered the landscape. These were surely the tents of the Army of Northern Virginia. Most of the Army was there, by the looks of it, and that meant Lee was there as well.

But what was he doing in this area? It was farther north than anyone had thought he would be. He should be protecting Richmond from attack. So what was he doing?

Nathaniel thought about the hungry prisoners he had seen. There was certainly nothing for Lee to feed them in Virginia or he would have done so. But the rich farmlands of Pennsylvania lay just to the north.

Lee was going to invade the Union again. Pennsylvania was pretty nearly undefended; even its state militia had been mustered to the Union cause. Lee could simply march in and seize fodder for his horses and food for his men. He would then be situated between the Union Army and Washington. He could easily assail the capital and capture it. He could then ask for any terms he wanted.

All of this occurred to Nathaniel Curry in the space of a few seconds as he beheld the tents of the enemy through his telescope. His next consideration was what to do about it.

If he simply transmitted a message to Headquarters, the Rebels on the line might overhear him and warn Lee. That would be worse than doing nothing.

He transmitted, MERKIN TELL THE MEN TO BRING ME DOWN. There was no response.

He leaned over the side and waved the green flag. He looked down, but there were no upturned faces. "Hi! Hi!" he shouted, but no one heard him above the gunfire.

He threw the flag over the side. The flag itself acted like the fletching of an arrow, keeping the staff vertical as it fell. The staff drove straight into the ground, startling the soldiers. They looked up at him and shook their fists. He waved at them, gesturing that he wanted to come down. They gestured back.

At last they set to the pulleys. Nathaniel looked back at the battle.

Where he had previously seen hundreds of horsemen there were now thousands. He hadn't known that both sides had so many cavalrymen between them. There was still a lot of shooting going on, but most of the fighting was being done with sabers. The battle looked much like cavalry engagements had looked for thousands of years.

If the main army of either side were alerted to this engagement it would throw in more forces and carry the day. If both sides were alerted at the same time the advantage would go to the Confederate forces, as they were much closer to the action.

Another message, a clear, strong signal from Headquarters, came over his instrument, but he ignored it. He glanced back at the battle but it was already hidden by the trees. He could still hear it, but it sounded like a small engagement.

He looked over the side. He was still a hundred feet up. He put his hands to his mouth and shouted, "Hurry it up down there!"

The soldiers stopped working to reply: "We're going as fast as we can!"

"You think this is easy?"

"You think you're sitting pretty up there, don't you?"

"You like to run a man through with that there flag of yours, boy."

"Just get me down," he said.

"We'll get you down," a man replied. "We'll get you down so's you don't get up again."

He considered letting some gas out to speed his descent, but *Intrepid* had precious little gas as it was. With him in the basket the balloon only had about twenty pounds of lift at ground level. There was no excuse for the men to take so long to get him down.

He jumped out of the car when he was still ten feet above the ground. He turned to the two infantrymen who had greeted them. "I need one of those horses, boys."

"You ain't taking our horses."

"One horse. I need to get to Headquarters lickety-split."

"How are we supposed to get back, then?"

"One of you can ride in the wagon with the balloon."

"What, with that thing ready to explode? I doubt it."

"It won't explode. Just don't smoke around it."

The man shook his head. "You ain't taking no horse."

"Listen," Nathaniel said, "I have an important message to deliver to General Butterfield. Am I going to have to tell him I couldn't get it to him because you didn't let me use that horse?"

The soldier leaned forward. He was several inches taller than Nathaniel and twenty pounds heavier. "How about I throw you *and* General Butterfield in this here river?" The other men laughed.

Nathaniel ended up riding back to Falmouth in the wagon with the balloon. By the time they had finished packing up it was past noon and becoming a very warm day. The soldiers bumped along in the bed of the wagon, complained about having been inconvenienced, complained about not being allowed to smoke, then fell asleep.

One man stayed awake and lay in the back of the wagon chatting with Nathaniel. "If you're in such an all-fired hurry to get back," he asked, "why don't you cut the balloon loose?"

"How would that help us?" he answered curtly.

"Well, it would make this here buggy lighter, wouldn't it?"

"No. Without the balloon, it would be about two hundredweight heavier."

"Oh. Because the balloon is lifting the wagon up, right?"

"That's right." The man was being polite so he decided, reluctantly, to reply in kind.

"Of course. That's perfectly obvious, in fact."

"Well, I don't think most fellows would get it right away."

"Well, it's just a matter of buoyancy, isn't it?"

"Say, it sounds like you know something about this stuff."

"Yes, I'm interested in science. I have some friends who will be very interested in what I've done today. Tell me, is this your personal balloon?"

"You mean my property? No, it's government-issue."

"It is? Well, I hope it's better work than the government-issue stuff that we have."

Nathaniel knew what he meant. War profiteers had made a fortune selling shoddy equipment to the Army: shoes with cardboard soles, wagons whose wheels fell off. He looked up at the balloon. He recalled Lowe saying shortly before his resignation that the Corps had made more than three thousand flights over the course of the war. *Intrepid*'s bag was patched in a dozen places and much of the wicker was broken but it was still serviceable. "Yes, it is," he said. "It's fine work."

"How did you come to be doing this?"

"You mean flying? Don't rightly know. It just sort of happened."

"Did you do it before the war?"

"No."

"Are you going to carry on with it after the war?"

Nathaniel glanced upward again. This seemed like a peculiar question, although it was actually quite natural. The truth was, he had ceased to think about a time when the war would be over. The war would continue forever, or at least longer than he would live. He shook his head.

"I'm sorry I was griping before," the soldier said.

He smiled. "That's a soldier's right."

"Truth to tell, this isn't bad work. It's better than a lot of work I get."

"Yeah? I should ask for you again."

"Yes, you do that. The name's Montgomery." Nathaniel replied with his own name and they shook hands.

It seemed to take an eternity to get back to camp, but the team drawing the wagon consisted of draft horses and they didn't care to hurry. It was the middle of the afternoon when they arrived at Headquarters. Nathaniel jumped off of the wagon and sought out General Butterfield.

He was shown into Hooker's command tent, the same one previously used by McClellan and Burnside. Butterfield met him with a sheaf of telegrams in his hand. "Curry!" he exclaimed. "Why did I hear nothing from you?" He bustled on, compelling Nathaniel to chase after him.

"Sir," he said, "there were Rebels on the telegraph line. I didn't want them to overhear me."

"Well, what did you have to say that was such a secret?"

"Lee is on the move, sir. He's way north in Culpeper County and it looks like he's going to go up into Pennsylvania."

"He is?" Butterfield paused to consider this. "What makes you think so?"

"I saw about a thousand tents about ten miles east of my position."

"A thousand tents? Are you being fatuous, or do you mean literally a thousand?"

"I mean literally a thousand, sir."

"Come with me. I want you to tell the general that."

"Yes, sir." Nathaniel had no desire to see General Hooker but he followed Butterfield out of the tent.

"What did you see of the battle?"

"Sir, it was the biggest cavalry engagement I've ever seen."

"Was it? How many horses?"

He hesitated. "Well, sir, you might think this is just my fancy, but I'd reckon it at about ten thousand on a side."

This was an extraordinary statement but Butterfield just nodded. A moment later they found Hooker conferring with his staff. Butterfield snapped a quick salute and Hooker nodded.

"Sir, this man says that General Lee is heading north into Pennsylvania."

"Yeah? And what do you know of it?"

"Sir," Nathaniel replied, "he's in Culpeper County, way north by the river. It looks like he aims to get between you and Washington."

Hooker looked at Butterfield, confused and alarmed. "Has this been confirmed?"

"No, sir."

"Well, have someone go out there and see." Butterfield turned and gestured to a young captain waiting nearby.

Hooker said, "What were you doing in Culpeper County?"

"I was observing the battle, sir."

"Stoneman, you mean?"

"Stoneman and another corps of cavalry up against the Confederate cavalry at Brandy Station."

"How did you observe this and make it back across the river so quickly?"

"I was watching from a balloon on our side, sir."

"A balloon?"

"Yes, sir, I'm a member of the Balloon Corps."

"I thought the Balloon Corps had been dissolved."

"No, sir. Mister Allen is –"

"I've spoken with you before, haven't I?"

"Yes, sir, I—"

"I know, it was back at Chancellorsville. You gave me that false report on Lee."

Hooker's face was suddenly a study in fear and wrath. Before Nathaniel had a chance to speak, Hooker called some soldiers over and had him placed under arrest.

"General, what I said was the truth."

"We'll soon see, young man. I have to make some inquiries but I'll get to the bottom of this."

Nathaniel was placed in the stockade. He had never been inside a stockade before and didn't much like it. It consisted of little more than logs driven into the ground in the form of a square about fifty feet on a side. Three feet inside the walls was a wire supported by stakes about a foot high. As he entered the enclosure a guard grabbed him roughly by the shoulder. "See that wire, boy?"

"Uh, yes?"

"That's called the deadline. Do you know why it's called a deadline?"

"No."

"Well, if you step over it, or touch it in any way, Jesus will be explaining it to you directly. You get my meaning?"

"Yes, sir."

"All right. You can step over it one time, going in."

He stepped over the wire and was instantly set upon by about a dozen men. They threw him to the ground and pummeled him for a few seconds, then quickly robbed him. First to go were his shoes, followed by his jackknife and his pocket telescope. The last item stolen was the locket from around his neck. The latecomers searched his pockets, then left empty-handed. The guards sat against the wall, watching in quiet amusement.

He slept under the stars that night without a blanket. It was not a very cold night but he still shivered.

The next morning he was taken out and brought to a small tent where two men awaited him. One glared menacingly while the other carefully closed the flaps. Once they were safely sealed in, they tied Nathaniel's hands behind his back, sat him in a chair and assailed him with insults. They called him a Rebel spy, a liar, a traitor and other, fouler things that he had never suffered before. One man pulled out a pistol, cocked it and held it to his head. "I could kill you right now, boy, and no one would say a word."

"What do you want me to say?" he said, half-choking with fear.

"Tell us who you work for."

"I serve the Union."

"That's not what we hear."

"What—what do you hear?"

"We've gotten the word that you're a Confederate agent, pretending to be a turncoat."

"That's not true."

"You tried to turn in a Union agent when you were in Lee's camp."

"No I didn't."

Red Sally again. Even as one of the men delivered a hard punch to his belly, he realized that she had once more turned on him.

The blow took his breath away. He leaned forward, expecting to vomit, and was unable to. He had after all not eaten in more than a day. He spat a drop of foul-tasting bile onto the ground as a man grabbed his hair and pulled him upright in the chair.

This unpleasant interview continued for about half an hour. Then he was dragged back to the stockade and dumped over the deadline. He lay there, one foot on the wire, half wishing that the guards would shoot him.

A few of the prisoners actually showed him sympathy at this point. They spoke kindly to him and pulled him off the wire. A bucket of water and rags were produced from somewhere and his wounds were washed. He even got a cup of goober peas for lunch.

In the afternoon his name was called again, accompanied by hoots and catcalls from the prisoners. He went to the wire and found Sally standing beside a guard. He stopped. "I don't want to talk to you," he said.

"Come on, Nathaniel," she said impatiently, and he followed her. A guard came with them and brought them to the same tent as before. The guard waited outside. There were two chairs this time and they sat facing each other. She breathed heavily, as if she had been running.

"I don't know what you expect me to tell you," he said.

"It's I who have something to tell you," she replied. She pulled a handkerchief from her sleeve and blew her nose.

He waited.

"First off, I'm sorry you got pinched. I didn't think that would happen."

"Well, it sure enough did."

"Why didn't you make reports? They said the line was fine."

"There were Rebels on the line. I could hear them. And I could see Lee was sneaking north into Pennsylvania. I wanted to tell them what he was doing, but I didn't want the Rebs to hear me."

"Well, that makes sense."

"It didn't make sense to Hooker. Too bad you weren't the commander-in-chief."

"I certainly couldn't do a worse job than he has," she replied. "I've been suspecting Lee was going to sneak north through the Shenandoah Valley."

"You have? You think he'll get a warm reception?"

"Oh, of course," she said sarcastically. "They'll welcome him with flowers and hosannas."

"Well, I should hope not."

"Why the Hell did you go see Hooker?" she asked, clearly annoyed. "You should have known he'd do this."

"It wasn't my idea. It wasn't even my idea that I fly yesterday."

"Are you mad at me for that?"

He shrugged. "Look where it landed me."

"Nathaniel, I thought I was doing you a favor by doing that. I got Butterfield to approve it and everything."

He had no answer to that. The Corps had been doing precious little flying of late so he should have been glad for her help. "When do I get out of here?"

"There's a problem with that."

"I know. You went and told them that I had denounced you to the Rebs last year."

"No, I did not."

"You didn't? Well, it was in your testimony, then."

"That testimony no longer exists, just like yours."

"That big guy, then?"

"No. Hooker went ahead and wired Washington. He spoke to Major Grover."

"Oh!" This made more sense. "He still has it in for me, does he?"

"Yes, he does."

"What's his beef with me, anyway?"

"Grover? Do you know anything about him?"

"No."

"He's charged with finding Rebel spies within the various spy organizations. He's found precious few to date. You were supposed to be his biggest catch so far."

"So in other words, the man's a fool."

"You could put it that way. Or you could say he's a political appointee, which is pretty much the same thing."

"Maybe there's just no Rebel spies in your group."

She shook her head. "About one in ten spies on the Rebel side is one of ours. We figure they're doing the same for us."

"Ever catch any?"

"Christian's killed several men he said were Rebs." She looked down at her hands. "Yeah, I bagged a couple myself."

"Christian?"

She pointed to her eye.

"Oh."

"Major Alphonsus Christian."

"He's an officer? When I saw him he had stripes."

"He's two officers. He's a major in the Pennsylvania Guards and he's a major in the Fourth Alabama Infantry. Under the same name both places."

"Jesus. You'd think someone would notice."

"Everyone notices. Everybody knows this. He's one of the few spies getting paid regularly. Both sides hope and pray he's really working for them and they think twenty-something dollars a month will keep him loyal."

"He as tough as he acts?"

She settled back in her chair. "You want to know?"

"Sure."

"I was with him when he lost his eye. One of our agents was bad."

"And Christian found him out?"

"He found out when the son of a bitch shot him."

"Oh."

"His name was Charlie Belcher. Him, me, Christian, Major Thomas and another man were in the woods between the armies. This was long about a year and a half ago. Belcher spins around and yells 'Ha!' and shoots. Little bastard, the gun was near as big as he was. No how-do-you-do, no nothing, just 'Ha!' and shoots him in the eye."

"Jesus. And he lived through that?"

She shook her head.

"What did you do?"

"I was right beside Christian. I got it all over me." Sally pantomimed a surprised woman splashed with something unpleasant, her hands up and her eyes wide. "I was pretty God-damned shocked." She pointed to a scar beneath her left eye. "I got pieces of bone in me."

"Too bad you weren't armed."

"I'm always armed. I consider myself one tough bitch, but I couldn't do nothing but stand there.

"But Christian, he just turned away for a second, then he went after him. Now, if you ever got hurt in the eye, you'll know you can't open either eye for your life. He didn't even try. He didn't have a weapon, but he reached out for Charlie, just groping around.

"Charlie couldn't God-damn believe it. He just stood there gaping at him like a scared nigger. Then he put the gun up and pulled the hammer back.

"That was all Christian needed. He heard the click and stepped up and grabbed the gun with one hand and put his other hand to Belcher's throat."

"Choked him? Broke his neck?"

She shook her head. "Pinched his Adam's apple. Just like this." She put her thumb and forefinger together. "Snapped his Adam's apple quick as you please and just held the gun while Charlie choked."

"Jesus Christ."

"Took him about a minute. He let go the gun and walked around, but there weren't nothing for it, so he turned blue and keeled over on the ground. We left him for the skunks."

She seemed very talkative but this wasn't what he wanted to know. "So what's next? Are they going to beat me up until I confess?"

She shook her head again. "I'll talk to the sergeant running the interrogation. They'll talk to you but they'll keep their hands to themselves."

"How will you convince him to do that?"

"Don't worry. I know what that swine likes."

He understood this and ducked his head in embarrassment. "But you can't get me out?"

"No, Hooker won't let you go. But have no fear. It won't be long."

"What do you mean?"

"Hooker's going to be back in Massachusetts commanding a plow."

"Oh. Good."

"Do you need anything? Are they treating you all right?"

"No. Somebody stole my shoes."

"Well, that wasn't very proper, was it?"

"No. Say, you mind if'n I ask you something?"

"No, what?"

"Last time I saw you, you looked, well, you looked pretty sick."

She smiled. "I changed doctors."

"You did? What did the new one do?"

"Well, the last one brought my fever down. The new one thought the fever was good for me. He sweated me and it seemed to help."

"Oh. Good."

He was returned to the stockade. As he stepped over the deadline his fellow captives greeted him with more cheers and catcalls.

Half an hour later a sergeant with four armed soldiers strode into the enclosure. They did not look like typical enlisted men. They were rugged, menacing individuals who glared arrogantly at the prisoners. The sergeant stepped up to Nathaniel and came right to the point: "Where's the man what stole your shoes?"

Nathaniel hesitated. If he pointed the offender out there would be no going back. He would be the man who had broken the code of all captives by openly denouncing a fellow prisoner to the guards. On the other hand, Sally had already paid the coin and he would probably be set upon worse than ever if he did not now take a stand. He walked over and pointed at the man.

The sergeant, his eyes blazing, approached the offender. "Take 'em off."

The man was as large as the sergeant and had thick, knotted arms. He stood eye to eye with him and said, "I'll see you in Hell first."

The sergeant stepped to the side and in a twinkling one of his soldiers flew past him and drove the butt of his rifle into the man's crotch. The man went down like a sack of shit and the soldier shoved his muzzle into his throat. The thief gurgled in pain, then kicked the shoes off.

The sergeant picked the shoes up and handed them to Nathaniel. Instead of thanking him, Nathaniel pressed his advantage. "I also had a telescope, a jackknife and a gold locket," he said. Before the sentence was finished the items were deposited at his feet. The thieves withdrew, murmuring hasty apologies.

The sergeant and his men left before he had a chance to thank them. The jackknife and the telescope went into his pocket. The chain of the locket was broken so he tied it in a knot and put it back on.

Nathaniel had no more problems with his fellow prisoners. Everyone deferred to him. At mealtimes he was allowed to eat and drink first. No one questioned or resented his sudden ascendancy; it seemed to be in the natural order of things that some prisoners were so favored by the authorities. The guards for their part ceased to abuse him.

There were no further interrogations. His questioners apparently decided that if they could not use violence against him the interviews were a waste of time.

A few days later the Army of the Potomac suddenly struck its tents and started moving north. The urgency with which this was accomplished convinced Nathaniel that Lee was indeed heading into Pennsylvania and that

Hooker was moving to cut him off.

This should have meant that he would be set free, with the commander's apologies. But that would have been the sensible thing; he remained a prisoner.

The prisoners were placed in manacles and marched under guard. This was more unpleasant than languishing in the stockade but it at least kept the guards from abusing the prisoners and the prisoners from fighting amongst themselves.

It was late June in Virginia and the heat and humidity were monstrous. At every step clouds of dust rose, choking man and beast alike. Every soldier's skin and clothing became caked with dust and sweat.

Walking all day in these conditions was an agony. At every halt men called for water, but there was little water to spare for prisoners. The men grew weak and began to stumble. The guards shot one man who fell and would not rise; no others fell.

More and more of the prisoners were freed. The men never welcomed their liberty because they knew it meant that they were being returned to the ranks and their services would soon be required on the battlefield. Nathaniel himself was always spared.

The sun told him that they were headed north. Rumor held that Lee had moved into Pennsylvania and captured Harrisburg and that his next prize would be Washington itself. Hooker was positioning himself to thwart this move. Hooker, however, had proven himself as incompetent as any of his predecessors and he would fail.

There were only a handful of prisoners left by the end of June. Nathaniel wondered what his fate would be. Would he be sent to the field like the others? Would Major Grover's advice finally be heeded and he, Nathaniel, summarily shot? Or would he just march along this endless road for all time, like the Flying Dutchman?

None of these things happened. Instead a great hue and cry arose from the army as some new intelligence passed through it. No one communicated with the sorry little band of prisoners, but it was easy to overhear what was being said: Hooker had resigned as commander in chief. General George C. Meade had taken his place.

Within the hour, the prisoners were overtaken by a mounted courier with orders in his hand and the column was taken out of line and brought to a halt. The sergeant in charge read the orders; then, without a word, he removed Nathaniel's bonds, shoved him roughly out of line and marched his charges off again.

Nathaniel sat by the side of the road rubbing his wrists and watching the might of the United States slouch past him. It was not a very inspiring sight: the men were tired of fighting, tired of marching and tired of being soldiers. To a man, they wished that the great conflict were over so they could once again be farmers, or tradesmen, or shopkeepers. They little resembled the glorious hosts of paintings and magazine illustrations.

On the other hand, they looked better than the Army of Northern Virginia.

So now Meade was in charge, was he?

This seemed a mark of how desperate Lincoln had become. He knew Meade by sight and he was not a very impressive figure. He was gaunt and haggard and sickly in appearance. His hollow cheeks and tired-looking eyes made him appear older than his years. He seemed like a competent staff officer, but he did not look like a man who could inspire other men to sacrifice their lives.

The dust made him even thirstier than he had been and he began to wonder where he would get his next meal. He suspected that it would be at the end of the column and he was right.

Nearly the last wagons in line were those of the Balloon Corps. In the lead was James Allen, driving a gas generator. Allen didn't recognize the waif by the wayside but Solomon Vogler, seated beside him, did.

Allen reined in and Nathaniel, throwing off his fatigue, sprang up beside them. They greeted each other warmly. "Nathaniel," Vogler said, "I had made sure you were dead. It's good to see you looking so fit."

"Solly, do you have any water?"

"Here, there's about half a bottle here."

"Is this here kosher water?"

"Water is always kosher unless someone has pissed in it. No, go ahead, it's fine."

"Thank you kindly."

"You get in a fight? You look kind of beat up."

"Oh, yeah, I guess so." He touched the bruises on his face.

"You been consorting with the enemy again?"

"No, this was the work of our side. The enemy generally treats me better than this."

"Well? You going to tell us about it?"

"Oh, just let me rest first."

"All right. Then I'll tell you our news: we've gotten our supplies. Wagon Four is carrying five hundred pounds of iron filings and sixty-five gallons of vitriol."

"Well, that's sure a blessing."

"Yes, if we ever get permission to use them."

The next day the Balloon Corps was ordered to report to Colonel Myers of the Signal Corps. He kept them waiting an hour, then brusquely informed them that General Meade had ordered the Corps transferred to his control. "I have no money, no men and no time for such folderol," he said. "You men are discharged."

"What are we to do, sir?" a shocked James Allen asked.

"Turn your equipment over to my transportation company. They can make use of the draft animals and the wagons."

"And the balloons and the gas generators?"

"Gas generators?"

"Yes, sir. I can't imagine that the transportation company will have any use of them."

"Was this expensive equipment?"

"Yes, sir. Tens of thousands of dollars worth."

"What is your base?"

"The Columbia Armory."

"Then bring it all there. Get paid off, then you're discharged. I'll write you orders."

The newly unemployed aeronauts returned to their wagons. Allen had them move the generators to a stream and drain them; getting rid of the old charging solution would lighten them by several tons apiece.

He then ordered them down the road they had just come up. When they reached Frederick, Maryland, they would take the turnpike southeast to Washington. They had to wait for a break in the traffic, so great was the northward passage of the Union Army. When at last they started moving they covered only a mile or two before more troops forced them off the road.

"Nathaniel, wake up. You have to drive a wagon."

"What? All right."

He sat up, trying to place where he was. It had been a warm night, the last one of June, and he had slept beneath the stars. As often happened to him, though, he awoke feeling disoriented. Wagon Two lay before him, but he was sure he had fallen asleep on the other side of it. He felt that he was facing west although he was looking into the rising sun. The sensation was an illusion, he knew, but still he felt confused.

The Balloon Corps had driven late into the night, stopping only when the mules and drivers had become exhausted. For all that they had only covered about ten miles. It was now shortly after sunrise, or a little after five in the forenoon.

"James, where are we again?"

"We're still in Pennsylvania, I think. Right down near Maryland. And we're between Lee and Washington."

"I need more sleep. I've only gotten a few hours the last few days."

"So have we all. But there are plenty getting more sleep than they wanted. Remember that."

"Yes. You're right."

"Nathaniel, I've made a decision. This will be my last order to you. It's slowing us down to keep together this way. We should go catch-as-catch-can to Washington. It's only forty or fifty miles as I reckon it."

"All right."

"So just drive to the Armory and find someone to take charge of your wagon. Get a receipt."

"Then what?"

Allen shrugged. "Go home."

"I would if I had a home."

Allen nodded sympathetically. "Well, *c'est la guerre.*"

As he was tying his shoes Solomon Vogler pulled up beside him. He was driving a gas generator. "Nathaniel, do you need a ride?"

"I'm driving a wagon myself, Solly."

"All right. I think the rest of the train has set out already. Nathaniel, I really have to go."

"All right, then I'll see you in Washington."

"Well, that's just the thing, Nathaniel, you won't."

"I won't?"

"Well, I'm going to return this generator, but then I'm getting out. I'm going to be on the first train to New York."

"Oh!" They looked at each other for a moment. "I always thought that we would have a more proper leave-taking, Solly."

"And so did I. I'll just say it's been a pleasure serving with you, Nate. If there is anything I can ever do for you, write to me at my father's company."

"Sol, let me borrow your Darwin book."

"What?"

"That way I'll have to see you to give it back."

Vogler smiled. "Well, that's novel," he said. He dug in his carpetbag and pulled the tome out. "Very well, Master Curry," he said sternly, "study this book carefully. You'll face examination when next we meet." They shook hands and he drove off.

Ezra Allen was already gone. Nathaniel looked around and discovered that he was the last of the Balloon Corps left in the vicinity. He was in charge of two conveyances, a gas generator and a wagon containing the balloon *Eagle* and their now-useless supplies.

There were also four mules. He removed their feedbags and hitched them to the wagons, wondering how he was going to drive two wagons at once.

He could tie the generator's team to the back of the balloon wagon and drive the rigs as a tandem. But while this was a good idea in principle it wasn't really practical. A wagon being led driverless this way was liable to drift off the road, especially on a curve.

Should he seek out a transport company? But they always had a shortage of both animals and drivers. Rather than provide him with a man, they would likely take his mules.

He finally decided to abandon the gas generator. Although the generators had been expensive pieces of equipment, they served only one purpose, to generate hydrogen on a battlefield. It was not likely that anyone would ever need to do such a thing again.

He would hitch the generator's team to the back of Wagon Four, but before he did that he looked the generator over to see if there was anything else he could salvage from it.

There was not. He stepped back and looked at the generator. It was certainly a unique conveyance, essentially a great wooden crate on wheels. He supposed that the battle would end with another Confederate victory and that the generator would be discovered by the victorious Rebels. What would they make of the thing? There was a pump to get water into it, but that was only its most obvious feature. If a hole were knocked in the box deep enough to penetrate its copper lining the dregs of the water and vitriol would run out, badly burning anyone who touched it, but that would be a puzzle to them as well. If someone went as far as to charge it with water, iron filings and acid, then turned the wheel, it would produce hydrogen, but even that would not be obvious unless someone held a match to the vent. No, if the Rebels captured it, they would not be able to make heads nor tails of it, and it would probably sit right where it was until it rotted.

Well, then, let it. It was no longer his concern. He turned back to the wagon.

"Well, if it isn't Nathaniel! Boys, this is the Nathaniel I was telling you about."

He looked up. Six soldiers had broken loose from the column and were approaching. The man in the lead was smiling, and as Nathaniel took his hand he recognized the firm shake.

"Montgomery! You're Montgomery who was at Brandy Station, aren't you?"

"The very same. Are you preparing to go up? My friends would love to see it."

"I'm afraid not. They've disbanded us."

"What, really? But this is too good an invention to let die."

"You should tell General Meade that."

"Meade? Well, disbanding you is his first gross error, then. Why won't he let you fly?"

"We were transferred to Signal Corps and they don't want to spend any money on us."

"Do you need money to fly?"

"Yes. Well, no. I could fly right now if I had a mind to."

"Then you should."

"D'you think so?"

"Sure. Steal a march on them. There's a big battle brewing, by all accounts. How would it look to General Meade if he suddenly started receiving reports of enemy positions from above the field?"

"Well, pretty good, I suppose. But I can't fly by myself."

"Why, what do you lack?"

"Well, I have no one to help me launch."

"Not so! We'll be glad to pitch in, won't we, boys?"

His friends eagerly signaled their assent, and their enthusiasm heartened Nathaniel. "Do you really think you could do that? Don't you have things you should be looking after already?"

"No, we're on casual status right now. We were looking for a place to pitch in and it looks like you've been nominated."

Even as he spoke they heard faint cannon fire coming from the north. They all turned practiced ears to the sound.

The sound and the sudden appearance of supporters stirred his blood. He turned back to his new friends. "All right, who knows this country?"

"I do," a man said, raising his hand like a schoolboy. "I grew up north of here."

"We need to head back up the road to where the armies are meeting. I need to get near a source of water, a small pond or a stream. I also need a telegraph line."

"There are a lot of streams and ponds around there, but I never took note of any telegraph lines."

"What about railroad tracks? They usually run beside them."

"Yeah, I know where there are tracks. They run east of the town of Gettysburg."

"Good. Who knows how to drive?"

"Anyone can drive Army mules," another man said. "You just have to cuss a lot."

"All right, you drive the wagon with the balloon. You ride with him to show him the way. I'll drive the generator, there's a bit of a trick to it, it's so large. Montgomery, you're with me."

"Aye, aye, Captain," Montgomery replied, and leapt into the seat. The others tossed their muskets and kits into the balloon wagon and climbed aboard.

They fell back into the advancing Union column. It was certainly easier moving with the current this way, but Nathaniel was getting tired of seeing the same houses and barns over and over again. They passed through Taneytown about noontime, then over the line into Pennsylvania an hour later. It was farther north than Nathaniel had ever been.

Nathaniel took the time to brief the men on their tasks. He found them eager students, quite unlike the soldiers who were usually detailed as ground crews. Although they numbered less than half of a normal crew he felt sure they would do fine.

These men were all students of the physical sciences and they had a lot of questions about the balloon and the gas generator. "How often do you have to charge the gasbag?"

"A charge will last about two weeks."

"How high will this thing fly?"

"Well, I always fly tethered, so I only go a few thousand feet at most. A lot of times it's only a few hundred."

"But if it wasn't tethered?"

"I've been three miles up in a similar one."

"How do things look from up there?"

"Small."

"Why doesn't the command structure appreciate what you're doing?"

He shrugged. "They're idiots."

"Why doesn't the vitriol eat through the wood of the generator?"

"It's lined with copper."

"I understand that water breaks into hydrogen and oxygen, but how is this effected?"

"I don't know."

"Do you put anything else in there?"

"Yes, iron filings. You turn that wheel and it stirs it up."

"Iron filings," another man mused. "Water and vitriol. Okay, I have it. The filings are oxidized by the water. Oxygen is pulled from the water, leaving hydrogen as a product. Hydrogen and rust. The vitriol's a catalyst."

"Yes, that must be it," the first one said. "Then you must have to change the stuff from time to time."

"Yes, we do."

The cannon fire grew louder, augmented now by musket fire. Nathaniel got off the gas generator, climbing down the back so that it would not have to stop, and ran to the wagon. "We're getting close, but I don't want to get too close to the action. I think the Union forces are to the south and east of the Rebels. Do you know this town?"

"Yes, this is Gettysburg."

"Isn't that where you said that railroad line ran?"

"Yes, it runs east of town. It's unfinished to the west."

"Then let's make our way east of town."

"All right."

"Say, what's your name?"

"Victor."

"Are there roads going there?"

"There are farm lanes. We may have to cut across fields, but we can do it, I think."

"Good. We'll want to stop at a pond or stream just before we get to the telegraph line, if there is one. We'll charge the balloon there."

"Yes, sir."

They used main roads at first, then moved onto lanes that were scarcely discernible. These paths had not seen any military traffic so far, and farmers and their families flocked to the roads to gape at the soldiers and their unusual vehicles.

There was now firing coming from many points, all to the west. The musket and cannon fire from some quarters was a steady roar.

It wasn't until well after noon that the party ground to a halt beside a farm pond in the middle of a pasture. Nathaniel jumped off the box and began to charge the balloon. He set two men to running a hose from the generator to the pond and manning the pump. Two more were detailed to lay out the balloon and bag. He and Montgomery ran the hydrogen hose to a cooler, then to the bottom valve of the *Eagle*.

He climbed atop the generator. "Boys, bring me four of those barrels of iron. That's right, the small barrels. I'll need the ax, too."

After he had poured the iron into the hatch in the top of the generator he called for eight gallon bottles of vitriol. These were passed up to him with great care and he held his breath and poured them in. Then he closed the hatch and called a man up beside him. "See this wheel?"

"Yes, it looks like the brake wheel on a railroad car. What's it for?"

"It stirs the mixture. Turn it for about five minutes. After that, give it a turn or three whenever the gas slows down."

"All right."

"Victor, you're with me. We're going to find us a telegraph line. Montgomery, you're in charge until we get back."

"All right. Is there anything else that can be done in your absence?"

He thought about it. "There are gunny sacks in the wagon. Fill twelve of them with dirt and tie them to the sides of the balloon car. Attach them to the top edge of the basket, here, but leave enough line that they'll hang beneath the bottom of the car. And use bow knots, like on shoelaces, so that they can be dropped in a hurry."

"Aye, aye, Captain."

Nathaniel grabbed his lineman's telegraph key, his climbing spurs and a small roll of wire. He and Victor each took a musket and an ammunition bag.

They worked their way north. At one point Nathaniel said, "Let's stay on this path."

"It would be faster to go across this field," Victor replied.

"Yes, but there's a stone wall there. I want to make sure there's a path the wagon could follow."

"All right. This way, then."

It was about half a mile to the track although it took them over an hour to get there. A telegraph line indeed ran beside the track. Nathaniel climbed the pole and attached the key. It immediately began clattering, proving that the line was intact and in use. He listened for a minute to be sure it was Union forces communicating with each other.

He broke the line and spliced in his own wire. He then ran the lines to the base of the pole, attaching them to two glass insulators and bridging them.

They started back. The sound of battle coming from the town was louder than any battle he had ever heard. Intrigued, he turned from the path and led Victor to the top of a hill. There was nothing to see, however, but smoke and dust rising a few miles to the west, so they turned back.

After a half hour he said, "Hey! We didn't come this way."

Victor looked at him. "Didn't we?"

"No. Don't you know the way back?"

"Well, we're going south."

"We should have gotten back to the balloon by now."

"It has to be right around here."

Nathaniel realized that they should have blazed a trail like Indians as they came, breaking branches so they could find their way back. "We're lost, damn it! And the battle will be over soon."

Victor pointed at the ground. "Can't you see the path we made going through this grass?"

"Oh, was that us? There were at least three men that went this way. Scouts, I think. But we didn't pass this way ourselves, I'd stake my life on it."

It took another hour to find the balloon. The ground crew had been diligently turning the mixing wheel whenever the gas slowed down, and as a result *Eagle* was quite full. Nathaniel had the men attach the balloon to the wagon, then led the wagon and the gas generator north.

He preceded the wagons on foot to make the path out. All the while he agonized over the time that had been wasted that day. The battle was still going on but it clearly couldn't last much longer. At the present rate of fire one side or the other would soon run out of ammunition or men or both.

With Victor's help he was able to follow their path north well enough, but *Eagle* had a hard time of it. Tree limbs blocked the path on several occasions. He had the men throw ropes over the branches and pull them down to clear the way.

The sky was overcast but he could tell the sun was approaching the horizon when at last they returned to the railroad line. Battles usually ended at sunset but this one was still going strong. He still had a chance of getting something accomplished today.

Nathaniel ordered that the rope be taken out of the balloon wagon and made fast to the wagon and two trees. He looked at the sky. The overcast was solid, but it was stratocumulus with a ceiling of about three thousand feet. The temperature was cool for the season, about seventy degrees, and it was very still. "Pay out four hundred feet of rope from each point and attach the other end to the basket. Attach it to these points at the top of the basket, here, here and here."

"That's twelve hundred feet of rope, sir."

"Yes, I know. I also need four hundred feet of telegraph wire to—"

"There's nothing like that much rope here, sir."

"What? Let me see that."

There were four coils of rope in the wagon, each containing a hundred feet of line. Nathaniel cursed his luck. "All right, we'll have to make do with less rope."

"What do you want to do, sir?"

If he ran a single line from the ground to the balloon, he could rise to four hundred feet. The Allen brothers always used a single line, although Lowe had always disapproved. If it was windy, his balloon would spin and bounce all over the sky. Conditions were perfect for flying at the moment but that could change.

If he ran two lines he could only reach two hundred feet. That would limit the distance he could see. On the other hand, the battle was only two or three miles away, four at the most. Two hundred feet might be enough.

He looked back at the sky. He really wanted to take it to four hundred.

Another problem occurred to him: he needed to run a telegraph line to the car and back to the ground. He had only uncoated wire. If he ran two strands along a single rope they would inevitably cross, "shorting" the circuit.

"I'll run two ropes. Tie two ends of those two ropes together. No, that's a granny knot. Use a square knot like this."

"That looks the same as what I did."

Another man spoke up: "No, Nathaniel is right, that was a granny knot. Let me help you with the ropes, sir." The soldier expertly joined the other two coils of rope, then affixed the ends to opposite sides of the car with bowline knots. He attached one of the ropes to a wagon wheel and the other to a small oak tree.

Nathaniel ran wires from the glass insulators on the telegraph pole to the wagon wheel and the oak tree. He had men take the middle of both ropes and pull them out to their full lengths, then ran the wires along the ropes and to the car. He attached the wires to his favorite camelback key, then threw the wire cutters to one of the men. "Cut the wire on that pole that runs between the two glass insulators."

"Won't it shock me?"

"No, those cutters have rubber handles. Hurry it up!" He turned to the other men. "All right, I'm going up now. The key is working so I'll be able to send reports. When I want to come down I'll wave to y'all. If it's after dark I'll holler.

"When I come down, I'll let out some gas. That will make me sink. You all just reel me in as I come. Try and set the basket right back here in the bed of the wagon. You understand?"

The men indicated that they did.

Nathaniel started to thank them for helping him but decided to wait until he came down. "All right," he said, "cast me off."

A man pulled out a Bowie knife and cut the basket loose. It shot into the air harder and faster than he expected it to. It ran up to two hundred feet, stopping with a jolt that sent him sprawling. He fell onto the floor of the basket.

> We will now discuss in a little more detail the struggle for existence. In my future work this subject shall be treated, as it well deserves, at much greater length. The elder De Candolle and Lyell have largely and philosophically shown that all organic beings are exposed to severe competition...

What? He was lying on Vogler's copy of Darwin. He must have put it in the basket when he borrowed it that morning. He closed the book, picked up his telescope and stood up.

What he saw took his breath away.

A few miles to the west of him a great battle was taking place. One of the armies was concentrated in the center, on a long low hill. The other was spread out in a great arc around it and was pressing inward. Both sides were firing incessantly.

Transfixed, he trained his telescope on the scene. On the far right, to the north, was a small town that he guessed must be Gettysburg. Soldiers were fleeing through this town in disorder. He focused as carefully as he could, trying to make out details, but it was difficult. The sinking sun was behind the running soldiers, making it impossible to see if their uniforms were blue or gray.

Then he saw a man bearing a flag as he ran. The sunlight behind it illuminated it and he could clearly see the red and white stripes. Their attackers, suddenly coming into view behind them, carried a flag that glowed red.

So the fleeing troops were Union. Well, he could have guessed as much.

Hundreds, perhaps thousands of these Union soldiers were fleeing the Confederates. As he watched, many were shot down or gave themselves up. Still others fled up the hill in the center where they were received by their comrades.

He looked the town over. Considering that it was now in the center of a battlefield it was holding up remarkably well. There seemed to be no burning buildings or shell damage.

He did see something that concerned him, though. There was a train of Union wagons that looked like a supply train. Although it was only a few streets over from the advancing Rebels, none of them had spotted it. It likely contained food and ammunition, the very things Lee had attacked Pennsylvania to obtain.

He transmitted, TO LT GEN BUTTERFIELD FROM CURRY BALLOON CORPS UNION SUPPLY TRAIN IN THE TOWN EXPOSED TO REBEL CAPTURE.

After twenty seconds came the reply, WHO SENT THAT MESSAGE. Another hand then sent, BALLOON CORPS IS DISSOLVED THESE ARE REBEL SPIES ON THE LINE DISREGARD.

Another hand, or perhaps the first one, said, THAT MESSAGE IS FOR LEE BREAK THE LINE. Seconds later his key went dead. He tapped it several times but there was no spark.

He raised an eyebrow. That was fast work, injudicious as it was.

Now what? There seemed no use in him even continuing to fly. He raised his telescope and was startled to hear gunfire and shouting very close at hand.

He looked down. About twenty Confederate soldiers were attacking his ground crew. They took the men completely by surprise and killed all of them in a few seconds.

One man raised his weapon and fired straight up at Nathaniel. He heard the bullet whiz by, missing the balloon by several feet. The soldier was using a rolling-block repeater, and as he was placing a new cartridge in the weapon another man touched his arm, stopping him. Watching his gestures, Nathaniel deduced that he was telling his comrade that the balloon would explode if a bullet struck it.

Another soldier cupped his hands around his mouth and shouted, "Come down, Yank!" Then all hands fell to despoiling the dead. They quickly went through the pockets and kits of the fallen Yankees, pocketing anything of value, gobbling up whatever food they found on the spot.

When this was done they set to pulling him down. It took six men on a single line to do so, but they were succeeding in reeling him in.

What was their intention? Nathaniel recalled the reward that was reputedly offered for the capture of a balloon, ten thousand dollars in gold. These men would be set for years with such a sum.

As for himself, he'd be a dead man.

He dropped two sandbags. One bag struck and killed a man. The balloon rose, pulling one of the six men right off of the ground. Two or three more joined them and succeeded in starting him down again.

Nathaniel did some quick calculations. Even if he dropped all of his sandbags there were enough men to pull him down by main force. They would have a hard time of it, but if they stopped and thought about it a minute they could certainly find an easier way to do it. They could drive the wagon over the line attached to the tree, for example, then drive the wagon forward, letting the weight of the wagon pull him down.

A man raised his weapon.

Spang!

"Gah!"

Nathaniel rolled back onto the iron plate. He had been hit, but he couldn't tell where or how bad. He hurt everywhere at once. Every place he touched on himself, his hands came back bloody.

How bad was he hurt? Was he going to die?

No, there was no time for that. He looked over the side again.

There were ten men on the line now. They were not working very efficiently, but they had pulled him halfway to the ground. He dropped another sandbag. They knew enough to dodge it this time.

Some of the men attacked the balloon wagon. One picked up a gallon bottle of vitriol and smashed it on the ground, spattering acid on several of his fellows. These unfortunates began screaming and tearing off their uniforms. Another man took the ax and attacked the gas generator. After three blows he broke through the side, releasing a stream of the mixture as thick as a man's arm. The stream hit him in the chest, instantly dissolving his shirt and the skin beneath it. Hearing his screams, other men turned to him and found their feet suddenly burning.

All of this had no effect upon the men pulling him to the ground; they were far enough away that the vitriol had not reached them. They were doing well at their task: he was now only about fifty feet above their heads.

He pulled out his pocketknife and began to cut the rope where it was tied to the top of the basket. The knife was about as sharp as a butter-knife, and the blood on his hands made the knife slippery. As hard as he pressed and as quickly as he sawed the rope parted only a strand at a time. At last the rope snapped and he could hear the curses of the men below him as they fell to the ground in a heap.

He shot up to the length of the second rope, jolting harder than before as he was several hundredweight lighter. He and the other contents of the car flew off the bottom, then crashed back onto the plate. He immediately set about his task of cutting the second rope as the men below him set about theirs. He vowed to himself that if he survived this day he would never again allow his knife to get so dull. He leaned on the knife, sawing for all he was worth.

The rope parted and he rose again. The only thing connecting him to the ground now was the telegraph wires, and this problem solved itself. When he reached the limit of the wires his telegraph key abandoned ship, flipping over the side with a crash, and he was flying free.

He looked over the side but it had become too dark to see the ground. He saw several muzzle flashes but he was already out of range.

Now to tend to his wounds. No, first he looked back at the battle.

The fighting was winding down for the night but both armies remained in position. He could see campfires everywhere. What he saw did not encourage him. The Union Army was surrounded, with the Confederates pressing it on three sides. The entire Federal force could be annihilated the next day.

He looked himself over. He seemed to have several small wounds, more like the effect of a shotgun than a musket. He looked at the edge of the iron plate and there was a notch in it. If the musket ball had struck an inch further one way, it would have hit the plate. An inch the other way and it would have hit his head.

He was still rushing upward. His ears popped and the air grew colder and still he rose.

Was he going too high? Should he vent gas? He didn't know. He knew that he did not wish to go back down to where these two great armies were set to murder each other, but beyond that he did not know what to do.

He recalled that at higher altitudes the air currents always went to the east. That direction would bring him to friendly territory. He was, however, going south at the moment. The campfires to his west were drifting steadily to his right.

It grew colder yet as he approached the ceiling. He took one last look at the battlefield, then it was gone. He was surrounded by swirling gray mists. His clothing grew damp from the moisture.

There was now a puddle of blood on the iron plate. If he didn't staunch his wounds soon he would bleed out.

He tore his shirt into strips and made bandages. One went on his left thigh, one on his right arm, and another, after careful examination. went around his head.

About this time he came out the top of the clouds.

The sun was nearly set. All that remained was a patch of blue sky on the horizon.

His ears were killing him. How high was he, anyway? He looked over the side but saw only clouds with blackness between them.

He looked at the silk strip. It was still fluttering downward. He grew concerned that he would rise so high that the bag would rupture. He wrapped his arms around himself and sighed. His breath came out as white steam and shot through the bottom of the wicker.

The gasbag was as round as a pumpkin. He touched it and it was harder than he had ever felt it. He vented gas until he was sure it would not burst. The balloon continued to rise, though not as quickly.

Maybe he should set down immediately. He was, after all, above Pennsylvania or perhaps Maryland. On the other hand, Confederate forces were likely in control down there. He would be better off riding the currents to the east, into Federally controlled territory.

The glow in the west slowly died and the stars began to come out. He heard a clattering above him and realized that the moisture in the bag was condensing. It sounded different than it had the time he had flown with LaMountain, however. He opened the lower valve for a moment and a handful of ice particles dropped into his hand.

He was thirsty and considered popping this ice into his mouth. Then he realized that the ice likely contained a trace of sulfuric acid. He tossed it over the side before it melted.

The silk strip now hung limp. He hung motionless in the air, suspended between the unseen, deadly ground below and the infinite heavens above. He sat against the basket, hugging his legs.

He popped his ears one last time. They still rang and whined with the battle below. The only other sound was his ragged breathing.

The starlight was bright enough that he could see his breath. It formed silvery clouds that drifted slowly out of the basket.

"Oh, Jesus," he said. His voice quavered like that of a coward. It was strange to hear it, to hear anything, in this vast emptiness.

He had never been in such a fix. He felt himself utterly incompetent to deal with the situation.

He tried to console himself with the thought that it could be worse. He thought of the six bright young men who had befriended him. They had assisted him and then died without even a word of thanks from him.

Tears welled up in his eyes. No, he told himself. The time for tears was after a battle. For his part, the battle was still going on.

He thought of the brilliant and resourceful Thaddeus Lowe. A man who could pick a teapot off of the ground and use it to charge a balloon would never be daunted by such circumstances. John LaMountain and John Wise, though erratic, were also courageous and great fliers.

No, LaMountain and Wise were brilliant fools. Both of them were apt to give in to emotion when coolness under fire was required. He had seen it himself.

Even Lowe, yes, even Thaddeus Lowe himself got carried away when the going got tough. He thought of all the times when fortune had turned against him and Lowe had sunk into impotent despair or even became physically ill.

Vogler? Smith? The Allen brothers? All good men, but they would all be as lost as he was in this situation. Worse, perhaps.

More to the point, none of these good men were even flying now. He was in this situation precisely because he had stuck it out. The thought occurred to him that he might, in fact, be the best person to face this particular task.

And what was this task? What should his goals be?

Well, he was in a balloon that was flying free, destination unknown. He had to bring it down on land, and preferably in friendly territory. Failing that, he would have to bring it down in Confederate territory, evade capture and make it back to the North.

All right, what were his resources? He looked around the car. He had a high-quality telescope, his pocket telescope, a jackknife and a copy of *On the Origin of the Species* by Charles Darwin. He was wearing civilian clothes.

And he had the balloon. *Eagle* had a good charge and nine of its twelve sandbags. There were, as far as he could tell, no bullet holes in the bag or any other damage.

He had the element of surprise. No one would be looking for him.

On the negative side of the ledger, he had no warm clothing. What he wouldn't give for a jacket right now, or even another shirt! He had no food or water and he had not eaten since morning. He had no weapon save a dull knife, and no money.

He looked over the side. The clouds had broken beneath him. His eyes had adjusted to the darkness enough that he could see the ground. He was indeed still headed south. The land beneath him was either Maryland or Virginia.

Why south? Lowe, LaMountain, Wise, Allen, all of these had been unanimous that the currents at the upper levels went eastward.

Or had they? No, he recalled Lowe saying that these currents tended *generally* eastward. Two years ago, in fact, Lowe had ridden an upper-level current that carried him southeast, from Ohio to South Carolina. And LaMountain had once ridden such a current into the north woods of Canada. There was plenty of room for variation.

So should he stay at this altitude? At some point the current should carry him eastward again. He might yet be able to land in the vicinity of Washington.

Perhaps he should descend. The currents at the lower levels might—

There it was again.

The first few times he had seen the light he had thought it a trick of the setting sun, or perhaps a distant bolt of lightning. Now he was sure it was neither.

It was right in front of him this time. A chill that was far different than that of the thin air spread through him. He was seeing something mysterious and mystifying.

A beam of white light swept through the air before him. It looked a limelight but it was not. It was much brighter and seemed to cover a great distance. Moreover, it did not originate on the ground. Its source, whatever it was, was at his altitude or higher.

The light pulsed silently before him, then flickered and was gone. Nathaniel was staring into the night sky and there was only blackness and stars before him.

Was this related to the tricks his mind played on him? Was he finally going completely mad? He didn't think so. He had always heard that madmen didn't consider themselves mad, that their wild hallucinations seemed perfectly normal to them. He thought no such thing.

Was he asleep and dreaming this? No: he was shivering too hard to be asleep.

Very well, then, the light was real. So what was it? Was someone searching the sky for him with powerful lights? That made a little sense, but not much. Lowe's limelights cast brilliant beams for up to half a mile, but not much farther. The beam he had just seen was at least twenty miles long. Also, he couldn't be sure, but he thought the light he had seen had undulated like a flag in the wind. He didn't understand how a beam of light could do such a thing.

He leaned out of the car, trying to see around the gasbag, and saw something coming down out of the sky right above him. It looked like a curtain at a theater being lowered. The curtain glowed a beautiful emerald green and it undulated. The sight terrified Nathaniel, it perplexed him and it amazed him.

The curtain came down until it seemed to be just above the balloon, then it stopped. It slowly flowed back and forth in the sky as if blown by a mighty wind. It was hundreds of miles wide and it was really there.

Then it wasn't. It faded to nothing in a few seconds' time.

Was this some act of Providence, sent to light his way? But why should Heaven aid him thus? Surely there were others more needing and deserving of its aid this night.

No, this was a natural phenomenon, the likes of which he had never seen. Another curtain, this one a deep burgundy red, was starting to descend. He watched it, trying to figure out what it was. Was it some trick of the atmosphere, like lightning? But no, these gossamer curtains had to extend far above the atmosphere. How high did they go, he wondered. A hundred miles? A thousand?

The horizon was now glowing. Lights like fanlights flared up beyond the mountains to his north, wavering in the dark. He leaned over the side. The clouds had broken and he could see the ground. Maybe his eyes had adjusted to the dark, or perhaps the mysterious lights were illuminating the ground. Whatever the reason, he could make out patchworks of farmland beneath him.

He looked at the stars, then carefully watched the ground. He was moving southeast now.

He began to plan his next move. It looked like he would have to land in Confederate territory. He would have to land near a city or a large town, somewhere a stranger would not be a very remarkable sight. He would actually have to land in open country, though; it would not do to be seen landing. He would have to get rid of the balloon and the easiest way to do this would be to let it fly away.

He could not see any large towns or cities. Well, these were more common near the coast and he would be getting there soon enough.

The worst thing that could happen would be to fly out to sea. He would have to keep a sharp eye out for the coast. One factor in his favor was that it was too cold for him to fall asleep.

He pulled the top valve, holding it open for about ten seconds. The air was so still that he could hear the hydrogen whistling out. *Eagle* drifted down a few hundred feet.

He vented again, watching the ground, until he had moved down to five thousand feet above the ground. The air was a lot warmer at this level.

It was also moving due east. Was it doing the same thing at five thousand feet over York County, Pennsylvania? If so, he had greatly erred by rising so high. He could have stayed low and flown to Philadelphia, Annapolis or perhaps even Washington.

Well, regrets were useless. He would watch for a place to land. With a little luck he would find Richmond. Then he would try his hand at steering by changing altitude. If he had learned anything the last two years he would be able to follow the James River and end up at Fort Monroe.

He knelt with his arms hanging over the top of the basket, watching for a city, watching for the sea. He also watched the shimmering lights overhead. One curtain had glowing red and white stripes, like the flag he had seen with the setting sun coming through it. The field of stars consisted of real stars. He looked to see if there was a Confederate flag up there as well. There was, and it was even bigger than Old Glory.

The two battle flags contended in the sky above him. He could hear men cheering, urging one flag or the other on to victory. "Huzzah the Union!" he heard, "Huzzah the Confederacy! Join the triumph of the skies!"

He returned in triumph to Washington where President Lincoln himself welcomed him. "Nathaniel," he said solemnly, "you remained faithful to the Cause when all others had fled. Your nation thanks you."

"Not so," said General Lee. "That message was for me..."

He opened his eyes.

Eagle's mottled brown gasbag looked dirty against the clear blue sky above it. He was sitting in the bottom of the basket, his back to its side. His arms were splayed to his sides, his head was tipped back and his mouth was open. It was full daylight.

He closed his mouth and it felt like he had a mouth full of cotton. He was very thirsty.

He had fallen asleep after all. It was full daylight now.

He tried to get up. He was very stiff from sleeping seated against the side of the car so it took a minute before he was able to look over the side.

"Oh, *shit!*"

He was at about six thousand feet. He was surrounded by cumulus clouds, but there were enough breaks that he could see the bright blue Atlantic Ocean beneath it.

The sun was rising before him. The temperature was perfect and the air was crisp and clear. It was a beautiful day for flying and he was flying out to sea.

Now what?

He recalled ruefully how he had congratulated himself on being the best person to handle his present situation. He could see now that he was probably the worst. He had erred at every turn. He had disobeyed orders by flying in the first place. He had risen too high back in Pennsylvania. He should have put down immediately upon escaping the Rebels, landing in Pennsylvania or Maryland. Barring that, he should have put down anywhere at all.

At the very least, he should not have fallen asleep. Not when he knew that falling asleep meant that he would fly out to sea and die.

So what should he do?

He looked at the broad Atlantic stretching before him. He was moving due east at about thirty or forty knots. For a moment he was tempted to just continue on his present course. In a few days he would arrive in Europe and would be the first person to have flown across the ocean.

He came to his senses. He would never make it. Dozens of aeronauts, Lowe and Wise among them, had attempted Atlantic crossings. The fortunate ones had never gotten as far as the ocean. All the rest had been lost at sea.

He was totally unprepared for such a trip. He didn't even have any food or water.

No, continuing on his present course meant death. He turned to the west.

In that direction he could see nothing but clouds. He vented and sank into the cloud bank, finally dropping beneath the ceiling at about thirty-five hundred feet.

The western horizon did not have the knife-edge sharpness of the eastern. He focused the large telescope on it. Yes, it was definitely jagged. There was land to his west, some thirty or forty miles away.

He looked below him. The waves were marching westward. He recalled something that Wendell Smith had told him: on warm summer days, the land heats the air and it rises, drawing cooler air off of the sea. An onshore breeze, he called it.

But this would only occur near the shore. He could ride the onshore breeze back to land, but only if he got down near the surface of the water quickly. He vented through the top valve.

Eagle sank rapidly. He wasn't used to flying over water and it was hard to judge how high he was or how fast he was falling. All at once he spotted his own shadow coming across the water at him. He was descending faster than he had intended and was about to hit the water.

Acting entirely on instinct, he snatched the book off the bottom of the basket. Seconds later the basket hit the water. Seawater rushed through the wickerwork with a sinister sizzle that grew to a roar as the basket sank.

He pulled the strings on two sandbags. *Eagle* stopped sinking. He stood in water up to his shoulders, holding the book above his head. He was very frightened. He was also surprised at how cold the seawater was, and how it stung his wounds.

He waited. The basket rose, inch by inch, out of the water. The last water drained out of the bottom of the basket and only the sandbags remained submerged. At last even these broke free of the surface.

Eagle rose about twenty feet above the water. He looked at the drops falling from the bags to the surface. They confirmed that he was moving west again at about five or ten knots.

He looked around. Both telescopes had somehow remained in the car, though the salt was probably doing them no good. He wrung out his stockings and hung them over the side.

The rising sun warmed the gasbag and dried most of the remaining seawater. *Eagle* rose to fifty feet. His speed increased.

He was still in a very dangerous position but he felt he was making headway. He imagined what it would be like to encounter someone, a fishing boat, perhaps. He pictured himself waving jauntily to the fishermen: Good morning, gentlemen, lovely day for a sail, hey what?

He scanned the western horizon with his pocket telescope. To his dismay the horizon was now a smooth line. He could not see land.

Had he been mistaken before? How could he have seen land earlier and not see it now? The answer came to him after several agonizing minutes: the world is round, you idiot. Several thousand feet up the horizon was a lot farther away than it was near the surface.

It took three or four hours for him to reach the shore. As he approached he dropped a sandbag, bringing his altitude to four hundred feet. He had now dropped six bags and had six left.

There was a narrow strip of sand at the shore. A man knelt with his back to him, digging in the sand. A ragged boy and girl watched the man. They looked up as the balloon went by, then looked back at their father.

The land beyond the shore was uninhabited woodland. That's good, he thought, as he flew above the trees. The air was warmer over the land. This expanded the gas and made him rise even more.

The land was rising as well. The woodland at the coast gave way to a rocky headland. A railroad track ran north and south along this.

Then he was over forest again. The forest was nearly level, rising but a little as he drifted west.

His progress slowed and he started rising again. Although he was going up, the silk strip fluttered upward. He was in a column of rising air.

He had no desire to go up and out to sea again. He vented gas until he was about two hundred feet above the ground. His forward speed was now a little more than a walk but he was still moving west.

His stockings were now dry and his shoes nearly so. He watched his progress as he put them on.

He passed over a town, barely glimpsed through the trees. There was no one in sight. A minute later he passed over a highway. There were two wagons and a man on horseback below him but no one spotted him.

All right, he would put down at the next practical place he could find. He was now passing over swampland. This gave way to a small lake. There was forest beyond the lake, and as he flew over the forest he saw a field beyond that. The field appeared to be cultivated.

He was now barely above the treetops. As he passed above the field – a cotton field, in fact – he gave a hard pull on the upper valve. *Eagle* sank to the ground and settled onto a cotton plant with a crunch.

He picked up the book and the telescopes and climbed out. *Eagle* sat on its sandbags. He put his hand under the basket and found he could lift the entire balloon off the ground. It weighed about twenty pounds more than the air it displaced.

He pulled the strings of three sandbags and *Eagle* rose. He grabbed the basket and held it for a second. "Thank you," he said, then let it go. Seconds later it was at fifty feet, then a hundred, then it was a black dot against the sky. It was bound for that column of rising air, he knew, and thence to the sea.

"Good-bye," he said. "Bon voyage. Give my regards to Queen Victoria." He looked at the three sandbags on the ground, all that now remained of the dream of military aviation.

"*Oo la mumbo jumbo?*"

The voice startled him. He spun around and found himself face to face with a Negro armed with a pitchfork. Although the man was dressed in the rags of a field hand he clearly knew how to handle a weapon. He held the pitchfork with the tines toward Nathaniel and the handle close to his body.

The man's hair was long and unkempt. His face wore a pattern of decorative scars. His eyes, showing fear and defiance, remained trained on Nathaniel as he bobbed and weaved before him.

He heard other voices and looked around. A crowd of frightened field hands surrounded him. They stood in a circle about twenty feet from him. A stocky woman of about forty years stepped forward. She held her hands up, her white palms toward him, and cried, "Tell us which one you be!"

"What...what do you mean?" Nathaniel replied. He found it hard to take his eyes off of the man with the pitchfork.

"Lord have mercy! Are you from God or the other place?"

"I'm from neither. Tell your friend here to back off with that fork, will you?"

"O Jesus! Ain't you a devil or an angel or something?"

"No, I'm just a man, a natural man."

"No! No natural man can fly."

"Yes, that's just a machine, a flying machine. It's a thing like a boat or something."

"A flying boat?"

"Yes, a flying boat. Look, I'm not going to hurt you. Have him put down that fork, okay?"

The woman spoke to the man in a language Nathaniel didn't recognize. The man backed away, keeping his eye on Nathaniel as he went.

The woman approached him. Although a slave, she did not hesitate to look him right in the eye. "You *is* a natural man," she said. "What you doing flying in here like this, scaring folks so?"

Nathaniel found this a bit forward and responded with a question of his own. "What was he saying to me there?"

"Oh, he just a crazy old African. He thought you be a mumbo-jumbo, a Africa magic man."

"Oh."

"Who sent you, master?"

"Well, I—"

"Was it Abraham Lincoln?"

He sighed. "Yes, yes, it was. He sent me but I got lost."

The woman turned and spoke to the other slaves. Some of the words were English, but most of it was the same odd language she had used with the pitchfork man.

"What's your name, girl?"

"Miriam, master."

"Miriam, fetch some water."

"Master, you gots to go to the well for that."

"I see a bucket right there."

"That *slave* water, sir."

"Fetch it here."

An old oaken bucket with a tin cup floating in it was placed before him.

He dipped the cup and drank a long draft. The cold water stung as it ran into his empty stomach. A murmur arose from the assembled throng and he looked up. The slaves were as astonished by this act as they had been by the sight of a flying man.

Miriam spoke to the people again, then approached him. She licked her lips, uncertain of what to say. "Abraham Lincoln," she said at last. "Is he sure enough the biggest man in the world?"

"He's a very big man."

"He really going to free the slaves?"

"He's a-going to try."

"Lord have mercy."

"Girl, I have to get out of here. Can you hide me until nightfall?"

"I done sent for the doctor."

"What?"

"Doctor Sullivan. He be coming directly."

"But I don't need a doctor."

She nodded. "Yes, sir. Excuse me, but you do need Doctor Sullivan. You come along with me now."

Miriam was certainly not shy about ordering a white man around. She brought him to an open shed in the middle of the field. "You can wait here, master."

"Miriam, don't you call that doctor, you hear me?"

"I done sent for him already."

"Shit."

"Can I get you something, master?"

"Yes, I need more water, and I need some food, and I need to get some sleep."

He got all three. When he awoke it was a blazing hot day and an elderly white man stood before him. He was bald on top and had a fringe of snow-white beard around the edge of his face. He was dressed very plainly in a homespun shirt and trousers and carried a broad-brimmed hat at his side. "Good afternoon," the man said.

"Doctor Sullivan?"

"You have the advantage, sir."

"Oh, pardon me. My name is Nathaniel Curry."

"I was told that you can fly like a bird, Nathaniel Curry."

Nathaniel rose from the gunnysacks he had been lying on. He smiled. "Not any more, I can't."

"Is there some service I can do you?"

"Well, sir, not to put too fine a point on it, I need to get away from here."

"I see. May I suggest that we retire to my home and discuss the matter?"

"Doctor, I have to warn you that it would be death for you if you were discovered to be hiding me."

"Come along, then."

His carriage was like the carriage of every doctor he had ever seen. The doctor laid him out in the back with a blanket over him. "If we are stopped, say nothing. Feign unconsciousness. Can you do that?"

"Yes, sir."

"Good lad." He got in the box and drove off. "We can speak as we travel, but if I tell you 'hush', you hush up, hear?"

"Yes, sir."

"That's good. Nathaniel, may I ask, how did you come to fly into the Claffey plantation in this manner?"

"I was a member of the Balloon Corps."

"That organization is part of the Union Army, am I correct?"

"That's right. Or it was. The Balloon Corps is dissolved."

"Is it, now?"

"Yes, sir."

"It was headed by one Professor Thaddeus Lowe, I believe."

"You've heard of him?"

"Oh, yes. The papers speak of him frequently. And not in very complimentary terms, I might add. But you are yourself, if I am not mistaken, a southerner?"

He sighed. "Yes, sir, I am, in fact, a turncoat."

"Tut! There are, I confide, greater sins. Now hush."

A minute later he heard the doctor exchange greetings with another driver. When the sound of hooves had passed the doctor said, "You appear to be wounded, son."

"A little, sir. It's not bad."

"I'll look you over."

"Yes, sir."

"Were you wounded in battle?"

"Yes, sir."

"May I ask what book that was that served as your pillow?"

"Oh. It's by Charles Darwin and it's called *On the Origin of the Species*."

"Ah. It's one I've wished to read, but it's hard to find."

"Yes, sir."

Within the hour they reached the doctor's home. It was a country house and was as plain and homespun as his clothing. His wife, a wrinkled old woman in an old gray bonnet, welcomed him warmly even before hearing his name. "Art thou a Friend, my son?" she asked as she took his hand.

"Nathaniel is a passenger," the doctor said.

Mrs. Sullivan looked surprised for an instant, then smiled even more warmly. "I hope you enjoy your passage," she said. "The doctor and I have never lost a passenger."

"Thank you," he replied.

"Good wife, is the kettle hot?"

"I shall put it on."

"Is Custis here?"

"Indeed," she replied, then called over her shoulder, "Custis!"

A Negro about thirty years of age appeared at the door behind her. "Yes, Mother?"

"Custis," the doctor said, "may I ask thee to drive to the Morgan home?"

"Of course, Father."

"We need to borrow a suit of Jonathan's clothing. Every stitch, shoes, hat and all."

"I'll leave right away."

"I'll write'ee a pass."

"I still have the last one."

"Thou shalt have a new one."

"All right." Custis withdrew.

When Custis had departed the doctor brought Nathaniel into the drawing room. This was perhaps too grand a name for it, as it had plain whitewashed walls and a bare floor, but there were also several wooden chairs where they sat as the doctor tended his wounds.

"Please to remove your clothing. Every stitch."

"Yes, sir."

"Nathaniel, you are surely wondering who we are and what our purpose is."

"Yes, sir." Mrs. Sullivan entered with a steaming pan of water and cloths. The doctor began to clean his wounds.

"We are Friends, that is, members of the Society of Friends of Jesus. Have you heard of us?"

"No, sir, I reckon I have not."

Sullivan took what appeared to be a screwdriver from his bag and probed the wound in his arm. "You may know us as the Quakers. One of our number once said that Man should quake and tremble in the presence of God, and others have called us 'Quakers' ever since." He drew out a piece of lead and dropped it in the pan. "While we do not embrace that name, neither do we dispute it." He dabbed iodine on the wound.

"Then I have heard of you, sir," Nathaniel said through clenched teeth.

"And what, pray, do you know of us?"

"Well, not much, sir, except that you don't make cannon."

He smiled. "Indeed we don't. We are in fact strictly pacifist. But there is much more that could be said about us. For example, we do not use molasses."

"What, never?"

"No."

"Is that, like, kosher law?"

"Not at all. Molasses, rum and the slave trade are tied together in a deadly triangle. To touch molasses or rum would be to support slavery. And slavery is anathema to us."

"Huh! Excuse me, sir, but that's a new idea for me. But who is Custis?"

"Who, indeed? Custis is in fact my slave. I purchased him from a local man."

"But you don't work him, do you?"

"No. His master was cruel to him. Custis did not take well to being a slave and responded to his lashes with defiance. I convinced his master to take a few dollars for him. We are all happier this way."

"I could tell he wasn't anyhow an ordinary slave. I never seen one call his master and mistress 'Father' and 'Mother' before."

"Custis never knew his true parents, being torn from his mother's arms in infancy. Mrs. Sullivan and I are happy to fill that role."

"So are you going to set him free?"

"I cannot. Virginia law now requires that all manumitted slaves be re-enslaved within six months of their being freed."

"What about…something else?"

"A very perceptive question, Nathaniel. Something else. As your life is in my hands, now shall I place my life in yours." He leaned closer. "We are members of an organization that has been called the Underground Railroad. Have you heard of it?"

"Yes, of course." Nathaniel, despite himself, expressed shock.

Sullivan took scissors from his bag and trimmed some of Nathaniel's hair. "What have you heard?"

"Well, sir, when I was coming up, the Underground Railroad was considered bad folks. Really the worst folks, in fact. They stole slaves from people. They cost folks a lot of money and it made the other slaves want to run away. It was a big insult to someone to say they were the Underground Railroad."

Sullivan had by now dug another piece of lead out of Nathaniel's scalp. "How do you feel about it now?"

"Well, sir, I haven't thought much on it lately, but I reckon you're doing good work. I've decided that slavery is bad."

Doctor Sullivan leaned back in his chair, wiping his hands. "Well, I'm glad."

"So is Custis going to be one of your passengers?"

"No. The Underground Railroad has not been running at its former pace during the present war. However, I think we can make an exception in your case."

"Mine!"

"Yes, indeed. For if I read your intention correctly, you wish to return to the North."

"Well, yes, sir, I do."

A few hours later Nathaniel left again with the doctor, riding beside him in the box this time. They now rode a shay, with Custis and the doctor's wife in the back seat. Nathaniel looked for all the world like any other Quaker in Jonathan Morgan's clothing; only the fancy shoes remained of his previous garb, as Morgan had none to spare.

After a few miles they stopped at a large, box-like house with several other buggies tied up before it. "This," the doctor said, "is our local meeting house."

"It almost looks like a church," Nathaniel said, "except there's no steeple."

"Well, it is the closest we have to what you would know as a church. But we like to keep things simple. We have no steeple, for example, as we consider it an affectation. And there are no stones in the churchyard."

Nathaniel turned to the yard beside the building. "You mean there are folks buried there, and no stone to tell who is where?"

"There is no need for such a thing. Christ knows the name of each of them. Shall we go in?"

The meeting house was as plain inside as it was outside. There was no organ and no altar. There wasn't even a pulpit, and in fact there was no minister, no leader of the group whatsoever. About a dozen people were there. The Quakers sat in chairs arranged in a circle in the middle of the building's single room.

And then they did nothing. It was the queerest church service Nathaniel had ever seen. Everyone simply sat and looked at each other in silence. Custis and another Negro, a young woman, sat with everyone else. As a stranger, he himself drew a few glances but no questions.

He sat and waited for anyone to do anything. No one did anything. Nathaniel, desperate to get out of Dixie, considered this a tremendous waste of time.

He realized, however, that as he had placed his life in Doctor Sullivan's hands, he really had to play it the doctor's way. He endeavored to stay as calm as he could.

On the face of it, what these people were doing made sense. Their odd church service was an oasis of peace in a turbulent world. This was a humbug, though. Outside a great war was raging. The greatest battle of that war either was still going on or had just concluded. They could deny the violence in the world with their little room of peace, but that did not change the world.

But there was always violence in the world. If it wasn't a war it was something else. Here at least, in this spartan room, no one was contending with anyone else. Here, in this circle of chairs, there was peace.

A man rose and began to speak: "Some of you have heard this tale before but I pray your leave to tell it again. Some years ago, when Indians still lived in this country, I encountered a man who seemed to be in great distress. I spoke none of his language and he none of mine but by various signs he told me that he had lost his horse. It was, he believed, in the local vicinity, which consisted of bracken.

"I indicated to him that he should remain where he was, on the path, whilst I sought the animal in the bracken. At last I found it. The poor beast showed signs of having been beaten and it rolled it eyes in fear of me as I approached. The horse fled from me into the road where its owner caught it.

"The man thanked me for my assistance. I for my part suggested to him that his horse would feel more inclined to serve him if he did not abuse it. He accepted my recommendation, then we each invoked the blessings of our respective gods upon one another. Then he mounted the horse and rode away. And all of this without either of us uttering an intelligible word to the other."

No one looked at the man as he spoke but there were now smiles among the company.

"I have always felt that the lesson of this encounter was that all men can work together, can do each other service and can spread the word of Christ's love, and of men's love for one another, despite the differences between us." He sat down.

The room again fell silent. In other circumstances, Nathaniel would have seen this silence following the man's strange story as awkward. But the silence seemed perfectly natural. It was hard to imagine anything else.

The colored girl stood up and began to sing. At first she just hummed. There were no words and no tune. As she warmed up, though, the words came. Strangely, however, Nathaniel never had any recollection of what she sang. What he did recall was the beauty of her song, and of her voice, and of her face and form. For although he had never had such thoughts for a female of her race, this young woman was the most beautiful woman he had ever beheld in his life. He felt that he was somehow privileged to simply sit in her presence and hear her sing.

Her song came to an end. The echoes of her voice on the walls of the meeting house died away. She sat down and all was again silent.

Nathaniel was no Quaker but it all made sense to him now. There was indeed peace, and it wasn't even within the room. It was within the people in the room and within him. That was, after all, the only place that peace could really exist, within someone's heart. He wanted to sit in that simple room forever. He was eager to see what would happen next.

A few minutes later several horses pulled up outside the house. Five cavalrymen under the command of a major tramped into the room. They strode arrogantly to the center of the circle.

Nathaniel found them a shocking presence in the room. The six men were dirty and smelled of human and animal sweat. They destroyed the silence of the room with their heavy boots and their heavy breathing. They glared at everyone with undisguised hostility. Even the bright yellow plume on the major's hat seemed an affront.

"Who is in charge here?" the major said.

"Christ Jesus," someone replied.

"Don't get gay with me, old man. Who owns that nigger?"

"Custis is my property," Doctor Sullivan said.

"More likely he's a runaway you're harboring. You're Sullivan, aren't you?"

"I am Doctor Sullivan, yes. And I have a bill of sale for this person in my pocket." He stood up.

"All right, I'm seizing him."

"But he's my rightful property. Don't you—"

"Shut the Hell up. Nigger, get out in front of the house."

Custis looked at Doctor Sullivan. The doctor nodded and said, "Yes, son, thou must go with them. Thou must bear this cross. It is useless to resist. But it will only be for a little while. Go with our love, and with Christ's." Custis nodded and rose.

"You, too, girl. We're taking you as well."

The colored girl did not go as willingly as did Custis. She gave a scream of fear and began to weep. The women on each side tried to comfort her. The old man stood and said, "This person is free. She has papers of manumission issued two weeks ago. If you—"

The major shoved the man roughly aside and grabbed the girl's wrist. At this she began to scream louder than before. It was a cry of fear and despair that was as moving as her song of a few minutes before had been. Doctor Sullivan attempted to speak to her as he had to Custis: "It is only for a little while, my child, and then it will be better."

"No! I can't stand it if they do that to me again! I'll *kill* myself if they do that to me again!" It took three men to carry her from the room.

The hoofbeats died in the distance. No one adjourned the meeting but it was clearly over. They stood outside in the field of unmarked graves. Nathaniel turned to the doctor. "I have to get back."

"That — that was always our intention, Nathaniel."

"You'll send me back to the North?"

"If that is what thou wouldst, yes. It will be for thy safety."

"You know that I'll fight, don't you?"

"I had hoped thou wouldst see that that is not the way. I had hoped that thou wouldst see that fighting is wrong." The doctor's voice, so calm and sure before, now sounded weak and shaky.

"Doctor, when you told them it was just for a little while, when did you mean it would be over?"

Sullivan licked his lips. "In Christ's Kingdom all wounds will be healed and all tears will be dried."

"I don't think that girl can wait that long." He turned and got in the buggy.

Chapter Fourteen:
The Elephant

Nathaniel Curry awoke to find Doctor Sullivan reading Darwin at the kitchen table as his wife minded her chores around him. The old man looked over his *pince-nez* eyeglasses at him and bade him good morning. Nathaniel nodded in reply and asked him how he was enjoying the book.

"Oh, it's enthralling. A very interesting theory, to be sure, and very well presented. He is the scion of a family of scientific minds, of course, and it shows."

"I would have thought, sir, that you would object to him on religious grounds."

"Oh, not in the least. This great conception magnifies the work of God."

"It does?"

"Certainly. That such a simple means should allow the Creator to produce this varied and wonderful world I find most agreeable."

"Sir, when can I get out of here?"

He closed the book and put his glasses in his waistcoat pocket. "Thou art chafing here, aren't thou?"

"Well, yes, sir, I am. I mean, you and Mrs. Sullivan have been very nice to me, but I have work to do."

Sullivan sighed. "Work indeed. A lot of work has been done lately. I have heard news from Pennsylvania and from Mississippi."

"You have? What have you heard?"

"Two very great battles have occurred. The one in Pennsylvania was especially deadly. The entire forces of both sides were thrown into the fray. They fought viciously for three days."

"Three days!" Nathaniel thought about the battle of Antietam, the greatest he had ever seen. That had lasted but a single day. He tried to imagine such an immense slaughter going on for three days. "Who won, sir?"

Sullivan turned wearily to the window. "We have not been able to drive thee north because of the weather. The rain has ended. We shall set out tomorrow."

"Are the roads that bad, sir?"

"No, the roads are not the problem, my son. All of the bridges across the Potomac have been destroyed by the combatants and only the fords can be used. The rains raised the river but it should be in its bed again by the time we get to it."

Nathaniel nodded. "I was wondering what to take with me. I promised my friend that I would get his book back to him so I should take that. But I'm not sure. Would a Quaker read a book like that one?"

"Well, this Quaker would, but I understand thy point. It might look queer to some eyes. Still, it would make thee look like a queer Quaker, not a false Quaker."

"What about the locket? That is fancier than anything you would have, I think."

"Yes, it is. I have seen that around thy neck but I have not inquired about it."

"It belongs to my betrothed and I bear it in token of her."

"Ah, such a young lad to be betrothed! The youth of today..."

"Doctor Sullivan," his wife said, "thou wast eighteen when we wed and I was but fifteen."

He raised an eyebrow. "True, true," he said. "So it is her heart that thou bearest, then?"

"More than her heart, it is she." He removed the locket and opened it. The doctor put his glasses back on to examine the tintype within. His wife set her broom aside and looked over his shoulder, smiling.

"My!" the doctor said. "She's certainly pretty."

"Yes, sir, thank you."

"Let me use thy glasses, Richard."

"Where are thine?"

Mrs. Sullivan responded by snatching the *pince-nez* from his nose and placing them on her own. She gave a coo of appreciation for Amanda's beauty.

Sullivan closed the locket. "I could not in conscience ask thee to abandon such a keepsake. In truth, it is something the youth of today would bear."

"Thank you, sir."

"What else hast thou?"

"Well, my telescopes."

"Those thou should not take."

"Very well. They're yours, then. What about this?" He handed him his pocketknife.

The doctor put his glasses back on and looked at the knife. The brass fittings on the ends and the dark rosewood handle made it the fanciest object in the room. He turned it over and looked at the tiny brass rose inlaid in the wood. He pulled the blade out and it snapped as it locked open.

"Well, it's not as plain as I'd like it, but it is hardly a weapon of war, is it?"

"No, sir."

He thumbed the blade, now honed to a razor edge. "Certainly we use knives. I use a many in my own trade." He closed the blade and handed it back. "What of thy shoes, son?"

Nathaniel looked down. The finely stitched English shoes, though badly in need of a shine, were still much more elegant than the rest of his outfit. He sighed and removed them. "These are yours as well, Doctor. Wear them in good health."

"Doctor Sullivan would never wear such shoes," Mrs. Sullivan laughed.

"Oh, but I might," the doctor said. "When I was a lad I was ever told

Use it up
Wear it out
Make it do
Or do without."

"So you'll wear them, sir?"

"I'll keep them, my boy," he replied merrily, "and I'll wear them the day slavery is abolished."

"Why, Doctor Sullivan, you surprise me," Nathaniel said, surprising himself with his boldness. "Next you'll sport brass buttons on your coat and gilt trim on your buggy." Husband and wife smiled in reply.

The sky was clear the next day and the roads were firm enough for them to begin the journey. Nathaniel had been surprised to find that he had flown clean over Virginia and into North Carolina, and they now had to cross the entirety of the Old Dominion to get to Washington. They passed west of Richmond around noon.

Riding beside the doctor on the box gave them opportunity to converse. Nathaniel described the strange spells that afflicted him from time to time. The doctor nodded as if familiar with the problem.

"This is an affliction of the brain, my son. In some ways the brain is a poor vessel for the soul."

"I thought the soul resided in the heart."

"I suspect it is the brain."

"Is there anything that can be done for it?"

"It can be endured, as can nearly anything. There are much worse afflictions. In time thou'lt learn to live with it. In time, perhaps, it will leave thee alone."

They also discussed the strange lights in the sky Nathaniel had seen. "I saw them as well, son. I had never seen such lights before but I am confident it was the aurora borealis, the Northern Lights. It is purely a natural phenomenon, though it is seldom seen this far south."

"Do you suppose the heavens were expressing grief over the great battles that day?"

"I think if Heaven had a comment on such a catastrophe it should have made it before the battle. But men would not have the eyes to read such signs."

They made fifty miles the first day, stopping overnight at an inn.

The next day they swung north. The doctor pulled over at one point to allow the horses to water at a stream. Nathaniel was lost in thoughts of Richmond, of Amanda and of bygone days of peace when the doctor interrupted him by asking, "What's it like?"

Nathaniel followed his gaze. A hawk was circling at four hundred feet, riding an updraft. As he watched the bird dipped a wing and swung toward the ground, then leveled and resumed circling. He shook his head. "It's like being God," he said.

They stopped again and set out at daybreak. It was early afternoon when they crested a hill and saw the Potomac before them. The river had clearly been running high and was sinking again.

On the other side of the river the Army of Northern Virginia was massed, preparing to return to Northern Virginia. The river was about four miles away but they could clearly see the cavalry, the myriad wagons and the great masses of infantry. Engineers were working to erect a rude bridge.

Doctor Sullivan reined in, struck with wonder at the sight. Nathaniel asked, "Is there another place we might ford?"

The old man shook his head. "Not for many a mile."

"Then we had best be gone from this place."

"Nay, we have no quarrel with this army. We shall give them no offense and they should treat us in like kind."

"Yes, Father." They had agreed that Nathaniel should stay in character as the couple's son until they parted ways. The doctor shook the reins and the team trotted toward the river.

At that moment the order was given to cross. Thousands of men crowded onto the bridge. Tens of thousands more pushed into the water, going chest deep and deeper. Nathaniel squinted at them, fascinated. Wagons, caissons and artillery pieces entered the water beside the struggling men. On the right, downstream, the cavalry forced its way into the current.

The doctor drove stolidly toward the army. They were only a few hundred yards from the river when men began to emerge from the bridge and from the water. As they approached, Nathaniel could see that they were fleeing in disorder. The vanguard passed them, soaking wet and their legs covered in mud. Their bare feet slipped on the damp road as they came. Their haggard faces wore expressions of terror and desperation as they plodded onward, hatless and unarmed, intent on nothing but going south as quickly as possible. They rushed by, ignoring the Quakers.

A man came up to the buggy and grabbed the reins of one of the horses, causing the poor beast to rear. A mounted officer approached and looked into the buggy. Seeing Mrs. Sullivan in the back, he ordered the soldier to release the horse. The man complied only when the officer drew his bloody saber.

"Mother," Nathaniel said, "you sit up here on the box with Father."

"But I always ride in the back."

"Do it, good wife. For they will not molest us that way."

"Yes, Doctor."

Doctor Sullivan, despairing of crossing the ford while the army was still using it, pulled up beside the river and waited. The mass of the infantry was crossing now, and although they did not look as desperate as the vanguard, they did not look happy. Nathaniel could make out the expressions of many of them. They were men who had looked the Angel of Death full in the face and fled from his awful presence.

The doctor turned and said, "When thou asked me who won the battles, my son, I did not wish to reply for fear it would seem to celebrate what I had heard. But thou canst see the answer now."

"Yes, Father."

"It is a grim sight."

"I know it is, sir. But I think you should shine those shoes when you get home."

The doctor hesitated, then nodded.

A minute later the doctor saw something that made him cry out. He set the brake and jumped from the box; Nathaniel was right behind him.

A soldier was helping a man with a head wound. The wounded man's arm was slung over his friend's shoulder and he seemed scarcely aware of where he was as the two struggled down the road. His wound was unbandaged and bleeding.

Doctor Sullivan stopped them. "This man needs treatment," he said.

"Leave us alone, old man," the other soldier said. "The damned Yankees are right behind us."

"He will die of shock if he is not treated. Do you have any bandages?"

"What do you know about it, damn you?"

"I'm a doctor. Let me treat him or he will surely die."

"He'll die?"

"Within the day. Do you have any bandages?"

"Help me get him out of the road." Nathaniel took the man's other arm and they laid him on the ground.

The soldier took bandages and lint from his kit. The doctor used the wet bandages to clean the man's wound as best he could, then stitched him quickly up. As he applied a dry dressing, he asked, "Who are you to this man?"

"He's my brother." Tears sprang to the man's eyes as he said this.

"Change this dressing when you are able. Keep the wound clean; clean it with soap and water. That's the best medicine for him. Make sure he drinks plenty of water. Boil it first if you can. You'll know when to remove the stitches."

"Yes, sir. Thank you, sir." Between them they got the unfortunate individual on his feet and the brothers headed back down the road.

The doctor turned to see a crowd of wounded men had gathered, all clamoring for his services. He sighed and turned to Nathaniel. "I thought this would happen. Nathaniel, tell thy mother to come and build a fire. I want thee to take a pot from one man and draw some water and set it to boil. We shall be here for some time."

"Father, I must speak with thee." He drew him aside and said, "Sir, it's death to me if I stay here. There are plenty of men in this army who might recognize me."

"If thou must flee, my boy, then do so."

"But you said you'd help me."

"And I have. Now I must help these men. Christ commands it. My conscience demands it." He turned back to his patients.

Nathaniel looked back at the clamoring wounded. *If thou must flee –* Sullivan hadn't meant to goad him, and anger wouldn't help him, so he quelled it. "Give me your mess kit, soldier."

As he worked, he thought about it dispassionately. He couldn't strike out north on his own – he would look decidedly odd crossing the river the wrong way. He didn't want to go the same way as the army, either. The safest place was with the doctor.

A while later – much later, for dusk was falling – an officer rode up. "What's going on here? Who the Hell are you people?"

"I am a doctor, sir," came the mild reply.

"You're no Army doctor."

"No, I am not, but yet am I a doctor."

The officer, a lieutenant colonel, saw Mrs. Sullivan and touched his hat brim. "Excuse me, ma'am. Sir, who are you? How did you come to be here?"

"My family and I are visiting relations in Pennsylvania. We but stopped to give these men aid."

The officer looked at Nathaniel. "Why are you not in the Army yourself, young man?"

Nathaniel felt himself flush and lowered his head in silence. The doctor answered for him: "We are Quakers and pacifists. We will not raise a hand against our fellow man."

Another man rode up and one of the wounded yelled, "Ten-HUT!" The others started to struggle to their feet when a gentle voice said, "No, be you men at ease. Colonel, what is this?"

"Sir, a civilian doctor is treating these men. Boy, remove your hat."

Nathaniel complied but kept his eyes lowered. He looked at the horse's forelegs. General Lee was again riding Traveller, the horse that had broken his wrists the year before.

"Colonel, take charge of these wounded. I'm ordering the Army to bivouac here tonight. See that these people are looked after as well."

"Sir!" replied the colonel, snapping a salute, and Nathaniel could breathe again.

Nathaniel awoke upon the ground. He had been given bedding by grateful patients; a tent had been erected for the doctor and his wife, one of the few in the vicinity.

It was very early; none of the soldiers save the sentries were up. Only the first light of dawn illuminated the scene.

Mist hung over everything. All around him horses and men slept. Beside him lay a pile of human limbs, the work of the previous day and evening. The flesh already stank and had collected an army of flies.

They had labored long into the night. The doctor was as tireless as a steam engine. Nathaniel had wanted to beg leave to turn in, but he would not as long as Mrs. Sullivan kept working. She had silently tended the fire, fetched water and assisted her indefatigable husband in his labors.

Nathaniel was still very tired but he felt anxious to get away from the Confederate Army. The doctor and his wife rose a few minutes later, none the worse for wear. Without a word they readied themselves to depart.

The lieutenant colonel walked up, buttoning his blouse. A young second lieutenant bore his hat and saber. When he had made himself presentable he came to attention and gravely thanked the family for its assistance.

"Sir," the doctor replied, "it is the only thing that a Christian could do."

"Nonetheless, my commanding officer would like a word with you." He glanced at the lieutenant, who snapped to and disappeared into the mist, returning a minute later with a man wearing the eagles of a full colonel. This officer returned the salute of his subordinate, who then introduced the doctor, his wife and Nathaniel. The colonel removed his hat at the sight of Mrs. Sullivan. It wasn't until he took the youth's hand and repeated his name, though, that Nathaniel recognized him. "Major Swanson!" he blurted out.

The colonel was momentarily at a loss; then he recognized him. "Nathaniel! But what is this?"

Nathaniel had no idea what to say or do. Colonel Swanson turned to his officers and said, "I need a few minutes to speak to this young man alone."

"Of course, sir."

"Nathaniel, will you walk with me?"

"Yes, sir."

They walked into the fog. Within a few paces they were quite alone. "Can you explain your presence here, young man?"

"Sir, I'll tell you, but first I have to say that you are looking very well."

"Thank you."

"I also beg you to bring no harm to the doctor and his wife. They're good-hearted people, the best I've seen in a long time."

"We would of course do her no harm in any case. But why should we?"

"They are smuggling me out of the country, sir, and back into the Union."

"Are they? But they hardly seem the type, unless they are themselves in disguise, as you seem to be."

"No, sir, they are genuine Quakers, the real article." He glanced down at his clothes. "I'm a fake, though."

"It's quite a convincing disguise. Please, time's a-wasting."

"Yes, sir. Well, to put it short but sweet, the Balloon Corps is no more. The Army fired all of us. I tried to make one last flight back in Pennsylvania but I had to cut my lines and fly away. I ended up in Carolina. The doctor and his wife took me in and agreed to carry me back to the North."

"Nathaniel, you do have a knack for landing in trouble."

"Yes, sir."

"Then you were at Gettysburg?"

"Yes, sir. I didn't see much of it, though."

"I saw more than I wanted. I saw the flower of the South cut down while advancing on a stone wall."

The fog was glowing yellow now with the dawn. The sun would soon burn it all away.

"Did it really last three days, sir?"

"Yes. Three days."

"Sir…how is Lemuel?"

"Lemuel?"

"Your son."

"He died on the second day."

Nathaniel burst into tears. Swanson was surprised and put his hand on the lad's shoulder. "Nathaniel, he died well."

"Yes, sir. I'm sorry, sir."

"I didn't think you knew Lemuel."

"I didn't, sir." He took control of himself. "Have you heard from David?"

"Yes. He writes a letter a week, he says, though we've only seen one of them. He's at a prison in Maine."

He nodded. "What will you do now, sir? With me, I mean?"

Swanson sighed. "Well, what are my options?"

"I don't think you have any, sir, except to turn me in."

"Turn you in? On what grounds?"

"I'm a Yankee spy."

"Are you? And what have you learned? That we lost the battle of Gettysburg?"

He looked at the ground. "I'm not a very good one, in any case."

They had wandered some distance into the fog but they were not disoriented. Behind them they could hear the groans and cries of thousands of wounded men. It was like standing outside the gates of Hell. Swanson turned toward the sound. "We shall be moving out within the hour. I have much to do. Come."

"Yes, sir."

It was a long hour. The three Quakers were placed under guard. As soon as Swanson left wounded soldiers appeared like magic. Doctor Sullivan rolled up his sleeves and ordered one of his guards to fetch water and firewood. By the time the colonel returned the three of them had set all of their guards to work and had treated a score of patients.

He spoke first to the soldiers. "All of you men fall back in. The wounded will be treated when we're farther south."

"What about us, sir?" one of the guards asked.

"You are relieved. Fall back in."

"Yes, sir."

Swanson stood in silence until he was alone with the Sullivans and Nathaniel. He addressed the couple first. "Again, your country thanks you for your service."

Rather than dispute this, the doctor nodded.

"I have learned something of your history, Doctor Sullivan. There is much we could say to each other of these present circumstances, but I doubt either of us could convince the other of anything. I shall simply say, 'Go and sin no more.'"

"We of course feel that we are doing no sin."

"It breaks the law of Man, if not of God. No matter; this is not an issue we can sort out right now. You must leave immediately. Nathaniel, you are in my custody. Say your good-byes."

Nathaniel turned to the elderly couple. All three had tears in their eyes at this parting and none could find words to speak. He kissed both of them and walked toward the river with Swanson.

"Nathaniel, I have always had a soft spot for you, you know that?"

"Yes, sir."

"At the same time, I find your opinions simplistic and your actions rash."

He nodded.

"While I fault you, I cannot deny that your intentions are good. Still, you seem to have outdone yourself this time.

"You insisted upon flying when the Union Army itself had declined your services. You then fell in with a company of notorious slave thieves. You helped them in their crimes and they helped you. Then, to top things off, when, inches from Union soil, you encountered the entire Army of Northern Virginia, you did not take evasive action but instead stayed to give aid and comfort to your own enemy. What would Professor Thaddeus Lowe say to that? What would General Meade or President Lincoln?"

"I don't know."

"My quandary with you is as great as it was with the Sullivans. Greater, in fact."

"If you let me go, sir, you know I'll sin again."

"I have no doubt of it, although I am not very concerned. Perhaps this is uncharitable, but I think you have done our cause little harm, nor will you in the future."

"Huh. Excuse me, sir."

"That is precisely what I am doing." He handed him an unsealed envelope. Nathaniel opened it and read, "Be it known by these presents that the bearer, Nathaniel Curry, is engaged upon purely scientific studies unrelated to the present conflict and should be aided and sped by all who meet him. Rob't E. Lee, Lieut. Gen., C.S.A." Beside the signature was Lee's embossed seal.

"Use this," Swanson said, "to return to the North. Once you get there, burn this letter. What you do after that is your concern. But if we meet again I can offer you no further succor."

"What did this cost you, sir?"

"Nothing, really. General Lee agreed with my case. Don't worry about it."

"Yes, sir. Thank you, sir."

"I noticed when we spoke this morning you did not inquire after Amanda."

"No, sir."

"Has your ardor for her cooled?"

Nathaniel pulled out the locket and dangled it before him. "Not in the least, sir."

"Know that she is well."

"Thank you, sir."

"I didn't know you had that. It looks like the chain broke."

"I've tied it back together, sir."

Nathaniel could have simply crossed the river into Maryland at this point, but he did not. If he had, he would have found himself with no means of transportation, no money and no prospects. Lee's letter had the magical effect of providing him passage on Confederate transports and he decided to avail himself of this. He rode the Virginia & Tennessee Railroad east, then took the Danville train to Richmond. Brandishing the letter even got him food.

The trains were full of men who had been invalided out of the Army. Most of them were in pretty bad shape, even on the edge of death. They lay around the carriages in all sorts of arcane positions. They reminded him of old paintings of ancient battles he had seen in books.

Many of them wanted to talk about what had befallen them. Nathaniel was pleased to lend an ear.

"My best friend was shot through the heart. I leaned over and took his head to say good-bye but he was already gone. Then I got hit."

"Both arms at the same time?"

"Yes. Right through the wrists. Hurt like Hell, it did. Look at me now. No hands. What am I supposed to do with no hands?" He shook the bandaged stumps before him.

Nathaniel shook his head.

"I got shot in the chest," another man said. "Right on through."

"In the back or in the front?" the man with no hands asked.

"In the front, of course," the man said. "What do you think I am?"

"The South is finished," another man said. "We can never win now."

"Who said that? God damn you!" another man exclaimed. He was a gaunt, toothless creature with a scraggly goatee. The stump of his left leg bobbed before him like a grotesque phallus as he waved his crutches in the air. "I killed me four Yanks and I'll kill you too, you bastard!"

"Sit there and shut up, Gramps," the man said. "The war is over for you and me."

The old man made a sound like a goat but said nothing more.

He found the city even more heavily fortified than before. Several times he had to undergo searches. Everyone was skittish from the Federal campaigns to capture the Rebel capital and from the Federal successes at Gettysburg and Vicksburg.

First he visited his family's store. The twins were working behind the counter; two colored boys were doing the toting. When he came in the girls did not recognize him at first; then both were overjoyed at his arrival. They came out from behind the counter to embrace him.

"Nathaniel, it is so good to *see* you!" Ada exclaimed. "But whatever are you doing here? Are you back for good?"

"No, I'm just passing through. Look at what I have."

The girls made admiring sounds at the letter. "Did General Robert E. Lee really write this?"

"Sure enough. Yes, that's his hand."

"And you're conducting scientific studies for him now?"

"That's what it says there, isn't it?"

How foolish females were, he thought. When last they had met he had been working for Abraham Lincoln. Now they blithely accepted that he was working for Lee.

"But where are you off to now?"

"I can't tell you."

This added a note of mystery that thrilled the twins. "You've grown up so, Nattie," Ada said. "You're a full-grown man now."

"Yeah, well, you two are, uh, all filled out."

Both looked scandalized. "You can't say such a thing to your sisters!" they said.

Embarrassed, he asked, "Uh, where's Maw?"

"She's upstairs," Ada said, her voice dropping. "She doesn't get out much anymore."

"She isn't well," Daisy added.

"What's the matter with her?"

"Oh, it's just a feminine complaint."

"Oh!" Nathaniel knew little about the workings of women's bodies but what he did know horrified and confused him.

"It's not really that," Ada said. "She's just really tired."

"Do you think we should send for her?" Daisy asked.

"Well, we should let her know that Nattie's here. If she wants to come down she can."

"All right. Philip, go see our mother. Tell her Nathaniel is here."

Philip turned to the side door that led to the outside stairs. He moved like he was a hundred years old, although he was not yet twenty.

"Hurry it up!" Ada barked, and Philip responded with a barely detectable burst of speed which quickly subsided.

Nathaniel recognized the tone she used in speaking to the boy. "We own slaves now?"

"Well, just the two right now," Daisy said. "We were up to four last week and down to one two days ago. But then we picked up Arthur. They don't stay long."

"Wait a minute, when did we become slave brokers?"

The girls giggled at this. "Some of our customers can't pay us sometimes," Ada explained, "so they give us slaves. We use them for a while and then sell them to someone else. It works out fine for everyone."

"I'll be glad when we're rid of Philip and Arthur," Daisy said. "They're a couple of stupid monkeys." Both girls giggled at this observation.

"Most of our business is trading things now," Ada said. "Someone will bring in a bag of rice and we'll give them some nails or something. It's called 'barter.'"

"Doesn't anyone have any money anymore?"

"Everyone has plenty of money," Daisy said, "but the money isn't worth a tinker's dam."

"Daisy!" Ada said.

"That's 'dam' without an N, so it's all right," her sister said innocently. "Nathaniel knows that."

"No, I heard the N at the end," he said. "What does Paw think of that?"

"Paw's in the Army," Daisy answered proudly. "He went in two months ago. He said it was either go in now or wait for the draft and he thought it would be worse to be drafted."

Nathaniel was quite surprised by this, as it had been his father with his denunciations of slavery who had induced him to fight for the Union. He actually opened his mouth to ask which army his father had joined but instead asked, "Has he written?"

"We've gotten three letters from him. They took over a month to get here. He mentioned other letters he had written but we never saw those."

Ada leaned forward conspiratorially and hissed, "He's going *north*. Isn't that exciting?"

Nathaniel nodded. "You've heard about Mellie, right?"

"Yes," both answered in chorus. Ada continued, "I hope he's all right."

"All right?"

"All we got was the one letter."

"Wait a minute, what letter are you talking about?"

"What are *you* talking about?" they asked simultaneously.

He closed his eyes and said, "All right, I haven't heard anything about Melrose. What have you heard?"

"He got captured," Ada said, "outside of some town with a funny name."

"He got captured?"

Both nodded. "They let him write a letter before he got shipped north," she continued.

"Except he can't write," Daisy said, precipitating a giggle from both. "So another boy wrote it for him. He got captured, he wasn't wounded bad, and the Yankees were making him go to a prison."

"Oh, that's good."

"Why is that *good*?"

"Well, it means he won't be killed in the war. And that's what I heard."

Both girls looked suddenly concerned. "What did you hear?" Ada asked.

"Well, it looks like it was wrong. Someone thought he had died."

Ada gasped and said, "Maybe he did," and Daisy began to cry.

"No, that's impossible."

"Anything's *possible*."

"Especially dying."

"No, someone thought he had died in a skirmish. But if he was put on a train for prison in the north, then that person is wrong."

"But what if they were *right*?"

Exasperated, he asked, "How could he have written a letter from a train after being captured if he was dead?"

"But he *didn't* write it, someone *else* did!"

"You're just trying to get us all upset. Wait until we tell Maw."

"You're a couple of ninnies," he said.

Philip slouched back into the store, cast his eyes down and muttered, "Missus don' want to come down."

Ada and Daisy looked at each other. "She's been like that," Ada said. "You better go up and see her."

The kitchen had little in the way of food in it but it was still a mess, as was the parlor beyond. The curtains were drawn and a lamp was lit. It was turned down so low that its light was barely visible.

His mother sat in her chair with her hands folded in her lap. She looked up at his approach. She managed a wan smile, then looked at her hands again.

He sat on the settee beside her. "Morning, Maw. How are you?"

Her eyes darted toward him, then away again. "Son," she said softly. "I'm sorry I didn't come down. It's so…hard."

"You sick, Maw?"

"Maybe I am, Nattie. I…well, I don't rightly know."

"You seen a doctor?"

She moved her head back and forth slightly. "Don't think a doctor would help," she said. "Besides, they're all with the Army."

"You been eating okay?"

She thought this one over. "There ain't nothing to eat."

She sat and looked at her hands. Her lips parted as if she was about to speak but she did not. She looked sad that she had nothing to say.

"Maw…I got to go again. You understand me?"

She turned to him, looking him full in the face for the first time. The lamplight softened her features. She was still a young woman but this light made her look even younger.

It was good to look upon her face, the first face he had ever known, the face he had seen every day of his childhood. Her face was warm, loving, beautiful, accepting.

But her eyes were bottomless pits and he feared to look into them.

"Son," she said at last. "Don't die, all right?"

"I won't, Maw."

He went back down to the store. "How long she been like this?"

The girls looked at him. "You see it, too?" Ada asked.

"Sure I do."

"It just sort of came on. We never saw nothing like it before."

"I have."

"You have? What do you mean?"

He went behind the counter and sat on a flour barrel. The girls came and stood before him, their hands clutching their aprons. Philip and Arthur, on the other side of the store, acted like they were not listening.

"I seen it in soldiers. It's called 'seeing the elephant.'"

"Seeing the elephant? What does that mean?"

He shrugged. "I guess it means that when you've seen an elephant you know you seen something big."

"So what's a-going to happen?"

He hesitated. "I don't know what will happen to her."

"Well, what happens to the soldiers who seen the elephant?"

"It means they're finished."

"What do you mean?" Ada persisted. "Honestly, Nattie, talking with you is like pulling teeth. What do they do when they're finished? Do they stop being soldiers?"

"Yes, they do." He stood up. "Listen, I can't tarry. Do you know where Amanda might be?"

"Yes, she works every day at the hospital now."

"Which one?"

"The Medical School Hospital. I don't know the address, but I know how to get there."

"I know it. I used to deliver telegrams there."

The streets had about as much traffic as before the war. Much of it was military but much was not. Many people seemed intent on living their lives as if their country and their city were not under attack. Ladies and gentlemen rode about on this beautiful July day in their fine carriages as if they had not a care in the world.

He did see, however, one remarkable concession to the war: women were starting to drive and even ride by themselves. In earlier times such behavior would have been scandalous, although he had never quite understood why.

The Medical School Hospital was a handsome three-story building about eight blocks from the store. A soldier with one arm sat on a chair inside the door; beside him a musket that looked to date from the War of 1812 leaned against the wall. Nathaniel told him that he was there to visit Miss Swanson. Without a word the man went into the building, leaving his weapon with the stranger.

Amanda returned with the soldier. She did not look in the least surprised to see her beau; rather, she said, "I thought it must be you. Give me a minute to clean up."

She returned with her bloody hands washed and her bloody apron replaced. Only then did she favor him with a smile.

"Is there some place we can go to talk?" he asked.

"Let's go out for a walk," she said.

The boardwalk was muddy due to the recent rains and a general lack of sweeping. Amanda's hem was a few inches above the ground, though, and she needed to lift it only when crossing a street. The day had grown as hot and humid as Virginia can get.

"You're looking well," he ventured.

"You as well," she replied.

"And look at you! You look so business-like. Is that what lady nurses wear now?"

"Yes, at my hospital."

"It looks almost like a uniform."

"Well, I suppose it is. We're as well regimented as a military unit, we may as well be in the Army."

"Uh-huh."

"And Lord knows we couldn't do any worse than the menfolk at conducting this war."

"Well, you're not the first to say so."

"And look at you, Nattie. Why, what is it that you are wearing?"

He looked down at his Quaker garb. "I know, this must look most queer."

They walked in silence. She may have been waiting for him to answer her question but he did not.

"I thought you could not come back to this city until all was done."

"I can't stick around. But it's all right for me to be here now."

"Why is it all right now?"

"I have a letter."

"A letter?" He handed it to her and stopped so she could read it. "Why, however did you get this? It appears to be genuine."

"It is genuine."

"Are you going to answer any of my questions?"

"Sorry. General Lee agreed to help me get back to the other side."

She handed him back the letter. "Like a smoky torch, your answers obscure more than they illuminate."

"Oh, that's good. That's a metaphor, isn't it?"

"A simile, actually."

"A simile, then. All right, let me answer you."

He stopped; she stopped. "I encountered Lee's army on its retreat from Pennsylvania. I was with a doctor and we helped a few of the wounded. I was given this letter in return."

"Well, that helps a little. The Army was retreating from Pennsylvania?"

"Yes."

She started walking again; they were headed toward the river. "We've seen some of the men from the Pennsylvania campaign in the hospital."

"I think you'll be seeing more of them. It was pretty big. I came here with the vanguard of the wounded."

"That's what some of the men have been saying." She hesitated before asking, "Was it really the biggest battle of the war?"

"It was pretty cotton-picking big. Your father..." He silently cursed himself.

She wheeled on him. "Yes, what of my father?"

"I saw him."

"You saw him after the battle? He was well?"

"He looked as good as he did before the war."

For the first time she looked genuinely happy. "Oh, Nathaniel, that is the greatest news you could have given me."

He smiled back at her. "Well, I'm glad to give you those tidings, then."

"It seemed like you didn't want to."

"I was going to when I found the opportunity."

She laughed. "Excuse me, I'm just so happy. You could have told me that straight away and I wouldn't have minded."

"All right."

They came in sight of the river. A number of ships lay at anchor or moored to the docks. Some of them were warships but not many. There were larger commercial vessels, stranded here by the Union blockade. A few were small, swift steam vessels, evidently blockade-runners. One larger warship was making steam in the river.

It was the *Merrimac*.

But it was not.

Nathaniel analyzed what he was looking at. The ship was a gray ironclad with sloping sides. She resembled the *Merrimac* in general form, but there were differences. She was low and rugged-looking but there were only a few guns. Evidently she was to be used primarily as a ram.

It also seemed to him that this ship was not a converted wooden ship but had been built from the keel up as an ironclad, like the *Monitor*. She did not have the cobbled-together appearance of her late sister. She was all of a piece, she was rugged and she looked like she was ready for business.

Clearly the naval engineers of the South had not been idle. They had taken what they had learned from their earlier experiment and applied it to this new ship.

Amanda followed his gaze. "That's a horrid-looking thing."

"I was just thinking that she looked beautiful."

"What, that bugbear?"

"Well, I've been thinking more in terms of science lately."

"Oh, and that is what you told General Lee, I suppose?"

"Well, that's what your father told him."

Amanda looked around; there was no one near them. "You had best tell President Lincoln about this."

"No need," he answered evenly. "He seems to know pretty near everything before it happens."

Her eyes flashed once but he was not taking the bait. She turned and walked down the river road. He stepped to her side.

"Did he mention Lemuel?"

He felt as if he were pinned down. There was no way to avoid answering this. "Yes."

She stopped, touched his arm and looked him straight in the eye. Her face was open and unguarded before him. For a moment it seemed like the good days, before the war and their estrangement.

"Tell me straight out."

He took a breath and said, "Your brother Lemuel fell on the second day of the Gettysburg battle. Your father said he died well."

Amanda turned from him and pawed at her bag, then snatched up her apron. She buried her face in it like a child, trying to suppress her sobs.

He touched her shoulder. It brought him back to the day he had departed to join the Balloon Corps, but it was different. He was touching not smooth flesh but her coarse cotton uniform. Her shoulder was no longer soft but hardened by hard work. And she was not accepting of his touch. She shook his hand free.

"Amanda…"

"Oh, leave me alone! Why did you have to tell me that? If you hadn't told me he could have lived a little longer in my hopes and my prayers."

"I'm sorry. I just thought that honesty was the best policy."

"How could *you* think *that*?"

He had no answer for this.

"I apologize. That was a horrid thing to say."

"No, it was all right."

"Is that why…is that why you were hesitant to tell me you had seen Papa?"

"Yes. Because I knew that when I told you about him, I would have to tell you about…the other as well."

She got her handkerchief out of her bag and dabbed her eyes, then discreetly blew her nose. "Then it was right to tell me."

"I had thought my own brother was dead. I just found out he's in prison."

"Then you have seen your sisters?"

"Yes, I saw them before I saw you."

"One is always closer to one's siblings."

"Yes, Amanda. But I'm very close to you as well."

She put the handkerchief away and turned back to him. "Nathaniel, you are not as close to me as you were."

"I know."

"Do you still bear my locket?"

He tugged the chain and it dangled before him.

"It looks a little worse for wear," she said.

"I know."

"I must ask you to return it."

"What? But why?"

"Because I no longer wish to marry you."

"Because I –" he glanced around "– because I support the Union cause?"

"That among other things."

"What other things? Or is it just that?"

"That should be enough."

"What about slavery? This war is the only thing that will end it, you know that."

"We Southerners will deal with slavery on our own terms."

"The South will never abolish slavery without the help of the Union."

"Oh, is that so? What about Lincoln's vaunted Emancipation Proclamation? Why did that only apply to the states that were in rebellion against the Union? Why didn't it apply to Missouri or to Kansas?"

"That was politics. He couldn't afford to have the Border States join the Confederate cause."

"Exactly. So he—"

"But there's a bill before Congress to make slavery illegal everywhere."

"Oh, and that will make everything better?"

"It won't solve every problem, but yes, Amanda, it will make everything better. The Confederacy is the only place in Christendom where there is slavery now. That must end."

She held out her hand, her eyes blazing. "Please return me my locket."

"No."

"No? But it is mine."

"You gave it to me."

"I gave it to you in token of a love that I no longer feel."

He dropped the locket into his shirt. "You'll have to fight me for it."

"Then I shall. I'm stronger than you know."

Her gaze was fiery but he returned fire. "I know you're strong. I'll never doubt that. But this little trinket has kept me alive."

"Don't speak nonsense, Nathaniel."

"It's not nonsense."

"In what wise could my locket possibly have kept you alive?"

"I've seen it with men that when they no longer care they die. A bullet finds them or some other mischance befalls them." He put his fingertips to his chest as he had a million times over the past two years. "When I do this I want to live."

She started to speak two or three times, then said, "Remember, then, that that is stolen property."

"I'll do that. Shall I walk you back to the hospital?"

"Don't trouble yourself. I know the way and I am in my own country. You have to get back to yours."

He turned toward the train station. He had stormed about twenty yards when he turned back to her.

Her golden hair had come partway out of its bun and now flew free in the afternoon breeze. She looked more beautiful than he had ever seen her, standing proud and defiant in the heart of her proud and defiant city. He pointed a finger at her.

"I'm going to win this war," he said, "and then I'm going to come back here and win you."

Chapter Fifteen: Good Company

It took a week to travel the ninety miles from Richmond to Washington. He did not dare ask anyone the best way to go so he sort of stumbled between the two capitals.

Lee's letter was meaningless to civilian railroad personnel but had an almost magical effect upon the military. He learned to look bored as soldiers snapped to attention and called him "sir." Once a private at a train station brought the letter to his captain, who summoned a colonel. These two then held an animated discussion that was not quite out of Nathaniel's earshot. It ended with the colonel solemnly declaring that this mysterious young man was certainly a spy. The colonel, an ancient and august personage with magnificent mustaches, then invited Nathaniel to dine with him.

He took the Richmond, Fredericksburg & Potomac north as far as Hanover Junction, then took the Virginia Central west to Gordonsville. There he picked up the Orange & Alexandria, taking that to Manassas Junction.

And there the railroad ended. Manassas Junction, the site of two brilliant Confederate victories, was still in proud Rebel hands, but points north were not.

There was certainly travel between the two capitals. Merchants in particular went between them, carrying goods possessed by one side and coveted by the other. Coffee, for example, was in short supply in the South, as was whiskey in the North. While some people objected to aid and comfort being provided to their enemy in this fashion, the merchants themselves simply bribed everyone in sight with gold and went their merry way.

Nathaniel Curry had no coffee, whiskey or gold, merely a letter and a book. As he approached the border area he became reluctant to use the letter. There seemed, after all, little opportunity for scientific research in that locality.

He hitched rides on wagons, both civilian and military, until their drivers demurred at carrying a stranger in the border area. He ended up walking the last ten miles from Fairfax Courthouse to Alexandria. And there, at last, he was firmly in Union hands, and on the outskirts of the city of Washington.

He found a military wagon train that was going to the Columbia Armory and sweet-talked his way aboard. At the Armory he reported to the Signal Corps, presenting himself to a fat, sweaty and most objectionable paymaster.

"Who the Hell are you? You're not even military."

"I'm Nathaniel Curry, late of the Balloon Corps, Sarge."

"Balloon Corps? You fellows still coming in?"

"Who-all have you had come in?"

"Why the Hell do you think you can ask me questions? I'll ask the God-damned questions around here."

"Yes, Sergeant."

The sergeant hauled out an enormous ledger book and dumped it onto the papers that littered his desk. He scratched the stubble on his vast cheeks with ink-stained fingers. "Let's see…Balloon Corps. Sounds like another boondoggle to filch government funds, if'n you ask me. When can I close this thing out?"

"Well, who reported to you so far?"

"You have to keep asking me that, don't you? Let me see, I've closed accounts on two Lowes, then there were two Allens…" He breathed noisily for a minute, then said, "Then there was this Vogler. And you're Curry, right? Are there any others?"

"No, I should be the last one."

"You should be turning in some equipment. A balloon and support equipment."

"I destroyed it all at Gettysburg to keep it out of Rebel hands."

The man looked sharply up at him. "Any officers witness you do it?"

"Yes."

"Did you get a signed order or receipt from one of them authorizing the destruction of Government property?"

"No."

"How come?"

"We were too busy killing each other."

He shook his head. "You can't destroy stuff like that without permission."

"Sarge, it was in the middle of a God-damned battle. With twenty Rebs all over me, you expect me to go and get an officer?"

The sergeant wheezed in annoyance. "You civilians are a *pain in my ass,*" he proclaimed. He reached around and scratched the afflicted portion of his anatomy, then took a pen and stroked through the words beside Nathaniel's name. "Destroyed," he muttered, writing the word above the obliterated listing.

"We quits, then?"

"Yes. No. One more thing, you want your pay?"

"Pay?"

"Yes, pay, or were you doing it for the fun?"

"Well, for both, of course."

The sergeant performed a rite that made no sense to the youth, bringing his fingertip up and down the columns and mumbling. He then wrote out a pay voucher. "Sign here. Or you can 'X' it."

"I can write."

"All right. You just sounded like a Southerner, that's all. Put the date, too."

"What's the date?"

"Ah, July the twenty-seventh. Eighteen-hundred and sixty-three."

"Where can I get actual money?"

The sergeant dismissed him with a flick of the fingers. "Any Federal Reserve Bank."

Nathaniel now had one hundred and eight dollars and the freedom of the city of Washington. His first act was to honor his word by burning Lee's letter. His second was to abandon the Quaker way of life and purchase new clothing.

He booked train passage north. He had never gone north of the capital before and he watched the passing landscape with interest.

In this country, eastern Maryland and Pennsylvania, it looked like the Civil War was not occurring at all. Farmers worked in their fields and merchants traveled the roads without a care in the world. There were no ramparts, no fortifications, no battle-scars upon the landscape. He was actually offended at how easily these states were getting off.

But they were not. There was a difference, although it took him a while to see what it was. Old men tended the fields; women drove produce to market. In one yard children were doing the washing. In another a man in his seventies worked the bellows of a smithy. There were no young men.

It took two days to make the trip to New York. His train journey ended on the Jersey shore where he took a ferry to Manhattan.

New York City was a stranger place than any he had seen in his life. For one thing, it was big. The docks stretched both directions along the shore as far as the eye could see. There was a forest in the center of the city that was itself larger than Richmond. People of all sorts crowded the streets and sidewalks, rushing in every direction like ants in an upturned anthill.

The people all seemed greatly agitated. Nathaniel at first attributed this to the war, but this was not the case. No one spoke about the war or even seemed to know that it was going on. Their excitement, which bordered on panic, seemed to be simply the result of living within this large and frantic city.

Nathaniel, wandering the streets with his carpetbag and his straw hat, felt very much the country bumpkin, but soon he realized that no one even noticed him.

After nearly an hour of walking it seemed to him that he had gotten nowhere at all. There was still street after endless street around him, some running east and west, some north and south. He sat on the stoop of a tenement and just watched the people for a while.

Most of the people were white. Some of these seemed well to do, even wealthy, while others were less prosperous or even poor. As he listened to people talking he came to realize there were a lot of Germans and a whole lot of Irish around him. These people, many of them fresh off the boat, were uniformly poor.

A barefoot boy of about eight dashed up, grabbed a handle of his carpetbag and tried to make off with it. He got a bad start because of the weight of the bag, giving Nathaniel time to snag the other handle. He then yanked the miscreant back and punched him in the head. The boy went down, then scrambled back into the crowd and vanished. He didn't seem to resent the blow to the head; it was apparently merely the cost of doing business. Nathaniel glanced around to see if he had any confederates, then resumed his inspection of the population.

There were many black people in the city as well. Many of them looked as poor as field hands. They were dressed in rags and were filthy and unkempt. Others were doing better than that, and some seemed to be as well off as the white people. In the South, the first question concerning a colored person was whether he was a slave or free; it was strange to think that every one of these people was free.

There were also Jews, or what he took to be Jews. There were men with what seemed to be carpets on their shoulders, or turbans on their heads, or side-whiskers that hung to their chests.

There were Chinamen in long silk robes, with long black pigtails and squinting eyes. Nathaniel had seen humorous drawings of such creatures and was a little surprised to find that they actually looked like that.

And then there were the just plain peculiar people. Several men were walking around with little black boxes tied to their heads. There were men dressed as women and women dressed as men. Some people were drunk, or on the point of death with consumption, or crazy. A lot of people walked along talking to themselves.

At last, having had his fill of this spectacle, he arose and continued his journey. He soon concluded, however, that he was helplessly lost. He hailed a cab and gave him the address.

After several miles of driving the cab entered a section of the city that was even more densely populated, though more prosperous. The driver pulled up before a brick edifice with handsome marble columns. He then demanded five dollars and fifty cents, which was greater than the price of the train ticket from Washington to New York. Nathaniel disputed this but ended up paying it.

The vestibule that he entered was the most opulent room he had ever seen. He barely had time to take in the velvet draperies, the gilt decorations and the richly patterned Oriental rug before he was accosted by what appeared to be an Army officer. The man's uniform was a deep burgundy red with gold braid running back and forth across the front of it. His shoulder-boards had gold fringe hanging from them. There were other accoutrements as well, but his eyes did not have time to take them all in. The only thing he lacked was a saber.

Although he was a civilian Nathaniel had learned to adopt a respectful reserve in front of high-ranking officers, so he automatically doffed his cap and straightened up. But then he realized that no army would dress even its most exalted officers in such a getup, not unless the intention was to dazzle the enemy into submission. This man was either mad, or on his way to a costume ball, or else he was some kind of servant.

The man gave him a haughty look and said, "May I help you...sir?"

"Yes, sir, I'm here to see Solomon Vogler."

"Do you have an appointment with Mr. Vogler?"

"No, just tell him I'm here."

"Your card, sir?"

"What?"

"May I present him with your card?"

"I don't have one."

His Excellency raised one eyebrow, then said, "Do you then have a name?"

"Nathaniel Curry."

"Please wait here. *Pray* ... don't touch anything."

"Yes, sir."

Vogler himself emerged a few minutes later. He wore a fine suit and gold-rimmed eyeglasses. "Nathaniel, it *is* you! How good it is to see you. But what brings you to New York?"

Nathaniel shook his hand, then took the copy of Darwin out of his bag. "I had to return your book."

Vogler took it, then smiled. "You could have mailed it, but this is you to the quick. It looks like it's been through a war."

"Yes, I'm sorry."

"Did you read it?"

"I puzzled over it a little. He's a smart fellow but he takes a long time to get to the point."

"Yes, he does. How long can you stay?"

"Oh, I'll head back tomorrow."

"Where's 'back'?"

"Washington, I guess. I can't go home until the war is over. I may not be able to go back even then."

"Well, will you have dinner with me? I can guarantee it will be nicer than our last meal together."

"Well, thank you kindly, Solly."

"Come upstairs with me. I have a few things to clear away and then I'll be free."

Vogler brought him up a fine staircase to another vestibule that was nearly as grand as the one at the entrance. "How do you find New York?"

"It's very nice. Everything is very grand here. Even the bad things are grand."

"Yes, *bon mot*. It's quite a place. London is larger but less interesting."

They entered an office where men bustled among tables or pondered enormous books. Here there were young men in abundance. Although they were all wearing handsome suits they jumped to their work like eager schoolboys. Not a thing they did, though, made sense to Nathaniel.

"What-all do you do here, Sol?"

"What do we do? Well, Nathaniel, you know there are various sorts of commodities. Cotton, for example, or beef or gold are commodities. They are things that are bought and sold."

"Okay."

"Well, at some level wealth itself becomes a commodity."

"Do you mean you buy and sell *money*?"

"Well, no, not directly. There are those who buy and sell money, but money is only the most visible manifestation of wealth. This company buys and sells wealth itself."

"How in Hell – excuse me, how on Earth is that possible?"

"I could explain it to you but it would take a couple of days and it would make your head hurt."

"Well, don't bother, then."

"Why don't you tell me your story? I'm sure you've been up to no good since last we spoke."

The carriage they were riding in was fancier than any that had ever passed him on the street. They were riding through a warm Manhattan evening to Nathaniel's hotel. "That was indeed a better meal than hardtack and goober peas. Thank you for buying it and thank you for ordering it."

"You're welcome."

"Thank Zeke for letting me use his suit, too."

Vogler smiled. "I'll also tell him you called him 'Zeke.' I don't think anyone ever has before."

"Does that old boy back there speak any English at all?"

"I don't know, I've never tried to speak English with Jean-Luc."

"Do you think I should stay here, try to find work in New York?"

Vogler frowned. "I don't know. It's getting pretty dangerous around here."

"We've been worse places, you and I."

"Do you know about the battle that was fought here a few weeks ago?"

"There was a battle here?"

"On these very streets."

"Who-all did that? I thought they never got any closer than Pennsylvania."

"It wasn't the Confederates. It was the citizens of this fair city rioting against the draft."

"I heard tell there were some riots."

"Not just some riots. The city was torn apart. They called out the State Militia, or what's left of it, but they couldn't stop it."

"Who was doing the rioting?"

"The Irish and the Germans, mostly. They didn't relish being drafted on behalf of the colored people. They were going around hanging coloreds, and not just the men. They were killing the women and children as well."

"Really?"

"A few blocks from here a colored orphanage was burned to the ground and they wouldn't let the children escape."

"That's terrible."

"You see that building? That's the New York *Times*."

"Really?" Nathaniel had often read the *Times*; it was usually on sale in camp.

"The publisher mounted a Gatling gun on the roof and manned it himself."

The building looked as staid and stolid as the newspaper that it housed. It was hard to imagine its publisher atop its façade, spraying lead onto the crowd below. "Did you see the riot, Sol?"

"Yes. I had to go through it to get home. You've noticed, I'm sure, that in addition to the driver, I have three other men with me."

"Yes. I thought it was all a bit much for the two of us."

"Those men are armed with pistols, as am I. There were some nights when they bore muskets. We've never had to fire a shot but we're ready to."

"So go back a minute here. You say the State Militia couldn't beat the rioters?"

"That's right."

"So what-all happened?"

"Army troops were marched in directly from Gettysburg. They fired on the mob for a full twenty-four hours before they established order."

"Whew!"

"Of course, 'order' is a relative term in this city."

"How many dead?"

"Two or three thousand. That's what they say, anyway. I've heard estimates as high as ten thousand. I saw the heaps of corpses myself."

"So if the Army hadn't of come in, the rioters would still be in charge here."

"Yes, it would have been mob rule. But it's worse than that. If the rioters hadn't been subdued and if Lee had gotten away from Meade, he could have marched right here. He would have had the freedom of the city."

"You think so?"

"Oh, yes. This city is a nest of Copperheads. They would have fed and armed the Rebels, bound up their wounds and sent them on their way."

"An entire army?"

"A few tens of thousands of men. That's nothing compared to the millions who live here. They could have camped in the park."

"But it didn't happen."

"But it could have. We like to say that anything could happen here, and that's for good or for ill. At its best, this is still a very dangerous city."

"Then why do y'all live here? Are you crazy?"

Vogler smiled. "New Yorkers are a special breed. Yes, perhaps we are crazy."

"So is the draft after you?"

"No, I paid the three hundred dollars. And I think I've already done my part in this conflict." He turned to watch a knot of people by the side of the road.

"Yes, I suppose you've done your duty to your country."

Vogler turned back to him. "My country? Is it that?"

"Well, isn't it?"

"Well, it is and it isn't. I feel just as at home in Paris, or in Bern or any of a half-dozen other places. And I feel just as not at home in those places as well."

"What do you mean?"

"I mean that no country is my country, nor can it ever be, unless Israel is re-established as a nation. My family isn't received in society here or anywhere. I attended a good college, but there are many others that would not have me because of my race. There are places I cannot go, people I cannot associate with, just as surely as if I were black."

"That's really stupid."

"So this is my world. I live in what may seem to you great wealth, but it is a gilded cage. And it may look like I have parted company with the Civil War but I have not, nor shall I ever."

Nathaniel had one more duty to perform before leaving New York. Solomon Vogler provided him with the address and as a parting gift paid the cab fare.

A maid greeted him at the door of a fine three-story home, then went to see her mistress. Within a few minutes he was ushered into a well-appointed parlor. As soon as he sat down he rose to greet the lady of the house. "Mrs. Spencer? My name is Nathaniel Curry, late of the Balloon Corps."

"How do you do, Mr. Curry?"

"Fine, ma'am, and yourself?"

"Fine as well. Won't you sit down?"

"Thank you."

"Would you like some tea?"

"No, thank you, ma'am."

Mrs. Spencer steeled herself and said, "I understand that you have some information on my son Mica."

"Yes, ma'am, I served with him. A fine young officer, I must say."

"And how is he?"

"Ma'am, I'm sorry to have to tell you, but he fell in battle."

She turned away in tears, but she was prepared: she bore a handkerchief in her hand and she used it. "How—how sure are you of this information, Mr. Curry?"

"Ma'am, I saw him after the battle at Chancellorsville. I'm sure."

"Did he suffer?"

"No, ma'am, he could not have. It must have been like—" He snapped his fingers and she winced.

"But his commander has written me," she said. "Mica's body was not found and he thought he must have been captured."

"Mrs. Spencer, I was on the other side after the battle."

"Do you mean in the enemy camp?"

"Yes, ma'am, and I was standing right beside General Robert E. Lee when I saw him."

"General Lee? But whatever could he want with my son?"

"He was attempting to identify the dead enemy officers, that is, the Union dead."

"To what end?"

"To notify their families."

"That is a very gallant thing for the enemy to do, is it not?"

"Yes, ma'am. General Lee is a gentleman."

"But he never sent me any word."

"He did not know your son. I was the only one who did but I could not say."

"But why not? Why did I have to hear it like this?"

"Ma'am, I wasn't supposed to be on the other side. Do you understand what I mean?"

"No...oh, but yes, I do." She stared into space for a moment, then said, "He had a pewter name tag engraved with his name and particulars. Why was that not found?"

"It must have been lost in battle, ma'am." It had certainly been scavenged by the Confederate soldier who took his boots.

"Do you know what they did with his remains?"

"Ma'am, I did not see it, but I know he would have been given a military burial."

"That, then, is a comfort," she said with an effort.

"Yes, ma'am."

Nathaniel knew that a "military burial" in this case would consist of being thrown into a ditch with a few hundred other unfortunates. Quicklime would be sprinkled on the corpses, then a foot or so of soil would be thrown atop them. It did not seem very dignified, but, as one member of a burial detail once told him, no one ever complained.

She smiled. "How well did you know Micah?"

"Tolerable well, ma'am. We weren't really friends as such because I'm not an officer, but we liked each other. He made a number of ascents."

"Ascents?"

"Oh, I was with the Balloon Corps."

"Oh, he mentioned that. Mentioned that warmly, as a matter of fact."

"I'm sorry I had to bring you such bad news."

"No, Mr. Curry," she replied, extending her hand. "It was very kind of you to tell me in person. Thank you for coming."

Nathaniel returned to Washington. He didn't really want to join the infantry so he looked around for other work.

There continued to be a crying need for telegraph operators, and those working for the Army could receive an exemption from the draft. He signed up.

Nathaniel could reliably send and copy twenty characters a minute and was therefore accounted a good operator. He expected to be sent back to the field but was instead assigned to the War Department in Washington. Here he communicated with operators throughout the theater of war. On the one hand it was boring because he spent most of his waking hours in a single large room. On the other hand, the telegraph allowed him to rove all over the South.

Although the brass was rightly worried about security on the line, the operators themselves tended to "chatter," exchanging pleasantries and gossip in addition to the official military traffic. He got a clearer picture of the progress of the war from his colleagues than he did from the newspapers, but one way or the other it was clear that the Confederacy was doomed.

He found himself again talking regularly with Morton Edge at Fort Monroe. Although the two had never come face to face he considered Edge a good friend, based entirely on the electrical clicks they sent to each other.

His life settled into a routine. Every morning, six days a week, he rose and went to the War Office. There he sent and received messages from throughout the theater of operations. Sometimes he would be required to send a reply to a message and he would find a soldier to run it. There were exceptions to this; if the message was intended for Secretary of War Stanton, he himself would run the message to his office, which was in the building, and wait for a reply. If the message was for President Lincoln, he would give it to a soldier to carry to the White House unless Lincoln was in the telegraph room, in which case he would simply hand it to him.

Lincoln continued his practice of spending several hours a day, time permitting, in the telegraph room. His presence went generally unremarked. The first time Nathaniel gave him a message there was a glance and a nod of recognition from the President, but neither spoke.

The most difficult messages to copy were the coded ones. Messages sent in "clear", that is, not coded, copied easier because if a letter was missed it could be deduced from the rest of the message. Not so with code, though: one missing letter might destroy the whole message.

Nathaniel Curry did not shy away from coded messages and developed a reputation for copying them accurately. He found himself writing down meaningless letters for hours on end. It wasn't merely boring, it required a lot of concentration. He would go to bed at night with the clattering still going on in his head.

Once he delivered a particularly long message to the officer in charge of the cipher division, one Captain Moran. Moran groaned, then said, "Thank you, Curry."

"Is it as much of a headache to reckon this stuff out as it is to copy it, sir?"

"Well, it's certainly not very diverting. And I'm up to my neck in it as it is."

"Where are those other fellows?"

"I'm alone today," Moran said. "Could you lend me a hand with it?"

"Shucks, I don't know how to do this and I don't know if I could."

"Oh, I'm sure you could. If you can work a telegraph you can do this." He sent a soldier to report that Nathaniel was with him, then said, "Pull up a chair."

Nathaniel said, "Now, I know that each of these letters stands for another letter, but I don't know which one stands for which."

"Oh, it's not even that easy. That would be a substitution code, and those are easy to break."

"They are?"

"Oh, yes. The Confederates use substitution codes and we always break them just like that."

"You do? How?"

"Well, with simple rules. For example, the most common letter in the English language is 'E', so we look for a preponderance of one letter. And the most common word is 'the', so once we deduce what 'E' is, we look for a group of three letters that ends in that. After that it's just hard work."

"So what do y'all do?"

"Well, we use a transposition code instead. With that, you use a keyword. The keyword for this week is 'honeycomb.' Now, that starts out like a substitution code, but it changes. Once a letter is used, it gets transposed and a different letter is used for that same letter. That way, there is no most-used letter. Do you follow me?"

"I reckon so, sir. No, I don't."

"Let me start at the beginning. A 'code' is the formula that is used to produce a 'cipher', which is a coded message. The process of producing a cipher is called 'encryption' or 'encoding.' Translating it back into clear is called 'decryption' or 'decoding.' Are you with me so far?"

"Maybe I should write this down."

"No, don't. You'll pick it up. And don't be afraid to ask me anything you don't understand. But never write any of this down and never tell anyone about it, you hear me?"

"Yes, sir."

"Maybe I should show you how it's done. We use a square to encrypt the message. Along the top I write the word 'honeycomb.' Now, the uncoded message, what we call the 'clear,' goes here…"

Bit by bit Nathaniel moved into the world of secret messages. The work was even harder and more tedious than telegraph work. At first he thought he would never learn how to use codes, but Moran was patient and repeated everything until he got it.

The messages often didn't make much sense even after they were decoded. In some cases that was because he wasn't privy to the rest of the conversation, but sometimes it seemed as if there were codes within the codes. One message read in its entirety, "THE TREE IS ON FIRE." Another said, "PROVIDENCE WILL REMEMBER."

The decoded messages were delivered to a different part of the War Office building. He left them with a sergeant who sat before a locked door.

Sometimes the sergeant would give him a message to be coded and sent. He would then sit down with the message, a pencil and paper, and a telegraph blank. Half an hour later he would have a page of unintelligible letters that some other poor fool would have to send down the wire.

In this manner he worked through the summer and autumn of 1863. There was not a lot of action going on in the war, at least not any major battles. Everyone knew after Gettysburg that the Confederacy was finished; it was just a matter of time. Still, the South refused to give up.

Things heated up in the latter half of September with the Chickamauga campaign. The Confederates, under Bragg, eventually drove the Union under Rosencrans off the field, but it was a bad experience for both sides. The lines chattered about it for weeks.

One afternoon in late October Nathaniel was carrying a sheaf of freshly-coded messages into the telegraph room when he heard someone say, "Aha! I thought I might find you here."

He turned to find himself face to face with Major Grover. "You!" he exclaimed.

"Yes, it's me," the officer said. He was even scrawnier than Nathaniel remembered him, and he still observed the odd habit of keeping his head covered indoors. "Thought you'd gotten away from me, didn't you?"

There was no proper answer for this, so Nathaniel merely said, "What do you want of me?"

"Isn't it obvious? I've always known you were a Confederate agent, and here I find you in the heart of the Federal espionage organization. I'm placing you under arrest, and if you don't give me the names of your contacts, you'll be dead by nightfall."

Grover stepped up to him. Nathaniel felt himself reacting to the man's presence in a purely visceral way. He had received nothing but contempt and physical abuse from Grover and expected worse from him now. While he knew he was innocent, every fiber of his being impelled him to strike out at the officer. The two would certainly have come to blows if a tall figure in the corner had not risen to his feet and said, "What is the matter here?"

Grover wheeled defiantly, then snapped to attention. "Mister President!" he exclaimed, then snatched off his kepi. He had only a few hairs on the top of his head and these stood on end like a hog's bristles. "Sir, I've just uncovered an enemy spy at the heart of our operation."

"No, Major, you have not. I'm sorry to disabuse you of this, but I have full confidence in this man."

"Sir, you have no idea of the bill of particulars against him."

"I know all that you know, Major, and a good deal more. The decision is mine. That will be all."

Seething with anger, Grover turned back to Nathaniel. "You've not seen the last of me," he snarled, then jammed his hat back onto his head and stormed out of the room. Nathaniel almost fancied he trailed smoke as he went.

All activity, all sound had been suspended in the room during this exchange and everyone now fell back to his work. After a few minutes Nathaniel approached Lincoln. The President looked over his reading glasses as he came up.

"I want to thank you for that, sir," he said. "It would have been pretty rough for me if you hadn't of spoken up."

"Well, of course, Nathaniel," Lincoln replied. "I couldn't in conscience suffer an innocent man to be interrogated by that fellow."

"Well, it was generous of you, sir, because you couldn't know for sure that I'm not a Confederate agent."

"Oh, I'm quite sure of that, my boy." He laid down the dispatch he had been reading. "So this is your new line of work since the Balloon Corps was disbanded?"

"Yes, sir. It's not much, but I reckon I'm doing something."

"You're doing a great deal. Work like this is as vital to the war effort as is the contribution of the infantryman."

"Yes, sir," he replied, although he certainly didn't believe it. He was about to turn away when Lincoln asked, "Do you remain in touch with Professor Lowe?"

"No, sir. I don't even know where he is."

"Well, he's in Keene, New Hampshire, if you ever get up that way."

"I'll remember that if I'm ever keen to see him."

Lincoln smiled. "That's a good trick."

"The only one of the Corps I've seen was Solomon Vogler. I went up to New York and visited him right after I got back from North Carolina."

Lincoln was turning back to his message as he said this. Nathaniel turned to resume his own duties when the President said, "North Carolina? When did you go there?"

His sharp tone alarmed the youth. He said, "Oh, I went there by accident, sir."

"How does one go to North Carolina by accident?" He took off his glasses and pulled a chair out from the table with his foot.

Nathaniel sat down beside him. Ten minutes later, Lincoln said, "That's quite a tale."

"I know I'm not a very good story-teller, sir. I'm sure I got everything out of order."

"No, you told it plain, and that's just the way I like it. I think Colonel Swanson and General Lee both acted with great charity toward you."

"Yes, sir."

"When all this is over I hope we can show them as great a charity."

"Yes, sir. Well, sir, I was thinking, there is a charity you could do for Colonel Swanson right away."

"And what is that?"

"He has a son in a prison camp in Maine."

Lincoln shook his heavy head. "We can't parole a man who would just bear arms against us again. More's the pity."

"Sir, he won't fight again. He had his eyes shot out at Ball's Bluff, and him only fifteen years old."

Lincoln's face clouded. Nathaniel had never seen him in such distress. "When will this cursed conflict ever end?" the President exclaimed bitterly. He put his hand to his forehead for a few seconds, then said, "Very well, I'll parole him. I'll have to dispatch a soldier to bring him back home as well."

"Sir, I'd volunteer for that duty."

"Then you shall have it. Come with me when I leave today and I'll write you the orders."

"Yes, sir."

Nathaniel informed Captain Moran that he was leaving with the President. An hour later Lincoln rose, tucked his glasses into his waistcoat pocket, set his old stovepipe hat atop his head, and headed for the door.

Nathaniel fell in behind him. The soldiers at the door gave smart rifle salutes as they went out. It was a crisp afternoon and Nathaniel threw on his jacket and cap as they walked. Lincoln said, "They're drilling on the Mall. We'll have to take the long way around, but it'll be on sidewalks all the way so we'll spare our shoes."

"Yes, sir."

They walked in silence until they passed a shop. "Look, sir," Nathaniel said. Lincoln followed his finger. A framed photograph of the President was displayed on a small table in front of the shop.

Lincoln held his glasses before him. "That's a nice frame, but they'll never get five dollars for that face," he said.

"I'd buy it," Nathaniel said, "if I had the five dollars."

They continued on their way. "You didn't see my picture for sale in Virginia, did you?"

"No, sir, but I know you can get it."

"You do? What do you mean?"

Nathaniel smiled, then said, "It ain't proper, sir."

"Out with it, young man."

"Well, sir, I knew a boy in a camp down there who said he was in the governor's office in his state. I don't rightly recollect which one it was. Anyway, he had to use the back house and there on the wall right across from the two-holer was your picture."

Lincoln smiled. "Well, then, I'm in good company."

"What do you mean, sir?"

"After the Revolutionary War, Ethan Allen visited England. He was staying with a gentleman there. He had to use the back house, or the privy, as it's called over there, and he found it was graced with a portrait of George Washington. He told his host that that was fit and proper because there was nothing that would make an Englishman shit faster than seeing George Washington."

Nathaniel laughed. He glanced over at the troops on the Mall. He could make out but faintly the sergeant calling orders to the men as they marched back and forth in formation. Soon, within weeks, these men would be marching back and forth on a battlefield somewhere while he sat safely in the War Office.

"They look good, don't they?" Lincoln said.

"Yes, sir, they do."

"Yet it breaks my heart to see them."

"I know. I keep thinking I'm a shirker for not being with them."

Lincoln glanced at him. "Yet you also serve, and serve well. But do you really think you could be of service in the field?"

"Well, sir, my eyesight isn't what you'd call the best. I doubt I'd ever be a crack shot."

Lincoln waited a few seconds before responding. "But there are other things you could be doing. Dangerous work to be sure, but extremely valuable for all of that. I know you've been approached."

Nathaniel flushed. "I'm not cut out for that line of work, sir. I'm not good at it. And it don't seem right to me somehow."

The President looked down at him, then away. "Well, I could not ask you to take on such a burden if you found it immoral. Consider the matter closed."

They walked in silence. Ahead of them two young officers approached them on the sidewalk on the other side of the street. One of them spotted Lincoln, touched the other's sleeve and they crossed over. They were very smartly dressed and both threw perfect salutes as they passed. One said, "Good afternoon, sir," as the other said, "Good evening, sir," then they looked sharply at each other. Lincoln doffed his hat and bade them good day.

"Mister Lincoln," he ventured, "you said you were well satisfied of my loyalty. How can you be so sure?"

"I knew it when I heard that you had given General McClellan that copy of General Lee's Order 109 at Antietam. I was glad when it turned out to be genuine, although it's a pity the Army didn't make better use of it."

"But General McClellan told everyone in that tent to keep it a secret that I …" The sentence trailed off into silence.

What was there that Lincoln didn't know? He remembered how surprised he had been when Lincoln had even remembered his name. Now he wouldn't think it odd if Lincoln ticked off the names of his brother and sisters.

Lincoln, he knew, was a very gifted and a very committed man. Both sides agreed that he was the only thing keeping the Union together. Yet with all his burdens he was going out of his way to help Nathaniel with what was by comparison a trivial task.

From the Mall came the sound of fife and drum. From the west came a sudden breeze that stirred the fallen leaves and sent them rustling and clattering around them. Nathaniel Curry felt that the forces of his life, internal and external, were somehow converging in this moment. He drew a breath and said, "Mister Lincoln, if you want me to do it, I will."

Lincoln turned, smiling, and clapped a hand on Nathaniel's shoulder. "Thank you, my boy," he said. It was the only expression of gratitude he was ever to get from his country, but it was enough.

Nathaniel's second visit to the city of New York was much briefer than the first. He dropped by Solomon Vogler's firm and presented a freshly-printed visiting card to the doorman. Vogler appeared a half-hour later, carrying a portfolio wrapped in red ribbon. "Nathaniel, I'm afraid you caught me at a rather bad time."

"Oh, that's all right, Solly. I won't detain you. Did someone in your family die?"

"What? No."

"Oh, I saw you were wearing that cap again."

"Oh, that. I wear that all the time now, Nathaniel. I've become an officer in my temple and I have to pass muster."

"In your temple? Really? Does that mean you believe in God again?"

"Well, the way I put it, it's not that I've gotten religion, it's more like I've lost my faith in atheism. It's hard to say what I believe right now."

"You're not religious, but you're an officer in your temple?"

"Well, that speaks more to the nature of Jewish culture, I suppose. Listen, I hate to be abrupt, but I –"

"I know, Sol. Look, can we go to dinner this evening?"

Vogler looked pained. "I can only eat at certain places now, Nathaniel, and you would not be allowed to eat there."

"But –"

"Nathaniel, this is difficult for me to express, but I have to be more circumspect in whom I associate with now as well."

This was a blow. "All right, Solly. Good-bye."

The first thing that Nathaniel did upon arrival in Keene, New Hampshire was to visit a men's clothing shop. The clerk, hearing his speech, correctly adduced that he was not used to the local climate and outfitted him accordingly. He left the store ten dollars lighter and twenty pounds heavier.

Nathaniel had seen snow but his experience was limited to the fluff that occasionally falls upon southern states, draws startled comments from the inhabitants, unlikey anecdotes from the oldsters, and then vanishes. Keene had ten inches of the stuff on the ground. No one found this in the least remarkable, however. People tramped through it without complaint, even little kids. Horses trotted along the snowy roads, steaming like locomotives, pulling sleighs of every description.

Everyone in the city seemed to know the name Lowe. He trudged a mile to the house. It looked exactly as described in Lowe's letter. In the South a dark servant would answer the door of a prosperous dwelling like this, but here it was Leonine Lowe who greeted him.

"Nathaniel, how good it is to see you."

"Thank you, ma'am," he replied. He attempted to snatch his hat off but it was attached to his head with a leather strap.

"Do come in. Please to leave the coat and the boots in this room. My husband and his brother are fishing."

Nathaniel pictured two men bundled against the cold sitting on a frozen shore with their fishing lines running into a frozen river. It wasn't until the next day that he found how one ice-fishes. He crowded into a hut the size of a two-hole outhouse with Thaddeus Lowe and his brother Joseph. The hut had no floor and the wind blowing across the river roared under and through the walls, putting a fine layer of snow over everything. A small coal stove threw a little heat but it was still cold enough that he thought he was going to die.

The Lowe brothers had bored a hole in the ice about nine inches across and had lowered lines into the frigid darkness. Nathaniel felt this was quite unfair to the fish. The poor creatures had to be having a hard time just surviving in the icy depths without these humans attempting to kill and eat them.

Thaddeus Lowe smiled at him. "What do you think, Nathaniel?"

"I think y'all must really like fish."

"Then you're no fisherman," Joseph said. "It's not the having, it's the getting that's the amusement."

"You're amused by this? Down South we wouldn't ask a colored person to do something like this."

"Well, for a true New Englander," Joseph replied, "this is the very trump of existence."

"I think I should warn you," Thaddeus Lowe said, "Maine is even colder than this."

"Oh, thankee much, sir. I won't stay around there a minute longer than I need to, I assure you."

"You're certain you know how to get there now?"

"Yes, your map made it very clear."

"That's good."

"That other map was very interesting, too."

"Yes, it was. It's too bad you didn't keep better track of your journey."

"Well, I shouldn't have fallen asleep. But I was studying on it again this morning and I think you were right. I must have come very close to passing over Fort Monroe."

"Yes, and that might have greatly simplified things for you. Still, all's well that ends well. And if you had seen the fortress and tried to land, you might have ended up in the water or in enemy hands."

"Yes, you're right, sir."

"All in all, you did very well. You have the makings of a first-class aeronaut if you're willing to pursue it."

"I don't see how I could do that."

"The war won't last forever," Lowe said. "I intend to resume exhibition flights as soon as peace is proclaimed."

"What will you do in the meantime, sir?"

Lowe glanced down at the string he held in his hand. "I'll fish," he said with a smile.

He knew he was approaching the prison by the smell. It was detectable two miles away. The odor spoke of human misery on a grand scale. It was the odor of garbage, degeneration and decay, but most of all it was the odor of feces.

The ladies in the coach, nurses all, put their scarves over their noses but removed them a minute later. There would after all be no escaping the odor soon enough. They stopped at the guardhouse and a sergeant pulled the door open and inspected the party. "You ladies I know," he said, "but who are you?"

Nathaniel said, "I have orders to pick up a couple of parolees."

"You with the Confederate government?"

He shook his head. "Union."

"Got anything saying so?"

"Here's my orders."

The sergeant took them out of the envelope. "Whoo-ee! That really his signature?"

"Sure enough."

"Well, that's good enough for me. The captain may have some more questions for you. You may pass." He saluted the ladies and closed the door.

The captain indeed had some questions but he passed Nathaniel along to a soldier who brought him to the warder. The warder perused the orders, then wrote two numbers on a slip of paper. The soldier conducted him into the prison proper.

"Does it always smell like this?"

"Nope. It's generally worse in the summer."

"Oh."

"Spring's bound to be nasty. We didn't have enough graves dug so we're leaving some cadavers in a storehouse. They're frozen now, but –"

"Yes, I understand. These are all young men. Why are they a-dying? Is it from their wounds?"

The soldier glanced at him. "No. Like everything else in this God-damned war, it's the niggers' fault."

"Niggers? Why?"

"The niggers just had to get into this war. Well, so Lincoln let them in. Myself, I don't think they can fight worth a damn, but there you go. Now, before that, both sides treated their prisoners all right. But the Rebs treat the nigger prisoners like they was slaves what took up arms, and who's to blame 'em? It has to be the biggest fear of any Southerner, the slaves rising up.

"But Honest Abe couldn't see it that way. He says, 'You treat my little dark friends like this, I'll treat your white boys in like fashion.' And then he goes and does it. So then the South treats the Union prisoners the same way, and here we are.

"And here we are."

They stopped before a cell that clearly contained many more men than its builders anticipated. The wretches inside were dressed in rags, despite the winter chill. As he peered into the depths a few men stared back at him. Their cheeks were sunken and their eyes were haggard; scurvy had claimed the teeth of a good many of them. Although most of them were standing – there was not room to sit down – none had the energy to move.

Nathaniel stepped up to the reeking cage. "Which … which one is this?" he asked.

"I don't know," the soldier said. "I was just told this cell and the other one. Try calling a name."

He braced himself and said, "Melrose Curry."

Nothing happened. Then an unseen man said, "He say Mel Curry?"

"I thought I done heard something else."

"Where Curry at?"

"I don't know…Mel Curry? He still in here?"

"Mel! They calling you."

"What? What you want, damn you?"

"Mel, you in there?"

Men slowly shuffled around and let a smaller man through. It wasn't him, though. It was an old man with a gray beard and a bald pate. He put his bony fingers around the bars and croaked, "What you want?"

"Melly? It's me, your brother Nate."

A look of puzzlement came over the man's face. "Nate? My brother Nate? They catch you too?" He pulled back. "No! It couldn't be! Or did you change sides?"

"Mel, I have orders to parole you. We can be on the train to Virginia in a couple of hours."

"Parole me? Virginia? What?"

"I got orders, Mel. You come along with me now."

"Orders? What the Hell you talking about?"

Nathaniel held the paper out. A hand reached from behind Mel and took it. A voice ran quickly through the order until it got near the end, slowly enunciating the last words: "'Private First Class David Swanson and Private Melrose Curry, to be released to Mister Nathaniel Curry, signed Abraham Lincoln, President.' Damn, boy, this is real." He reached the order back to Nathaniel.

"Abraham Lincoln? Your dear friend?" Melrose said bitterly.

"I got him to let you out, Melly." Nathaniel said.

Melrose choked, then said, "I'd die before I took an order from him."

"It's not him letting you out, Mel, it's me."

The haggard creature sobbed and let go of the bars. As he turned away Nathaniel said, "Melly ... I'm your brother."

Melrose turned back to the bars and for a moment he was his true self again. He would clearly have assaulted Nathaniel if he had had the opportunity. "Brother?" he asked, spitting the word out bitterly. He waved his hand behind him. "*These* ... these are my brothers."

Before he received his wound David Swanson had probably resembled his father. He had the same square jaw and the same erect carriage. The upper part of his face was now a wreck, though. The bullet had caved in his left temple and blown out the right one. It left the bridge of his nose intact, creating a literal, free-standing bridge of bone and skin from his forehead to his nose. Behind that was a morass of folded skin that used to be his eyelids. It was a wonder that he had survived this wound. Nathaniel had seen men die from much lesser injuries.

David's morale was high and he conversed brightly with Nathaniel, although he was barely strong enough to sit up in the seat of the railroad car. "Is this farm country we're passing through, Mr. Curry?"

"Call me Nathaniel, David. I reckon so. It's hard to tell with all this snow."

"Yes, it must be beautiful."

"Mostly it's cold. Yes, that's a barn. It's kind of ramshackle, but it's sure enough a barn."

David turned back to him; Nathaniel had the creepy feeling that he was looking at him. "I still don't understand why it is that I'm being paroled. You didn't explain it very well."

"I'm a good friend of your sister, that's all. And I had the opportunity to get you out."

"There was another name on the order, someone with your last name."

"My brother Melrose. He chose to stay."

"He wanted to stay in prison?"

Nathaniel shrugged. "I reckon he knows everybody there."

"Still, it's most peculiar." He gave a brief laugh. "I'm happy enough to be leaving, don't worry. But I don't understand how you got my parole."

"I just asked President Lincoln to let you out. I saw on the roster he had that my brother was in the same place and he told me he would let him go too. But Melly wanted to stay."

"Did you know the President before the war?"

"Oh, I've known him a long time. I guess I can tell you, we've gone too far for you to turn back. I'll be working for President Lincoln and he owed me a favor."

"Well, I'm happy you chose this way to allow him to repay it." He turned his face to the sunlight coming in the window, smiling at this simple pleasure.

After they were safely away from the prison Nathaniel had stopped at an inn and given David an opportunity to clean up. Here he bathed and shaved. His Citadel cadet's uniform was now in ruins and didn't fit in any case, so it was replaced with a set of clothes from Nathaniel's carpetbag.

Orders from Abraham Lincoln had nearly as great an effect upon Union troops as orders from Robert E. Lee had on Confederates. Additionally, David Swanson's wound drew compassion from everyone he encountered. The two young men rode second-class carriages south and dined on hot meals all the way.

"I think we just crossed over into Maryland."

"Oh, that's good. Is there still snow on the ground?"

"I think we've seen the last of it. Beg pardon."

"Of course. It's warmer just within this carriage."

"Yes, and they don't even have a fire lit. I don't know how the Yankees put up with it."

"I know, and you said the children were playing in the snow."

"Yeah, I would think they'd hate to live like that, or they'd all die of chilblains or something."

"I know. It's most peculiar. Perhaps the soil is especially fertile here."

"Fertiler than back in Old Virginny?"

"Well, that's true."

"And the farmers have to do it all by themselves there. There are no colored people at all."

"None at all?"

"I never saw a single one north of Boston."

"It's hard to imagine a life without them."

"Yeah."

"It just shows once more how important it is that we win this war."

Nathaniel glanced at him. He didn't conclude this at all. In fact, if anything he saw the opposite: slavery, even in this grim country, was unnecessary. Perhaps David was looking for some justification for his injury.

They went through Washington and into Alexandria. Here they were fortunate enough to fall in with a truce party. They accompanied six officers and a single enlisted man in an open coach flying a white flag. A few miles down the road they stopped at a roadhouse and met five officers in gray. There were cordial greetings all around and the exchange of documents. When business was concluded drinks were called for. Only then did Nathaniel present his orders to the ranking Confederate officer.

The officer was a genial colonel with a trim white beard. "Aubrey," he said, turning to his Union counterpart, "what do you know of this?"

"No more than you do, I'm afraid, Angus. It looks like Lincoln's signature and his stamp. The boy's certainly been wounded and I doubt he'll do much more fighting."

The colonel donned eyeglasses and read the order over, his lips moving silently. "Yes, we can take him in hand, I suppose. I thought I had taken my last orders from Abraham Lincoln but I'll be happy to obey this one."

"Please, sir, I'd like to accompany him."

"You mean alone?"

"Yes, sir."

"Well, that would be a help. A relative of your'n, is he?"

"More or less, sir."

"He a war prisoner?"

"Yes, sir."

"But he's in mufti."

"There wasn't much left of his uniform, sir."

The colonel removed his glasses. "How come you aren't in uniform yourself, young fellow?"

"Well, that will happen soon enough, sir."

"One side or the other, but jump to it."

"Yes, sir."

"I'll write you some orders for the train."

The colonel's orders got him into Richmond the next morning. To Nathaniel's surprise, Federal money was accepted there as cab fare. The driver didn't even flinch at the sight of a "greenback" dollar, the new currency generally derided as worthless in the Union.

David was quite excited and compelled his guide to tell him what landmarks they were passing. "There's the Capitol. Jeff Davis' house is down that street on the right. Here's the Broad Street Hotel with the Catholic Church across the street. The Market Depot is right up ahead, but we should be turning before we get to it."

They got out at the Swanson house. "All right, take my arm. Mind the hitching post."

"Hitching post?" David found it, then ran his fingers over the shiny brass ball at the top.

"Nathaniel?"

"Yes, David?"

"I think I should have a cloth over my head or something."

"What? Why?"

His hands moved down and lifted the iron ring. "I'm afraid I'll frighten my family."

"Maybe dark glasses would have been a good idea, but it's a little late now."

"Yes, maybe later." He placed his fingers atop the brass ball again.

"Does it feel good?" Nathaniel asked. It seemed like a foolish question.

"It's strange," David said, "but right now I'm sorry I can't shed tears."

Rachel answered the door. Her hands flew to her face to stifle a cry as she saw David. She repeated the sound and the gesture a moment later when she saw Nathaniel. "Lord have mercy!" she exclaimed. "Lord have mercy!"

"What's the matter here?" said another voice. Titus was coming down the stairs. Nathaniel was surprised at the change he had undergone. When last Nathaniel had seen Titus he wore the workmanlike apparel of a house slave. He now wore a cutaway and was clean-shaven and neatly groomed. He also had a very commanding air.

Titus was surprised to see who had arrived, but only for a moment. "Master David, welcome home."

"Thank you, Titus."

"Rachel, do you tell the mistress that Master David is home." Rachel gave a bob and rushed out the front door.

They led David into the parlor. A few minutes later a cab clattered to a stop outside. Amanda, her mother and Rachel flew in the door in a great rustle of petticoats. These three retained the ability to shed tears and they produced a great quantity of them in the next few minutes.

Rachel went to the kitchen to prepare an impromptu meal as Mrs. Swanson brought David to his room. Silence fell upon the parlor.

Amanda and Nathaniel sat side by side on the settee. It was a large settee and they sat at opposite ends.

"He's so thin," Amanda ventured.

"I know. I tried to fatten him up a little on the way but it didn't take."

"I don't like those sores on him one little bit. He wasn't well tended."

"It was a terrible place. He's lucky to have a sister who's a nurse."

"A sister and a mother."

"Yes, all the better."

Silence.

"Is your mother in uniform? I didn't notice."

"She doesn't wear a uniform but she's every inch a nurse."

"Oh."

Another pause.

"Nathaniel, however did this come about?"

"Huh? What?"

"You waltzing in here with my brother. It's a wonder to me."

"Oh. I have orders from President Lincoln. It was a favor from him."

"President Lincoln did this as a favor?"

"Yes. Well, he owed me a favor, that's all."

She pondered this for a moment. "Will you join us for dinner?"

"I would be much obliged. I hate to put you out."

"It won't be very good fare."

"I know."

More silence.

"You, Nathaniel, have been eating well. Why, you're nearly fat."

"I just sit all day now. I'm little more than a clerk these days."

"We must all serve in our own way." Her voice seemed thin and strained, much like the platitude she uttered.

"I know."

"Will you see your family?"

He shrugged. "I don't rightly know what I'd say to them right now."

"Oh."

"And my orders don't mention them. I'm on thin ice here."

"Yes. Last time you had the permission of Robert E. Lee. This time…"

"Yes, it's not the same."

He looked at her face, catching her in the act of looking at his chest. "Yes," he said. "I still wear it."

"I dreamed of it last night. I never remember my dreams but I remember this one. It woke me up."

"It did?"

"I dreamed that the chain was broken. It broke and you tied it back together. But the knot came loose and you lost the locket. You were flying and it fell to earth." She sat back, clearly upset by the recollection of this dream. "It was me in the locket and it was me falling to earth. But it's only a picture and I'm sure I don't even look like that any more."

Nathaniel pulled the locket out and pressed the tiny latch. Although the locket itself was battered and scratched the image within was pristine.

"You must not open this much."

"Not much. Sometimes, to get a look at you or to show it to someone."

"To whom have you shown my picture?"

"Not many people. Just my friends. And Mister Lincoln."

"You showed my picture to Abraham Lincoln?" she said indignantly.

"Yes'm."

Pause. "What did he say?"

"He said I was a lucky man."

"Hmph!" she said primly, though she was clearly pleased. They moved closer together and looked at the tintype.

The girl in the picture wore her hair free, cascading in billows over her shoulders. She looked at the camera with an open expression of happiness and anticipation of the world she was entering. Her pretty dress and the chair of the photographer's studio were lost in the dazzle of her beauty.

He looked at Amanda and she at him. He did not know what she saw, but he saw a young woman with her hair in a bun and in a plain dress and apron. She looked at the world with as much intelligence as the girl in the picture but with a lot more experience.

But it was still her. The fire in her eyes and her unquenchable spirit were the same.

Amanda looked at the tintype longingly, as if she wished to be once more the girl in the locket. "I was wrong," she said, her voice little more than a whisper. "The chain never broke."

"It broke," he said, "but I had it mended." Then, very swiftly, he stole a kiss.

Chapter Sixteen: Starlight and Dewdrops

In March of 1864 Nathaniel Curry purchased a pair of eyeglasses. He was tired of not being able to see anything more than ten feet away without squinting.

The process was more involved than he expected it to be. He had anticipated simply going into an eyeglass shop and buying a pair. Instead, the merchant examined his eyes with a large magnifying glass, then made him read letters of varying sizes on signs placed at various distances. He then repeated the process with a series of lenses held before his eyes. This was followed by a prolonged measurement of every conceivable dimension of his head. Nathaniel wondered if much of it was merely for show.

When this ordeal was completed he had to choose the frames. He paid the man two dollars and seventy-five cents and returned the next day for his finished glasses.

The arms of the glasses rested upon his ears and did not wrap around them, but rather around his head. They gave him a headache at first but they allowed him to read shop signs a full city block away.

He did not need the glasses to read or write or operate the telegraph. Because few people his age bothered with the devices he carried them in a shirt pocket and took them out only when needed.

He wore them a few days later to attend a ceremony at the White House. He had not been invited but neither was he refused admittance.

Ulysses Simpson Grant was being installed as General in Chief of the Union Army. He wore a full dress uniform for the occasion and not the private soldier's garb that he usually affected. He was sober and he looked like he didn't much like the sensation. President Lincoln gave the requisite address and Grant responded in kind. The myriad officers in attendance, all decked out in gold braid and shining medals, did their level best to look important.

After the ceremony Nathaniel felt a tug at his sleeve. He turned to see Colonel George H. Sharpe, head of the Bureau of Military Information. Joseph Hooker was long gone but the Bureau, his creation, lived on.

Nathaniel had been dreading this encounter for months. He came to attention. "Good evening, sir."

"Are they keeping you busy, Curry?"

"I'm earning my keep, sir."

"Good. Come around to my office at one o'clock tomorrow, will you?"

Nathaniel was admitted to Sharpe's office at the appointed hour. It was a small office, even tinier than the one Thaddeus Lowe had occupied. Everywhere there were piles of paper and dispatches. One small table was piled high with unopened envelopes. Whatever else Colonel Sharpe did for a living, he didn't read his mail very much.

He saw a young woman was there already and excused himself. "No, Curry," Sharpe said, "come in. Miss Emmer, may I present Nathaniel Curry. Curry, this is Miss Clarabel Emmer."

"How do you do, Miss Emmer?"

"How do you do, Mister Curry?" Miss Emmer had dark, curly hair framing a face with a ready smile. She spoke with a Southern accent.

"Sit down, Curry. I have an assignment for you."

"Yes, sir?"

"First of all, this information is not to leave this room. General Grant has ordered General Sherman to reduce Georgia in the next few months. Preparatory to this, Grant himself will assail northern Virginia in order to engage Lee's forces."

"I see."

Nathaniel did not in fact see. He had heard of forts and garrisons being reduced but never a whole state. Was the grim-faced Sherman now planning to reduce the entire state of Georgia to smoking rubble? If so, it was a monstrous intention. That Sharpe could discuss it so easily made him shudder.

"It is my desire that you should enter Virginia in the guise of a slave-catcher. Clarabel here will disguise herself as a Negro boy. You will be furnished with documents indicating that she is a slave you are returning."

Nathaniel turned to the woman, expecting that she would object to this preposterous proposal. She did not. Nathaniel was left to murmur a weak, "Yes, sir."

Accompanying the Union Army southward was a young married couple. By their dress they seemed to be sutlers, though they had no wares. They kept to themselves, avoiding discourse with enlisted men, officers or other sutlers. They were provided good accommodations and good food, indicating that they had greased the palms of many an officer.

The army crossed the Rapidan River. The young couple vanished, replaced by a young man in the garb of a Southern farmer, and an even younger man clad as a colored field hand, straw hat and all. The white man carried a Sharps carbine, a small repeating rifle favored by cavalrymen and anyone who needed to travel light and shoot quickly. He could crank out seven shots just like that by working the lever; he carried additional rounds in his kit.

This pair left the vanguard of the Union Army early one morning and headed west on the Orange Turnpike alone and on foot.

"Ever done this before?" he asked her.

"Yes, several times. No one pays any attention to a darkie."

"Well, let's hope no one starts to."

"It's a pleasant day, anyway."

It was indeed a pleasant day. It was the first week of May. The road was dry without being dusty and they strolled along at a good pace. The army coming behind them would be moving more slowly.

She glanced at the forest on either side of the road. "How long will this jungle last?" she asked.

"I don't know," he replied, "but it has to end sometime."

They knew that Grant had ordered his army, a hundred and twenty thousand strong, to make its way through the heavy forest to meet the enemy on the flat countryside beyond. There had been reports of isolated Confederate regiments in the forest and Nathaniel and Clarabel had been sent to assess their strength.

"I'm not moving too fast for you, am I?"

"Don't worry about me."

"Sorry. I keep forgetting you're a woman, that's all."

"Well, you can forget it entirely. I can keep this pace up all day."

"All right."

Nathaniel glanced over at her. She had done nothing to darken her skin and despite her black, curly hair she hardly looked like a Negro. In point of fact, though, many of the nominally African slaves in the American South were so light that they could easily pass as white. This was due to centuries of white slaveowners availing themselves of their female slaves. This practice was, of course, a shameful betrayal of both their wives and their race, and as such was never discussed.

The pale skin of the progeny of these unions was never discussed, either. The fiction that such persons were still "darkies" was one of the anomalies of Southern culture. Men, women and children were often hauled onto the auction block who would have gone unremarked in a white church or school. No one ever objected to their white skin; to do so would be to strike at the very foundations of the institution of slavery. Saying "Why, he's as white as I am!" would be to say "I am as black as he."

What made Clarabel's ruse work was the fact that no white person would ever try to pass himself off as black or as a slave. She admitted to being a Negro, therefore she was one.

They could never see more than a few hundred yards ahead through the woods; thus it was hardly a surprise when, about a mile west of the Wilderness Tavern, they came around a bend and found elements of Ewell's Corps blocking the road.

"Halt! Who goes there?"

Nathaniel cupped his hands around his mouth and shouted, "Slave catcher. I got me one. Let me by, boys."

"Approach and be recognized."

A sergeant who was at least sixty years old took charge. "What do we have here?"

"Runaway nigger." He yawned as he spoke.

"What the Hell are you doing catching niggers around here?"

He shrugged. "I catch 'em where they is."

"Shoot, boy, Yankee army is coming down this pike."

"I know it. I don't want them to get my nigger."

"Ain't that a Yankee gun?"

"Yep."

The old man looked uncertain, then said, "All right," and stepped aside.

"Just a minute." Another man stepped up. "This looks mighty fishy to me. Where you catch this here nigger?"

Nathaniel looked annoyed. "Up by the river. He couldn't get across."

"Where you taking him?"

"I got a newspaper ad. You want to see it?"

"Sure do. Don't move too quick-like, I'm mighty nervous."

Nathaniel displayed a perfectly legitimate advertisement. "Satisfied?"

The soldier regarded the ad with suspicion. "This picture don't look like your nigger."

"I reckon not. They use the same picture for all of 'em."

"Someone who can read come up and look this over."

A freckle-faced lad of twelve came forward and read the ad aloud: "'One hundred dollars reward. Ran away from Bell Meadow Farm, on Tuesday, 18th instant, a very light-skinned Negro called Brutus Cook, about five feet two inches in height and about fifteen years of age. The above reward will be paid upon his live return. Cornelius van Pelt.'"

The soldier looked at the slave. "Your name Brutus?"

"Yes, master," came the soft reply.

"What's your master's name?"

The slave looked at the ground. "Master."

"Damn you!" A fist swung out and cuffed the woolly head. "Master what?"

"Master Cornelius."

"Happy?" Nathaniel asked.

"One more thing," the soldier replied, turning back to Nathaniel. "Why ain't you in uniform?"

All eyes turned to the slave catcher. "Well, you tell me, why are we fighting this here war in the first place?"

This required a moment's thought – both sides were indeed starting to forget the reasons for the war. The soldier stepped aside. "Go ahead, I guess."

"Say, you boys better light out yourselves. If'n the whole Union Army is coming this way they'll roll right over y'all."

"Don't worry your head about that," the soldier said with a sneer. "Our whole Corps is here, and more a-coming."

"All right, then. Move it, boy." He poked his charge in the side with the muzzle of his weapon.

He had gone another twenty yards when he turned and asked, "Hey, what's the best way around to Richmond?"

"You know this area at all?"

He shrugged. "Passable."

"Take the next road south to the Plank Road. Take that east to Parker's Store. Take that road south."

He knew all of that already. "Thank you."

Another man shouted, "Don't go too far on the Plank Road, A.P. Hill and Lee are on that."

And that was what he wanted to know. "Okay."

Once they were out of sight of the soldiers they quickened their pace. "All right," Clarabel puffed, "what now?"

Nathaniel pulled his eyeglasses out. "Keep your eyes peeled for a telegraph wire."

"What are you going to say?"

"Well, Grant thought there were only a few regiments out here. There are at least two corps, probably three."

"What did you think of those troops?" she asked.

"Well, they looked hungry, skinny and they don't like Yanks."

"And that was a picket, but there were only eight men there. And four of 'em were little boys. And did you see how they were dressed?"

"Yes," he said. "Only one of them was in uniform. The sergeant."

"That's right. They don't have the money for nice things like uniforms any more."

"Yeah."

"Was that a Union uniform he was wearing?"

"No," he said. "That's Stonewall Jackson's old corps, under Ewell now. They wear blue."

"Ewell's Corps, A.P. Hill's Corps and Lee's Corps?"

"That's right. And more a-coming, he said. I suppose that means Longstreet."

She looked behind them. "Too bad we couldn't have just turned around and gone back to our forces and warned them."

"I know. But it would have looked mighty peculiar to those boys if we had gone back up the road. We could do it, but we would have to go through the woods and that would be slow going. And even if we found our forces, we'd have to convince them who we were, then convince them to get a message to Grant, then hope it makes it in time. It would be faster to find a telegraph. Grant would be reading a wire message ten minutes after I sent it."

"Really?" she asked. "What route would it take?"

"Well, let's see," he replied. "Most telegraph traffic around here would go toward Fredericksburg, and we have an intercept line on that line. That would send it to Fort Monroe on the peninsula, and it would go directly to the War Office in Washington from there. Then they'd send it back down the railroad line to Grant."

She thought it over. "That's two or three hundred miles."

"Yep."

"Telegraph really as fast as all that?"

"Yep. Fast as lightning."

"I've never worked with a telegraph operator before."

"Well, I don't know if one has ever done this type of thing before."

"Where is there a telegraph line?"

"The only one I know for sure is on the railroad line just south of the Plank Road about two miles from here," he said. "But getting there would take too long. I'm hoping to see a wire before that."

A mile down the road they encountered an army coming the other way at double-quick time. Without a word both moved off of the road and into the woods. Rather than wait for the army to pass they struck out southward through the trees. "Do you know where we are now?" Clarabel asked.

"I think so," Nathaniel replied. "The Plank Road is about a mile south of here."

"Who was that army?"

"I don't know, I didn't see any banners."

A minute later she raised her hand to stop him. They halted and heard a pattering of musket fire. As they listened the pattering mounted to a roar. Soon artillery joined the chorus.

"There's Grant's little surprise," Clarabel said.

"Yes," Nathaniel replied, "but we still have to report on what we seen."

After half an hour they crossed the Plank Road. A short time later they found the unfinished railroad track. Nathaniel searched the trees beside the track and found a telegraph line. He climbed a tree and attached a lineman's key.

He transmitted, FROM STARBUCK TO GEN CUSTIS LEE FREDERICKSBURG AP HILL CORPS RE LEE CORPS AND EWELL CORPS ENGAGING GRANT STOP OTHER FORCES MOVING IN SUPPORT 73

Custis Lee was not at Fredericksburg so the operators there would ignore the message. There were Federal agents listening on this line, however, who would not ignore it. Still, Nathaniel doubted that it would do Grant much good.

He sat in the tree, feeling very anxious and exposed, until he received a brief message: 13 CAPTAIN SMITH. "13" was the telegraph code for "I understand." He put the key back in his kit bag and climbed down.

"What now?" Clarabel asked.

"I thought you were the old hand at this."

"It sounds like the firing to the east is getting pretty loud."

"Yes, let's head over and have a look at it."

They went back to the Plank Road and headed east. When they were sure they were near the fighting they moved into the woods.

Their intention was to watch the fighting from the safety of the forest. They did not anticipate that the fighting would spread into the forest itself. They were wrong. In the late afternoon Confederate forces crashed through the woods, closely followed by Federals. Gunfire erupted all around them. Nathaniel and Clarabel stumbled west, intent only on staying alive.

As darkness fell they lay hidden in a thicket on the south side of the Plank Road. They were west of Ewell's forces; the Yankees appeared to have withdrawn.

"Sounds like the action's dying down," Clarabel whispered.

Nathaniel listened. There was still shooting, some near at hand, some farther away. Men were shouting, though he could not make out the words. "Most likely nobody has a hankering for running around the woods in the dark. It's one thing to get shot, it's quite another to get a branch in the eye." Like her, he spoke only in a whisper.

"I reckon you're right."

"Do you think we should spend the night here?"

"Reckon it's as good a place as any."

Indeed it was. They lay in a thick bramble. They were below the most lethal barbs, but any approaching soldiers would be easily induced to go around them.

"Look at all the smoke," she said.

"That's not all gunpowder," he said. "I think the woods are on fire."

"I think you're right," she said. "Another God-damned way to die."

"Want some hardtack?" he asked.

"Yes, thank you. Let's get comfortable first."

They spread a blanket under them, another atop them, then had a frugal meal. They agreed that one of them would stay awake listening for troop movements while the other slept. "Before morning," Nathaniel said, "I should find that line again and get another message off."

They lay on their stomachs, facing the road. "I'm cold," she said. "Are you cold?"

"Yes."

She moved closer, pressing up against him. The warmth of her body felt good.

"Nathaniel?"

"Yes?"

"Do you have a sweetheart?"

"Yes. Well, I sort of do. She's Secesh and I don't know if she'll take me back."

"She'd be a fool not to."

"She says she won't marry me."

"I think she'll do it or she'll be an old maid."

"What do you mean?"

"I mean all the young men are dying." She turned her head to the east, toward the darkness.

"Oh." A minute passed. "Do you have a beau?"

"No."

"Oh."

"I had a husband but he's dead."

"Oh, that's too bad."

"Yes, it is. Sometimes I miss him a powerful lot."

"Did you like it?"

"What?"

"Being married. I'm sorry, that's not a proper question."

She thought before answering. "Yes, I liked it. I think it's what people are supposed to do."

He opened his mouth but it took him a long time to find the words.

"We're not doing what people are supposed to do, are we?"

"You mean this war?"

"Yes."

"No," she replied after a moment. "No, I think it's a very wicked thing we're doing."

"But we're doing our duty."

"Those men out there are doing their duty. They're standing up and shooting and being shot. What we're doing is something more than that. We're really trying. If you and I are good at this, we'll kill more men than any common soldier."

"But…is that really bad?" he pressed.

"I suppose you mean that it's good that we're helping to end the war and save the Union?"

"Yes."

She considered this. "Yes, that's good, I suppose."

"Yes. And we're freeing the slaves."

"Yes, that has to be the greatest good we're doing. This war is terrible but it won't last forever. And if it ends slavery that will be a good thing."

Nathaniel thought of the heaps of corpses at Antietam. "Good enough for the price we're paying?"

"Ask a slave that question, Nathaniel."

He thought of Uncle Sammy and the scars upon his back. It was one terrible thing balanced against another. It was hard to see the right thing to do in this morass of bad choices. "I hope…" he began.

"Yes?"

"I hope some day I can just be an ordinary person again."

"An ordinary person living an ordinary life?"

"Yes. Yes, you understand me."

"Yes, that would be nice."

Later, he didn't know how much later, he was awakened by an elbow in his ribs. He raised his head and looked.

An army was quietly passing a few feet from where they lay. They were Confederate troops, moving forward to reinforce Lee and Hill. The men groped their way along the dark road by moonlight, doing their best to move silently. Nathaniel and Clarabel were off the road proper, but either could have reached out and touched a man.

Still, it wasn't quite an army. The men passed in single file. It was a regiment of men, no more. If Longstreet was coming, he was running late.

He cupped a hand over her ear: "You sleep now." She nodded.

He lay there watching the passing troops. Later he awoke cursing himself. If he ever stood sentry duty he would probably fall asleep. He'd be shot for it and he'd deserve it.

He looked up. The sky was no longer black but a very deep blue. The land was still dark enough that no passing soldiers would see them, but there were no passing soldiers.

Clarabel was pressed against him, her arm thrown over him. He looked at her face for a moment. It was odd to see someone from only an inch or so away. It felt strangely intimate and even intrusive. She looked very sweet and innocent as she slept beside him. What was her past, he wondered? Did she start out whoring? Had she killed men? How did her husband die? Had she any children? And most of all, how did someone who looked so childlike find herself in this extraordinary line of work?

He touched her cheek and she came awake with a start. Her eyes flashed to his mouth, then to his eyes. "I'm going to send a message," he whispered. "I'll come down this road again. Keep an eye out in case I don't see you."

She nodded. "You won't see me," she replied, "but I'll see you." She began to cover herself with leaves.

He began to work his way through the woods, headed south, or so he hoped. He put his eyeglasses on to ward off tree branches and held his rifle before him as he went, but it was still rough going. It was getting brighter with every passing second.

Within five minutes he had reached the telegraph line and affixed his key to it. He sent a message to Custis Lee: REINFORCEMENTS GOING TO SUPPORT OF HILL AND LEE STOP LONGSTREET STILL COMING 73.

He considered leaving the telegraph key behind, as there was little likelihood that he would get to send another message and it would be embarrassing if it were discovered on his person. He ended up putting it back in his kit bag.

He got back to the road; it was full daylight now. He did not know if Clarabel was east of him or west. He took a chance and ran west down the road.

He ran smack-dab into three mounted men approaching from the west. He considered running into the woods but instead cradled his carbine and waited for them.

The horsemen passed him without a word. Right behind them came

General James Longstreet at the head of his army. The sight was very similar to his encounter with Longstreet just before the second battle at Manassas: Longstreet and a few officers rode at the head of a column of men marching ten abreast, crowded onto the forest road. Longstreet must have thought him a straggler because he called out, "Soldier, fall in with my corps."

"You General Longstreet?"

"Yes, I am. Why do you want to know?"

"General Hill sent me to look for you. Sir."

"Tell him that I'll be along directly."

Nathaniel threw a salute and ran up the road before anyone could remark on the oddity of a Confederate soldier wearing glasses and carrying a Union weapon. He passed the three horsemen at full steam.

The battle resumed. Although the fighting was more than a mile away he could follow what was happening by listening to the firing. First Grant began with artillery and musket fire. Lee's, Hill's and Ewell's forces answered with musket fire. He was close enough to the battle that he could tell the guns on one side from those on the other by the loudness.

Nathaniel ran along the Plank Road as fast as he could, stopping only when his ribs cramped up. He hobbled on until a stone tossed from a bush landed at his feet.

He stopped and Brutus, alias Clarabel, crawled out. "You catched me fair and square, master," she said.

"Never mind all that right now," he said. "You hear that fighting?"

"How could I help it? Want to go up and have a look?"

"I was afraid you'd say that. Let's go into the woods first."

"Why?"

"Longstreet's coming up behind us. I'd rather let him pass us by."

"Oh. All right."

They went deep enough into the woods that the passing army had little chance of seeing them; they could scarcely make the soldiers out themselves. Half an hour later there was a sudden roar as thousands of muskets opened up at once. "I think Longstreet just got to the party," Nathaniel said. They could hear the yip of the Rebel yell coming through the woods.

"Want to move closer now?" she asked.

"Yes," he said, "but let's stay in the woods."

"All right. But stick close to the road."

The sound of battle moved away from them. Cautiously they moved forward through the dense forest. They began to encounter casualties. Soon dead and wounded men littered the ground, and still the line of battle moved away from them.

He said, "I'd say Johnny Reb was having a good day here."

"Yes," Clarabel replied. "I'm seeing two Union fallen for every Confederate."

"Yes, and they're pushing them back, too. The line has moved pretty near a mile in three hours."

"Do we dare go a little faster?" she asked.

"Yes, let's."

They walked through the woods, passing the dead and dying. The Confederates were skinny and in rags. The Yankees were in fine new uniforms, shoes and all, and had fat, rosy cheeks. Yet the Rebels were winning, if the toll of the fallen was any indicator.

"I have to say it's a caution how well the Rebels are doing, the way they are and all," he said.

"Yes."

"Where you from, Clarabel?"

"Virginia."

"Whereabouts?"

"Floyd County. Down by Roanoke."

"I'm from up in Fairfax, but lately of Richmond."

"I know."

"I was going to say, I know these boys have to lose, but at the same time I'm proud of how well they're doing."

"Yes, me too."

By noon they were approaching the fighting. The muskets dead ahead of them were roaring like a typhoon. All at once everything seemed to change. The forces closest to them, the louder muskets, ceased fire abruptly. He could hear men's voices crying out, but it was not the Rebel yell, they were crying in alarm.

"What just happened?" he asked.

"I don't know," Clarabel replied. "It's like the Rebs have broken."

"But all at once like that? If the other fellows were making a bayonet charge they would have stopped firing first, and they didn't. Also the attackers would be raising a ruckus. This is all most peculiar."

"I don't know," she repeated.

They stepped out onto the road. Soon they could hear men rushing in their direction, shouting in confusion as they came. As always the vanguard of a retreat was in a mad rush to set a speed record, and these individuals flew by without weapons or kit bags. It was only when other soldiers came by who did not look like they were in mortal terror that he stepped forward and asked, "What happened?"

"It's Pete!" a man cried as he rushed by. "Pete was hit!" cried another man.

Clarabel looked at him. "Pete?"

"That's what they call Longstreet," he said. "Hey, what happened to Pete?"

"Pete got hit," another man called. "He's dead and the Yankees are rolling over us."

The two spies looked at each other. "Now what?" she asked.

"I don't know," Nathaniel replied. "I suppose it wouldn't do to be killed by our own friends. I suggest we move to the rear."

"All right. You ready to run?"

His ribs still ached from his last bout of running. "I suppose so," he said. "Just don't run away from me. I wouldn't want to have to shoot you."

They joined the exodus, perfectly disguised as two more unfortunates in the rout. After about two miles the road ran into a large clearing. Here the retreat stopped. Men milled around in the large open space, uncertain of what to do next.

Nathaniel asked man after man what had happened. None knew, but at last a man was able to tell them. "I saw it all. Pete was in the back and he was shot by his own men!"

"No!" Nathaniel exclaimed. "Why, that's just like Old Jack!"

"Yes, and you know what? I was here a year ago when Jack got hit. I was right at the spot where he was shot, and I was just remarking that it was almost exactly a year ago. Longstreet died just the way Jackson did."

"Oh, God, what bad luck!"

"Yes, and we were doing so well, too. We saved Hill from being routed and we had just smashed the Union center. We would have had the whole Yankee army on the run if'n Pete hadn't of been killed."

"Are you sure he's dead?"

"I saw him go down. It rolled him right off the back of his God-damned horse. I ran over and looked at him. He was alive then but he must be dead by now."

"Why, where was he hit?"

"In the throat. Nobody could live through that."

They sat by the side of the road for over an hour until a great wail arose from the assembled masses. They got up to watch as a procession wound its way along the road.

Four men came bearing a litter with the body of the unfortunate upon it. He lay upon his back with his hat on his face. Every soldier stood silently and at attention, though no order was called, and tears streamed down their faces.

Then a miracle: the dead man's hand rose to his face and removed the hat. He lifted it a few seconds only, then returned it, but that was enough. Hearts that had been despairing now soared, and the silent throats burst forth with a cry of joy. Hats were flung into the air and rained back to earth. The ground trembled beneath Nathaniel's feet as the Confederacy jumped for joy around him. Pete Longstreet yet lived!

Nathaniel and Clarabel sat on the ground, discussing what to do next. "I'm glad I nabbed that telegraph key after all," he said. "It looks like I'll get some more use out of it."

"I just don't know what we can tell them that they don't already know," Clarabel replied.

"Do you suppose they know about Longstreet?"

She shrugged. "If they don't, they will soon enough. I'm sure they caught some stragglers. Shoot, it will be in the papers within a few days."

He looked at her. "The stragglers'll say he's dead. That's what everyone thought."

"Well, with a wound like that he will be soon enough. What can they do to treat it? They can't put a tourniquet around his neck."

"Well, no," he said, "but I've seen some mighty peculiar things. Johnston got shot through the chest and everyone said he was a goner. Now he's back fighting again."

"Nathaniel, it's not very likely."

"No, it's not," he agreed. "Have you heard anyone say where Lee is?"

"No, but he can't be far. He has two choices: split his forces and hold the Yankees here while guarding Richmond, or concentrate his forces and counterattack."

"He could split them up, run around Grant's rear and hit him from two sides. It worked at Chancellorsville. Hell, this *is* Chancellorsville. Beg pardon."

"But he can't use the same men to do it. Ewell's no Jackson."

"No, no, he's not."

She looked up at him. "Maybe we should press on to Richmond ourselves."

"You think that's a good idea?"

"Well, that was our intention, wasn't it? It would be good to see how the city's doing."

"I reckon it's doing mighty poorly."

"I reckon you're right. But how are the defenses? If Grant wants to hit it, he'll want to know that."

"How do we get back?"

"How about if I was a slave you had caught and were bringing north?"

He shook his head. "Slaves don't run south. Even the dumbest darkie knows where north is."

"Well, I could find me a dress, turn into a lady again. You have other advertisements for runaway slaves. That would give you a reason to go north again."

"Split up?"

"Or together. We work well together."

"Why would a slave catcher have a white woman with him?"

"I'm your wife and I'm helping you catch runaway girls."

"Okay. Yes, that makes sense. I have ads for a couple of girls."

"Or I could cadge me a uniform and be a soldier."

"You could do that?"

She shrugged. "Done it before."

"Huh!" This woman was full of surprises.

"Do you want to head out?"

"You mean right now?"

"Yes."

He thought about it. "Maybe we should stay around here another day. Get a feel for what these boys are up to. See if Pete dies, see where Lee is."

"All right. I think we could both use the rest anyway."

They sat and watched the Confederates for a few minutes. At length he asked, "Are you hungry?"

"Yes," she replied, "but I don't think it would do to pull out any food right now."

"You're right, these boys would find the sight most remarkable."

"Didn't Napoleon say something about…"

"'An army moves on its stomach,' yes."

"Well, this one is moving on an empty stomach."

"I know. I never saw such a skinny lot."

She looked at him. "Let's play a game."

"Now?"

"Let's pretend we were Lee. What do we do now?"

"Oh. All right. Well, he's running out of options, isn't he?"

"He can't continue like this. He needs a bold stroke."

"You're right," he said. "Something audacious. That's his stock in trade."

"He needs food and fodder. He needs ammunition. Where does he get it? In the North?"

Nathaniel shook his head. "Every time he goes up North he gets spanked."

"All right, then. Something different than what he's done before." She thought about it. "I've got it. Do you know how Napoleon would conquer a country?"

"No."

"He would go into a country, win one battle, then take the capital."

"The capital? What do you mean?"

"I mean Washington, of course."

Nathaniel looked at her. "Are you serious? He couldn't do that."

"That's every reason for him to try. And he doesn't have much else that he could do now."

Nathaniel thought about it. Washington was of course ringed by defenses, but these were heavy gun emplacements. Aside from the gun crews there were few soldiers; the soldiers were all needed in the field. A Confederate commander would have to silence or evade a gun emplacement, but after that he could march right into the city.

If Lee took Washington he could capture Lincoln, most of the members of Congress and a good deal of the bureaucracy. If the city were burned it would destroy much of the nation's records. The United States would be crippled.

He started to speak two or three times and ended up saying, "I hope Lee isn't thinking along your lines."

The approach of darkness brought an end to the fighting. Men falling back gave conflicting accounts of the day's progress. Some thought that the day had gone to the Federal forces; others felt that Lee had once more out-maneuvered the enemy. The only thing that everyone could agree on was that it had been a deadly day.

The woods were burning quite merrily now and the dense smoke made sleep difficult.

The next day began with news that Longstreet had not died after all but neither was he in any condition to resume command. General Richard Anderson came before the men and announced that he had been appointed to temporarily replace Longstreet. Anderson had always enjoyed the men's favor and this announcement was greeted by cheers and hats thrown into the air. The general was moved to tears by this response.

The troops formed up and marched back into the burning forest. Nathaniel watched them go, thinking that he had never seen such a noble sight.

A sergeant accosted Nathaniel, demanding that he fall in. Nathaniel replied that he was a slave catcher and had to bring his charge to Richmond, just as soon as the soldiers cleared the road. The sergeant made a rude sound and let him be.

In the early afternoon Nathaniel and Clarabel went together to the railroad line. Nathaniel sent a message describing Longstreet's injury and Anderson's appointment. When he got down from the tree Clarabel suggested that they eat before returning to the bivouac. They sat on a fallen tree and had a meal of hardtack and jerky supplemented with water from a stream.

Clarabel sat rather closer to him than necessity dictated. He wondered if she wanted him to kiss her. "What did you think as the men went back into the woods this morning, Nathaniel?"

"I thought it looked like they were marching into Hell."

"You know what a soldier told me once? He said, 'When I die, I know I'm going to Heaven because I've done my time in Hell.'"

He nodded. "I think every soldier says that. I reckon it's true."

"Even the enemy?"

"Yes. Even the enemy."

She chewed her food. "What do you reckon it's like?" she asked.

"What?"

"Heaven. You think it's all clouds and angels playing harps, and you get a crown of gold?"

He sighed. "I don't know. I used to think like that but I don't know any more. There has to be something, though."

"Maybe. I wonder, because they talk about people going to Heaven, but then they talk about them resting, about them sleeping. It's like they don't really know."

"Yeah," he said.

"But if you ask a preacher about that, they just get mad at you."

"I don't think I ever asked."

She had a swig of water. "I did. I said it would be horrid if I remembered all the things I saw here on Earth and it would be horrid if I sat on a cloud for ever and ever with no end."

"And the preacher got mad?"

"Yes. Said I was a sinful girl and I was a-going to Hell."

He thought for a moment. "So what do you think now?"

She replied, "I think maybe it's like a dream. You don't think about the passage of time in a dream and you don't think about real things. You sleep and you dream and you do it forever." She said all of this quickly and with no forethought, as if it were something she had long worked out and was waiting to tell someone.

He turned to her as she turned to him. "I hope they're sweet dreams," he said.

They looked into each other's eyes. The moment stretched on; then it was over. They got up and headed back to camp.

That evening at about midnight the entire camp was roused. The men were ordered to fall in for a quick march to the south. "What is it?" the soldiers asked. "What's happening?"

"The Yankees," they were told. "They're moving on Richmond and we have to head them off."

There was no question of staying behind. Nathaniel and Clarabel fell in with Longstreet's, now Anderson's, corps and moved out at the double quick time.

As they puffed down the road in the dark, Nathaniel glanced around, then said, "Do you think we ought to drop out now?"

"You mean skip?"

"That's exactly what I mean."

She shook her head. "This is something new. This is just the situation where we want someone in the enemy camp. We should stick with this and see where it gets us."

"All right. Say, it looks like this march is a surprise to the brass, not just the enlisted men."

"Yes, what's that all about?"

"Well," he said, "every time a Union commander won a victory before this he would withdraw. Grant decided to attack again."

"Damned inconsiderate of him."

"Damned right."

After about half an hour they saw a person standing and coughing at the side of the road. They thought it was one of the walking wounded until they saw it was a woman in a gray dress, jacket and bonnet. They approached the figure and Clarabel reached out and touched her shoulder. The woman turned and Nathaniel saw that it was Red Sally.

This was the first time he had encountered her since becoming a spy. He knew that he had to be friends with her now but he still had not known how he would react to seeing her.

The woman's cheeks were hollow and she was unsteady on her feet. It took her a moment to recognize Nathaniel; when she did she offered him a weak smile.

"You poor thing!" Clarabel said. "Why, you have a fever. You're in no condition to be walking like this."

"Do you have…some water?" Sally asked. Nathaniel offered his canteen. She took a long draft and said, "Do you know how much farther we have to go tonight?"

"I reckon it's another four miles," Nathaniel replied.

Sally looked at the passing columns. "I'll never make it," she said. "I'll have to drop out."

"You'll do nothing of the kind," Clarabel said. "The thought of a poor woman sitting beside this road with no one to take care of her—" She clicked her tongue reprovingly. "William," she said, using Nathaniel's alias, "find a wagon for this lady."

A covered wagon was passing at the moment and Nathaniel flagged it down. The driver did not want a passenger but found it quicker to acquiesce than to argue. As they helped her into the back, Sally quietly asked Clarabel, "What's your name?"

"Brutus," she replied. "I'm a runaway slave boy."

Sally nodded and crawled into the dark wagon. Nathaniel slapped the boards and the driver shook the reins.

He turned to Clarabel. "She didn't seem surprised when you said that. She must have known you were a lady."

"Oh, I know her," Clarabel replied. "And I know you know her. But I didn't know she was along on this little trip."

"She's getting really weak."

"I know," Clarabel said. "She's determined to die in the traces. I wish I had her gumption."

The armies tramped along the dark road all night, trying to make haste with as little noise as possible. By morning they had reached their objective: the crossroads at Spotsylvania Court House. If Grant was going to Richmond he would have to go through here, and he would not go through here without an argument. The Confederate troops had beaten the Yankees to the crossroads and they knew the importance of what they had just accomplished. They took a minute to cheer their accomplishment; then they set to work.

Some men improvised breastworks. They did this by felling trees and stacking the trunks in the form of a log cabin with no roof. These improvised fortresses had worked for the Yankees at Gettysburg and would now work for them. Other men made abatis, sharpened poles, and placed them in the ground before the breastworks. Nathaniel was amazed at the speed with which the Rebels set up a defensive line more than a mile in width.

By the afternoon the Confederate defenses were taking shape. The lines were in the shape of a ragged V. The apex of the V was round, in the rough shape of a horseshoe; indeed, the men were already calling it the "mule shoe." Here the forces were concentrated, inviting a Federal attack.

The Union troops were trickling in by this time. They stayed out of rifle range and watched the Confederates work.

Nathaniel and Clarabel hung in the rear, watching the goings-on. "All right," he asked, "what do you suppose we should do?"

"Maybe we should skip now."

"You think so?"

"Well, this is going to be one Hell of a pitched battle. We'll be pushed into the fighting if we stay around."

He nodded. He thought it was a strange contrast, her sweet, childlike voice and the language that she used. "Is there anything we could do besides fight or skip?"

"I could hang in the back. I could be a camp darkie and listen in on the officers at dinner."

"Well, then, I could help out at the telegraph tent. If you find anything out, I can make sure it gets sent out. I don't know if Fort Monroe will copy it, though."

"Fort Monroe? You mean your line there?"

"Yes."

"That's not necessary."

"It isn't?"

She shook her head. "Anything that goes on the line ends up being copied to Jefferson Davis, and we have someone in his office."

"We do?" He blinked. "Who is it?"

"Do you really need to know?"

He waved his hand. "No. Say, have you seen Sally?"

"Sally? Oh, I know who you mean. No, not since we got here."

"I reckon she made it here but she was looking mighty peaked."

They retired to the makeshift headquarters at the rear. While Clarabel went to the cook-tents, Nathaniel sought out the telegraph office. This was not hard to find; it consisted of a tent with a wire running into it.

He entered the tent. Two men in civilian garb stood and stared at the key as if they did not know what it was. They looked sharply up at their visitor. "Howdy do, boys," he said. "Have a problem?"

"Who in Hell are you?"

"Name's Jones. I just joined up and thought I might be more useful working a key."

"Can you work a key on a dead line?"

"Not hardly."

"Well, neither can we."

"Are you an operator?" the other man asked.

"Yes, I worked for American in Richmond before the war."

"American? Under Rogers?"

"Yes, why?"

"What's your name?"

"Jones."

"What Jones?"

"William Jones."

"I don't recollect you. I worked for American in Alexandria before the war. Name's Benjamin Rush, and this here's Dylan Finney."

Nathaniel recognized both names. He had in fact conversed with both men numerous times; now he actually knew what they looked like. "How'd you do? Why's the line dead?"

"Don't rightly know. They just ran it in to this tent an hour ago. Most likely they don't have the other end tapped in yet."

"Where would they branch in, the railroad?"

"I suppose so," Finney said, "but that's about five miles away. It would be a weak signal."

"Are there any repeaters?"

"Not that I've seen," Rush replied. "I'm going to go out and chase it down."

Rush departed. As yet there was no sound of battle. Nathaniel sat and talked with Finney for half an hour until the line began to clatter.

It was only routine traffic from Richmond but it came through loud and clear. When the message ended a new one began: FROM CSA AT SPOTSYLVANIA COURT HOUSE TO WAR OFFICE RICHMOND WE ARE ON LINE STOP TELEGRAPH TENT ANSWER.

Finney looked at Nathaniel. "Want to send an answer?"

Nathaniel sent TELEGRAPH TENT COPIES YOU WELL STOP DO YOU COPY RICHMOND. Seconds later came the reply, FROM WAR OFFICE RICHMOND TO CSA AT SPOTSYLVANIA COURT HOUSE WE COPY STOP HOW ARE YOU BOYS DOING.

Nathaniel answered, ARMY IS DIGGING IN YANKEES ARE SHOWING UP NO SHOOTING YET STOP LONGSTREET SHOT IN THROAT BUT ALIVE STOP. This last was not for the benefit of Richmond but Washington.

The reply came: ALL TRAFFIC GIVE CSA AT SPOTSYLVANIA HIGHEST PRIORITY PER ORDER WAR OFFICE STOP GOD BLESS YOU BOYS AND KILL LOTS OF YANKS THE NATION DEPENDS ON YOU 73.

Nathaniel answered, THANKS WAR OFFICE 73.

Rush returned a quarter hour later. "I chased down the gang stretching the wire," he explained with a smile. "No one knew how to splice into the railroad line. I had to go up the pole and do it myself."

The day drew to a close. There was a bedroll laid out in the tent, so the operators needed leave only to eat or relieve themselves.

Nathaniel let Finney and Rush take their meal first so that he could go alone. It was dark before he went to dinner. Telegraph operators were so important a resource to the Army that they were given the same rations as officers. While better than what the men got, it was still very poor fare. He held out his plate for a dollop of grits accompanied by a spoonful of "nigger peas."

"Thank you, boy," he told the mess hand.

"Yes, sir. Our friend is better."

"Well, that's good."

"I think she was just real tired from the road. She's resting now." She touched her side. "I laid some victuals by for her."

"All right."

"You talk to Richmond?"

He nodded. "I told them about Pete."

"Good." She turned away to serve a lieutenant.

He pulled the night watch while Rush and Finney slept. He expected the attack to begin at dawn but it did not. The Federals were still trickling in and were still assessing the Confederate defenses.

Finally, at about four o'clock, the assault began. Nathaniel and Finney stood outside the tent and told Rush as much as they could discern of what was happening. Their vantage point was nearly a mile away, but it was on a rise and there was fairly clear land between them and the line of attack.

The initial blow fell, as expected, upon the Mule Shoe, the strong salient in the center of the line. Neither side had managed to bring any artillery along on their quick march, so the assault was made by infantry. The Union forces advanced upon the breastworks, drawing a lot of fire but unable to hit their entrenched foe. They ended up withdrawing, leaving several thousand casualties upon the field.

A greater force formed up. These men screamed across the field, and across their dead and dying friends, and struck at a single point upon the Confederate breastworks. They managed to break through. Several thousand men poured through the narrow gap, only to find a second line of breastworks in front of them. From this they received a murderous fire.

The beleaguered Yankees fought like demons, but if they were expecting reinforcements they were disappointed. They ended up having to fight their way back out of the salient, and this was even harder than fighting their way in had been. The Rebels fired at their fleeing backs until they were out of range, then cheered and waved the Stars and Bars from the battlements. The day belonged to the Confederacy.

As darkness fell men descended into the salient with torches; Nathaniel joined them. There amidst heaps of tangled limbs and rent bodies thousands of wounded men begged for aid. These unfortunates were piled onto litters and moved to the rear. The dead, in all states, were left for another day.

The Union wounded were treated with no less regard than the Confederate, though they were destined for the Purgatory of Andersonville. Although treated with respect, they were relieved of their shoes and other valuables before being led away.

When the wounded had been removed the men washed themselves in a stream and retired for the night. Nathaniel was visited by nightmares of moving through a dark landscape lit only by flickering torchlight. All about him he saw severed heads, their faces frozen in expressions of surprise or agony; shattered limbs; torsos burst open with wet intestines spilling onto the ground. Wherever he walked in this slippery tableau, arms and legs rolled beneath his feet and men in various states of mutilation begged him to rescue them, or to give them water, or to kill them.

Grant spent the next day thinking about what to do next. The Confederates licked their wounds, dragged their dead away and dug in deeper. Dugouts were hastily constructed, with log walls and roofs and earth piled atop them.

The three telegraph operators kept busy, but they did have time for conversation between messages. Rush asked a question that everyone was asking with increasing frequency: "Do you think we can still win the war?"

"Yes," Finney replied instantly. "We just need to keep our noses to the grindstone."

"I think we can win," Nathaniel said. "We still have the better officer corps. Grant is the best they have thrown against us so far, but he's supposed to be a drunk."

"He fights pretty well for a drunk," Rush said.

"Actually, he fights poorly," Finney said. "He continually loses two men to every one of ours that he kills."

"But is that so wrong?" Nathaniel asked. "I mean from his point of view, of course. He may have calculated that he can afford to lose twice as many men as Lee does."

"Then he needs to lose more," Rush said defiantly. "At some point the North will decide it's lost enough men. Sentiment will turn against the war."

"It may be turning already," Finney said.

"What do you mean?" Nathaniel asked.

"Well, the Copperheads might win the presidential election. If Lincoln gets voted out we'll have won the war."

"All right," Rush said, "maybe Northern sentiment will turn against the war. Will it ever turn toward us?"

"Do you mean will the folks in the North ever start to sympathize with us?" Finney asked.

"Yes."

"I think they're starting to already."

"Really?"

"I was with Longstreet as we came into Pennsylvania, just before Gettysburg. Most of the Pennsylvania folks were just watching us march by, but a girl came running out and gave Pete a bouquet of posies."

"A girl?" Rush said. "Really? What kind of girl?"

Finney shrugged. "She was one of them Pennsylvania girls. You know the kind?"

Rush said, "Pennsylvania girls are pretty much like other girls, aren't they?"

"Well," Finney said, "I mean she was wearing one of those Pennsylvania bonnets."

"What's a Pennsylvania bonnet?" Nathaniel asked.

"Some of them girls up there wear real plain gray bonnets that cover their hair and hide their faces."

"Oh, you mean she was a Quaker."

"A what?"

"They're a religious group, they like everything real plain. I reckon she must have been one of them."

"I reckon she must have been."

"Well, it was nice of her to do that, but it was hardly a big outpouring of enthusiasm."

"Well, it was still important," Finney said. "I heard from an officer that that bouquet had a note in it. The note told of the disposition of Union forces in the area, and it turned out to be accurate."

"Well, I'll be darned. Really?"

"Sure enough."

Morning came and Grant had decided what to do. An enormous force, some twenty thousand strong, struck at the toe of the Mule Shoe. The Federals broke through but were met by forces pouring in from other places on the line. This was head-to-head and toe-to-toe fighting, the fiercest Nathaniel had ever seen, and it raged all day. The Federal forces managed to surround and capture a full division of Lee's forces. Meanwhile, other Union forces attacked the weakened line but could not break it.

At the end of the day the Yankees were again obliged to withdraw. Although the field was once again ceded to the Rebels, it was a bitter victory. In two days of fighting both sides had lost about ten thousand men. Grant paid the price with a smile, knowing Lee could not.

Nathaniel met with Clarabel at the mess tent again. Both were so stupefied by what they had witnessed that they found it hard to speak of it. "What have you been sending?" she asked him.

He shook his head. "Nothing they haven't asked me to," he replied. "I found out something last evening that was kind of interesting."

"What was that?"

He told her what Finney had said about the Quaker girl and her note. "Do you think they'd find that interesting back home?"

"They well might. I think it would be worthwhile telling them that."

"All right, then." He started eating.

"Do you think Grant can win?"

"I think he will in the end. I don't know if he can win here and now. His supply lines are getting longer while ours are getting shorter."

"What do you think he'll do, then?"

Nathaniel shrugged. "He'll try to break Lee here, but if he finds it hard, he'll move on Richmond. That's always been the Federal prize."

"And Lee?"

"Lee? He'll lose if he keeps on like this. He's always counted on his enemy being a fool, but Grant's no fool. Unless Grant makes a big mistake Lee's a-going to lose."

She thought about it. "Or he might do the other thing."

He nodded, then put his plate and spoon down. He had eaten breakfast, the only meal he would have that day, in half a minute.

He made his way to a dugout. The back door was open and the soldiers were firing through slits in the front. Though he was unarmed and not even in uniform the Federals took a bead on him. Bullets whistled around him as he ran for the door. Inside it sounded like a hundred carpenters were working on the outer wall.

A second lieutenant saw him come in and inquired as to his business. "I'm a telegrapher," he said, shouting above the din, "and I need to encode a message."

"Why can't you do it at the telegraph tent?"

He shook his head. "This is so secret I can't let the other operators see it."

"Go to it, then, son."

Son, he thought. That lieutenant was younger than he was. He sat down and took out a message blank. He wrote his message out in clear, signing his own name to it. Then he took out a second blank and drew an encryption grid. He used the code word he had been given, POSEIDON, and encoded the message onto a third blank, using the Union encryption technique.

He nodded his thanks to the lieutenant and left. He dropped the clear message and the encryption square into a campfire, then returned to the telegraph tent. He sat down without a word, pulled out the blank and sent it.

Rush and Finney didn't ask what the message was. He assumed that somewhere down the line a Union operator would pick it up and forward it to the War Office.

The battle wore on for a fourth day, then a fifth. The lines of battle twisted and squirmed on the map. One day they faced each other north and south, the next it was east and west.

Finney returned from the mess tent and told them, "I heard that Ewell made a reconnaissance around the Federal right, looking for the end of the line. You know what he found?"

"No, what?" Rush and Nathaniel responded.

"Yankee artillerymen, pulled out of the defenses of Washington. They brought them down here and gave 'em muskets."

"Well, damn," Nathaniel said. "Those boys wouldn't know one end of a musket from the other. If they got into a scrap, they'd have to swing the damned thing by the barrel."

"That's what this boy was telling me," Finney said. "Ewell's men were killing them two to one."

All three ruminated on this for a moment. "I guess what matters," Rush said at last, "is that Grant has the two and Lee doesn't have the one."

"Something else," Nathaniel said. "Washington doesn't have as many artillerymen as it did a week ago."

"Can't see as that makes no never-mind," Rush said.

"It just might," Nathaniel said. "Here's another question: was that the end of the line, or was it just Yankees and more Yankees?"

Finney hesitated. "I don't know," he said.

On the sixth day Nathaniel met Clarabel at the mess tent. She told him, "Don't be surprised if I'm not here tomorrow."

"What? Why not?"

"They're looking for hands to carry ammunition to the lines. They were looking at me as they said it."

"Well, what the Hell," he said. "Are the officers supposed to feed themselves now? Because they'll starve, to a man."

"I don't know," she said. "They're within an ace of starving now."

"Well? Is it time to skip, then?"

She shook her head. "Don't know if I could skip now. There's troops all around the back country here. Besides, things are just getting interesting."

"Have you seen Sally?"

"I saw her yesterday. She was caring for the wounded and listening in on the officer corps. I told her what that fellow told you about the Quaker girl."

"What did she say?"

"She seemed very interested. She asked me what you were going to do with the information. I told her you had sent it to Washington. She said that was the right thing to do." She moved away and served two lieutenant colonels.

He spent another evening dragging wounded from the Mule Shoe, another night having nightmares, and another day reporting the battle to Richmond and Washington. It was a relief to get to the mess tent and see Clarabel. He smiled at her. "You're still here."

She did not return his smile. "Nathaniel, I need to speak to you in private. Is there a place we can do that?"

"How about the telegraph tent?"

"Can you get those other fellows out of there?"

"I think so." He bolted down his meal – an easy task – and went with her to the tent. As he went in he turned and looked to the west. The sun was just touching the horizon and the firing was abating for the day.

He offered Rush and Finney no explanation as to why he wanted them to leave but they left without a word. Clarabel closed the flaps and tied them. Then she turned to him, putting her hands to her face, then her hair. "Oh! It's just so long since I did anything without there being people looking at me."

"Ain't I people?"

"No, you're not. You're my only friend in the world. Put your arms around me."

She hugged him, laying her head on his chest. He hugged her back. A volley of shots flared up a mile away, then faded to silence.

"Do I frighten you, Nathaniel?" she asked. Her voice was soft, almost musical.

"No. Well, yes, I reckon you do."

"Your heart is going like a trip-hammer."

"Clarabel, do you want me to kiss you?"

She laughed softly. "No, you fool."

He tried to pull back but she wouldn't let him. "What, then?"

"Oh, you're such a gentleman! Or maybe you just don't know any better."

"Better than what?"

By way of response she moved his hands to her chest. Her breasts were bound up somehow and they were small in any case, but touching them had an effect upon him like an electric current. He had a thousand objections but they all melted away before the sudden overwhelming desire he had for this woman.

When all was done they lay together on the rumpled blankets at the back of the tent. She lay on her side, her head on his arm. The dying daylight coming through the muslin behind her lit up the profile of her body. She was a smooth line of white in the darkness of the tent, curving in at her waist, out at her hips, and she was the most beautiful thing he had ever seen in his life. He was afraid that Rush and Finney would enter the tent unannounced...but yet he was not.

> *Beautiful dreamer,*
> *Wake unto me*
> *Starlight and dewdrops*
> *Are awaiting thee*

His eyelids fluttered but he didn't open them. He was surprised that he had fallen asleep.

> *Sounds of the rude world*
> *Heard in the day*
> *Led by the moonlight*
> *Have all passed away*

He smiled to let her know that he heard her.

> *Beautiful dreamer,*
> *Queen of my song*
> *List' while I woo thee*
> *With soft melody*

She didn't sing as beautifully as the Negress, but it was beautiful in a different way, one he could never explain, even to himself. Her voice was teasing, ironic, and flirtatious. He knew the person behind the voice and she knew him.

> *Gone are the cares of*
> *Life's busy throng*
> *Beautiful dreamer*
> *Awake unto me*
> *Beautiful dreamer,*
> *Awake unto me*

"I'm sorry," he whispered.

"For what?" Her fingertip ruffled the hairs of his chest.

"Didn't I hurt you…before?"

"*Hurt* me? What gave you that idea?"

"It sounded like…I thought I was hurting you."

She laughed softly. "My dear boy," she said, "you have a lot to learn."

They lay in silence. It reminded him in an odd way of the Quaker meeting. That was a blasphemous thought, of course, but lying with her like this was similar to that religious service in its silence, its peace, its sense of communion.

Her hand lay flat on his chest. "Something's wrong," she said.

"It seems to me that things are right just now. No," he amended, "I guess you're right. A whole heap of things are wrong."

"No," she said, "something in particular is wrong. I didn't see it before but I think I see it now."

"Want to tell me about it?"

She shook her head. "Not until I'm sure."

He ran his fingertips down that curve of white. She moved beneath his caress like a cat. "Do you think this is what people are supposed to do?" he said.

Her head nodded against his chest. "This is close, anyhow," she said. "Find someone and care about them."

He nodded.

"I'm glad you're here with me right now, Nathaniel," she said. "Even if we both die in this place, I'm glad you're here."

The next day began with an infantry major drafting Nathaniel and Finney to carry ammunition and water to the men. They joined a line of other men, young boys, women and Negroes similarly employed. These people were actually in a more dangerous situation than the fighting men. The soldiers at least were dug in.

As Nathaniel was bringing yet another pail of water forward he looked up in time to see a figure spin around and fall. He squinted at the crumpled heap on the ground, his heart in his throat. Dropping the pail, he rushed forward, stumbling over the broken ground.

A woman knelt before the broken body. At his approach she rose and turned to him. "She's gone, Nathaniel. It's too late."

Clarabel lay on the ground as if resting. Her face was turned to him and her eyes were open but she didn't see him. "No!" he cried, "No!"

Sally took his wrists. "Turn away," she said. "You can't help her."

"Are you sure? Look at her, she looks fine."

"She's dead."

"Oh, God! Did she say anything?"

Sally put her bloody hands to her face. "She said one thing but it was nonsense."

"Fall in!" a colonel shouted as he ran past. "You men drop what you're doing and fall in! We're headed south!"

"What?" Nathaniel persisted. "What did she say?"

"She said to tell you that she'll dream of you."

Chapter Seventeen:
Old Tom Fool

The Army of Northern Virginia marched south again, grimly moving ahead of the Army of the Potomac. The Rebels turned at bay at Hanover Junction and again offered battle. After a few more deadly days the Federals swung past their foe and headed south again. The Rebels ran south and blocked them again, this time at Cold Harbor, just north of Richmond.

The Southerners were hungry, weary and ragged; every day their numbers diminished as men fell or fled. The Confederacy was doomed, and while no one wanted to be the last man to die in a losing cause, few wished to abandon that cause.

Grant attacked like the warrior that he was. His initial assault was ferocious and reckless. Two corps of infantry attacked across the seven mile wide front, charging forces that were well dug in, quite expecting to be charged, and ready, willing and able to resist. Seven thousand Union soldiers fell in the space of twenty minutes.

The Rebels were motivated by hatred, bitterness, grim determination and a host of other, baser feelings. For many of them, this war was all that life now consisted of: kill until you die. They killed and they died with little more thought than the beasts of the jungle.

Nathaniel Curry had fallen in with the forces of Jubal Early. He had lost his carbine and now bore a regular rifle musket. He was now indistinguishable from any other Southern soldier. He was dead tired, he was hungry, he was rotten with fleas, and he was on the edge of madness. Still he soldiered on.

Nathaniel retained enough of that divine spark we call humanity that he refrained from killing his friends, though they did their earnest best to kill him. He took care to aim directly at the Union soldiers, knowing that the ball would strike the ground before reaching its target. If he had in fact killed a Union soldier he would not much care. If a Union soldier killed him he would not much care.

Three miles behind him the spires of Richmond rose pristinely. He longed to go there, to lie in his bed again, but the city may as well have been at the North Pole of Mars. Other young men could abandon the battle and go home but he could not. He could never openly return to Richmond as conqueror or as vanquished, but only as a slinking spy.

In a few bloody months Ulysses S. Grant had driven from the Virginia border to the outskirts of the capital. He was willing to risk defeat in the pursuit of victory; he was a clever tactician; he was determined and patient; he had advantages in men and materiel; he did not reckon his dead. It was but a matter of time before he would crush the Confederacy.

Then Lee spoke a few words and everything changed again. Jubal Early was ordered north into the Shenandoah Valley. His mission was to clear the Valley of Yankees before the harvest, draw attackers from Richmond, and, if possible, threaten Washington. His forces numbered a mere eight thousand, but many of them were seasoned veterans who had two years before marched with Stonewall Jackson.

The first goal was nearly a moot point. The Union Army had adopted a scorched-earth policy toward the breadbasket of the Confederacy, burning crops and anything else of value. Early's forces encountered the chief of these vandals, David Hunter, and sent him packing. Encouraged by this success, Early invaded Maryland, setting his sights upon Washington.

As had been anticipated, the North was nearly stripped of fighting men. A makeshift force was assembled under Lew Wallace and placed before Early at Monocacy, Maryland.

The Confederates crossed the Monocacy River and entered the town. Wallace's forces fought bitterly but they were too few in number and too poorly organized to carry the day. They ended up retreating toward Baltimore.

Early resumed his march on Washington. Two days later he reached the outskirts of the city. He sent skirmishers forward to reconnoiter Fort Stevens, one of a string of fortifications ringing the city.

Nathaniel Curry joined one such band. His intention was to break loose from his fellows and make it to his own lines. This sounded simple but experience told him it would be difficult.

The skirmishers moved across a broad, flat plain. Nathaniel knew the area well; he had tramped these fields when he had been stationed in Washington. He was actually only about four or five miles from the White House.

The skirmishers kept together and kept a sharp eye out for Union forces. They met only token resistance, men who usually did support work of some kind but who had been abruptly handed weapons and sent into action. They were not good fighters and there were only a few of them.

Early's men also kept an eye on the fort. It had not as yet fired its cannon, but if it did it was sure to make a lot of noise. An infantry attack against a fortress was suicide, so the principal task of these men was to find a way around it.

Suddenly more seasoned Yankee troops began to appear. These men rushed into the battle as if they had just arrived upon the scene, and indeed they had. They had been diverted from the battles around Richmond, shipped to the capital, quick-marched through the city, and were showing up just in time to stop Early.

The skirmishers fought with the vanguard of the Union forces. Both sides rushed in more troops. Meanwhile the reconnaissance of the fort continued.

Fort Stevens was so placed as to command a sweeping vista of the northern approaches to the city. It was impossible to get past the fort without exposing oneself to the installation's firepower. If Early had sought another approach to the city, he would have found another fort that was just as deadly.

True, the fort was undermanned, but seasoned infantrymen were now pouring into the city every second. Early determined to make an assault while he still could.

Nathaniel was with a group of men that had fought its way to within a few hundred yards of the fort. As yet the fort remained an *eminence gris*. It had not yet fired a large gun, although it was producing musket fire. Still, it dominated the landscape as it dominated the thoughts of every attacker.

The men around him were reloading when a lone Yankee burst out of the brush before them. Nathaniel put one in his chest and he went down. Someone said something he didn't catch and the other men laughed.

Unit by unit, defenders were joining the battle. Field artillery was being driven in, unhitched from the mules and made ready. Early was still doing well but he would soon start doing poorly.

Suddenly a cry went up from the soldiers, Rebel and Union alike. Everywhere men ceased firing and pointed at the fort. Nathaniel heard what they were shouting but could scarcely believe it. He set down his musket and pulled out his eyeglasses.

There before him, upon the parapet of Fort Stevens, stood the President of the United States. He was about a hundred and a half yards away. It wasn't just another man in a stovepipe hat; Nathaniel knew the way Lincoln moved and this was he. He stood alone, a black silhouette against the sky, looking down upon the battle. Nathaniel could not see his face but he fancied he wore an expression of sadness.

The outcry lasted but a few seconds. The Confederates took aim upon the parapet and unleashed a thunderous volley, quite ignoring the Union troops that resumed fire upon them. Lincoln stood and watched them. He was beyond the reach of even a well-aimed standing shot, although not out of range of a lucky one.

Sharpshooters rushed forward. One of them, a young blond man wearing glasses, stood and looked at Lincoln for about ten seconds. He shouted, "I make it one hundred and sixty-five yards," and died. Several men hastily lay on their backs, placed the muzzles of their rifles on their feet, and focused their globe sights upon the parapet. Nathaniel started to turn back toward Lincoln.

"Well, look, boys, it's old Tom Fool. How you doing, Tom?"
"Morning, boys."

"Why, Tom, it's the evening now, don't you know!"

"Morning, boys." The boys all laughed.

"Come along now, Natty."

"Why Tom, isn't that your Paw?"

"Yes I am, fellows, and he's no fool."

"Why, he sure enough is. Tom, you friends with Abe Lincoln?"

"I sure am. He around here today?"

"Why, he's in the next cell, boy."

"Send him around in the afternoon, then."

"We sure enough will, Tom." More laughter.

"Tom, where you get captured?"

"I don't recollect. Somewhere, I guess."

"Come on, boy, you got to remember that. Who were you with?"

"I was with Longstreet at Manassas, I remember that. We charged old Fitz-John Porter."

"Yes, that was the second Manassas, wasn't it?"

"Sure was."

"You broke him there, didn't you?"

"Broke him bad, boy."

"They court-martialed him for that, Bill. Did you know that?"

"Yes, I heard that, and they convicted him, too. Kicked him out. Did you know that, Tom?"

"Wait a minute…yes. Yes, I do recollect that. In a great big old room with lots of paintings on the walls."

"What, was you there, Tom?"

"I think so."

"Did you talk to General Porter?"

"Um, yes, I did."

"What you say to him?"

"I told him I was sorry I done charged him that-a-way."

The other soldiers laughed. "And what did Fitzy say to that?"

"He said he'd forgive me."

"Natty, you have to wake up now."

"Aw, Paw, let me sleep a little longer. Can't Melly work the store today?"

"Now, Nat, you know there ain't no store here. But you've been sleeping all day."

"What time is it?"

"I don't know, but it's after noon. How does your head feel?"

"It's sore today, but it's not as bad as yesterday."

"Get up and move around a little. That will make you feel better."

"All right. Say, Paw, is there anything to eat?"

"Yes, I cadged you a little breakfast."

"Give it over, will you?"

"Only after you walk around a mite."

"So you're the new fellow?"

"Sure enough."

"Well, welcome to our little corner of Hell. My name's Curtis and this is Jenner. This here fellow we call Tom Fool. It's not his regular name, but he's a foolish one."

"Pleased to meet you, boys. My name's Johnson and I was with Ewell's cavalry, and Jackson before that. What did y'all do in the Army?"

"We was all infantry. All except Tom here. Tom got a bump on the head and his story keeps changing. Tom, you recollect any better what it is you done?"

"I think so. I seem to remember that I was a spy."

"Oh, a spy, was it? For which side, boy?"

"Uh, the Union side. I was a Yankee spy."

"And what did you find out about us?"

He searched his memory. "Y'all lost the battle of Gettysburg."

"Tom, we were just talking about Gettysburg. Were you there?"

"Gettysburg? That in Virginia?"

"No, up in Pennsylvania. You were there, weren't you, Henry?"

"Sure enough. Marched in with Longstreet."

"You did? Say, how did them folks receive y'all?"

"Well, they didn't much appreciate us coming in, for the most part. My sergeant spoke up to a shopkeeper, told him, 'How you like us coming back into the Union, mister?' The old boy just looked away."

"Yes, same thing here. But some folks liked us. I saw one girl run up and give old Pete some posies."

"She did? Pete Longstreet?"

"The very same."

"Pennsylvania girl, was she?"

"Sure enough. She was one of them Quakers."

"A Quaker? Sure enough?"

"Yes, she had the plain dress and the big bonnet and all."

"Yes, I remember that, too. She gave Pete some posies."

"You remember that, Tom? You were at Gettysburg?"

"I think so. I recollect a Quaker girl giving Pete posies with a note in it."

"Why would a Quaker give a general flowers? I thought they was agin war in all its forms."

"That's right, they won't fight."

"So you know about that, too?"

"Yep. I was a Quaker once."

"What, you was a Quaker boy?"

"Yes, for a week or maybe a month. I don't recollect too well."

"I don't think you was, Tom. You don't do a hitch as a Quaker. You either is or you isn't, like being black or white. Or being a boy or a girl."

"Oh." Tom frowned; he seemed to recall someone who changed color and sex at will, but he wasn't sure.

"Where was you at Gettysburg? Who was you with?"

"Wasn't with nobody. I was the commander."

"What, you have troops under you?"

"Couple."

"You an officer in those days?"

"Civilian. I think I still am."

"Why would a civilian be commanding troops, Tom?"

"I don't know. I just remember getting away."

"Well, how did you get away?"

"I flew away. Bunch of God-damned Confederates was trying to kill me."

"Man, it gives me a turn when he starts in a-talking like that. How you fly away, Tom?"

He shrugged. "Cut my drag lines."

"Okay ..."

"What about Fredericksburg, Tom? Was you at that one?"

"Umm ... I think so. Yes, that was marching up that long hill, wasn't it?"

"No, that was the Yankees that marched up the long hill. We shot 'em as they came. You remember that?"

He frowned. "I do recollect it, yes. They was just mowing the Yankees down, but they just kept a-coming. That was Burnside. He was a fool."

"Sure enough. You know, boy, you must be getting better. I asked you about Fredericksburg before and you didn't know nothing."

"Well, it hurts my head if I think too much. But yes, I do remember Fredericksburg now. I remember looking down at the Bluecoats."

"Do you remember what unit you were with?"

"No…wait a minute. Yes. Yes, I was with the Balloon Corps."

"Why, boy, there was no Balloon Corps then. There used to be a balloon, but that was back on the Peninsula."

"You sure? Because I remember at Fredericksburg, they tried to hit the balloon with a shell. And it landed in the latrine instead, and everyone got covered in shit."

"Covered in shit? You're thinking about this place."

He shook his head. "No, they were covered in shit worse than we are here."

"You too, Tom? You get covered in shit, too?"

"No, because I was way up in the air in the balloon. Shit couldn't reach me."

"Tom, your mind's addled again."

"My name ain't Tom."

"Paw, how long I been here now?"

"As well as I can recollect, it's about three weeks."

"And how long you been here?"

"Over a year. I got captured after Gettysburg. I told you this before."

"Yes, but I forgot. What's the date now, do you know?"

"I think it's the first of August or thereabouts."

"Do you think I'm getting better?"

"Well, your mind is. Your body's getting weak, but we all are. Your mind, though, it's like night and day. When you first got here I hardly knew you. It was like you were drunk all the time. You'd laugh and sing and talk nonsense. Now you seem addled sometimes but not so much as before."

"Paw, do you remember what I told you before?"

"What, about how you want to get out?"

"Yes."

"Now, son, that was nonsense. There's no way to get out of here. This ain't no garrison camp, and it ain't no stockade. This here was a prison before the war and it's good solid brick. Besides, it's way in the North. You'd have to make like the Underground Railroad running backwards."

"I think I can do it, though."

"What, and just walk back home?"

He turned to his father, dropping his voice low. "Paw, do you remember the work I was doing?"

"Yes, I do."

"Well, I have to get in touch with some of those folks, that's all."

"How do you plan to do that?"

"I don't know just yet."

"Tom, you done said you seen Lincoln at Fort Stevens, didn't you?"

"Yes, I think I said that."

"Well, that might be right. I talked with another fellow who says he saw Lincoln there, too."

"I saw him just standing there. He was wearing his big old hat. It's funny, but that's how I recollect it."

"He was on top of the fortress, right?"

"Yes, that's right. Yes, yes, I remember it now. That must have been about the time I got hit."

"You don't remember that? Getting hit, I mean?"

"No. I don't think I want to, either."

"What about after?"

"I just remember being in this place."

"Oh."

"Wait, there's something else I remember from right after I got hit at Stevens."

"What's that, boy?"

He frowned. "You'll just say I'm talking nonsense again."

"I promise you I won't, Tom."

"I saw Uncle Sam. He was there on the battlefield and he helped me get up."

"Uncle Sam? The old boy with the white whiskers and the braces?"

"Yeah. No. He was an old colored boy."

Curtis shook his head. "I should know better than to make a promise like that."

"So what do you want, soldier?"

"Sir, I'm not a Confederate. I'm a Union agent."

"You're a what?"

"A Union agent, sir. I was sent south to reconnoiter ahead of Grant."

The commandant looked him up and down. "You hardly look the part, son."

"Sir, should I?"

"What?"

"Should an agent look like an agent?"

"Well, I don't plan to bandy words with you, my boy. You've been here nearly a month. Why did you just decide today that you're a Union agent?"

"I got hit on the head, sir, which occasioned my capture. It pretty much knocked the sense out of me until lately."

"Is that all you wanted to tell me?"

"No, sir. I need to get out of here and get back to Washington."

"What, just like that? What kind of a fool do you take me for?"

"I don't take you for a fool at all. I—"

"Do you think I'm going to release you based on that cock-and-bull story?"

Nathaniel sighed. "Can I send a letter to someone, sir?"

"To whom would you like to send a letter?"

"President Lincoln."

The commandant frowned at him. "No, I'll not bother the President with a joke like that," he said.

He thought about it. "Well, then, sir, I'd like to write to Colonel George Sharpe at the War Office. He's the head of the Bureau of Military Information."

"If you say so. Yes, I'll go along with that. Write your letter and I'll look it over and if I like it I'll send it along."

Nathaniel's head hurt as a memory forced its way to the fore. He saw again Sharpe's office with its piles of unopened correspondence. "No, wait, sir. I want to write to someone else. He's also at the War Office."

Nathaniel wrote to Major Grover and gave the letter to the commandant. The commandant must have sent it with the military dispatches because less than a week later a telegram arrived from Washington. The commandant had it in his hand when he arrived at Nathaniel's cell with three guards.

He pointed at him through the bars. "That's the one there. Get him out of there."

As the guards entered, the other prisoners spoke up: "What are you up to, boys? What did Tom do?"

"He's a spy," the commandant said.

"A spy? Which side was he a spy for?"

"He was supposed to be working for us," he replied, "but it turns out he was being crafty."

The word spread quickly among the Rebel soldiers. "Tom Fool! Tom Fool a spy? Tom Fool a spy for the Yankees! No, he was really working for us. He's no fool. He was just *playing* the fool. He made fools of the Yanks. Huzzah for Old Tom Fool!"

The cheers died away as Nathaniel was moved to an isolation cell. He sat alone in this tiny cage for a full day, then was manacled and transported under guard to Washington. He was brought on an open wagon to the War Office where Grover warmly received him.

"Well, Curry, it looks like I have you at last. I have witnesses this time." Several privates with very practiced hands came up and removed his manacles, then applied new chains. He now had a chain from each wrist and ankle, all meeting at a ring in the center. He had to stand hunched over and could only walk at a shuffle.

"What do you think I've done, Major?"

Grover shook his head. "Not think, Curry. Know. Don't worry, the charges will be specified."

"Have you told Colonel Sharpe about this?"

Grover responded with a sneer. Nathaniel was left in a cell to ponder his situation another day.

The next day he was brought before Grover and Sharpe in the very room where Grover had first interrogated him. Grover wore a triumphant air; Sharpe looked thoughtful.

"I *have* a *witness*!" Grover exulted. "He's a Confederate soldier. The man says he saw this man kill David Miller."

"He says this of his own free will?" Sharpe said.

"I didn't hold a gun to his head. He in fact volunteered it to a guard. The guard then approached me."

"What unit was he with?" Sharpe asked.

"He's of Longstreet's corps. He was captured during the Wilderness campaign."

"Can I speak to this man?"

"I would be most pleased. He's being held in this very building."

"Good. Please take Curry's bonds off."

Grover was surprised. "You want to bring him?"

"Do you mind?"

"I suppose not. A defendant should have the right to face his accusers."

As they left Grover's office Sharpe encountered two private soldiers and told them to fall in. They then went to a cell in another part of the prison. As they approached, Sharpe turned to the others and cautioned them to hold their silence.

A large man with long blond hair and a great red beard sat alone in a small cell. It was hard to make him out because the light from the barred window above his head was full in their faces. Sharpe addressed him: "You are John Warner?"

The man stood up. "Yes, sir."

"I hear that you have some information on the death of one David Miller."

"Yes, sir."

"You men step up to the cell beside me. You too, Grover. Keep silent, now. I'll do the talking. Now, then, Warner. Tell me what happened."

Warner said, "The day of the Second Manassas I was marching with Longstreet to the battlefield. I was in the back of the column. During a rest I met two men who had just met up with the column and General Longstreet told them to fall in. They said their names were David Miller and Nathaniel Curry.

"Miller and Curry hung back from the rest of the army. I thought they were going to desert and I wanted to watch them so I could report it. I hid in the trees beside the road. When Miller and Curry were alone they started to quarrel. I could not hear what they were saying, but I saw Curry raise his musket and shoot Miller. He left him lying on the road and went and caught up with the column. I went and caught up with them, too."

"Why are you telling us this?"

"After I was captured I was interrogated. One of the things they asked me is did I ever meet a David Miller. I said yep."

"Did you get a good look at these men?"

"I reckon so."

"Would you recognize them if you saw them again?"

"Well, I won't be seeing Miller again this side of Judgment Day, but I'd know Nathaniel Curry if'n I saw him again."

Sharpe stood there a few more seconds, then said, "You're looking at him now."

"What? I am?"

"Yes. One of us is Nathaniel Curry. Can you say which one?"

Warner stood mute for ten seconds, then sat back on the bench. "I ain't a-saying nothing," he said.

Sharpe dismissed the two soldiers, then led Nathaniel and Grover back to the interrogation room. He sat wearily in a chair. "I'm satisfied," he said, "that the man is lying."

"What?" Grover exclaimed. "Why? Because he didn't recognize Curry?"

"Precisely."

"Then why did he say that?"

"That, Major, is for you to determine. Clearly someone did put a gun to his head and gave him that story. A prisoner in his situation will say or do anything under duress, as we both know."

"I can assure you I did no such thing!"

"I am well assured of that," Sharpe said. "You would not have allowed things to reach this pass if you were the father of this scheme."

"Then who did, if you're so sure of yourself?"

"You figure it out. I would caution you to treat as suspect any other information this John Warner gives you. For the moment, I wish to have these charges against Curry dismissed."

Grover looked like he was about to explode in wrath. He turned purple and blood vessels stood out all over his face and neck. "There is still the other matter," he said tensely.

"Yes," Sharpe said. "Where is this witness?"

"In Armory Square Hospital. It's about a ten-minute walk. Shall we?"

They walked in silence to the hospital. They passed through the wards, which as always were very unpleasant places. The bedpans in hospitals were emptied but seldom and the large rooms stank of feces and urine. The men stank of infection, gangrene and general filth, but more than anything else of feces and urine. Everywhere flies swarmed around men's wounds and mosquitoes tormented patient and doctor alike. Major Grover made a quiet inquiry of a female attendant and was pointed to a woman sweeping the floor at the other end of the room.

At their approach the woman turned. It was Red Sally. "Well, Mrs. Pettijohn," Grover said, "you seem to be doing much better."

"I have my good days and my bad days," she replied.

"You're supposed to be a patient here, not an attendant."

She shrugged. "Someone has to do this."

"Will you speak to us alone?"

"Certainly."

The administrator surrendered his office to the four of them. The men waited until Sally was seated before sitting themselves.

"Mrs. Pettijohn," Grover said, "will you repeat to us the charge that you made to me before?"

"It's not really a charge, Major," Sally replied. "It was more in the way of hearsay."

"Please let us hear it, in any case. You were with the agent Clarabel Emmer at Spotsylvania Courthouse when she died, were you not?"

"Yes, I was." Sally lowered her head.

"Would you recount to us what she said as she lay dying?"

"I'm sorry, Nathaniel. She had her back to the enemy when she was shot. I saw that very clearly. I approached her and I could see the bullet had struck her in her front. I went up to her and she told me that she thought that Nathaniel had shot her."

Nathaniel felt such a shock that he nearly fainted. The room went black for a moment and he tottered in his chair. "What?"

Both men turned to him. "Might you have shot her?" Sharpe asked.

Nathaniel opened his mouth but could not speak. He had fired at so many men over those few weeks that it seemed possible that he might have hit a friend, yet … "No," he replied firmly. "I was carrying a bucket of water in one hand and a bag of ammunition in the other."

"Did you have a weapon at that time?"

"Yes, I had a Spencer repeater. But it was slung over my shoulder."

Grover said, "Then how do you explain what this witness has said?"

"She was mistaken. Or Clarabel was mistaken. I would never have shot her." He lowered his face as tears came to his eyes.

Clarabel had been facing him and not the enemy when she was hit, he remembered that. And he had seen blood soaking the front of her clothes.

"Sally," he said, "was that all she said?"

Sally hesitated. "Yes," she said firmly. "That was all she said."

"What exactly…" He swallowed hard and went on, "what exactly did she say?"

"She said, 'I'm hit. I think Nathaniel shot me.'"

"That was all she said?"

"Yes, that was it."

"Did she say that other thing as well?"

"The other thing?"

"You told me at the time that she said something else."

"Oh. No, she did not say that. She only said the one thing."

He buried his face in his hands, weeping uncontrollably. It was the first time he had really wept for Clarabel and he was ashamed that he could not stop himself. At last he was able to say, "Then why did you tell me that other thing?"

"I had to say something. I couldn't tell you what she told me. I thought you'd shoot me as well."

"Oh, God!" He got to his feet and struggled toward the door. The other two men stopped him. "I don't care any more. Take me away, shoot me. Do what you want. I give up."

"So you admit it?" Grover said.

"No, I don't admit it. I never shot her. But I just don't care about anything any more."

The three of them went to Grover's office at the prison. Grover sat at his desk and pulled out a piece of paper. "I'll start the bill of particulars on this matter immediately," he said. "I'd like to thank you, Colonel Sharpe, for your help today."

"Don't mention it, Major," Sharpe replied, "but I'll be taking young Curry here with me."

Grover looked up. "You will? After what you just heard?"

"I heard the word of one whore quoting the word of another, and there was equivocation there in any case."

"But she was one of your agents!"

"Major, I don't know what happened at Spotsylvania that day. I do know that I have gotten a lot of good information from this young man. Even if he indeed killed her, her loss to me would be worth it in his utility."

"Then you're a fool, sir!"

"Be that as it may. Curry, you're with me."

It was a hot August day. It hadn't rained in weeks and the roads were redolent of horse manure. Hospital tents were pitched on the Mall where eight months before troops had drilled. It was good to be walking out in the open this way although the sun still dazzled him. "Thank you for sticking up for me, sir," he said.

"I didn't really do you any favor, Curry. I just found that on balance you were of more value to me alive than dead."

"My allegiance is to the Union, sir."

"Curry, have you ever killed anyone?"

"Yes, sir."

"Like it much?"

"No."

"I've killed six men. They were all men I knew, men who in fact worked for me. I've always insisted on doing it myself. It's hard, but it's less hard each time I do it."

"Yes, sir."

"Don't play me false, Curry."

"I won't, sir."

"You can take three days furlough, then it's off to Atlanta."

"Yes, sir."

Nathaniel approached Atlanta from the northwest, riding on the Western & Atlantic Railroad. This rail line roughly followed the path that had been recently blazed by General William Tecumsah Sherman. Looking out the window of the car revealed a path of devastation, for what the retreating Confederates had not destroyed, the advancing Federals had.

The rail line no longer extended into the city itself; Nathaniel and the other passengers had to debark where the track suddenly ceased to exist. Nathaniel joined a wagon train headed south of the city.

They came to the town of Ezra Church. Here, a few weeks earlier, Sherman had faced General John Bell Hood and beaten him badly, killing five thousand men at a cost of a mere six hundred of his own. Nathaniel was shocked to learn this; it was a reversal of the usual pattern of the war, in which canny Southern generals killed two Union soldiers for every one they themselves lost. The very train he rode carried troops whose sole purpose was to bury the dead from this latest battle. Talking with the men he discovered there had been several recent battles in which the Union had badly beaten the city's defenders.

He rode with the wagons south of the city, then left the Army and headed east. When he reached the track of the Macon & Western Railroad he started north. He came to White Hall Tavern, where a rail station was still in operation.

He fell in with a company of rebel soldiers. A few deserters and stragglers were continually repenting of their ways and trickling back to the Army. Many of these men were in civilian clothes and appeared unarmed, like he himself. As a result his presence was not questioned.

Nathaniel was in fact armed. He carried a small pistol and forty rounds of ammunition in a shoulder holster under his shirt. He had five dollars in his pocket and another fifty in a pouch hidden where he hoped no one would search.

He also wore Amanda's locket. It had in fact returned to Washington with him, in his prison papers, and Colonel Sharpe had given it to him just before he left for Georgia. The locket had been open when he took it out of the envelope and he fancied that a soldier had intended to steal it but held back when he saw the beautiful and innocent face within.

The rosewood-handled jackknife was gone, vanished into the hand of a Yankee soldier, but that was where he had found it in the first place, so he was even there.

Atlanta had had its start in 1845, a year before Nathaniel, and had outgrown its britches many times. At first glance it was a queer combination of Richmond and New York. It was an entirely Southern city, but it had a bustle and an energy few other Southern cities had. It was not only an important rail center, which was its original *raison d'etre*. It was also a major manufacturing center, with mills turning out weapons of war, locomotives, textiles and other strategic products.

Sherman had failed, despite his victories, to either capture the city or to disrupt the rail lines in and out of it. The city's defenses were too difficult to defeat and too extensive to encircle. He could win any battle but he could not, as yet, win the campaign.

Nathaniel simply walked into the city. Pickets were out but they didn't even challenge him and the other stragglers. They strolled in, chatting amongst themselves.

Upon arriving at a camp within the city Nathaniel followed a wire to a small brick building. A captain and a corporal looked up as he entered. "Can y'all use an operator?" he asked.

"Depends," the corporal said. "What can you do?"

He shrugged. "I can run wire, charge a battery, hook up a key, send twenty characters a minute, copy twenty, and dance the shoo-fly all night long."

The men smiled. "Shoot, boy," the captain said, "sounds like you can do anything except walk on water."

"I never tried that one, Captain."

"Well, Francis," the corporal said, "shall we give this young fellow a try?"

Nathaniel had never heard a corporal address an officer by his first name before, but these two appeared to be old friends. "Sure enough," the captain said. "Boy, here's the key. Let's hear what you can play."

Nathaniel sat at the key and waggled his fingers like a man warming up to play the piano. Then he transmitted, FROM WILLIAM JONES ATLANTA TO GENERAL WT SHERMAN USA I HAVE ARRIVED AT THE CITY SAFE AND SOUND STOP LIVE AND LET LIVE 73.

The soldiers laughed at this message. "What was that all about?" the captain asked.

"I just thought it was polite to warn him I was here."

"Do you think he'll get it?"

"He'd be a plumb fool if he did not, and he's no fool, unlike the mass of the Yankee officer corps. Sir."

"I take no offense at that, I assure you. I quite agree, in fact. And I hope he does get that message, if only for the perplexity it will cause him. Well, William Jones, my name is Francis Conroy and this here is Billy Margate."

"Pleased to meet you both." They shook hands.

"We can't call you Billy," Conroy said.

"Beg pardon?"

"We have one already. Can we call you Willy?"

"Oh, of course."

"Now, who are you and how did you get here?"

"I worked for the Atlantic Telegraph Company before the present hostilities, Captain. I've never really joined up, but I've done a lot of work for the Army."

"Where you been?"

"All over. I was lately at Spotsylvania and Cold Harbor. I was about to go to the defense of Petersburg when I took a trip up north instead to try to capture an ape." Both men nodded at this. "I got a bump on the head at Fort Stevens that had me down for a while but I'm back now.

"As to how I got here, I was with various units fighting around the city. They pretty much all got wiped out, so I made my way in here."

"Ever been to Atlanta before?"

"Never, Corporal. It looks real pretty."

"It sure is. And with God's grace it will continue to be the anchor of the Confederacy."

"There are six operators here in all," Conroy said. "Seven counting you. Two of the others are on temporary duty with the Army, the other two are off duty now and are sleeping."

"Or whoring or drinking," Margate interjected.

"Or all three," Conroy said. "Since you can fix wire, we may ask you to patrol the city if communications go down."

"All right."

"We'll see how you work out before we decide how to assign you. Do you have any questions?"

"Yes, sir. What's the state of the city?"

"Well, it's pretty good. Now, bear in mind, about nine citizens in ten have left town, but those who remain are performing yeoman's service, producing ordinance and defending the city. We're still getting goods in and moving war materiel out.

"The Yanks are doing a lot of damage around us but they don't have the strength to break through the defenses and invade the city proper. Our hope is that they'll get tired and go home."

"There are a lot of strange niggers in the city," Margate said. "They seem to be primarily occupied with filling their own stomachs and their own pockets. That's to be expected, of course; they have no stake in the success of our Cause. They're a danger to the women of the town, but there are precious few women left. They've been tolerated because they can be used to dig defenses and move goods."

"Got a place I can bunk?"

"Sure do," Margate said. "We're all rabbits here; everyone sleeps underground. Just outside this building, on the right, there's a bombproof we all use."

"The bombing much of a problem?"

"Well, you've probably heard a little already." Nathaniel nodded. "Billy Sherman throws shells in here but he hasn't done much damage. Some folks have died, but most folks end up dying anyway."

"Can a fellow still get a bite to eat around here?"

"Yes, if you have the yellow for it," Conroy said. "Confederate currency is pretty much scorned, but gold is still, well, good as gold. Just don't expect fancy fare."

"I won't. Can I have a few hours leave?"

"Sure enough."

If nine out of ten citizens had quit the city it was hard to tell. The streets were full of traffic, both military and civilian. Most shops were shuttered, though, and those that were open didn't have much on the shelves.

A group of six soldiers accosted him: "Halt! What's your name and what's your business?"

"I'm William Jones and I'm a telegraph operator."

"Do you have anything that can prove this?"

He did indeed. He handed him a letter from an aide of General Longstreet identifying him as a civilian telegraph operator for the Army. The letter was a forgery, but with Longstreet busy in Virginia it was not likely that inquiries would be made. The soldier read it and handed it back.

"Have anything to eat?"

"No."

"In a pig's ass. All right, be on your way."

The city was laid out in a sensible grid, with broad avenues interspersed with pleasant open areas. Many of the homes had once been quite prosperous, although times were clearly hard.

A dollar got him a decent rabbit stew at a restaurant. The restaurant was owned by a free colored man who had several white employees. The owner had a formidable forehead liberally decorated with frowns and blood vessels, and great white eyebrows. He ordered his staff around like an overseer. Nathaniel had never seen such a situation before; surely Atlanta was a remarkable place.

As he returned to the telegraph building another soldier approached him and asked his name. When he replied that he was William Jones, the soldier said, "Is this not Nature's bounty?"

Nathaniel replied, "Rejoice in the day the Lord hath made."

"I do, every day," the man said, smiling. "You're Nathaniel?"

"Call me Willy," he replied. "Yes, you have the right fellow, but they know me as Willy Jones here. What's your name?"

"Just call me Bobby. What do you think of the place?"

"I think it will be a hard nut to crack."

"Well, I've had a good look around myself. I have a few concrete suggestions I could make to Sherman."

They shook hands. In the process Nathaniel received a small piece of paper and put it in his pocket. He found a quiet alley and read the paper. It provided the locations of some important facilities in the city: a powder magazine, a house where several high-ranking officers slept, a rolling mill.

He couldn't simply get on the key and report this without being detected. He started walking again, following the telegraph wire through the streets.

At an intersection it joined three other wires. One wire, going south, clearly followed the railroad out of town. Another went to the train station, which was occupied by the Army. He followed the fourth wire.

It went into a three-story brick building. The building was shuttered and the doors were locked. The back door, however, had been knocked down by looters.

The third story had previously been occupied by P. NASH ATTORNEY AT LAW. The door was conveniently open. The offices had of course been ransacked, but a length of coated wire hung by the window in a small room at the front.

A careful search of the room produced a very old camelback telegraph key that may have been constructed by Samuel F.B. Morse himself. It was in a closet containing spare parts, including a coil of wire and a crow's-foot battery, though no juice.

He cleaned the contacts on the key as well as he could. Then he attached the wire coming in the window to the key. Looking around the office, he discovered it had indoor plumbing, something he had heard of but never seen. He ran the coil of wire to the water tap and from there to the key.

The key started tapping. The ground was good enough that he did not need a battery.

He listened to the traffic. The train station had just received three officers of General Hood's staff; Sherman was attacking south of the city; Richmond and Petersburg continued to resist the besieging Yankees.

When the key fell silent, he sent a message without a header ordering guards at the magazine, the officers' quarters and the rolling mill. He appended their addresses. With any luck, this message would appear to be part of the message before it. He removed the key and hid it, then exited the building.

He returned to the telegraph building. Margate was on duty but he was reading the newspaper and paying scant attention to the clattering key. The two of them chatted for a while, exchanging war stories and gossip about various officers of their acquaintance.

"You worked for American, Willy?"

"Yeah."

"Where?"

"Richmond, mostly. What about you?"

"Alexandria, Manassas. A little while in Washington."

"Yeah? I been to Washington."

"Nice city, isn't it?"

"Well, it sure enough was pretty, but I don't plan on going back there soon."

"No, me neither. Who was your boss at Richmond?"

"A Mister Rogers."

"Oh, I remember the name. So you've been working for the Army? Which one?"

Nathaniel did not want to get into particulars. "Well, a couple of them. For most of the war I been a nigger-catcher."

"Oh, you like that?"

"Well, it was good when a man could make a living at it. Catch one nigger, get a hundred dollars, shoot, a fellow could do just fine. But the Yankees are putting me out of business."

"How did they pay you?"

"Well, that's the other problem. I wanted gold but they always insisted in paying me in Confederate money. Jeff Davis' money says that it's 'legal tender for all debts public and private,' but it's not. The stuff is getting to be downright worthless."

"Oh, you've never read the fine print?"

"What fine print?"

Margate pulled out a Georgia five-dollar bill. A tiny line of letters arced above the engraved image of a battle scene. It read, "Two years after the conclusion of a treaty of peace between the Confederate States and the United States of America." Beneath this was the larger text, "The State of Georgia will pay to the bearer on demand FIVE DOLLARS."

"In other words," he said, "this note won't be worth five dollars until two years after the war ends."

"Oh. And that's only if we win."

"Yes, there's that little detail as well." Margate put the bill back in his pocket. "Well, it's still better than a corncob in the outhouse."

Nathaniel thought about it. "Oh! Is that what the 'legal tender' part means?"

The next day began with a rousing artillery attack upon the city. Rather than just a few random shells tossed in, this was a sustained barrage against three particular points.

They were the wrong points. At first light Nathaniel joined a crowd of curiosity seekers that viewed one of the scenes of destruction. The bombardment had leveled a large livery stable, killing a dozen horses and three stable hands. The bodies lay interspersed with the large planks of the stable, stacks of hay and piles of manure.

Nathaniel listened to the people around him:

"Mercy sakes! What a waste of horseflesh."

"Was anybody hurt?"

"Nope, just horses and niggers."

"That's a blessing, anyway."

"I think I knew that nigger. Well, that's a shame."

"Why did they hit a *stable* like that? Where's the sense of it?"

"I don't know. Sure looks like it was done on purpose."

"Yes, there must have been twenty shells hit this one spot."

"We'd best be careful in case they start in again."

"Maybe they're out to kill all our horses."

"All our stable hands too?"

"Yes, I thought that big monkey loved niggers."

"Well, it's mighty peculiar."

"Don't make no sense at all."

It made sense to Nathaniel, who had only to look beyond the stable to see the powder mill half a mile down the road.

Something else that made sense, more so than ever, was the utility of military aviation. He looked at the sky. It was overcast, with the ceiling at eight thousand feet. He pictured himself in a balloon a thousand feet up and four miles away at Ezra Church. He would be able to see this stable and the powder mill and he would be able to correct the aim of those guns in ten minutes time. Every military target in the city would be at his mercy. The city could be taken in jig time with little loss of civilian life.

Well, the generals were fools. He turned away, knowing he would have to see the other targets and tell Sherman how far wrong his gunners had been.

At the third target he met Bobby. The two of them found a quiet corner to compare notes. They agreed on the corrections needed to the aiming points.

"Don't you want to write this down, Willy?"

"Not really. I wouldn't want to carry around a note like that. I can remember all this. It just makes my head hurt a mite."

"All right. I'll see you outside the First Congregational Church at noon tomorrow."

"All right."

Nathaniel returned to the telegraph room in time to relieve one of the other operators, a boy of about fifteen who was so weary he could scarcely hold his head up. The lad went off to the bombproof, yawning all the way.

He didn't get a break until one in the afternoon when Margate relieved him for lunch. Instead of eating he ran to the law office and set the telegraph up.

He waited as message after message came through. At last he heard what he was waiting for. It was a long message from a general operating south of Richmond to his supply chief fifty miles farther south. The operator was inexperienced and made a lot of errors. He would spell a word wrong and send the standard "error" code, EEEEEEEE, then laboriously send the word again.

By the time he was finished it was likely that not even the intended recipient was still listening. The operator finished without sending a "73" and Nathaniel seized the moment.

He sent TARGET ONE THREE HUNDRED YARDS NORTH TWO FIFTY YARDS EAST TARGET TWO FOUR HUNDRED YARDS NORTH TARGET THREE ONE HUNDRED FIFTY YARDS NORTH THREE HUNDRED YARDS WEST 73. If that was not good enough for Sherman, then to Hell with him.

He removed the wires from the key and picked it up. He heard a sound behind him and looked over his shoulder. Three of the largest Negroes he had ever seen in his life stood watching him. He said, "What do you boys want?"

The largest of the three said, "What you got we could want, man?"

There was no deference in his voice at all. He had not called him "master" or "sir" or even "boss," he had addressed him as an equal. And that was not a good sign.

"I got nothing you could want."

"So you say, man. So you say."

The man stood with his thick arms crossed. Nathaniel made some quick calculations. The men were about eight feet away from him. They were dressed as laborers, not field hands. Their clothes were in good condition and they wore shoes. They were not armed or their weapons would be displayed.

The Negroes themselves had not decided what do to and were playing things by ear, just as he was. Things could still go either way.

The largest man was the ringleader and he would make the first move.

"That's what I say. I was just looking for anything of value in here. There's nothing but this thing." He held up the telegraph key.

"What's that?"

"I don't know. It clicks when you tap it."

"It clicks when you tap it. I must look like one dumb nigger to you."

"No you don't."

"What you doing with a telegraph, man? Here alone in this empty building this way? Shit."

"Why don't you tell me?"

"You a Yankee spy."

He moved the key to his left hand. "Well, what if I am? That means I'm on your side."

"Shit, man. Ain't no white man on no nigger's side and you know it."

"If I'm a Yankee spy, then I'm working for your freedom, ain't I?"

"Freedom. You telling me that if the Yankees win, I going to be free?"

"Yes. I seen it. I seen whole plantations of slaves get freed. It's the federal law now."

The man shook his head. "You a Yankee spy," he said, "and you no better than any other white man. I know these people will pay me if'n I turns you in. I want to know what you'll give me not to turn you in."

"I told you, I have nothing to give you."

"More white lies," the man said. His tone told Nathaniel what he had to do next.

He dropped the key, tore his shirt open with his left hand, reached in with his right and pulled the pistol out. The large man started to spring toward him but checked the motion. The other two Negroes started but did nothing.

Nathaniel pulled the hammer to full cock. The ringleader, realizing his missed opportunity, muttered, "Shit."

Nathaniel kept the weapon trained on the large man. "The three of you turn around and march out of here," he said.

The largest man remained crouched before him. "You think a little fellow like you can get all three of us before we gets you?" he asked.

Out of the corner of his eye Nathaniel saw one of the other men moving to his left. The desk was between him and this man but it would only be a momentary hindrance. Nathaniel shot the man before him. The Negro fell on his back, the soles of his shoes rising into the air. Nathaniel pulled the hammer back with his left hand, aimed carefully and shot the man scrambling over the desk in the top of the head. He fell on his side, his head thrown back, and jerked like a hooked fish.

The third man turned and ran from the room, crying, "Don't shoot me, master, don't shoot me!" Nathaniel cocked the weapon but never had a shot.

He looked at the fallen. The man on the desk was no longer in play. The other man lay on his side, hugging himself. He put the pistol and telegraph key away and started to leave.

"You ain't going to leave me here like this, are you?"

Nathaniel answered with a sneer; then, whatever vestiges of a Christian soul that remained to him came to the fore and he turned back.

"Help me up."

"Okay. Sit in this here chair." He put his hands under the man's arms and moved him into the office chair he had just vacated.

The man sat there for a few seconds, then pulled up his shirt and looked at his wound. "It not very big," he said.

"No."

"Look like a bee sting."

"Yeah. Big enough, though, I reckon."

The man gave him a searching look. "What about a doctor?"

He shook his head. "The best doctor in the world couldn't save the King of England with a wound like that."

The man nodded and turned to look at the man on the desk. "That nigger dead as an old coon."

"Yeah, I got him clean. Y'all should have left when I said."

"Yeah. He a big talker, he know where everything be in Atlanta."

"He your friend?"

He shook his head. "Never seen him before two days ago." He gave a wet cough that spoke volumes to Nathaniel.

"What about the other fellow?"

"He my brother. Me and him left the farm four days back."

"Oh."

The man looked at his arms resting on the arms of the chair. "Well, this all three things."

"What?"

"When we lit out I said I wanted to do three things: kill a white man, fuck a white woman, sit in a chair with arms. I done it all in two days." He smiled up at his killer. "You really a Yankee spy?"

"Yes, I am."

"I promise I won't tell nobody."

It took the man half an hour to die, and he may have still been alive on the floor when Nathaniel left. He figured he had come out of this well enough, but he could never use this office again. Two dead Negroes would not raise much suspicion, if they were even found, but the third man might talk.

He found a dry-goods store and bought another plain white shirt. He no longer had the time or the appetite for lunch so he went back and relieved Margate.

The next morning he awoke to the sound of incoming artillery. At first he thought that Sherman must have gotten his message, but after a few minutes he began to doubt it. The bombardment went on too long.

He went outside and stood in the early morning light listening to the firing. It seemed to be striking all quarters of the city, near and far, with no discernable pattern.

He went into the telegraph room and said good morning to Margate. "You sleep well?" Margate asked.

"Until this ruckus started," he replied. "You know, I grew up on a farm and I would wake up to a cock crowing."

"Yes, me too. This isn't as good."

"No."

"Want some coffee?"

"Thank you kindly. Is that cornbread?"

"You know it is."

He relieved Margate and sat sipping coffee, listening to the shelling with one ear and the telegraph traffic with the other. An hour passed. To his surprise the shelling did not abate. It continued at the same pace as before. Moreover, it seemed to Nathaniel that the shells were louder than they had been.

A twelve-year-old boy stuck his head in the door and asked if Nathaniel needed relief. He replied, "Well, I need to relieve myself, if that's what you mean."

The boy smiled. "It wasn't, but go ahead."

"All right. You know how to work this thing?"

"Sure do," the lad said proudly. "It's as easy as the multiplication tables."

"Well, I'll take your word for that, I never learned them too well. Listen, I have a message for General Hood. I'm going to deliver that and find a bite to eat. I'll be back in an hour."

"All right."

He went down to the army headquarters. General Hood was in the city, preparing to go out to do battle. When Nathaniel arrived Hood's aides were affixing him to his horse the way a man would attach a bayonet to a musket. Hood had lost his right leg and had shattered his right arm in separate battles, so it was necessary to tie him to a board attached to his saddle in order for him to ride at all. The result didn't look very pleasing or comfortable, but it made him the very picture of determination.

Nathaniel approached and saluted, saying, "Dispatch for you, sir."

"Read it, I don't have my glasses."

Nathaniel read it. The message was a waste of paper and time. Hood nodded, said, "No answer," and rode painfully out of town.

Nathaniel met up with Bobby on his way back to the telegraph room and related this encounter to him. "What did you think of Hood?" Bobby asked.

"He looked like he wasn't enjoying himself."

"Yes, but he always looks that way. He has a naturally tragic face. He looks like he was born to play King Lear."

"Well, I don't know King Lear. I just thought he looked like an old hound dog, but he was still handsome for all that."

"Have you met up with Sherman yet?"

"No."

Bobby shook his head. "Ugliest man in America. Bar none."

"Really? I thought Abraham Lincoln was the ugliest man in America."

"Well, Lincoln is ugly in an appealing sort of way, yeah, like an old hound dog. You see Lincoln, you want to be his friend. Sherman, though, is bad ugly. Sherman is enough to scare children."

A shell landed in the next street. The concussion broke windows in nearby buildings. Nathaniel said, "Is it my imagination or are some of these shells louder than the others?"

"Yes, some of them are louder. Those are siege guns. Sherman is still using field artillery against us, but he's brought in siege guns from Chattanooga as well. He's trying to reduce the city like you'd reduce a fortress."

"That's too bad."

"Yes, this is a beautiful city. Won't be for long, though."

"Say, does Hood know his business or doesn't he?"

"He's a political appointee, does that answer your question?"

"Oh, God, really?"

Bobby shook his head. "Joe Johnston had the job before him. Johnston had plans to withdraw into the fortifications around the city and wait Sherman out. It might have worked, too. If the city doesn't fall by Election Day, the Democrats might win the presidential election, and that could end the war."

"Really? If Atlanta doesn't fall the Confederacy could win the war?"

"Sure enough. But Jeff Davis didn't like Johnston withdrawing all the time so he kicked him out and put in his old friend John Bell Hood. Trouble is, Hood is a fighter. He keeps running out and attacking Sherman. And we've seen the results."

Nathaniel had never had the situation laid out for him as well as this. "All right," he said, "so what should each side do now?"

"Well, Sherman has to cut the rail lines in and out of the city. It's the middle of August now; the election is in three months. If he can starve the city by then and take it, or shell it into submission, or take it by invasion, then Lincoln wins the election.

"Hood has to prevent this. Even if they lose the rail line, the city has to hold out. They can slaughter the horses and dogs and cats and live on them if they have to. Anything but surrender. Then the Democrats might win. The Democratic platform calls for a treaty of peace with the Confederacy."

Nathaniel nodded. "Who are they running for President this time? Is it Douglas again?"

"No, didn't you hear? It's Mac."

Nathaniel was astonished. "What?"

"General George McClellan. Mac is back again, and now he's running for President."

"Wait a minute, McClellan is running as a Copperhead Democrat?"

"Well, no. That's where things really get funny. Despite the Democratic platform, McClellan says that if he's elected, he'll prosecute the war better than Lincoln, and he'll win."

Nathaniel thought that over. "Yes, but you know he won't. If he's elected, the South will win."

"Yes," Bobby said, "and although I'm a Southerner, I want the Union to win."

"Yes, so do I. I think it's the only way that slavery will end."

Bobby looked around. "Yes, I think so too. But to me what's important is the strength of the Union. If this country remains united, it can form a great empire from sea to sea, from the north woods of Canada down to South America. It would be the rival of the world."

Nathaniel went to bed that night to the sound of shells. He was awakened several times by close hits and he got up to the sound of shells.

Sherman was continuing the bombardment. It appeared that shells would fall on the city until Judgement Day.

Before his watch he took a walk around the city. The shells were causing a little damage but not much. They were falling at random, putting a hole in a road here, knocking a tree down there. A few dwellings and business establishments were hit, but everyone seemed to accept this as the price of doing business.

He stopped by the law office. Without going up the back stairs he knew that the survivor of his attackers had kept quiet about what had happened, because the two corpses were still up there. The sweet, sickening odor of death flowed down the steps like an unholy river. He could hear thousands of flies buzzing in the office on the upper floor.

He stood looking through the doorway. He really wanted to go up there and send a message, but the thought of doing so in a room with two rotting corpses terrified him.

He steeled himself, took a breath, put his foot on the step, then spun around and vomited on the ground. No, he realized, he could not go back there again. He returned to the telegraph house.

When he was alone with the key he sent a message with no header: ATLANTA IS HOLDING UP UNDER THE BOMBARDMENT STOP THERE IS PLENTY TO EAT AND WE CONTINUE TO DO OUR JOBS 73. He hoped that any Confederates who saw this message would see it as an expression of defiance but that the Federals would understand that it was a message.

He met Bobby the next day. Neither had any news to report. The bombing continued, but Sherman already knew that. The city resisted, but he knew that as well.

He returned to the telegraph hut. He could tell, coming through the door, that something was wrong. Conroy and Margate sat looking at him.

"Afternoon, boys. What's up?"

"What did you say your name was?" Margate asked.

"Well, I said it was William Jones."

"Might it be something else?"

He looked perplexed. "What do you mean?"

"I thought I knew every operator from Roanoke to Baltimore. I never knew any William Jones. There were operators I didn't know their names, of course. But what I did know was everybody's fist.

"I recollected a Richmond fellow who had a certain way of sending '73.' He would make that last dash twice as long as the dash just before it."

"Yeah?"

"Yeah. So I contacted Rogers at Richmond, asked him if he recollected that as well. He didn't, but he did say that he once had an operator there name of Nathaniel Curry. This fellow Curry up and quit in '62. Rogers said he just vanished."

"Do tell."

"So what we were speculating on, to make a long story short, is why a fellow would change his name and say he was a nigger-catcher when he was in fact a telegraph operator."

"Why don't you fellows tell me?"

Conroy spoke up: "We were wondering if'n you might be a spy."

The clock ticked about twenty times. "Well, if I was, you know I couldn't tell y'all."

Conroy looked at Margate. "Told you," he said.

Margate said, "Shoot, boy, you could trust us."

"Hell, Billy, Major Norris would shoot me if he heard me tell you this much," Nathaniel replied. He was referring to the head of the Confederate espionage organization, William Norris.

"What's your mission?" Conroy asked.

"Well, I'm supposed to keep Richmond appraised of how well the generals are doing. They can't depend on their staffs to be objective."

"That's it?" Margate asked.

"That's not it by a long shot." Nathaniel poured himself a cup of coffee and sat down. The other two let the subject drop.

At Nathaniel's insistence they continued to call him Willy.

The days dragged by. The shelling continued day and night. Targets were hit and people were killed but the city of Atlanta stood firm.

The telegraphers sat in their small brick building listening to the concussion of the shells and the clattering of the key. The key gave them more to be concerned about than the shelling. It told them that Sherman was extending his tentacles south of the city, seeking to break the rail line even as he bombarded the city.

Then, astonishingly, the shelling stopped. Atlantans walked the streets greeting each other and surveying the damage. Everyone shook their heads at the ruined buildings but smiled because they had after all prevailed. The Yankees, it was soon learned, had given up and headed south of the city. General Hardee had been sent to beat them once and for all.

Five days later a great clamor arose from the south. When it died away the citizens of Atlanta congratulated each other on another magnificent victory. The joy everyone felt was dashed a few hours later, however, when deserters began to straggle into the city. Hardee had been smashed at Jonesboro, they said, they had fled for their lives, and do you have a place to hide? The Union had taken the last rail line in and out of Atlanta, and with it the city's last hope of remaining out of enemy hands.

Nathaniel Curry and Captain Conroy were in the telegraph hut that afternoon when a message arrived by courier from Army headquarters. Conroy read it and handed it to Nathaniel. It was addressed to General Lee and it proclaimed General Hood's intention to evacuate the city and link up with Hardee.

"My God," Nathaniel muttered. "It's really all over."

"I wonder if we should even send this," Conroy said.

"Why shouldn't we?"

"Well, if Jonesboro is in Sherman's hands, he's broken the last telegraph line to the rest of the Confederacy. The only person who will get this message is Sherman."

"Oh, yeah, I suppose so. But do you really want to take the responsibility for not sending this? After all, Hood must know the line has been broken."

"That's true enough, I suppose."

"And the message might be intended for Sherman. It might be misdirection."

"You're right there, too."

"Here's something else, and you did not hear this from me: we have plenty of people in Sherman's army."

"What do you mean? Oh!"

"Any message that gets into his hand will be on President Davis' desk before it reaches Lincoln's."

Conroy smiled. "Well, send it along, then."

Nathaniel leaned forward and took the key. He smiled. "I feel like I should put 'To General Sherman' in the header."

When he had finished, Conroy said, "I'm ordering all the operators out of the city."

"You are? Are you leaving too, sir?"

"No. There will be a small Army staff left behind, I'm sure, and they'll need an operator."

"Might they need two, sir?"

Conroy smiled. "I could not ask you to stay, Jones, but your help would be appreciated, I'm sure."

Conroy went to the bombproof and mustered the telegraphers. They fell into a ragged line in front of the dugout. "You are all released, boys," he said. "The Army is leaving and the city will be taken by the Yankees." There was a defiant murmur from the men, although all had been expecting this. "I'm ordering all of you to leave with the Army. You can see if they need operators or you can fall into the ranks."

"That's too bad," Margate spoke up. "That's a damned shame."

"I suppose so, soldier," Nathaniel replied. "But it has a bright side."

"And what's that?"

"Well, Sherman will get the city, but he was likely to, anyway. And this way the city won't be destroyed."

"That's a Hell of a bright side, soldier. For my part I'd rather see it destroyed than to end up in enemy hands."

Nathaniel sighed. "I suppose you're right."

As the men gathered their kits, Nathaniel told Conroy, "I'm going to go down to headquarters."

"Change your mind?"

"No. You got me thinking about misdirection. I'm going to see if Hood is really pulling out."

"Oh. Good idea."

Hood was indeed quitting the city. His army, long idle, marched out just before sunset, followed by the Georgia Militia and Stewart's Corps.

The marching men looked sadly around the empty and darkening streets. One man started singing in a clear tenor voice and the whole army joined in:

> *The years creep slowly by, Lorena,*
> *The snow is on the grass again,*
> *The sun's low down the sky, Lorena,*
> *The frost gleams where the flow'rs have been.*
> *But the heart throbs on as warmly now,*
> *As when the summer days were nigh;*
> *Oh! The sun can never dip so low,*
> *Adown affection's cloudless sky.*
> *The sun can never dip so low,*
> *Adown affection's cloudless sky.*

Nathaniel had heard the song many times, but for the first time the lyrics truly made sense. It was as if the marching army was speaking directly to him, communicating the sense of loss every man felt, asking if he felt it as well. No song had ever done this to him before.

> *A hundred months have pass'd, Lorena,*
> *Since last I held that hand in mine,*
> *And felt the pulse beat fast, Lorena,*

Tho' mine beat faster far than thine.
A hundred months, 'twas flow'ry May,
When up the hilly slope we climbed,
To watch the dying of the day,
And hear the distant churchbells chimed.
To watch the dying of the day,
And hear the distant churchbells chimed.

A hundred months? About eight years. In eight years it would be 1872 and he would be twenty-six years old. Would he even be alive then? And would the pain get easier to bear or would he be like the man in the song?

We loved each other then, Lorena,
More than we ever dared to tell;
And what we might have been, Lorena,
Had but our lovings prosper'd well
But then, 'tis past, the years are gone,
I'll not call up their shadowy forms;
I'll say to them, "lost years, sleep on!
Sleep on! Nor heed life's pelting storm."
I'll say to them, "lost years, sleep on!
Sleep on! Nor heed life's pelting storm."

He watched the Confederacy leave its greatest city, then returned to his post. He and Conroy manned the telegraph together the rest of the evening. The key was silent; they talked much.

Talking to Conroy was frustrating. He wanted to open his heart to him but could not. He continually found himself talking about experiences he had had, things he had done, only to find himself brought up short, unable to continue. He was, after all, his best friend's enemy, and he could not reveal this to Conroy without immediately killing him.

Conroy seemed to accept that there was much in Nathaniel's past that he could not discuss and never pressed him.

One evening they shared a watch and a flask of whiskey. Conroy asked, "Have you ever seen anything that seemed divine? Any sort of godly intervention or the like?"

"No. What do you mean?"

"Oh, I've heard tales of men saying that they saw angels minister to the fallen. Another man swore that at sunset after a battle he saw the souls of men mounting to the sky."

"You know, I think that if I ever saw that, it would be time to give it up."

"I know what you mean."

Nathaniel thought about it. "I did see something that was mighty peculiar. I never knew how to explain it."

"Oh? Do tell."

"You're going to think I'm cracked for saying this."

"Well, let's hear it."

"All right. I was with Jubal Early and we were attacking Washington. We were at Fort Stevens. That's where I got hit."

"All right, I know about Fort Stevens, and that was a damned shame you got so close to catching that monkey and he got away."

"Yes. Now, as time goes by I recollect it better and better. I got hit in the head with something and it mixed me up for a long time. At first I couldn't even remember that day. Little by little I remember the day and everything that led up to me being hit. I don't remember being hit, but I remember something that happened right after that. It was passing strange."

"And what was that?"

"Well, there was an old colored boy I knew back in Virginia, name of Sammy. Uncle Sammy. We took a shine to each other. Now, we got split up and I never did find out what happened to him. He might have been sold off or gone down the river or died, I don't know."

"Yeah?"

"But after I got hit I saw him there. I was just lying there half dead and next thing I knew he was standing over me. He told me, 'Boy, you gots to get up, them Yankees will kill you, and if'n they don't, the Rebels will.' Well, I thought he was dead and so was I, so I figured I didn't need to get up at all. Because everything was funny and I didn't hurt at all.

"Well, old Sammy kept on a-yelling at me to get up, waving his hat around the way an old nigger will. And finally I could see he was right, because I commenced to hurting about as bad as you can hurt, and I could hear the shooting again. And I got up and got out of the line of fire. It was just into a gully, but it was isolated against anything but a direct hit with a shell. And then everything was black again for a real long time. And by the time I come to and knew who I was and what I was about, Sammy was gone."

"Do tell."

"And I never could figure out if that was all real or not."

"You mean maybe it really happened and maybe you dreamed it?"

"Yes."

"Well, any army has niggers traveling with it."

"Yes, but if he was with Early I should have seen him before that."

"Not if you were in the ranks and he was with the niggers."

"Well, yeah."

"And maybe he was with the Yankee army."

"What, out doing fetch-and-carry on the battlefield?"

"Sure. The Yanks use niggers in the army, same as us. The Yankees use 'em as soldiers. Hell, we're going to have to start signing 'em up and swearing 'em in pretty soon."

"Could be. But the Yankees have enough soldiers they shouldn't have to use a broken-down old black man like that."

"I suppose not. Well, it may have been some sort of dream. Or it may have been something else."

"Something else?"

"Yes." Conroy paused, then continued in a low voice: "I've heard tell that sometimes when someone gets a good bang to the head, it's like the soul leaves the body for a little while. It gets freed of its earthly bonds and it can go places and see things that it can't in life. Maybe that's what happened to you."

"You reckon?"

"And people see folks that have passed on, and sometimes they say, 'Go back, it ain't your time yet.' Maybe this is what happened to you."

"Oh, Lord."

Conroy sat back. "Or maybe your head just got addled. I don't know."

"Huh."

"So what transpired after that?"

Nathaniel hesitated. "I better not say."

Conroy graciously changed the subject: "You have a sweetheart, Willy?"

"Yes, well, I do after a fashion. We're sort of on the outs right now."

"Oh? Problems between you?"

"You might say."

"Is it anything you care to talk about?"

"Not really. I don't understand it too well myself."

"They're a mystery, aren't they?"

"Women? Yes."

"I don't think any man has ever really understood women."

"I reckon you're right. I sure don't."

"But you know, I suspect they don't want us to understand them."

Nathaniel smiled. "Yes, I think so, too. And if we ever did figure them out, they'd change so we didn't understand them again."

"Do you figure they're like that on purpose, so that we can't understand them, or is it just their nature?"

"I figure it's just their nature, because I suspect women understand each other. It's like we men are missing something essential in our natures that would let us figure them out. The way that dogs and horses can't understand us when we talk."

Conroy sighed. "I guess you're right. But you know, for all that, they sure are interesting."

Nathaniel smiled. "They sure enough are."

Conroy filled their cups. "You ever hear tell of Charles Darwin?"

"Sure. I've read his book."

"Well, I read a book *about* his book. It makes a lot of sense to me. What I was getting to is, I suspect women are more evolved than we are."

"I suspect they are. So you hold with the theory of evolution?"

"With one exception: I may be descended from an ape, and you may be descended from an ape, but Robert E. Lee is not descended from an ape."

Nathaniel raised his cup, Conroy clinked it and they drank.

At about eleven o'clock a message came in for General Hood. It was from General Hardee and it inquired as to Hood's intentions. The two operators looked at each other. "What are we supposed to do with this, sir?"

"Well," Conroy said, "I don't suppose we can just ignore it."

"Hood must be having trouble getting south," Nathaniel said. "He should have linked up with Hardee by now."

"I don't even see how Hardee could have sent it if Jonesboro is in Sherman's hands."

"I don't know either, sir, but it's sure enough possible. I'm talking from experience here."

"Well, let me ask you, Will. What do you think we should do with this?"

Nathaniel took the message from Conroy's hand. "I'll run down to headquarters and see if anyone's still there. They may have a courier or something. But I suspect this is a fool's errand."

There were exactly two soldiers left at headquarters: a colonel who looked older and more befuddled than Winfield Scott and a fat sergeant whose hairless head made him look like an evil baby. The sergeant looked at the message and in an evil baby voice asked, "What do you want me to do with this?"

"Sergeant, I have no idea. Do you expect a courier from the general?"

"No. Well, let me see. There are a few cavalrymen left out at the rolling mill. You might get one of them to carry this."

"Out by Oakland Cemetery?"

"Yes."

"What are they doing out there?"

"How the Hell should I know?" The sergeant handed the message back. "You got a horse?"

"Do I *look* like I got a horse?"

"No."

He hitched a thumb over his shoulder. "You can jump on the colonel's back here if you have a hankering."

The colonel leaned forward. "What?"

"Nothing, sir."

"Oh. All right."

It was a moonless night and the city was dark. Nathaniel headed north until he found the tracks of the Georgia Railroad, then turned east. After half an hour he could see the smokestacks of the rolling mill ahead of him.

He heard the hoofbeats of galloping horses coming from the direction of the mill. The riders were going down Decatur Street, which ran parallel to the tracks. He ran across to the street. Six men were hightailing it down the road. He called for them to stop but they drove right past him.

Nathaniel went down Decatur to the mill. At first he saw no sign of life. Then he spotted a flickering light from the direction of the railroad tracks.

Whatever the light was, it was not a torch. He put on his glasses. He could dimly make out a line of boxcars before him. The light was on the other side of the cars.

He went to the end of the line of cars. There were two lines, actually, two sets of cars on the parallel tracks, something like eighty in all.

There were five steam engines backed up to the cars, all throwing off heat. He went around in front of the engines and saw that the last boxcar in the line was on fire. Flames were licking up the back end of it.

So that's what those men were doing. That car must contain something of strategic value they didn't want to fall into enemy hands.

But why were these engines backed up to the cars this way? Even if all of these cars burned, that wouldn't destroy the engines, would it?

Another thought occurred to him: why were these cars right in front of the rolling mill? That was also a strategic target, one that Hood would not want to surrender to the Yankees.

The answer came to him in a flash. He turned and ran away from the tracks.

Before him rose the stone spires of the cemetery. He ran along the wrought-iron fence until he found a gate and dashed through it.

There was a flash behind him and he glanced over his shoulder just as the blast reached him. He saw half a boxcar spin into the air, spewing flames like a rocket.

Echoes of the blast came back from the surrounding buildings. He ran between the headstones toward a large family crypt formed in the shape of a miniature church.

A much larger flash came from behind him. It lingered and lit the cemetery up like the noonday sun. The crypt had a low fence; he vaulted over it as the blast struck his back.

The flash died away. He saw a flight of steps going down into the crypt. As he went down the steps he looked back at the railroad tracks.

Burning pieces of railroad cars hung in the air. The air itself glowed with burning powder. Cars lay scattered around the tracks like kindling. He saw this for but a second; then there was a brilliant flash, far brighter than the other two. Suddenly blinded, he tumbled down the stone steps and landed on his back.

He remembered what a Pennsylvania soldier had told him once about surviving an explosion in a mine and opened his mouth. The blast hit him like a mule kicking him in the chest. It deafened him and shook the ground. Stones fell from the walls of the crypt.

He could see nothing but a bright purple glow flickering before him. His ears whined but he could still hear pieces of cars landing around him. He crawled back against the gate of the crypt.

Something large struck the ground near him. He shrank against the gate, panting. The air was thick with sulfur.

There were two more large explosions in quick succession. Gravel from the track bed pattered down the steps, followed by a powder keg.

The flickering purple glow before his eyes faded enough for him to see a little. He stepped cautiously back into the land of the living, peering above the steps like a man in a dugout.

"Jesus Christ and Joseph." He could not hear his own voice.

The shattered railroad cars were piled up and burning like logs in a hearth. Explosions continued to rip through the cars; behind them the rolling mill was a sea of flame. It was like any number of battles he had been in except that he was the sole participant.

He came out of the crypt and grasped the bars of the fence. A big piece of metal landed behind him and bounced around the gravestones, making a great clatter. The sky was full of an orange glow interspersed with burning embers. Another keg hit the ground before him and exploded. As he watched, the embers burned out and the glow in the sky faded. The rolling mill would clearly keep burning all night.

He went back to the telegraph hut. "Did you hear those explosions?" Conroy asked as he came in.

"Yes."

"What happened to your hair?"

"My hair? What's the matter with my hair?"

"And your clothes. And your face looks like Jim Crow. Damn it, boy, what have you been up to?"

"I've been out losing a war."

"Did you find a courier?"

"No. Here's General Hood's message back." He went down to the bombproof and went to bed.

The next morning the telegraph line was dead. Nathaniel and Conroy abandoned their post and took a tour of the city. They had become good friends by this time, with little pretension of rank between them.

About noon they returned to the bombproof and Conroy opened a locker that had been concealed beneath the floor. From this he retrieved a suit of civilian clothes, a small pistol and a purse containing twenty gold Napoleons. He divided these coins into two stacks and asked Nathaniel to take one.

"No, thank you, Francis. I have money of my own and it might be impractical to carry more."

"Really?" Conroy said as he pulled off his uniform. "Where do you keep it?"

"In a pouch under my pants."

"Oh, I have a pouch like that, but I keep jewels in it, not gold."

Nathaniel nodded; he did not get the joke until several hours later. "What are you going to do now, sir?"

"Well, first off, you can stop calling me 'sir.' For the moment I'm a civilian again. I may just stay that way, too; the war is pretty much over.

"As for my intentions, I'm going to just play this tune by ear for a while. And I'll stay in Atlanta for the moment."

"I'll do that too if'n you don't mind."

"I don't mind in the least, Will."

Nathaniel looked around the bombproof. "Do you suppose it's okay to keep living in this place if we're supposed to be civilians?"

"I don't see why not," Conroy replied. "Civilians are living in every other cellar and hole. And if we're living in a former military facility, well then, we're just beating our swords into plowshares."

The Army had given up its stores to the citizens, who had carried off anything they could find. These same citizens now extended this policy to the rest of the city. They broke into any store they could find and thoroughly looted the place. Men and women, young and old, black and white dug through the remains of these establishments in a savage frenzy. The authorities did nothing to stop them because the authorities did not exist. Although there was a civilian government, enforcement of the law had long been the province of the Confederate Army.

Stragglers from the recent battles filtered into the city, telling tales of woe and looking for food and cellars to hide in. Negroes of unknown origin also came in, reveling in their first taste of freedom and desperate for food of any kind. At last, in the afternoon, came the Union Army, moving quickly to establish control, then to distribute food to the masses.

It was strange to see bluecoats in the city; it was stranger still to see them embraced by the people. Atlantans were nothing, however, if not practical. The Federal government was again in charge, and if the price of cornmeal and sorghum was to watch Old Glory getting hoisted to the top of City Hall, they would pay it.

Sherman entered the city. Nathaniel and Conroy watched from a crowd as he rode by. Bobby was right, Nathaniel decided: Sherman was easily the ugliest man in America. His eyes glowered; his mouth was a bitter gash across his face. He looked more like he had just lost a campaign than won one.

The Union Army moved easily into the role previously occupied by its foe, keeping order in the city. As if by magic the looting stopped. The strange Negroes remained in the city, though they mended their ways. They put away their criminal activities and found gainful employment among the victorious troops.

Now it was Union soldiers that accosted people on the street, demanding to know their identities and their business. Nathaniel stopped showing the letter identifying him as a telegrapher for Longstreet. Instead, he simply played the fool. At some point, of course, he would have to come clean to the Federals. It would not do to tell private soldiers that he was a Union spy, though. None of them would believe it, thinking it was just another civilian trick to curry favor with the city's new rulers.

The Union soldiers accepted that Nathaniel was another ignorant Southerner and let him be.

September drifted into October; October became November. Abraham Lincoln was re-elected to the Presidency with fifty-five percent of the popular vote and a landslide in the Electoral College. The city of Atlanta received this news with a shrug; as far as Atlantans were concerned the war was already lost.

Atlanta itself came back to life. Commerce resumed. There were after all profits to be made under the new regime.

This was not good enough for Sherman, however. He was quite aware that there was more fighting to be done out there and that as soon as he and his army left the city it would return to its previous occupation of providing for the insurrection. Therefore he decided that Atlanta must be evacuated. All citizens were ordered to quit the city. Those of Union sympathies could flee to the North and find succor; those of a secessionist mien were on their own. Additionally, Atlanta was to be stripped of anything of value. The departing citizens could take what they wanted, except for the cotton, which was ill-gotten in the first place and was therefore Government property. As a final indignity, any property within the city that could be of value to the enemy would be burned.

The city did not receive this news quietly. Citizens formed committees that remonstrated with the general, but to no avail.

Sherman prepared to march out of the city, heading toward the southeast. It was assumed that his intention was to catch Hood. Nathaniel and Conroy went down to the rail yards to see him off.

Conroy had expressed skepticism that Sherman really intended to destroy anything within the city. As he put it, "Atlanta is Union property now. The Stars and Stripes flies from City Hall. You don't capture a city intact and then destroy it."

"Maybe he doesn't intend to hold the city."

"Of course he does. He has plenty of men, he can keep a garrison here. Do you suppose he doesn't want it?"

Nathaniel shrugged. "Maybe he doesn't."

As they watched the Federal Grand Army forming up a man lit a torch and walked across the rails to the main buildings of the rail yard. This was too much for Conroy, who ran after the man with Nathaniel hot on his heels.

"Stop! Stop!" the lieutenant cried, and the soldier indeed halted, puzzled by the two men in civilian clothes who approached him. He stood with the torch dripping pine tar onto the ground.

"Don't fire those buildings, soldier," Conroy panted.

"Who the Hell are you?" the soldier demanded.

"I'm a citizen and a native of this city and I can't let you destroy this place."

Nathaniel turned. Several mounted officers were picking their way across the tracks with a dozen infantrymen behind them. When they were still twenty yards away, the ranking man called out, "What's going on here?"

"Colonel," Conroy said, "in God's name, tell this man not to fire those buildings."

"On what authority? General Sherman says they should be burned."

Conroy waved his arm. "There are other buildings right beside these," he said. "If these burn, the others will catch as well."

"That's no concern of mine, mister, nor of yours. Say, who are you, anyway?"

"I'm a citizen of the city."

"You look like a military man."

Conroy made no reply to this and the colonel ordered the soldiers to search him. They quickly found his pistol and the purse of gold coins. They found nothing else, but these few items drew attention.

"Out with it!" the colonel demanded. "Are you a soldier or what?"

Conroy came to attention and said, "Sir! I am First Lieutenant Francis Leonardo Conroy of the Georgia State Militia."

"You're out of uniform, lieutenant. And you should have declared yourself when we took the city. You must know that orders were posted to do so. An enlisted man I could let this go, but I'll have to treat you as a spy. Who is this other man?"

"He's a civilian telegraph operator, sir."

"Hmph! Well, we'll hold him until we get this sorted out. As for you, we can't take you and we can't leave you behind. I never had much truck with spies in any case. Take him in hand, boys. We'll find a brick wall on the way."

The soldiers grabbed Conroy roughly and started to haul him off when Nathaniel cried, "Wait! He's no spy. I am!"

This startled everyone. Conroy and his captors turned to look at him. "What?" someone said.

"I'm a Union agent. I can tell you that this man is no danger and you should let him go."

"Young man," the colonel said, "it's very noble of you to want to protect a friend in this manner, but—"

"Sir, I'm a Union agent and I can prove it. You can wire Colonel Sharpe at the War Office to confirm it."

The colonel made a dismissive gesture and started to turn away when he saw Sherman riding up. "What's the delay, colonel?"

"Sir, one or the other of these men is an agent, and we can't tell who or what side."

"Well, time's a-wasting. Take them both in hand and we'll sort it out on the road. As for you," he said, indicating the man with the torch, "get to work."

Nathaniel didn't want to have his hands bound again but there was no way out of it. Fortunately, he was becoming a minor expert on the subject. He crossed his wrists before him as a soldier approached, not giving the man time to wonder if his hands should be behind him, then clenched his fists hard. The soldier tied the rope as tight as he could, using a knot unlike any known to Man. Nathaniel relaxed and the rope loosened. He would have to inspect the knot better later, but he might be able to do something with it.

This same soldier searched him, doing a particularly poor job of it. He relieved Nathaniel of the twelve dollars in Confederate money in his pocket, and welcome to it, but found nothing else.

Conroy was also bound. No sooner was this done when both saw a most unusual sight. The Union Army's entire stores, loaded into several score wagons, were marshaled together in the center of the rail yard and put to the torch. Only the ammunition wagons were spared; everything else, including foodstuffs, was burned. The horses were shot.

As the flames rose, soldiers tore rails from the tracks and threw them into the fire. When they were good and hot, the rails were pulled out and twisted into arcane shapes. The men who did this spoke not a word; they clearly had a lot of practice at it.

Sherman came forward and commanded that a line be run from a nearby telegraph pole. An operator established a link with Union forces and nodded to the general. Sherman then dictated a message to the effect that he was departing Atlanta for Savannah as planned. As the operator was tapping this message out soldiers wrapped several rails around the telegraph pole. The operator received an acknowledgement for his message and removed the key, leaving the wire to spark against the twisted rails.

Nathaniel and Conroy turned from this odd ceremony and watched the flames of the rail yard buildings rising. "There's no way on God's green earth that that won't spread," Conroy muttered.

"It doesn't matter a great deal," Nathaniel replied. "Look."

Conroy looked. They were standing in a large open area and could see much of the city to their west. At a half dozen places slender columns of smoke were rising. They saw this for only a second; then, prompted by a pair of bayonets, they turned and began walking out of the city.

After two hours of walking their guards had become bored with them and shouldered their weapons. They began speaking, keeping their voices low.

"Can you smell it?" Conroy asked.

"The smoke? Yeah."

Nathaniel looked over his shoulder. "Look behind you," he said.

The remark was meant for Conroy but their two guards looked over their shoulders as well. All four stopped and turned around.

It was still an hour until sunset and the sky was very bright to the west. A cover of clouds hung above the city at eight thousand feet and reflected the orange light of the sun off its lower surface.

A column of smoke five miles wide rose straight to that cloud ceiling. The sun itself was blocked from their view by that wall of smoke. Looking carefully, Nathaniel could see that the column of smoke had punched a hole in the cloud cover as it drove through it.

A line of trees blocked their view of the city itself. They could see no flames, no images of destruction, just that black curtain of smoke.

It looked so simple, so benign. From where they stood it was merely a rectangle of black. It seemed paradoxical that it embodied the destruction of an entire city.

The four men turned and resumed their march. "My God," Conroy muttered.

"Nothing we can do about it, Francis."

"It's still a damned shame."

"You were crazy to try to stop it."

"Maybe so, but I had to try. I couldn't have lived with myself if I had done nothing."

"Uh-huh."

Conroy looked at him. "Willy, it was good of you to speak up like that. It probably saved my life."

"Well, I hope so. It may have just cost me my own."

A minute later Conroy said, "Have you seen how this army is marching? It's most peculiar."

"What do you mean?"

"Well, they're spread out along a wide front. It looks to be a couple of miles wide, and that's just what I can see."

Nathaniel glanced to his left and right. "Yes, I can see that."

"Why do you suppose they're doing it?"

"Well, here's a better question: what do they plan to live on? They're going to be hungrier than General Lee's men in a few days."

"You think they intend to forage? That's why they're spread out so?"

"I reckon so. Reckon they'll take what they can and destroy the rest."

"Yes, I reckon so. It's monstrous cruel."

A few minutes later Conroy said, "You really think they're fixing to shoot the both of us as spies?"

"Well, they haven't yet, but they might. It depends."

"Depends on what?"

"Depends on if I manage to convince them that I'm really a Yankee agent."

"Well, do your best, boy."

The army halted for the evening and prepared to bivouac. Foragers who had set out that morning on foot now returned mounted or driving every sort of conveyance. They led other horses, plus cattle and anything else that would come along. The wagons were piled with freshly-slaughtered hogs, calves and chickens and freshly-stolen cookware.

Every officer now had a mount and a spare in tow. Every wounded man could now ride. Sherman did not wish, however, that his infantry should spontaneously become a cavalry, so the camp rang with gunfire as the extra horses and mules were put down.

Then the feast began. All the food animals were slaughtered and the soldiers picked what they wanted for their meal. Wagons were broken up and burned. The men laughed as they took their ease and passed around tobacco and whiskey.

Nathaniel and Conroy stood in silence, waiting for the soldiers to eat before begging their own meals. Around them black plumes of smoke rose into the darkening sky. The nearer ones were cook-fires; the farther ones were farms.

The colonel who had arrested them rode up with another soldier who turned out to be Nathaniel's contact, Bobby. Bobby now wore blue and had been promoted from private to captain. "Yes," he said, "that's the man. How'd you do, Nathaniel."

"How'd you do yourself. Good evening, sir." Both men dismounted.

"Good evening, Curry," the colonel said. "We've received good reports on your service."

"You have, sir? Did you get through to Colonel Sharpe?"

"No, we're out of telegraphic communication with anyone, will be for some time."

"Oh." Nathaniel had become so used to the telegraph that it felt odd to be cut off from communication this way. "I thought what I did was nothing special."

"Oh, quite the contrary. Soldier, release this man and see he gets something to eat." One of his guards came up, pointed his musket at him and cut his bonds with his bayonet.

"Wait a minute," Conroy said. "Do you mean to tell me you really *are* a Yankee spy?"

"Yes," Nathaniel said. "I told you that."

"God damn you! I thought you were just shitting them. You son of a bitch turncoat! I could kill you where you stand!"

"Well, we mustn't have that," the colonel said genially. He stepped forward and shot Conroy in the forehead with his pistol. Conroy fell onto his back and did a little dance.

Nathaniel gasped. "Couldn't you have just kept him prisoner, sir?"

The colonel shook his head. He and Bobby rode away, leaving the soldiers who had been cooking behind Conroy to complain about their ruined meal.

Nathaniel had never dug a grave before. The folding shovel he borrowed from a Massachusetts boy was too small for the task and the soil was rocky. It was also very vexing to dig in the dark. He could see that he would never produce a hole that was six feet long, six feet deep and three feet wide. He ended up scooping out an area of earth a little larger than the victim himself and barely two feet deep.

By the time he had finished Conroy had stiffened into an awkward position. He wore a startled expression, his eyes and mouth wide open, his bound hands open before him. As Nathaniel dragged him into his grave he rolled over, exposing the back of his head. Wendell Smith used to say that human beings died like grass and Nathaniel had once observed men dying like corn. Francis Conroy had died like a melon. The back of his head looked like a honeydew melon that had been smashed with a hammer.

Conroy still had gold coins in his pocket. Nathaniel didn't want them.

It felt strange to shovel dirt onto his face, to see it fall over his unblinking eyes and into his mouth. He piled the dirt on him first, then stacked the stones on top of that. It didn't look like a regular grave, it looked sort of pagan.

He stood over the grave with his hands clasped but no prayer came to him. He tried to feel sad but no sadness came.

Three Confederate soldiers now knew his secret, but two of them were dead.

If he had spoken more quickly to that colonel he might have let Conroy go. He and Conroy had been friends, although he himself was something of a false friend. Shouldn't he feel bad about killing a friend?

Colonel Sharpe said that every time he killed a man it felt bad, but it got easier each time. The same thing was happening to him. It was becoming easy to kill.

He was losing his humanity and he knew it. And to what end? Victory? The preservation of the Union? To free the slaves? To please Lincoln?

He said, "The Good Book says, 'What profiteth it a man if he gains the world but loses his soul?'" He returned the shovel, washed his hands and bummed some fried chicken from some soldiers.

Nathaniel awoke to the strains of Reveille. He had spent a restless night lying on a goosedown tick with another atop him, an eider pillow beneath his uneasy head. The soldiers were happy to share breakfast with him and he had his fill of bacon, eggs, sweet potatoes and cup after cup of real coffee. As he ate, foragers set out on another day of pillage.

Nathaniel searched the camp for Bobby or the colonel but found neither. It appeared that he was being left to his own devices. The army had by this time broken camp and he was left to follow in its wake.

The camp was a mess. Abandoned army camps were seldom a tidy scene, but this one looked like an enormous garbage dump. Crows were already busy with the dead animals. He made up a bedroll from some abandoned blankets and packed some food into a kit bag. On impulse he searched for a pistol and found a nice one within five minutes. He hid it beneath his shirt and headed south.

He came to the remains of a farm. All of the buildings had been burned to the ground and the crops trampled. Hogs lay dead in their pen and a dog lay in its own blood beside what had been the front door of the house.

A man and woman in late middle age were poking through what was left of the house with sticks. They looked up sharply as he approached. "There's nothing left here," the man said, waving him away. "Y'all took it all yesterday."

"I don't want to take anything."

"What do you want, then?"

"I just wanted to see. What happened?"

The man sat heavily on the ground. "They took it all. They went through the house and barn and took everything." He looked at Nathaniel. "They stole our Bible. Can you imagine what the world has come to when they steal your family Bible?"

"I can't see that. Stealing a Bible? It ain't right."

"That had my family's names in it back four generations. The End of Time better come soon, because I –" He broke off and began sobbing like a child.

"Come on, old man," his wife said. "You'll accomplish nothing like that."

"They didn't harm you, though?"

"No," the man said. "They even tried to sound kind, saying they was sorry but they was under orders. I was in the army, too, in Mexico, but I never did nothing like this." He looked around. "I can't start over. I'm too old to start over."

"We started with less, Levi," the woman said. "And while you're alive you're not too old." She plucked a teacup with a broken handle from the ashes.

The road crossed a small stream a mile farther down the road. The stone bridge must have been constructed in colonial times but it was broken now. A mile beyond the bridge there was a rail depot. Every building had been burned and the track torn up and wrapped around trees.

A colored family huddled under a tree. The man tottered toward him. "Master," he said, "do you have any food?"

Nathaniel shook his head and kept walking. The man stood despondently with his hand out until he had passed. Nathaniel thought, Why are you so sad? You're free now.

Acting on impulse, Nathaniel turned north. He was now cutting across the swath made by the army. He walked the whole day that way, curious to see how wide the path of destruction was.

It appeared to be endless. Every farm he saw was burned out, every town had been pillaged and torched, every steel rail had been torn up. He estimated that he walked fifteen miles that day and did not come to the edge of Sherman's path.

The next day he did. He found a village that was still standing. Its citizens were in the street, guarding their community with shotguns and pitchforks. He raised his hands to show that he was unarmed.

This was not good enough for the townsfolk. "Keep moving, boy," a man told him. "There's nothing for you here."

"All right."

A woman asked, "Are you with the Union army?"

"Not hardly. I just want to get out of their way."

"Well, you can pass through," the man said. "You ain't no Yankee?"

"No, I'm a Virginia boy." These people had never heard a Yankee speak.

"How come you ain't in the Army?"

"I was," he said. "We been licked." He could feel their eyes on his back as he walked out of town.

He came to an abandoned rail depot. There was a telegraph station there but no key or battery. He set his own key up but the line was dead.

He followed the tracks north. In the afternoon he came to another depot. An old man in a stationmaster's uniform looked up as he came in.

"Are the trains still running?"

"Depends," the man said. "Who are you?"

"I just want to get home to Virginia."

"Deserter, are you?"

He had no answer to this.

"Well, can't say as I blame you. I reckon the Yanks licked us fair and square."

"When's the next train north?"

"Hard to say. One is due in but it's over a day late. And it goes east, toward Charleston, but you can get connections north."

"Did you wire them to see what the delay is?"

"Can't."

"Oh, the line down?"

"No. All the telegraph operators have gone to the Army. I don't know if the line is good or not."

"Mind if I take a crack at it?"

"What do you mean, use the telegraph?"

"Yes."

The old man looked puzzled. "There ain't no key."

"I have one of my own."

"You do?" His voice went up a full octave. "Well, the line's out here."

The stationmaster led him to the telegraph office, which was right off of his own. Nathaniel found a dry battery and a small bottle of vitriol. Within a few minutes he had set up his key and had a good spark up.

He sent out a CQ message and got responses from operators as far away as North Carolina. He talked back and forth with them for twenty minutes, then signed off.

As he stood up the stationmaster asked, "What did they have to say?"

"Well, nothing has been heard from the operators in Atlanta since Sherman pulled out. Some refugees have shown up north of here who say the place was leveled to the ground. Nothing is left there now and if they rebuild it they'll have to start over someplace else.

"Sherman's army is moving to the southeast. I think they're heading for Savannah and they'll do the same thing to that place.

"There are no Yankees north of here, but there aren't any Confederate troops either. The Carolinas are up for grabs.

"Richmond and Petersburg are besieged but are holding on by the skin of their teeth. They still have telegraph contact with the rest of the Confederacy and are getting trains in and out, but it's only a matter of time."

"And the train will be in by tomorrow."

The stationmaster's mouth worked beneath his gray mustache. "And what about south of here?" he asked at last.

"South of here? There ain't nothing. I seen it. It's all burned out."

"You seen it? You been through it?"

"Yes. There's a swath about fifty miles wide with nothing in it. No one's eating but the carrion-fowl, and soon they'll have nothing."

"Are they coming here next?"

"No. They've passed by. You'll be left alone here, I think."

"How did you come out of it so well?"

He shrugged. "I been careful." He pulled out a gold dollar. "Can I get a ticket with this? Maybe a meal as well?"

He was directed to a roadhouse where he had a stew of some small mammal. It was purported to be rabbit; he doubted it but he didn't want to consider the alternatives.

About nine o'clock that evening an engine drawing a carriage and two boxcars pulled in to the station. Some sorghum and cornmeal were loaded into one of the cars, a single passenger boarded and the train went back east.

Although Nathaniel never knew it, he became a subject of legend in the community. Over the years the story grew of the mysterious young stranger who appeared unscathed from Sherman's ruin, laden with gold and bearing baleful tales of destruction. The visitor re-established telegraphic contact with the outside world and warned it of the town's hunger, saving it from annihilation. He spake words of wisdom, predicting that the town and the South would rise again, then vanished as suddenly as he had come. By the dawn of the Twentieth Century the legend had it that he had convinced Sherman, through suasion or subterfuge, to spare the town from being sacked and burned. By the dawn of the Twenty-First he had been forgotten.

The next afternoon Nathaniel was several hundred miles away. He was traveling north of Sherman's army and roughly parallel to it. He had not really worked out where he was going or what he would do; he knew only that he was finished with the war. Thousands of Confederate soldiers had abandoned the Cause and were scratching out a living on its leavings; he could do the same. He was in fact deserting the winning side, but the approaching victory held no appeal for him.

Was he a deserter, a coward? He didn't know or really even care. He was sick of struggling, sick of killing, sick of facing his own death. He had done his fair share and more. He would be quite content to sit in a room and do nothing until the whole wretched affair was over.

It felt like a great burden had been lifted from him. He felt relaxed and at peace as he had not in years. He curled up in the wooden seat and took a nap.

He was asleep when the car he was riding derailed. He awoke to a great rumbling and shaking as the rear wheels left the rails and bounced along on the ties. He and the six other passengers held on as best they could.

The engineer threw the brake, sending the two boxcars and the caboose forward and throwing the carriage and the car behind it entirely off the track. The two cars folded up like a jackknife.

The experience was quite beyond anything Nathaniel had ever experienced. Of all the ways to die he had seen in the past three years none resembled a train wreck. That speed itself could be lethal was a new experience for him.

The carriage, turned nearly perpendicular to the track, slid sideways across the ground until the whole train ground to a stop. Without a word everyone exited the train and looked things over. The carriage and the boxcar had been knocked off of their trucks but were otherwise in decent shape. The ends of the two cars had dug a deep furrow in the ground, knocking down small trees that had sprung up beside the track.

The engineer took the corncob pipe from between his teeth and grinned. Several teeth were gold and several were gone. "Y'all all right?" he asked. "Still gotcher balls on?"

Everyone was shaken but uninjured, except for a man with a sore elbow. Someone asked, "Did Sherman's cavalry tear up the tracks?"

"No, the track was just bad. I knew it was kind of poorly so I was only doing about forty per when I hit it."

"What's 'forty per'?"

"Forty miles per hour."

"Oh!"

"Oh my."

"It felt like a hundred."

"Well, a hundred would have been a lot worse, I'm here to tell you."

"What will we do now? Wait for a new train?"

"I wouldn't recommend it. It might be quite a spell before another train comes down this way. Y'all are going to have to ride in the tender."

"Aren't you going to try to put the cars back on the track?" another man asked.

"With what? I ain't Samson. They'll have to send fellows with jacks and teams to do that. We'll just have to leave them for now."

"I don't want to ride on coal," someone else averred.

"This-yere train burns wood. You can ride on that or you can walk."

They rode in the tender. It was less than half full so there was plenty of room. Everyone arranged himself atop the split logs as well as he could. It was a very warm day and they were glad when the train started moving again.

Riding in the open tender felt kind of like flying. Nathaniel looked up. There were thickening cumulonimbus at about three thousand feet. He hoped it wouldn't rain.

"Well, this isn't doing my elbow any good."

Nathaniel nodded politely and looked away.

"I paid good money for a train ticket. Not for this."

No reply.

"I hope there's someone at the other end who can reimburse me. I'm getting splinters in me and look here, these pants are ruined."

Nathaniel of course agreed that the man had suffered as none other had ever suffered but he confined his reply to a nod.

"This isn't fair, and this isn't doing my elbow any good."

"Yes, sir. Excuse me."

He stepped across into the cab. "Anything I can do to help you?"

The engineer cocked an eyebrow. "Know how to fetch wood?"

"You need some now?"

"Well, throw a couple pieces in. I'll let you know when I need more."

Nathaniel complied.

"Interested in trains, are you?"

"Well, I reckon. I reckon most young fellows are."

"I saw you looking at the gauges."

"Which one is the pressure gauge?"

"Well, both are. One's boiler pressure, one's jacket pressure."

"Oh."

"There's a difference, but it's hard to explain. If you did this for long you'd understand, but you couldn't get it from outside. You probably think that's crap, don't you?"

"No, I've seen things you have to get into to understand. You done this a long time?"

"I was about your age when I started."

"You like it?"

He shrugged. "Reckon. It was really exciting when I started doing it."

"Was it the traveling around or the working the engine that you liked?"

"Neither, really. It was what it did to me. It made me different than other folks."

He fiddled with the valves for a minute, apparently adding water to the boiler.

"We'd pull into a town and I'd see the same people I'd seen the last time, and I could see most folks are born in a town and never leave. Die there."

"Oh."

"And I was out and all over the place. I wasn't stuck farming the same patch of dirt all my life."

"Okay."

"Also ..." His gaze drifted off across the fields. "Well, you look at a hill or something, it just sits there, and you can wonder what's over it and never know. But I could make the hills change. I went over that horizon." He looked at the horizon and Nathaniel had a glimpse of that young man of years ago.

"You still feel that way?"

"Not so much, or else I'm just used to it. Well, let's see. Throw a couple more sticks in there."

The old man raked the fire around, closed the door and said, "When I started, the train was the new thing. It was going to change everything, and it sure enough did. But it's not new anymore. I think the next new thing is going to be the sky."

"The sky!"

"I read a story by Edgar Allan Poe set in the future where some fellows were traveling in a balloon. One of them was complaining that they were only going a hundred miles an hour. Now, I've done well over a hundred. It's fun but it isn't really pretty. I always expect the train to jump the track. And it's even done it a few times." He glanced at the track behind them and grinned.

"But what if you could go around like this with no track? There'd be nothing to jump."

"Yes, sir."

"And as for watching these hills change? That's still good, but all we're really doing is crawling around on top of them. Imagine watching the hills roll under you."

Nathaniel opened his mouth, then closed it.

"Want to drive for a while?"

"I sure would."

"Okay, this here's the throttle. When we go up a hill push it forward a little. Pull it back when we're going down. Keep the speed steady."

"So did you ever even have a home?" Nathaniel asked a few minutes later.

"Sure. I had three of them." He gave a conspiratorial grin.

"What do you mean, three wives? Three families?"

"I ain't proud, but yeah."

"All at the same time?"

"Well, that's why I'm going to Hell when I'm through doing this."

"You better hope they never get together."

Two colored boys stood beside the track. The taller one pumped his hand in the air and the driver blew the whistle. "The women are all dead now. Kids are scattered."

"Oh. Sorry."

He put the throttle forward as they started up a mountain.

The driver glanced forward, then toward the western horizon. "Sometimes I'll come into a town and find myself looking at a young woman, seeing if I recognize the face. Or if I get a new fireman I'll look at his eyes."

"Aren't firemen usually colored?"

"Well, he would be."

The sky was solid overcast now. Nathaniel looked up the hill. About a mile ahead the track ran up to that overcast and disappeared. "We're going into the ceiling," he said.

"The what?" The engineer looked forward. "Well, that's a clever name for it."

"Well, that's just what they call it," Nathaniel muttered.

"Who calls it that?"

He shrugged. "Some people."

"Hmph! Reckon there's more to some folks than meets the eye." He grabbed the vertical bar at the back of the cab and swung out onto the outside. Nathaniel watched him make his way like a fat old monkey to the front of the engine. Just as they entered the swirling fog the yellow glow of the headlight shone forth.

The ceiling always looked real flat from down below but up close it was always just fog.

They crested the hill and ten minutes later went back through the ceiling. The track leveled out and they were in farm country again. A little while later someone in the tender called out. Nathaniel glanced back and saw him pointing ahead to where plumes of smoke were rising. Half a mile farther the engineer brought the train to a halt. About a quarter of a mile south of the track a farm was burning merrily. The house was fully involved and collapsed in a fountain of sparks as they watched. A barn and several outbuildings were about half burned. The fields were also burning, although not as fiercely. People were milling around in confusion.

"What in tarnation is all of that?" someone asked. There was a puff of smoke followed by the report of a firearm.

"It must be the God-damned Yankees," another man said.

"Either that or it's a slave uprising."

As they watched a figure ran toward the train. It was a woman, they saw; as she got closer they could see that she was black. They got off of the train and went to meet her.

"This has to be Sherman," one of the men said. "He's been killing and raping all through this region."

"How do you know it's not an uprising?"

"Niggers wouldn't burn everything like this. They'd rape the mistress, sure, but after that they'd just want to get away."

"Let's us be on our way."

"No," said the first man, "let's stay awhile."

His firm tone decided the issue though the other man still asked, "What if it is Sherman? What do you intend to do about it? Fight him?"

"I don't know. I fought in Mexico and I thought my fighting days were over. Maybe I was wrong."

The woman was entirely out of breath and fell twice as she covered the last hundred yards. She rose crying, "Masters! Masters!" and waving a hand over her head. Her other hand held a baby to her chest.

"What's the matter, auntie?" someone asked.

The woman was weeping. "They's all a-dying," she sobbed. Two more gunshots came from the direction of the farm.

"Who's dying?"

"They's all a-dying," she repeated.

"Yes, but who? The white folks or the black?"

"All of 'em." The baby lolled limply in her arms as she held it to her face.

"Damn you, nigger! Who's doing the killing?"

The woman cast the baby on the ground before her. Its eyes were vacant and its skin gray; there was a patch of dark blood on its chest. "The master's doing the killing! He killed the missus and his own babies and he set fire to everything."

"What, and everyone just let him?"

"He put us all up in chains, said we was all going down the river. Then he commenced to shooting. He shot his own missus as she was running to him and he shot his babies as they was a-running away into the fields. The niggers he was a-shooting and a-stabbing. I … I got away."

"Girl, I can't believe that. No white man would do that to his own family."

"He kept saying the Yankees was coming and he wouldn't let them take it all. He said he worked all his life for what he had and he wouldn't give it up. He done lost his senses, and Jesus, he killed his own family."

"Jesus Christ Almighty."

"Masters, you gots to stop him. My husband Bill be down there, and my baby."

"That's your baby there on the ground."

She shook her head. "That my grandbaby." She sat heavily on the ground and buried her face in her hands.

The men looked at each other. "Maybe we ought to look into this," Nathaniel said.

"Why? What are we supposed to do?"

Nathaniel shrugged. "Stop him."

"It's the man's farm and the man's niggers. Man can do what he wants with his own property."

"I don't think so," another man said. "I don't hold with just killing niggers like that. They're still human beings."

"No, they're not. They have no more soul than a dog or a horse."

"Well, there's slave cruelty laws, you know."

"To Hell with that! I ain't dying for no stupid cruelty law."

"And if'n he killed his family he should be brought to accounts for it."

"I don't know if I want to face the guns of a madman. It wouldn't bring his babies back in any case."

The other man shook his head. "I couldn't go home and tell my wife I saw this and did nothing." He pulled a pistol from his belt. "You boys coming?"

Nathaniel replied by pulling out his own pistol and every man followed suit. The woman picked up the dead child and led the way.

As they approached the farm another shot rang out. Nathaniel saw the solitary figure fall to the ground. The train passengers came up and looked at the man lying face down with the Navy Colt pistol beside him. He would not be getting up again this side of Kingdom Come.

There was nothing for them to do. About thirty feet away a white woman lay on her side, her skirts spilled up over her. She was not wearing stockings and her legs were shockingly white and beautiful. A boy of about ten lay across his little sister at the edge of the burning field.

Beside the blazing barn a score of Negroes lay chained together like a string of catfish. The colored woman screamed and threw herself upon the corpses.

One of the slaves stirred and Nathaniel went over, ignoring the heat of the fire. The man had been shot twice in the chest and once in the head but still lived. He was old and as wrinkled as a raisin, with a snowy beard. He tried to look around despite the blood running into his eyes.

"You just lie still," Nathaniel said, knowing he could do nothing for him.

"Wh-what?" the man said. He struggled to focus as Nathaniel knelt beside him. Nathaniel pulled a bottle of water from his pocket and held his head up so he could drink.

"Thank you, Master," the man said. "Master, why you do this to old

Caesar?"

"I didn't do this. I'm not your master."

"You not Master?"

"No, I'm not."

"Who you be? You a Yankee?"

Nathaniel didn't know what to say.

"You a Yankee? Yankee soldiers come?"

"Yes. Yankee soldiers come."

"Then … I free."

"Yes. You're free."

The old man smiled and died.

Chapter Eighteen: The Cat in the Window

The day after he arrived in Petersburg Nathaniel met with Colonel Sharpe, with one of Grant's staff officers and with three agents whose names he never learned. The six of them were at different locations around the country and they conferred by telegraph. There was the additional inconvenience that everything had to be encrypted and decrypted, but everyone was patient and saw it through.

The Army telegraph operator at Petersburg knew the keyword, which was "CLINTON." Armed with this Nathaniel was able to encode his own transmissions and decode the responses. The conversation consumed two and a half hours. When it finally came to an end he sat and rubbed his wrists.

The operator sat behind Nathaniel as he worked the key, occasionally helping him out with the ciphers. When everyone eventually sent "73" – the only part of the conversation that was sent in clear – the operator shook his head. "A meeting by wire. I've heard of such things but I've never seen it."

"It sure took a long time for the result."

"Well, yes, but the result is clear. They must think a lot of you in Washington, Curry."

"Not everyone does. Some do, I guess. Tell me, how could I get into the town?"

"Well, that might not be so hard. There are places along the line where our forces are in contact with theirs all the time. They're not just swapping tobacco and coffee, they're taking meals together and playing cards. You could just walk over there."

"Yes, but everyone would look at me as the fellow who came over from the other side. How else could I get in?"

"Well, there's the trains."

"The trains? The Secesh trains from the south?"

"Sure."

"I already done rode them. I came up from the Carolinas that way."

"Yeah? Didn't ride it all the way into Petersburg, though?"

"No, I got off at a whistle-stop about ten miles south and hoofed it."

"Well, we can run you back down there on a mule cart, you can pick them up again. What were those boys saying about 'cover?'"

"That means who the Rebs think I am. The last name I used, anyhow. That's still intact, so I can go back there and be welcome."

"Well, shoot, boy! Reckon you must get to losing track of who you really are sometimes."

"Reckon so. Colonel Sharpe says I should meet with someone in the command structure here before going in to the town."

"Well, I'll talk to Headquarters, see if they want to see you."

The operator raised the installation at City Point, where Grant and the other top officers stayed. The operator at City Point came back ten minutes later to say 2 CURRY TAKE TRAIN TO CITY POINT IN TWO HOURS 44. The "2" designated the message as "very important;" the "44" meant "Answer promptly by wire."

The operator glanced at Nathaniel. The latter reached over and keyed 32, the telegraphic shorthand for "I understand."

While waiting he wandered the fortifications. Petersburg, on the east bank of the Appomattox River, was surrounded on its eastern flanks by a semicircle of Confederate fortifications. These fortifications were of a type known as redans, three-sided structures with an open end facing away from the enemy. The redans were further fortified with sharpened stakes, pits and other obstacles. Though only a few thousand men guarded the city, they easily held tens of thousands at bay.

The city itself was the connection between the existing rail lines and the city of Richmond. Not much was getting into and out of the capitol, but what was making it was allowing the city to survive.

The assault on Petersburg was the brainchild of General U.S. Grant. Stopped at Cold Harbor, at the very gates of Richmond, he divided his army and sent half of it to the south, around the Army of Northern Virginia, with the intention of taking Petersburg. It was a move worthy of the great Robert E. Lee himself. He used it against Lee and he succeeded. But this brilliantly conceived and brilliantly executed plan was undone by a foolish subordinate.

On the night of June 15, 1864, General William Smith broke through a mile-wide section of the redans with a great mass of infantry. Instead of exploiting this breach, as nearly any other commander in history would have done, he stopped, allowing the Confederates under Beauregard to construct a new line of fortifications. Smith could have sent his troops running across the last mile of ground and into Petersburg, destroying the city, strangling Richmond and giving Grant an easy path into the capitol. He did not, however, and the result was a ten-month siege.

Nathaniel had never seen anything like Petersburg. Both sides had dug an intricate network of trenches. Soldiers in both camps waited behind piles of earth or wooden palisades, training their rifles on the opposing trenches. Any head that rose above the level of the trenches was liable to be blown off.

This was in fact an entirely novel form of warfare, one grown out of the accuracy and the rapid rate of fire of the modern firearm. Gone forever was the venerable mode of battle in which lines of brave men would face each other and nobly blast away until one side broke. This new way of fighting was to see its greatest development fifty years later in what was simply known as the Great War.

Within the warrens of the trenches life went on as it always had for the enlisted men. They ate and slept, played cards, read and wrote letters. They talked and laughed, prayed and sang. They did everything except leave their maze of dugouts or expose their head or anything else to the enemy.

At one point in the line, however, this rule was broken. A man had climbed onto the open ground and stood unarmed and in full view of the enemy, inviting a shot. A Negro sat in the trench beneath him, plucking a banjo and keeping a wary eye on the fool. No one bothered to shoot the man, though, and he was still alive when Nathaniel left the vicinity.

The train consisted of an engine, a tender and a single car; the only other passengers were four senior officers. The journey lasted about ten minutes. A private soldier took him in hand as he stepped off the train and led him to a plain log cabin. "Go on in," he mumbled, and departed.

Cautiously, Nathaniel opened the door. He was struck by the odors of whiskey and tobacco. Before him was a wooden structure like a barn door, painted red and supported by four flour barrels. Upon it were stacks of paper, a whiskey bottle and glass, a kerosene lamp and the head of Ulysses Simpson Grant.

Nathaniel cleared his throat. Grant remained insensible. He called the general's name, which produced no response.

He steeled himself, went up to the general and shook him, calling his name. Grant tried to brush him away but Nathaniel persisted.

At last Grant came to his senses. The head rose heavily from the table, a scrap of paper clinging to it, and a throaty voice said, "Yes, soldier, what is it?"

"I don't rightly know, sir. I was told to report to you."

"And who are you?"

"Nathaniel Curry, sir."

Grant's expression passed in an instant from bleary to alert. "Curry. Good. Sit down."

"Thank you, sir."

Grant plucked a telegraph message from the table. "You're ordered into Petersburg to serve as a telegraph operator for the Confederates."

"Yes, sir. I've spoken with Colonel Sharpe. I –"

"I don't take my orders from colonels. President Lincoln orders you in there."

"Lincoln? He's in on this?"

"He was watching over someone's shoulder while you were on the line this morning. He sent me a detailed order. Where have I seen you before?"

"Sir, I was at the White House when you received your appointment."

"You were at Fort Monroe as well. Always in mufti, as I recall."

"Yes, sir."

"Been an agent from the start, have we?"

"No, sir, I was with Professor Lowe's Balloon Corps before that."

"Oh, that. You're much better off as an agent than bobbing around in the air, Curry."

"Yes, sir." Nathaniel knew that upon taking command Grant had approved Meade's order disbanding the Corps.

Grant took a cigar from a barrel the size of a powder keg. His movements were swift and sure. He deftly produced a match and struck it on the sole of his boot. "General Lee is as short of operators as he is of nearly everything else. He should take you to his bosom."

"He already has, sir."

"Beg pardon?"

"Oh, I've met him and worked for him. That could be a problem."

"How so?"

"Well, I told him before that I was a farm boy. He might think it strange if he saw me working a key."

"Many a farm boy is doing things he never anticipated a year ago."

"Yes, sir."

"What's your grade, Curry?"

"I'm a civilian, sir."

"No, I want you in. You're a corporal."

"Yes, sir. Who am I under?"

"My Lieutenant Drummond. Him or me, or Colonel Sharpe. One of us will tell you if there's anyone else."

"Yes, sir."

"Your primary objective is Lee. Find him, let me know where he is and tell me what he's doing."

"Yes, sir."

"Don't kill him. He's the only one who can compel a surrender. But don't let him get away from you either."

"Yes, sir."

"Your secondary objective is to tell me what is going on in Petersburg and Richmond."

"Yes, sir. Are you listening in on his telegraph?"

"We have men on it, yes. Be careful what you say on the line. The Confederates will be listening for just such communications. They're sure to—"

"I've done this before, sir," Nathaniel replied, shocked at himself for interrupting the officer. "I'll seem to be saying nothing, but it will mean something to an outsider. 'I sure am hungry' and the like."

"Good."

"And a man down the line will always ask, 'How are you boys today?' A fellow is likely to let something slip at such a moment."

"That's fine. If you can work your way into their spy operation, all the better. Even give them good intelligence if it helps you."

"Richmond would be dangerous for me, sir. I'm from there and folks know me."

"That's no matter."

"But they know I was in the Balloon Corps."

Grant turned to his papers. "Then let them think you've repented. Now go see Drummond. Dismissed."

He took a step backward, then asked, "Sir, will I have a contact?"

"I imagine so. Keep your eyes open."

Nathaniel hesitated. "Sir," he said, "will you burn Richmond?"

Grant looked up at him. His eyes glowed like blue beacons in the dim light. Nathaniel turned and fled the cabin.

The soldier was waiting outside and brought him to another cabin, where he met Drummond. "Are you all set as far as your orders go, Curry?"

"Yes, sir. I guess so. The truth is, sir, they're kind of sketchy."

"Well, you're going to be on your own for the most part. I'll let you know if someone else is coming in."

Nathaniel nodded. "One thing I could use, sir, would be a telegraph key."

"I'm sure the enemy will provide you one."

"I mean a little one, sir. A lineman's key."

"I don't know what that is but we should be able to find one around here."

"That should be it, then, sir."

"One other thing we should give you, Curry, now that I think about it."

"Yes?"

"You should have a hot meal before you go."

While receiving said hot meal – and a better one than he had had in many a month – Drummond tracked him down with another officer, a second lieutenant, in tow. "No, don't get up, Curry. Nathaniel Curry, this is Lieutenant Manchester. Washington called up and said you should see him.

Do you want some more coffee?" He snapped his fingers at a soldier at the cook-stove and pointed to Nathaniel's cup.

Nathaniel could tell who and what this Lieutenant Manchester was with a single glance. The officer waited until Drummond and the cook had left, then said, "So, you ready for a little vacation, Curry?"

"Is that what this is going to be?"

"Sure enough." Manchester was a southern boy, although Nathaniel could not tell where from. "Things are getting pretty grim over there. It's hard to say whether they'll collapse from within or whether we'll lick them. It shouldn't be long one way or the other."

"We have many people over there?"

"A couple. Most of what we know is from contraband slaves."

"Contrabands are coming out?"

"They sure are. We have more niggers walking around here than you can shake a stick at. Pity we don't have any cotton."

"And they're talking?"

"Talking up a storm. You have to sort through it, of course. My old man used to say that nine tithes of anything is crap. It's sure enough that way with these slaves. Chaw?"

"No, thanks."

He bit a piece off of a plug. "But if'n you sift through it, it's clear that Johnny Reb is in a bad way."

"Well, too bad for Johnny Reb."

"The key to everything is Lee." Pieces of tobacco flew from his mouth as he spoke. "When he realizes it's time to quit the whole house of cards will come down."

"That's what Grant said."

"So you've met our mighty leader?"

"Yes."

"What did you think of him?"

"I think he might be a fighting son of a bitch but I'd never invite him into my grandmother's drawing-room."

Manchester grunted. "Got a sidearm, Curry?"

Nathaniel patted his armpit.

"Let's have a look at it."

Nathaniel laid the pistol on the table. "Well, shoot, boy, I've shit things bigger than that. Hope you didn't pay money for that piece."

"I sure did, soldier. Damn near a week's pay."

"Why, look at the bore on this thing, a rat couldn't fit his pecker in there. This one of those policeman's pistols?"

"Sure enough. I could shoot you with it if you'd like a little demonstration."

"Well, if you do, warn me aforehand so I notice it."

"You don't think this would stop a man?"

"It wouldn't have much stopping power, no. A, let's see, a board with a nail in it would be deadlier than this thing. But the sight of it would still slow a fellow down. No one ever wants to be shot by anything. Now put it away before a gust of wind comes up."

"Do you know Red Sally?" Nathaniel asked.

"The hooker? Sure."

"She any good?"

"If you mean is she a good spy the answer is yes. If you mean does she put on a good show in bed I'd have to say I've had better."

"Ever suspect her?"

"Sure. I suspect everyone. Do you have anything on her?"

"Listen to this. Do you know that Longstreet got a note when he came into Gettysburg?"

"I've heard that, yes."

"Where did he get it?"

"A girl gave him a bouquet."

"Yes, but what kind of girl?"

"You tell me."

"A Quaker. Now, no Quaker would do such a thing, it's supporting a war and that goes against the grain for them. But Quaker bonnets cover a woman's head up, hair and all."

Manchester looked impassive. "You think that was Sally, and she wore the bonnet to cover her hair?"

Nathaniel shrugged. "Could be."

"Well, any woman in that situation might dress up as a Quaker. It would be a good idea, in fact. That don't mean nothing."

"All right."

"That's a thought, though. I'll think that over. Thanks."

"You're welcome. Tell me, have you met Alphonsus Christian yet?"

Manchester spat on the ground.

"Like him that much, do you?"

"He's a fighting son of a bitch, too, but most of all he's a son of a bitch." He thought about it. "You'll be playing with him over there, I suspect."

"He goes over?"

"Back and forth all the time. He's pretty high up in their organization. They can have him, for my say-so."

"What name does he go by?"

"His own name. He's a major over there, too."

"Will he be my boss, I hope not?"

"I don't think so. Not unless Grant said so."

"He didn't."

"Okay. Then the chain of command is me by telegraph, then Colonel Sharpe, then Grant. Christian has his own organization. You can work with him, or you can tell him to go pound sand up his ass."

"There's a second organization?"

"There's a passel of them. There's one, well, I'll tell you nothing about it, except they're very good but they're crazy."

Nathaniel stuck half a loaf of bread in his shirt. "Okay."

"You know the area?"

"I'm from Richmond."

"Not good. Got another name?"

"Yeah. William Jones."

"Okay. Don't use either of those names in your dispatches. Sign your stuff Joshua, okay?"

"Okay."

"And encrypt with Joshua. Decrypt with it too." Manchester pointed the plug at him. "One thing to keep in mind, Curry: remember who you are. Remember who you're working for. It's easy to get lost in all this shit."

Nathaniel held his cup before his mouth and spoke low: "You think Christian's on the up and up?"

Manchester chewed on both this and his tobacco for a few seconds. "Do you mean what I think you mean?"

Nathaniel set his cup down.

The officer pushed away from the table and got up. "Christ! Why did I even talk to you?"

"Wait! Hold on, lieutenant." He finished his coffee and stood up. "Tell me more about what it's like over there. How's Richmond?"

Manchester stood in silence for a minute, then turned back to him. "They're eating rats, that's how's Richmond. There must be about ten niggers left in the city, and hardly more whites than that, but still we can't crack them."

"Are you taking the train down to Petersburg?"

He sighed. "Yes. Yes, come along."

Manchester grew voluble again on the train. "These niggers are coming over with anything of value they can hide on their persons. We find them with silverware and gold and silver jewelry. They always say it's their own, of course. Seems like every nigger in Richmond gets a gold watch as soon as he can walk."

"You let them keep it?"

"Sure, why not? We don't mind them robbing their masters. The sutlers and the Jews will end up with it all sooner or later anyway. One nigger in Petersburg walks around in fancy gentleman's clothes, shiny shoes and everything. We put him to work same as everyone else, and you should see this old boy, done up like something from a minstrel show, mucking stalls. It's a laugh."

"No fooling."

"Now, if you make it into Richmond and you see some rich man walking around bare-ass, you can tell him where his clothes are."

"Manchester, you know the telegraph?"

He shrugged. "Ten characters a minute."

"Are you going to be listening on the lines?"

"Yes. I've heard you before, Curry. Plenty of times. I know your fist. Don't trouble about identifying yourself, I'll know when it's you." The train came to a stop. "And you'll know it's me when you see the name Maccabee. You want to see that fancy-ass nigger now?"

"Sure."

Manchester led him to a line of makeshift shacks behind the train station. Before these shacks a variety of Negroes lounged and smoked. He indicated a well-dressed young man who leaned back in a chair, reading a newspaper. "Look at him! He may as well be a white man."

Nathaniel looked at him for a few seconds, then exclaimed, "Titus!"

The Negro started and tucked the paper under his arm. "Do I know you, sir? Why, it's Master Nathaniel!" He crossed the ten yards between them. He retained the haughty air that he had the last time they had met, though he favored Nathaniel with a nod.

"Titus, you've come over!"

"Yes, sir, I have. About a month ago."

"But what of your mistress? And Master David and Miss Amanda? Who's taking care of them?"

Titus smiled. "They can all go to Hell as far as I'm concerned."

Despite himself Nathaniel grew angry at this. "I thought they treated you pretty damned well, Titus."

"Yes. I had everything I could ever want. Save one thing." He took the paper out and returned to his chair. Manchester laughed.

Nathaniel rode south of the city in a donkey cart driven by an old Negro. He lay under a blanket in the back, surrounded by melons and squash. If stopped, he would lie silent unless discovered. If discovered, he would say he had been out foraging and had fallen asleep in the wagon.

He in fact slept for most of the trip. His driver came right up to the city's defenses before being challenged. He told the sentries that he wanted to sell his wares to the soldiers and was allowed to pass.

Nathaniel emerged from his cover once they were in the city. It was his first look at Petersburg since the war began. He had remembered it as a town of some twenty thousand souls, a place where a river and three railroads converged south of the capitol. In those days it had been prosperous and businesslike.

Now it was an armed camp. Its only reason for being was to defend the city of Richmond; indeed, there was not much left of the Confederacy besides these two communities.

Although Petersburg had few men to defend it, these men had made the best of the time the enemy had graciously provided them. Trenches were dug everywhere and especially in the direction of the Union forces. Every fortification was faced with sharpened sticks driven into the ground or with pits containing sharp stakes.

The soldiers looked defiant but they also looked desperate. Their uniforms were more ragged than ever and the men were skinny and dirty.

Nathaniel jumped out of the cart and waved to the driver. The old man nodded and went off to sell his wares.

He found a telegraph line and followed it. The line led to a structure of pine logs with ten feet of earth on its roof. In its dim interior he found Dylan Finney and Billy Margate. Both rose joyfully to greet him.

"Jones!" Finney exclaimed. "I'd counted you among the honored dead. I'm glad I was wrong."

"Howdy-do, boys," he said. "It's good to see you, too."

"When did you get here?"

"Just now. Reckon I can find some work here?"

"Sure enough, boy, and glad to have you. But I'm afraid your only reward will be in Heaven and in the hearts of your countrymen."

"Well, that will have to do, I reckon."

"How did you get out of Atlanta?" Finney asked.

"It appears Billy here has told you about me."

"Sure enough."

"Well, I walked out. I wasn't in uniform so when Sherman and his boys got to town they left me alone. Then when they burned it I just left."

"You left the day it burned?"

"Yes."

"Well, that was back on November the fifteenth. It's a few days before Christmas now. What have you been up to?"

He shrugged. "This and that. I thought of dropping out but I decided to see things through."

"Did they really burn the place to the ground?" Margate asked.

"I didn't look back much. It was too painful. But from what I saw it was a pretty big fire."

"That's a shame. That's a damned shame."

"I know it."

"What happened to Francis?"

He hesitated. It would have been safer to say that he didn't know, but he like Margate. "He's dead," he said. "Yankees killed him."

Margate looked at the floor. "Why they do that?"

"No reason, really. He was in civilian clothes. An officer said he looked like a military man. He confessed he was and the officer shot him. It was quick."

"Well, that's a mercy," Margate said softly.

"Providence save us from such mercies," Finney said.

"Where's Ben Rush?" Nathaniel asked.

"He skipped," Finney replied. "After Cold Harbor he said he seen the elephant and he just walked away."

"Well, that's good. I mean I'm glad he's not dead. And who can say but that it's not wiser to skip now anyway?"

"I know," Margate said. "The Army's down to a few score thousand. Sure, a lot of them are fallen, but I think most have just gone home."

Finney sternly pointed a finger at Nathaniel. "You, young man, are out of uniform. You don't want to suffer Francis' fate."

"I reckon I don't. Can you fix me up with a uniform?"

Finney and Margate were the two principle operators at Petersburg and they gladly accepted Nathaniel as a third. They provided him with a tunic and kepi, allowing him to keep his civilian pants and shoes. The tunic was well-worn and had a hole in it right over his heart.

The three of them alternated shifts at the key. A few boys there were with rudimentary telegraphic skills, but they only served as runners for the most part.

During the first shift he had alone with the key, he fulfilled the first part of his commission. He copied an urgent message from Richmond to General Lee and the other operator told him to report back upon delivery. He replied that the general was in the town and he would see that it made it into his hands.

Christmas day dawned with the Union guns fallen silent. As Nathaniel watched, a man climbed out of his trench, stood on the open ground and waved his hat at the Union side. A minute later a Union soldier got up and waved his own hat in reply.

A commotion arose as the soldiers saw what was happening. Soon soldiers were pouring out of the trenches on both sides and warily crossing the narrow strip of land that divided the two armies. They had to jump over trenches and work their way through the sharpened sticks and other obstacles, but they did so without injury. Soldier met soldier with empty hands; they shook hands and wished each other a merry Christmas.

Nathaniel didn't take part in this impromptu truce. He was afraid that someone on the Union side would recognize him and ruin his cover. He took a turn at the key instead, allowing Finney and Margate to walk around in the sunlight for a change.

On December 26th the Yankees resumed shelling the Confederate trenches. The day of peace had passed.

On New Year's Day a message in clear arrived from Richmond ordering Nathaniel to report to the War Office. It was signed Maccabee.

The train moved at little more than a walk, such was the state of the track. It took more than two hours to cross the fifteen miles to the city.

A variety of vehicles were waiting at the York River station. One of them was a fairly elegant carriage. The driver, in smart green livery, caught his eye. It was Carl Morgan.

Nathaniel, surprised, approached the carriage. Carl descended from the box without a word, his eyes downcast, and opened the door.

Nathaniel had gotten to know Carl fairly well after Chancellorsville. He found him intelligent and witty, but ultimately unsuitable as a friend. This was due not to his color or his northern background, but to his love of killing. He was good at it, particularly with a knife, but even in wartime no one should take so much pleasure at the death of his fellow man.

Nathaniel got into the carriage and found himself sitting opposite a small woman in late middle age. She had a pointed nose, a pointed chin and dark, piercing eyes. She was dressed as a somewhat dowdy matron, with a white shawl around her shoulders and gold spectacles perched on her nose. She looked as puzzled at his presence as he was. Carl clucked to the horses and they were off at a walk.

He glanced around. It was very much a lady's carriage, with velvet cushions and gilt fittings, but it was old and poorly maintained. Glass bud vases hung on each side of the door, each containing a dead flower.

The lady looked out the window, then back at him. He felt like she was assessing him like a horse at an auction. "May I ask your name, young man?" she said at last. Her tone was harsher than it needed to be.

"William Jones, ma'am. Private William Jones." He took off his cap.

"I am Elizabeth van Lew."

"Pleased to meet you, Mrs. Van Lew."

"It's Miss, not Mrs." Her frown suggested that he should already know that.

"I beg your pardon."

She cocked her head to the side. "It is not the song of a bird," she said.

"Pardon?"

She waved her hand in dismissal. "Never mind. I say things … I hear things."

"Uh, yes, ma'am. Ah, may I ask, do you know why I'm here?"

"I'm afraid none of us know that, young man."

"Yes, ma'am."

They rode in silence for a minute, then she seemed to remember that he was there. "You must excuse the state of my carriage, Private Jones," she said, "but the war has made it difficult to keep up appearances."

"It's fine, ma'am."

"Well, I don't think so, but it's very gallant of you to say so, Private. Are you a resident of this city?"

"Yes, ma'am."

"You'll doubtless find it much changed, and not all for the better. Still, when the war is won I trust it will become as lovely as ever." She opened a parasol and put it over her shoulder, although there was no sunlight in the carriage.

"Yes, ma'am."

"There are a great many ruffians in this city now. They make it hard for a decent woman to … do you know, a man came up to me and insulted me on the street. And this happened only yesterday. No. The day before. Whatever day Tuesday was."

"He did? Do you know why?"

"Why, for my political views, of course."

"Your political views?"

"Yes, I know I am not supposed to have them, but I can't help … I am one of the city's leading abolitionists, you know."

"Oh, of course."

"The situation has become quite dreadful, quite insufferable. One can only hope that this dreadful conflict is resolved soon."

"Yes'm."

"I could not ask him that," she said. "Yes, I know what Joshua did. I—I—I … Private Jones, are you Joshua?"

"What?"

He was suddenly on guard. This befuddled woman knew things she should not.

He tried to put things together. Carl must have told her he was Joshua. That meant she knew he was an agent.

Why would he tell her that? For that matter, why did Carl know? Was he in Grant's graces? And what was he doing as this crazy old bat's slave?

None of this made sense. He would just have to play the cards as they came up.

"I know I get a great many things wrong, but I feel certain you are Joshua."

"Where did you hear that, ma'am?"

"A little bird told me," she said. She didn't smile; she looked as confused as ever. Then she glanced beside him, as if addressing someone sitting there. "Oh, be still! Yours is not the voice of a seraph, fool. Oh, very well, then. Private Jones, you shall be our Joshua, and Richmond shall be your Jericho."

"If you say so, ma'am."

"You must be on the watch for messages addressed to General Hill."

"I ... I must?"

"Yes. Because for these purposes, and to this end, it is you who are General Hill."

He considered this. "Which one, ma'am?"

"Why, is there more than one General Hill?"

"Yes, there is. Are."

She looked out at the passing rooftops. "What? Very well, then, I'll tell him. One of these is an Ambrose Hill, is he not?"

"Yes'm."

"Then messages addressed to him may actually be messages addressed to you. Do you understand?"

"Yes, ma'am."

"Splendid," she muttered. She suddenly noticed the parasol on her shoulder and took it down.

For the first time he indeed understood. This curious creature was part of the Richmond group. The way she talked, she could even be the head of it.

She regarded the rooftops again, as if looking for something to say there. Then she looked sadly at the seat beside her. At last she perked up and turned back to Nathaniel.

"When you see such a message, one addressed to General Ambrose Hill," Miss van Lew said, "if such message is not in code, why, then, you will be free to read it. If, however, it is encoded, then you must translate it. Use the keyword 'Hamlet' and employ the method of translation used by the Federal forces. It is my understanding that you are familiar with this process."

"Indeed I am, ma'am."

"That is wonderful."

She sat back, a faint smile on her lips, and watched the city roll by. "Wonderful," she muttered sadly.

They were on one of the nicer streets of the capital. They were in fact passing the three-story brick mansion of the President. The lady tried to peer in the windows, then turned back to Nathaniel.

"Be also watchful of anything that you may find of interest to me or my circle. If you wish to communicate with me, send a telegraphic message to General Joseph Finegan in Florida. It is likely that the general himself will not be troubled by the message, as he is at present greatly vexed by Union forces, if he is even still in play. I shall leave it to your discretion as to whether such messages should be in code or not."

"Yes, ma'am."

She turned slightly, addressing the person beside him again. "If you are in Richmond and unable to reach a telegraph, a message sent to President Davis might also reach me."

"I understand."

"I beg your pardon?"

"I said I understand."

"Thank you. By all means bear in mind that the message will also reach the President and … such others as will be dismayed by receiving it." She sighed and folded her gloved hands in her lap. "I have to beg your indulgence, young Joshua. People say that I am mad. I suspect that I am indeed mad, as I constantly hear the voices of people who are not there. It can be most distracting at times."

"Yes, ma'am."

The carriage pulled up beside the train station. The train he came in on was getting ready for the return run.

"At first," Miss van Lew continued, "I thought the voices were real and that it was a visitation of God. As time went on, however, I came to realize that I was simply crazy."

"It … must be a great burden to you."

"In some ways it is," she said sadly. "But it protects me marvelously in my work." She looked at the parasol in her hands and carefully furled it as Nathaniel got out of the carriage. He looked back to take leave of her, but she looked like she had already forgotten that he even existed.

He nodded to Carl. The latter doffed his top hat and drove off. Nathaniel sighed. Once again he was in over his head.

He looked at the waiting train and decided, against his better judgment, to walk around the city for a while.

So this was the Richmond operation. They knew him before he knew them, and just like that he was working for them.

He puzzled over what Miss van Lew had told him. The strangest part was that a message sent to President Davis would reach her. Was there a Union spy in the President's office? One who saw all the President's messages? If so, it would have to be someone placed very close to Davis, probably a high-ranked officer or civilian.

He could see why Manchester had said that the Richmond organization was crazy. Elizabeth van Lew was also clearly pretty rich and well placed in society. Still, couldn't the Union have found someone who wasn't cracked in the head?

He went past the Swanson house. It looked as fine as ever, though he thought the shutters needed painting. He wanted to knock on the door but wisdom prevailed. If Amanda was home she would hardly receive him well and she was the only one he really wanted to see.

He went to his own home instead. He was as surprised to see his mother behind the counter of the store as she was to see him. She threw herself upon him, weeping with joy.

"Maw, it's good to see you! You look so much better." He was a hand taller than her now.

"Oh, Nattie! Oh, thank God you're all right! You are all right, aren't you?"

"Sure I am, Maw."

She indeed looked better than she had the last time he had seen her. At the same time she looked worse. She was thin, with her cheekbones standing out prominently. Her hair was gray and thinning. Still, she looked like she wanted to live again, and that was paramount.

"Oh, Nattie, I'm sorry I was that way when you came here before. I was just in a state, but I'm better now."

"Well, I should say so! You recollect that?"

She nodded. "It's like recollecting a dream or something."

"What happened to fix you up?"

She stepped back. "I know exactly what did it. It was when your sister Ada died."

This hit him like a rifle butt in the stomach. He staggered back, unable to breathe. "What?"

"She just up and died a month ago. First her legs became cold and numb and she couldn't move them. Then her chest hurt. Then she was gone. It all happened in the space of a day. There, child, it's all right. It's all right. She's with her father now."

"Did a doctor see her?" he asked, wiping his eyes on his sleeve.

"There ain't no doctors left in Richmond, at least not for the likes of us. We didn't think it was that bad, either, right up until she died, and then it was too late."

"Was she sickly? Had she been eating right?"

"Nobody's been eating right. She was getting thin, yes, but no thinner than anyone else."

"Just one of those things, was it?"

"I reckon so."

"Paw's not dead."

"He ain't?"

"Maw, I got captured and went to a Yankee prison."

"The one in Michigan?"

"Why, yes. How you know that?"

"A soldier came to the store. He had been paroled from that prison. He said you had been paroled a month before him. A man named Murdock, I believe."

"Yes, I knew a Murdock there."

"He said the guards had killed your father."

"Oh, God! Paw dead too?" He began bawling again.

"Yes, Nattie, and we never heard from Melrose. We just got that one letter saying he was going to prison. We don't even know if he got there."

"Maw, I saw Melly in a prison in Maine. He was fit as a fiddle when I saw him." He thought as he said this of the emaciated figure he had seen behind the bars, but damn it, he *was* fit. If he had been let out, he would have beaten the tar out of his brother.

"Oh, thank God!"

"Maw, where's Daisy?"

"She's a sutler with the Army now. I don't know where she is but I pray every night that she's well."

"Give her my best."

"Nattie, you'd be real proud of me. I'm learning my ciphers."

"You are?"

"I can run the store all by my lonesome. I can reckon the accounts myself."

"Huh! Can you read now, Maw?"

"No, I can't do that yet. That's next, I reckon."

"One thing at a time. If you can't read, how do you keep track of the accounts?"

"I draw pictures, look."

She opened the ledger book. A spiral was a bolt of cloth. A square with XXXX in the center was a bag of flour. A line ran through four stick figures holding hands like paper dolls.

"What happened to them slaves that was here?"

"It was awful, Nattie. We lost all kinds of money on them. We lost four niggers in a fortnight."

"Lost 'em? How?"

"They went over to the Yankees, like as not. They just up and disappeared, and there's no nigger-catchers anymore."

"Well, can't say as I blame 'em."

"Well, neither can I, but it sure hurt us. We settled some accounts by taking them. I suspects them folks knew all along those boys had a hankering to run away."

"Yes, the Yankees have plenty of food and will pay them cash wages."

"The Yankees think they can get their moncy's worth paying wages to niggers?"

"Reckon so. They got money to burn."

"Folks ask for you, Nattie."

"Maw, don't tell anyone you seen me."

"But why? That old balloon business? I'm sure--"

"There's other things."

"Like what?"

"I won't be able to tell you until after the war. Tell Daisy but no one else, all right? No, don't tell Daisy either. Not 'til it's over."

"But the war won't end for another ten years. Everyone says that."

"It will be over within the year and likely less than that."

"Oh, Nattie, do you think so?"

"I know so. Just keep mum about seeing me, okay? I got to go. Happy New Year, Maw."

He kissed her and turned without another word. As he left he saw a cat and two rats hanging in the window.

Life in Petersburg sank into a routine. Messages came in from other parts of the Confederacy for Lee and the other officers. Some were in code and some were not. In all cases Nathaniel dutifully copied and delivered them, knowing that Union agents had already intercepted them.

In the second week of January Nathaniel received a message addressed to General A.P. Hill. After first determining that the message was not actually for himself he ran it to Hill's tent. There was no sentry so he brought it in.

To his surprise Hill was speaking with Lee. He saluted, apologized for the intrusion and handed Hill the message form. As he waited for Hill to read the message Lee said, "Wait a minute, soldier. Is your name High?"

"No, sir, well, yes, sir. I'm William Jones. High is my middle name."

"High is your middle name?"

"Yes, sir. Hiram is my middle name. Folks call me High so as not to confuse me with my father."

"Oh. He is also William Jones?"

"Yes, sir. Or he was."

"Very good. Thank you, Jones."

"Yes, sir."

Hill lay the message aside. "No reply," he said.

"Yes, sir." Nathaniel left the tent, his heart beating like a triphammer.

He worked the overnight shift that night and slept in the next day. He was awakened about noon and ordered to the telegraph hut. Margate and a major with a thick beard and wavy black hair awaited him; two armed soldiers with steely expressions stood by. "Willy," Margate said, "this is Major Norris, the chief of information."

"How do you do, sir?" he said, throwing a salute.

Norris looked Nathaniel up and down. "Jones, I hear you've been decoding messages."

"Yes, sir."

"Who taught you how to do that?"

"An operator back in Atlanta."

"Yes, who?"

"A fellow name of Conroy, sir."

"Agent?"

"Just a telegraph operator as far as I know, sir, but he had learned the ciphers."

Norris cocked his head at Margate. "Get a hold of this Conroy."

"Do you know where he is, Jones?"

"Yankees shot him leaving the city, sir."

"Shit," said Norris. "Well, I want you in Richmond."

"Yes, sir. When?"

"I have a train waiting for me. I want you on it."

"Yes, sir. I'll pack my kit."

Norris waved to one of the soldiers. "Give him a hand."

"Oh, I can handle it, sir."

The soldier followed him anyway, watching as he packed his bag and even looking his cot over before they left. Mighty kind of you, Nathaniel thought.

Norris set Nathaniel up in a telegraph hut near the War Office. He was given such tasks as working the key and encoding and decoding messages. For the first day or so it seemed that someone was always watching him. If he was under suspicion, though, the suspicion abated in the face of the serious problems the Confederacy was facing.

There were two other operators there, each younger and less experienced than he was. Though both Enoch Cartwright and Phineas Ness were also privates he naturally took charge of them. Whenever he was on duty he worked the key himself, setting the other men to encoding and decoding messages and running them.

Ness was from Richmond. Nathaniel did not tell him that he was also from the city but he did ask him if he knew Elizabeth van Lew. "Sure I do," Ness replied. "They call her 'Crazy Bett.'"

"She crazy, then?"

"Sure enough. She walks around talking to herself. Nobody pays it any mind, though."

"Because she's harmless?"

"Well, that and the fact that her family's one of the richest in Richmond. And she doesn't mind helping the boys out. That's why folks forgiver her … her ways."

"Her ways?"

"She's an abolitionist," Ness said, the word sticking in his craw. "She talks about it out in the open. Wants to set our little nigger brothers free, let 'em run around like God-damned chickens. But she's crazy and she's a lady and she's good to the troops, so folks don't pay her no never mind."

"Good to the troops? How so?"

"Oh, she's always holding socials for the officers and raising money for soldier hospitals. And she gave her maid to President Davis."

The messages coming in were bleak: everywhere forces were experiencing hunger, lack of fodder for the horses, ammunition shortages and, increasingly, desertion. The many Armies of the Confederate States were simply melting away. No one wanted to be the last man to die in a lost cause.

The messages going out were even worse. Rather than issuing real orders, Richmond was telling the troops everywhere that victory was imminent, that they had merely to hold on a little longer. The fact that the lie was transparent made it no less a lie.

Occasionally he would engage in chatter with the other operators. One of the first such messages he sent was I SURE AM HUNGRY. His counterpart replied that he would send him a baked ham with all the fixings by the next morning's post.

On his second day at this post Christian walked in like he owned the place. He wore a major's uniform, of the sort officers sported when they didn't want to attract attention in the field. "Come with me, boy," he said. Nathaniel left with him.

"Come into this alley with me."

"No."

"No?"

"The street is good enough. No one can hear us and I like being seen right now."

"What's your name?"

"William Jones."

"Jones, I'm going across the street tomorrow and I want to tell them boys what you've been hearing. Make it quick."

"No."

"God damn it, you say that a lot. If'n you've grown a set of balls I'll gladly relieve you of them."

"They told me who my boss would be and it wasn't you. I don't have to like you and I don't. I don't even know if your hands are clean."

"They won't be in a minute."

Nathaniel shrugged. "If my orders change I'll talk to you. I got work to do." He went back to his key.

A few days after this Nathaniel was ordered to Norris' office. The major was not there and Nathaniel took the opportunity to look the place over. There were piles of correspondence everywhere. He didn't dare pick anything up – Norris might arrive at any moment – but he read what was in sight.

To his surprise he found a telegram that mentioned his name. It was at the top of a sheaf of new messages lying on the major's desk. Nathaniel snatched it off the table and stuffed it in his tunic pocket.

Seconds later Norris entered the room. He came to attention. "Good morning, sir."

"Good morning, Jones. What are you looking at?"

"Uh…this, sir."

He held up a letter that had been mailed from an Ohio family to its soldier son. Printed on the envelope was an inspirational and patriotic image. It depicted a balloon upon whose gasbag was the word SECESSION. The balloon was on fire and falling. Tumbling from the tiny basket were Jefferson Davis, Robert E. Lee, Thomas Jackson and James Longstreet.

Norris glanced at it. "Not a very pretty sentiment, is it?"

"No, sir."

"Jones, what's your grade?"

Nathaniel glanced at his bare sleeve. "Buck private, sir."

"Well, you're a buck sergeant now." Norris wrote a quick order and handed it to him. "Go see the quartermaster."

"Is that all, sir?"

"Yes." Norris picked the sheaf of new messages up and started flipping through them.

The quartermaster had a shirt with three stripes on it. He gave it to him in exchange for his old shirt.

The new shirt was far too large for him. Like its predecessor there was a hole in it as well as a large stain the color of port wine. Still, he was a sergeant! He walked proudly back to the telegraph shack, keeping an eye out for lower-ranking men to terrorize.

There were plenty of private soldiers in the streets but they were already terrorized. Most of them were on the edge of starvation. Their cheekbones stood out in stark relief, they had dark circles under their eyes and their hair and teeth were falling out. They were getting so weak that they could hardly walk, much less fight.

There were still plenty of civilians left in the city but most of them kept out of sight. Some people, the prudent and the well to do, looked like they still had food, but none of them was sharing.

He thought about the military situation. The prospects for a Rebel victory were getting quite bleak. The Confederacy was nearly all in Union hands; only the capital and a few other places held out. The Union now fielded nearly a million men, the South less than a hundred thousand. The South was starving while the Union was fed by the bottomless cornucopia of its fields and factories.

Why did they not surrender? It seemed utter folly.

Or was it? Was it perhaps some nobility in the human spirit which compels men and women to do things that seem beyond natural limits? A horse, after all, would lie down and die under such a burden. The proof of that could be seen on any corner of the city.

He stopped in his tracks. What, then, was the noble purpose that impelled the Confederacy? What was the Cause? Why, it was that white people should own colored people as their chattel slaves. This noble struggle was to an utterly corrupt end.

Cartwright and Ness glanced up as he came in, then snapped to. "As you were, fellows," he said. "I'm not that kind of a sergeant."

"Are you really a sergeant now, Nathaniel?"

"Yes, and when anyone's about you call me sergeant, you hear? But not behind closed doors."

"Sure."

He went into the office, closed the door and pulled out the telegram. It read:

TO MAJ WILM NORRIS RMND
FROM CARDINAL PBURG
SEE MY EARLIER MESSAGES RE UNION AGENT NATHANIEL CURRY IN YOUR CITY 73

Cardinal? Who the Hell was that? It didn't even sound like a person's name. As far as he knew the word only applied to a kind of bird.

The message blank was different than what was used in his office. Well, the message had not come through his office, he would surely have noticed it. This Cardinal knew he worked at the telegraph office, then.

Or did he? If so, the message would say that. Cardinal knew only that he was in Richmond.

But what telegraph office was this message sent to? As far as he knew all of the Confederate lines in Richmond came through his office. Was there another one he didn't know of?

Yes, he realized, there was a different line in this area. If the Union was listening in on the Confederate lines, they had to have a separate line running to their own headquarters.

Did this message then originate at Union headquarters?

The message referred to "earlier messages" about him. Had Norris read these messages? Perhaps not: like Colonel Sharpe, he was overwhelmed with information. These earlier messages might be sitting in his office, unread.

Or maybe Major Norris was looking for Nathaniel Curry and took no note of William Jones. His cover was safe.

Or was it? Perhaps Norris knew exactly who he was and was keeping an eye on him. If so, he had neutralized a Union agent without the Union realizing it. Nathaniel was no longer watching Lee and reporting his movements. In fact, he wasn't doing anything Norris didn't want him doing.

But why hadn't he simply shot him?

Maybe he intended to use him somehow. Perhaps he would feed him false information that he would then pass on, using the Union codes.

He didn't know. All he knew for sure was that he was in over his head. Again.

He considered fleeing back to the Union lines but even if he made it alive Grant would shoot him. No, he would just have to bide his time and watch his back. He burned the message in the stove and went back to work.

Cartwright worked the overnight shift that night. He was dozing beside the key when Nathaniel came in. Cartwright started at the sound of the door closing and sprang to attention.

"At ease, Phineas. I ain't a-going to shoot you."

"Yes, Sergeant. Uh, is it morning?"

"No, it's two o'clock at night now."

"Sorry, Nathaniel."

"Listen, I can't sleep. Go ahead and bunk down. I'll take the key."

"All right. Nothing's coming in anyway."

"All right. Good night."

He wrote a message out in plain:

TO MANCHESTER PBURG
FROM CURRY RMOND
I HAVE BEEN BETRAYED STOP MESSAGE ARRIVED FOR
NORRIS NAMING ME AS UNION AGENT STOP I INTERCEPTED
MESSAGE STOP MESSAGE WAS SIGNED CARDINAL STOP PLEASE
ADVISE 73

He then made up a code square using the word Joshua, encrypted the message and sent it to General Finegan in Florida. As he watched the clear message, the code square and the cipher burning in the pot-bellied stove he felt that he could at last sleep. He could not, though; he was on duty and even when serving the enemy he had become too diligent to fall asleep on watch.

When Ness took over at six in the morning he told him to be on the lookout for any encoded message for A.P. Hill, saying that he would decode it himself. He slept until noon and learned that no message had come in.

Four hours later Carl Morgan entered the hut. Cartwright and Ness were surprised at the appearance of the well-dressed, well-groomed young Negro with his intelligent and refined bearing. He spoke not a word but smiled at Nathaniel who rose immediately and went out with him.

"Well! How are you, Private Jones?"

"It's Sergeant Jones now, Carl. Are you impressed?"

"Oh, quite. My congratulations, of course. Did you get a raise in pay as well?"

"Yes, from nothing to twice nothing. How much are you taking in these days?"

"Oh, just what your average slave makes. By a remarkable coincidence, it's precisely what you're making."

"What's new?"

"Miss van Lew needs to speak with you."

"By all means. Where is she?"

"Come right this way."

Carl led him down the street about half a block to a private residence. It was a handsome brick townhouse with a flight of stone steps running up to the front door. The building looked deserted. "This is the place," he said.

Nathaniel glanced at him. "She's in here?"

"Yes."

The two started up the steps together.

Nathaniel's mind was racing. He had just seen a peculiar light in Carl's eye, one he had only seen a few times before. Nathaniel burst forward, running up the steps.

"Hey!" Carl cried, running up behind him. He had his knife out but he had already lost the element of surprise. Nathaniel turned at the landing and kicked at his face.

Nathaniel spotted two soldiers on the other side of the road and called to them, "You men! Help me out over here!"

Carl knocked Nathaniel's foot aside with one hand and lunged at him with the knife. Nathaniel grabbed the knife hand and swung his fist at Carl's head. Carl ducked and they both lost their balance and tumbled down the steps.

Nathaniel landed on his back in the street with Carl atop him. He still gripped Carl's wrist but the latter took the knife with his free hand and stabbed at Nathaniel's chest. Nathaniel got his forearm in front of him and took the force of the blow on it. Carl drew back for another stab just as the soldiers arrived.

The soldiers grabbed Carl and threw him on his back, pinning his arms down. Something metallic flew out of his hand and landed on the street beside him. "Hold him!" Nathaniel barked. "Don't let him up!"

The men kneeled on Carl's forearms. "You all right, Sergeant?"

"I think so."

"No, you're not," the other man said. "Jesus Christ, look at your arm."

Nathaniel's arm was bleeding on both sides. The knife had gone right through his forearm and had cut his chest. As he watched the blood began to gush freely from his arm. It also began to hurt.

"Let me help you with that, sir," the second man said.

"No, hold that nigger down, I need to talk to him."

The soldier picked the knife up, plunged it into the ruffled lace on Carl's chest and pulled it out. Carl gave a wide-eyed gasp and fell back limp. "He'll stay down now, sir. Let me look at your arm."

"God damn it, I told you I needed to talk to him!"

"Sergeant, you're going to be dead in about two minutes. Let me see you." The man used Carl's weapon to cut Nathaniel's sleeve open, then raised the arm straight up and pressed a thumb on each side of it just below the wound. Like magic the bleeding stopped.

"You need to see a doctor, sir."

"You look like you're a doctor yourself."

"Well, my daddy's a doctor. I reckon I'll be one if I live out the war."

The other soldier said, "This here nigger's not getting up again." He stood up and kicked Carl in the ribs. Carl made no complaint.

"There's a hospital in the next street, sergeant. Maybe we should get you over there."

"Yes, thank you."

"Let me check this first." He lowered the arm and removed his thumbs. Blood came out, though not as freely as before. The soldier took lint and bandages from his kit and bound the wounds up. While he was doing this Nathaniel told the other man, "Drag that body off the street. Someone will have to clean it up later."

"Yes, Sergeant." The soldier picked up a small object lying beside the corpse. "What's this?"

"What did you find?" Nathaniel asked.

"He dropped this. Let me see that knife, Ezekiel. "

"It's not a knife, it's a spoon."

"Really? Let me see. " He held it up. It was a metal spoon whose handle had been sharpened to a knife edge on each side, with a wicked point at the end. "Look, you stick it in this wooden handle and it's just a spoon. Wonder where he got it."

"He probably made it himself," Nathaniel said.

He dropped the spoon and shook his head. "Niggers aren't smart enough to make stuff like this." He grabbed Carl's collar and dragged him away.

Nathaniel looked at the bandaged arm. "Thank you," he told the other soldier. "You boys saved my life twice in the space of a minute. I'm much obliged."

"You're welcome. Are you going to the hospital now?"

"Yes."

"I'll come with you."

"Well, thanks again."

"Your chest is bleeding, too, sir."

"Yes, I see it, but I don't think it's deep."

"You'd best hope not, sir." The soldier gave him a piece of lint and Nathaniel held it against his chest as they walked. "What possessed that nigger to take after you that way? I swear he wasn't drunk."

"I don't know. Just took a fit, I suppose."

"And did you see how he was dressed? He was a house nigger."

"Yes, someone will miss him. I wish y'all hadn't killed him. I wanted to find out why he done that."

"Well, it was him or you. I couldn't hold him down and treat you at the same time. And it's death for any nigger what goes after a white person like that. You can't abide that."

He sighed. "I reckon you're right."

"Does your chest hurt?"

"A little. It feels like I got stuck with a knife."

"That's all? That's good."

"Why is it good?"

"If you were stuck in the lung you'd be hurting a lot more."

"Or the heart."

"If you'd gotten it in the heart it wouldn't hurt at all. Ah, here we go."

A set of stone steps identical to the ones he had just scaled was before him. He had an instant of anxiety, then climbed the steps.

"Do you feel light-headed?"

"No, I don't think so. I'm just a little flustered still. I think I'll be all right. Thanks again. You can return to duty now."

One of the last male nurses in captivity took him in charge. The old man set Nathaniel in a chair, clicked his tongue as he listened to his story, then ordered him to strip to the waist. He examined his arm, then removed the dressing. He looked the wound over, then put on fresh lint.

"Now, sergeant, touch your thumb to the tip of each of your other fingers."

"Like this?"

"Good, it looks like none of the tendons has been severed."

"It hurts a lot to do that."

"Well, that's fine. That means the nerves are all right." He examined the chest wound. "The chest cavity wasn't penetrated," he said as he dressed it. "I think the real danger is in your arm."

"Yeah? What's the danger?"

"Infection, as always. Keep it clean is the best advice. If it turns pink you're infected, but that's not the worst of it. If it turns black the arm has to come off."

"Do you take arms off?"

He made a face. "I have but I'm not good at it. A doctor would have to do it and more likely than not it will be a Yankee doctor."

"Well, let's hope neither of those comes to pass."

The nurse raised his eyebrows. "I know. I keep thinking that—"

"Nathaniel?"

Two lady nurses, their arms linked, were passing on their way out of the hospital. One of them was Amanda Swanson. He could but gape at her in astonishment.

She recovered first. "Can you walk home alone, Mary?"

"Of course I can, my dear. Good evening."

Amanda then turned to the male nurse. "I can take over here, Raymond. Thank you."

"Well, thank you, Miss Swanson, and good luck to you, sergeant."

"Thank you." Belatedly he rose.

"Please don't rise. You are after all a patient."

He remained standing. "How do you do, Amanda?"

"Well, I am the same as ever. What have you done to yourself now?"

"A colored boy took after me with a knife."

"Hmph! And on which side of the conflict is he?"

"Don't rightly know. He may have just been crazy."

"Are you speaking of him in the past tense?"

"Yes'm. Is there someplace we can speak in private?"

"This is as private as any place in the city, I believe. Yankee spies are everywhere."

"More's the pity."

"Indeed."

Her words were baiting but her heart wasn't in it.

Nathaniel was suddenly conscious of how he must appear to her. He was half-naked, but she had seen him half-naked before and it was the other half. He was bloody and dirty and unkempt; his hair was a mess. He knew that women considered men some sort of dangerous beast, and he now looked the part.

He was for the first time several inches taller than she.

She looked wonderful. She had cleaned up when her shift ended and was in a crisp light grey dress with matching bonnet. She was every inch a woman now.

She didn't seem hostile at all toward him; in fact, she looked unsure of herself. He suddenly recognized the look she was giving him. He had seen it before, when a man met someone he had thought dead.

She steeled herself to say something, then hesitated. Her eyes went to the locket, the only part of either of them that hadn't changed.

"You can take it back if you want to."

She met his eyes. "Do you no longer value it?"

"More than ever. But I am not worthy of you."

"Nathaniel … I understand that you have to lie to do what you do, and I know there are many things that could be called treason, and many that could be called loyalty."

He shook his head. "I have done things …"

"Worse things than any man around you has done? I doubt it."

"I've betrayed …"

"No," she shook her head. "One man's treason is –"

"Amy, there is a betrayal that can only occur between you and me."

She didn't understand; then she did. She sought confirmation in his eyes and found it.

She took a tiny step back. They had never discussed carnality, what we would call sex, and she was taken aback. She was suddenly as cold and distant and beautiful as Saturn setting over the Antietam Creek.

Her demeanor started to crack and he wondered wildly how to react if she began to cry. Then she mastered herself as one would a willful horse. He had never seen her do this, and it was a remarkable sight. She seized control of herself, and she suddenly became Grant, her blue eyes blazing.

"Who is she?"

"It's over, Amy."

"Don't let me prevent you –"

"She's dead."

"Oh!"

Neither could meet the other's eye. "You'll have to take it off me. My hand is …"

"How did she die?"

"She fell. At the Spotsylvania Courthouse."

"Did you … love her?"

"No. I never understood it. But it happened." He stole a glance at her. "You're the one I love, Amanda."

"Does it still … keep you alive?"

He nodded. "So far."

"Then wear it in good health."

"Thanks."

She turned to him and for the first time they looked each other in the eye. "Will they – will they burn the city?"

"He wouldn't say. But you'd best get the family out."

She shook her head. "Mother and I have too much work to do."

"On the other side there are hospitals full of wounded Rebs. Confederates. And they'd feed you there."

She shook her head again, smiling ruefully. "It's too interesting here."

"How is your family?"

She straightened and took a breath, and she was suddenly herself. "What remains of it, you mean? Titus and another boy have run away, lured by the blandishments of the Union. Rachel remains, though she threatens to leave at any time. Mother is well though she is as thin as a switch."

"That's good. And David?"

"David is thriving. He alone has plenty to eat. Our neighbors and friends continue to give him any morsel they come by. We can see that they are starving themselves to do so, though he cannot."

"That's good. That was a thought that's been running through my mind lately, that I may have brought him from one Hell to another."

She hesitated and looked him full in the face. He was suddenly overwhelmed by her presence and felt the urge to crush her to his chest. Her words came to him as if from a great distance, or from underwater, or through the influence of one of his spells.

"He will never go to Hell, Nathaniel, nor will you. Whatever else I may say or feel about you, I would never forgive myself if I did not say that Mother and I thank God every day that you brought him back to us."

Nathaniel chose his words carefully. "I was glad to do it," he said. "I did it in part to settle accounts with your father but I'm glad I did it because David's a good man."

She was suddenly distant again. "What's wrong?" he asked.

"My father died at Cedar Creek in September."

He came awake slowly. He was lying on the floor and the male nurse was back. "What happened?" he asked.

"You took a header," the old man said cheerfully, knocking his pipe out onto the floor. "Looks like you lost more blood than you thought."

"Help me up."

"You're going no farther than this chair for a while, sergeant. Here, drink this."

His head throbbed, whether from lack of blood or striking the floor he knew not. The draft of liquor went through him like a flame. "Where's Miss Swanson?"

"She left. She went home."

"Oh."

"She bade me tell you that she could do no more to help you."

Chapter Ninteen: The City Falls

He walked through the streets of the city as quickly as he could. He tried running a few times but each time his vision went black. His left arm hurt and bled unless he held it higher than his heart. His body and mind still glowed from the brandy, but that was waning.

He turned down another street but Christian wasn't there. He looked in every doorway, down every alley. The bastard probably thought he was dead by this time, so he would have the advantage of surprise, but that would vanish when he saw him, arm bandaged and pistol out, alive and angry.

He stepped out of the alley into the daylight. He stumbled back from its brilliance, turning to see his reflection in a shop window.

"Ahhh…"

He looked like shit. No, he looked like a madman. No, he looked like a madman with a gun.

His clothes were ripped, cut up and covered in dirt, blood, and a little horse manure. His raised left arm made it look like he was greeting everyone.

His hair was all over the place.

While it was perfectly normal to see soldiers with muskets in the center of the city, it was unusual to see someone brandishing a pistol. Now he understood why people had been staring at him. Everyone knew how the story of the Confederacy would end, and people had been looking at him and thinking, "Is this it?"

God damn it, he was uncovered.

He knew he had put his kepi on when he left the shack. It must be lying in Broad Street. He swore under his breath. Shortly after coming to the city he had received a public dressing down from a full bird colonel for being out of uniform. After that he never went out with his head uncovered. And here he was.

Probably the worst part of the refection was his face. He had a look of desperation and despair that shocked even him.

He looked at the overall effect for another second. He was waving a bloody, bandaged arm in the air, he had a cocked pistol in his other hand, his uniform looked like he had been dragged behind a horse, his face was crazy and he didn't have a hat on. Perfect. He could just stand here now and wait for them to come and take him away.

He put the pistol away, washed his face and right arm in a trough and straightened his uniform as well as he could. He got his bearings and found his way back to the scene of the fracas. His hat lay in the middle of the dusty street beside a pool of blood and a spoon. He gave Carl a final glance – he had settled comfortably into the alley and had turned grey – and walked away, thinking.

After considering all angles he went to the Presidential Mansion, three blocks away. The two sentries at the front door waved the wounded soldier through without comment. You're a couple of fools, he thought. How do you know I'm not a Yankee spy?

President Davis' secretary occupied a small anteroom just outside the President's office. He sat at a desk that was nearly as large as the room itself. On each side of him stood a handsome Negro in a gold-braided uniform. The secretary glanced up from his correspondence at Nathaniel's approach. "You need to see His Excellency, sergeant?"

"No, sir, I need to see his maid."

"What?"

"He has a maid he received from Miss Elizabeth van Lew, doesn't he? I need to talk to her."

The secretary pulled off his glasses. "May I ask why?"

"Well, sir, it's a private matter involving her mistress."

The secretary looked skeptical but waved to the servant beside him. A few minutes later he returned with the maid.

Nathaniel thought at first that he had made a mistake. The maid looked no more or less than any other house servant. She wore a kerchief and an expression of surprise and confusion. "You wants to see me, master?" she asked, ducking her head.

"Yes," he said. "Is there someplace we could speak in private?"

"Well, come with me to the library, sir."

Nathaniel had never seen a room like this library. It was about the size of his parents' entire home and was filled floor to ceiling with books. There were even ladders to reach the more inaccessible volumes. He had no idea why anyone would need so many books, except as an affectation.

The maid stood apprehensively before him, her hands beneath her apron. "Your mistress is Miss van Lew, is that right?"

"Yes, master."

"What's your name?"

"Mary Elizabeth, master."

"I am Joshua."

Her eyes gave the slightest flick. "Yes, sir."

"Can you get a message to your mistress? I mean quickly."

"I can have it to her within the half-hour."

"Tell her that Carl Morgan attacked me."

Her eyes flicked downward. "Is that what happened to your arm?"

"Yes."

"Where is Carl?"

"Lying on Broad Street."

She gasped, then recovered. "He say why he did it?"

"We never had time to discuss the matter. Mary Elizabeth, did he work for Alphonsus Christian?"

She seemed to shrink. "We don't trust him. But Carl? I never understood him. He might—"

"Is there any—"

"Mary Elizabeth!"

They turned to the door. Jefferson Davis stood there, his glasses in one hand, a newspaper in the other. She turned and dropped a quick curtsy. "Yes, master!"

"I'll have my coffee now."

"Yes, sir." She bustled out, looking silly and distracted.

The next day another young colored man in the same livery Carl had worn appeared at the telegraph shack. By the time Nathaniel made it out the door the servant was unfolding the steps of a closed coach. Nathaniel, his hand inside his tunic, shook his head and waved him into the box.

A soldier sat in the box, his musket beside him. Another soldier rode the footman's position at the back. Nathaniel entered the coach, taking out his pistol as he went.

Elizabeth van Lew sat looking at him. She was dressed nicely, with a fur muff in her lap. The driver clucked to the horses and they were off.

"How do you do, Private Jones?"

"I'm pretty sore, ma'am."

She looked more confused than she had on their previous meeting, though her dark eyes watched him sharply. "Do you ... intend to shoot me?"

"No." He kept the gun pointed at her but slipped his finger behind the trigger.

"Would you mind telling me what happened?"

"Carl came to my office, said you wanted to see me. He led me to an empty building and tried to kill me with a knife."

"And then what happened?"

He shrugged. "He died."

"That is most extraordinary. Both in that you survived an attack by Carl and in fact killed him, but also in that he assailed you in the first place."

"Do you have any idea why he did it?"

"None whatsoever."

"You reckon he just went crazy? No offense, ma'am."

She smiled softly. "Yes, perhaps he went crazy. It's as good an explanation as any."

"Miss van Lew, do you know of an agent with the code name Cardinal?"

"Did you say 'carnival?'"

"No, Cardinal. Like the bird."

She thought it over. "No. I know of no agent with that name."

"Does it mean anything to you?"

"Well, it means the songbird, of course. The male is red and the female is yellow and both have the tuft of feathers at the peak of the head that gives them the name. There is also the religious figure."

"Religious figure?"

"Yes. A cardinal is a prince of the Roman Catholic Church. There are other Christian denominations that appoint cardinals as well, I believe. And cardinal is a mathematical term as well, though I am unsure of its application." She frowned. "It was once a kind of shawl as well, though it has not been worn since my mother was a child. Why do you ask?"

"Someone signing his name as Cardinal is sending messages to Major Norris naming me as a Yankee agent."

She looked sternly to Nathaniel's right. "It was none of you and you know it. Sergeant, do you think the assault upon you was related to this denunciation?"

"I reckon so. I sent a message addressed to General Finegan telling them about the message from Cardinal. Carl attacked me the next afternoon."

"I have not seen that message yet though I doubt not that you sent it. Did the Federal command structure reply to your message?"

"No."

"Apparently someone intercepted it and induced Carl to assault you."

"Do you suppose it was Alphonsus Christian?"

"Carl, Cardinal. Christian, Cardinal," she said absently. "Perhaps. I doubt it, though."

"Why?"

"Very well, I'll tell him, hold your peace. He is deadlier far than Carl was. If he wished to kill you he would have made another attempt as soon as the first one failed. Additionally, he usually does his own killing."

"Oh. Do you reckon he could have turned Carl?"

She looked even more confused than before. "Does Major Christian have reason to kill you, Private Jones?"

Nathaniel merely grunted at this.

She peered at the pistol. "Is that the kind that takes the little brass cartridges?"

"Ah, no. You have to load each cylinder like a little musket."

"Oh." She lost interest. "How are your wounds?"

"They hurt. I think I'll get better, though. My arm is the worst of it, you can see the bandages, but it's my left arm so I can still work."

"May I ask why you approached my maid instead of coming to see me?"

"I didn't know what kind of reception I'd get at your house. I figured the maid wouldn't be expecting me."

She looked down at the muff, then at him. "How did you know that she was an agent?"

He waved his hand. "Ask me something else."

"Very well," she said evenly. "Do my eyes deceive me or are you now a sergeant?"

"Yes'm. This is three shirts I've worn in as many days. Are you taking me prisoner?"

"What?"

"These soldiers. What are they here for?"

"Oh. They are for my protection. A man threatened me with violence a few days ago and I asked President Davis for help."

"Why did the man threaten you?"

"Why, I'm certain it's for my abolitionist views."

"Your ... abolitionist ...?"

"Of course. I have made no secret of my feeling that slavery is a sin. The citizens of this city are often frank in their demurral."

Are you crazy welled up in him but he held his tongue. The carriage stopped before the telegraph office. He nodded to her and put his piece away.

As he turned from the coach she called his name and pulled her hand from the muff. It held an ugly black pistol nearly as large as she was. It was cocked and her finger was on the trigger. The piece seemed totally out of place in the carriage but looked perfectly natural in her hand.

"I at least do not want to kill you, sergeant."

He smiled for the first time. "I'm glad there's someone, ma'am."

Major Norris also demanded a description of the assault. Nathaniel described Carl as being drunk at the time and demanding money from him. Norris heard him out and dismissed him without comment.

Weeks passed with no further assaults. He heard nothing further from Christian, Miss van Lew or anyone else involved in the sordid business of espionage. He settled once more into the life of a telegraph operator.

One afternoon in late January he delivered a message to Major Norris. He went into his office to find the major talking to a youth in the uniform of the American Telegraph Company. The young man turned around and said, "Hey, Nate! How are you?"

"Oh, nice to see you, Willie."

Behind the desk, Norris said, "You two know each other?"

"Yes, sir," Willie said. "Nate and I worked the key for American before the war."

"Nate? Isn't his name William Jones?"

"No, sir, it's Nate Curry. Nathaniel Curry."

Norris frowned. "Nathaniel Curry," he said. "Where have I heard that name before?" He thought a moment, then his eyes opened wide. "Guards!"

Two privates with muskets rushed in from the anteroom. "Yes, sir?"

"Arrest this man! Nathaniel Curry, I know I had some correspondence on that..." He pawed at the letters on his desk as the soldiers grabbed Nathaniel's arms. "Yes," Norris said, "here it is. 'Nathaniel Curry, Union agent in this city.'"

"What's the matter, sir?" a young officer said, rushing in from the outer office.

"I just captured a Union agent, one Nathaniel Curry."

"Nathaniel Curry? I recollect that name."

"It was in my correspondence, have you been sneaking peeks at my desk?"

"Never, sir," the young captain said, stiffness in his voice. "No, it was from the start of the war. I know," he said, snapping his fingers. "It was that assault that the Union made with the balloons on Falls Church. It was that Yankee, Thaddeus Lowe, and a young Richmonder, Nathaniel Curry, helped him. Telegraph operator. We all had orders to arrest him." He looked at Nathaniel. "And this is him?"

"Yes, sir," Willie said, looking at Nathaniel with wide eyes, "this is him."

"Well, that's good enough for me," Norris said. "Let's take care of this son of a bitch right now." No sooner had he spoken the words than one of the sentries let go his arm and rammed the butt of his musket into his gut. Nathaniel bent over and began to puke on the floor.

"Not here, you idiot, I don't want any corpses on my floor, and you're going to clean that up. Take him outside and kill him. Wait, I'll come with you." He drew his pistol and came around the desk.

"Sir, I can explain!" Nathaniel said, or tried to: the words came out as "Oog! Ag! Oog!" He was dragged, struggling, out of the building and into an adjoining alley.

"Let me do it," Norris said, and cocked his pistol. "Don't stand behind him, you moron!" As he stepped up a voice behind him calmly said, "Hold on a minute, there, sir."

Norris hesitated, then said, "Yes?"

Alphonsus Christian said, "Why are you killing Jones?"

"He's no Jones and never was. His name is Nathaniel Curry and he's a Union spy."

"His name is Nathaniel Curry and he's both a Union spy and a Confederate one."

"Well, he's really working for the Union."

"No, sir, he's really working for me. I'm quite certain of his loyalty."

Norris lowered the pistol and turned to Christian. "How can you be so all-fired sure of that?"

"When I had that little problem with Charlie Belcher it was Curry who tried to warn me. I was sure Belcher was full on our side and Curry just had it wrong. Wish I had listened to him."

Norris said, "God damn you, Christian, here's another of your God-damned people magically appearing before me. You know I hate that. If I let him go, he's your responsibility, you clear on that?"

"Entirely, sir."

"Well, then, Curry, get the God-damned Hell out of here." He dropped the hammer to half-cock.

"Yes, sir," Nathaniel said. The soldiers let go of his arms. He had his feet beneath him though his legs were wobbly. He knew, though, that this weak feeling would give way to the peculiar exhilaration a close brush with death always seemed to give him. "Sir, if it's all right with you, I'd like to keep going by the name William Jones."

"I don't give a shit. You," he said, pointing to one of the sentries, "go clean that puke up." He turned around but Christian was gone.

One morning in February Nathaniel was ordered to report to the Presidential Mansion. The secretary in the anteroom recognized him and ushered him into Davis' office. There he saw Davis sitting at his desk, with Major Norris and Major Christian seated before him. Christian was dressed as a staff sergeant. Completing the scene was Mary Elizabeth in a white maid's cap, her eyes lowered.

"Sit down, Curry," Norris said. "This is him, Mister President."

Davis glanced up, then gave him a second look. "You're Nathaniel Curry?"

"Yes, sir. I go by the name William Jones over here."

"Weren't you here a few weeks ago?"

"Yes, sir."

"Well? Why?"

"I had to get in touch with Elizabeth van Lew and I knew she gave you that nigger girl. One of her niggers attacked me and I killed him."

"Why did the nigger attack you?"

"Sir, why do niggers do anything? Excuse me, sir."

"Norris?"

"Yes, sir. Curry, Christian, General Lee needs information on the Union lines at Petersburg. We need you to go over there and look things over."

"You want us in blue suits, sir?" Nathaniel asked.

"That was the original intention. I'd like to suggest another approach, though, if I may, Mister President."

"What's that, Norris?"

"I'd like to attach these two men to Vice President Stephen's peace delegation that's meeting with Lincoln at Hampton Roads tomorrow."

Davis looked annoyed. "You know I'm not sanctioning that. He said he'd meet with you only if it was agreed beforehand that we are abandoning secession."

"I know, sir, but hear me out. The stipulation of abandoning secession is a political fiction, both sides recognize that. The peace mission is going anyway and these two can go along as aides to the delegates."

"Stephens is ready to sell me out for thirty pieces of silver."

"Nothing of the kind, sir. He's a loyal Confederate and a servant of Your Excellency. He just gives voice to his opinions. This is after all a free country."

Nathaniel felt uncomfortable at this last exchange. Alexander Stephens had been increasingly free in his criticisms of the President and of the Confederate government in general, but Davis should not be discussing this in front of enlisted men.

"So why these men?"

"These men are professional agents, sir. Anything they see or hear in the normal course of their duties could be of great value to us. However, they are both known among the Yankees and could be compromised in a more conventional spy mission."

"Why not a more conventional spy mission, then, with other men?"

"We're doing that as well, but we'd like to do this too."

"Go ahead, then," Davis muttered.

The next morning found a delegation consisting of Vice President Stephens and several other members of the government boarding a boat flying a white flag to take them down the James to Hampton Roads. Accompanying them were two noncommissioned officers bearing their portmanteaus and other papers. These two had the additional duty of observing the shore on both sides with telescopes.

The boat picked its way down river, carefully avoiding the sunken ships and other obstacles placed there to thwart Union gunboats from attacking Richmond. Nathaniel and Christian could clearly see the extensive Union works at City Point and Petersburg. Beyond the Union lines they could see part of the Confederate defenses.

Some of these defenses were under attack. "Hey! Look at that," Nathaniel exclaimed.

"What?" Christian asked.

"I saw a projectile going through the air. It went from the Union trenches into the Rebel ones and exploded."

"So?"

"I never saw a projectile moving through the air before. I mean, cannon fire and musket fire moves too fast to see."

"That was mortar."

"Mortar?" Nathaniel had seen mortars before but had never seen them in use. They were very peculiar-looking cannon, about three feet long and three feet wide, a hemisphere of solid iron but for the ten-inch bore down the center. They could not fire a round very far or very fast but they could do so with great accuracy. Union forces were now dropping rounds right into the enemy trenches with them.

"None of these delegates is even looking at the shore," he observed.

"That's not their job."

"Yes, but you'd think they'd still keep their eyes open. You and I are the only ones on this boat who aren't fools."

Christian turned to him. "Curry," he said, "don't get familiar with me. Remember our difference in rank."

"One stripe?"

"I'm an officer and you know it."

"Should I start saluting you, then, sir? Oh, wait, I'm a civilian. I never joined up."

"Don't get gay. You're in uniform, that makes you a soldier."

"Sorry, but I've come to feel that this officer and enlisted man business is all pretense. As for you and I, the pretense at the moment is that we are both noncoms."

Christian looked out the window again.

The boat moved into the broad estuary of the James. A Union gunboat, also flying a white flag, came within hailing distance and formed up as an escort for the rest of the journey. Several hours later they rounded the point and came up to Fort Monroe. They did not land, but pulled alongside a ship, the *River Queen*. There a major received the delegation, courteously saluting Stephens. He led the three delegates to a large stateroom. The two sergeants brought up the rear, toting the delegates' briefcases and portmanteaus.

Lincoln, accompanied by Secretary of State Seward, received the delegation with great courtesy, shaking the hand of each delegate. He greeted Stephens and another man by name before they were introduced. For their part, the delegates were as effusive as Republicans. Lincoln invited the delegates to sit; the spies remained standing.

They sat down and got right to business. The first issue at hand, and the one that was the official pretext for the meeting, was a bizarre proposal that the Union and the Confederacy, under the authority of the Monroe Doctrine, should jointly attack Mexico and drive the French out. This was discussed, but everyone knew it would be rejected.

At last they got to the real purpose of the meeting. What, Stephens asked, would it take to end the current hostilities?

"The only thing that would end this war," Lincoln replied, "would be for those resisting the laws of the Union to cease that resistance."

"To what laws in particular are you referring, sir? After all, there are many issues between our two countries."

"I can only recognize one country," Lincoln said evenly. "That is the United States of America."

"Given that, sir, in what wise are we in violation of the law?"

"By not admitting Union forces to the city and by taking up arms against the Federal government."

"So allowing occupation of all our lands would end the war?"

"Yes, sir. That, and acceptance of Federal laws outlawing slavery, among other issues."

"Sir, upon that matter we can not compromise. Chattel slavery is in no way prohibited by Scripture and we have always employed it. Indeed, our way of life, our very existence, depends upon it. It is to the benefit of both races."

Lincoln shook his head. "The law of this nation demands its abolition."

"We must find another course, sir."

"Upon this matter, Mister Vice-President, there can be no compromise."

Stephens raised his hand in moderation. "Compromise, Mister President, is the soul of politics, as we both well know. Surely there is some middle ground we can seek."

"There is indeed much that can be discussed," Lincoln assured him. "Upon one matter or another we can seek a middle ground. But prior to that, the Confederacy must lay down its arms, cease all resistance to the government of the United States and its laws and accept immediate reunification of the nation."

"Do you mean to tell me, sir," Stephens said evenly, "that you have nothing to offer this delegation but the acceptance of our unconditional surrender?"

Lincoln had been sitting with his legs crossed. He put both feet on the floor, leaned forward and said, "Yes, sir. Your only course is to surrender. The alternative is for our forces to reduce Richmond. That is the message you must take back to President Davis."

The delegates looked at each other. "Sir," someone said at last, "we have no commission from President Davis."

"Do you have any authority to treat with me at all?"

"No, sir. Not beyond discussion of the proposed assault upon Mexico."

"Then I'm afraid this meeting can be of little utility, except that we have all established our *bona fides*."

The meeting ended shortly thereafter. Each of the delegates shook the President's hand again, with less enthusiasm but perhaps with more respect than before. Lincoln asked leave of Stephens, then greeted the two enlisted men as well, taking their hands and asking their names.

The next morning, after the delegates had reported upon their meeting with Lincoln, Nathaniel and Christian made an oral report to Norris and Davis. Christian was able to give detailed descriptions of the Union fortifications and supplies based upon what he had glimpsed from the boat.

On their way out of the office Christian pulled Nathaniel into an alley and Nathaniel quickly told him all he had gleaned from recent telegraphic traffic.

No one attacked Nathaniel again, and this puzzled him. Was the instigator of Carl's attack himself out of play? Had this person repented and decided that Nathaniel was worth more alive than dead? Would there be an attack from another quarter? Everyone in Richmond walked around in a state of great anxiety, but he looked over his shoulder more than most.

In March telegraph traffic picked up. A great assault upon the Union forces besieging Richmond and Petersburg was in the works. The Union of course knew of the coming onslaught and was making preparations.

The last great Confederate assault began a few days later. Striking out before dawn from Petersburg, Lee's forces quickly overran Fort Stedman.

Nathaniel followed the attack from the telegraph hut, sending a steady stream of eager boys running to the War Office as reports came in. At first the reports were all good: Stedman was firmly in Rebel hands, as were a number of smaller outposts surrounding it. Striking out from the fort, the Confederates captured other outposts and further widened the gap in the Union lines.

By 7:30 in the morning, however, the tide had turned. Federal attackers drove the Rebels back into Fort Stedman. Seeing that he could not hold the fort, Lee ordered a retreat half an hour later.

By this time, however, the fort was surrounded. Many Confederate troops stayed in the fort and surrendered rather than fight their way back through the lines. The Rebel Army lost three thousand men it could ill afford; worse, it had failed in a last, desperate effort to break the Federal stranglehold.

Now the initiative passed to the Union. Its forces gathered for what all expected to be a crushing blow. Spies were sent out to descry the Union positions and intentions.

Nathaniel Curry worked the key as much as his constitution would allow. Cartwright and Ness were getting better at the key and could copy messages in clear most of the time but they could not receive encrypted messages. With a clear message one could miss a quarter of the characters and still get the sense of a message. An encrypted message, however, could not be read if even a few characters were received wrong.

Nathaniel taught the younger operators the essentials of encryption and decryption. He would receive a coded message and pass it on to one of them. Soon they were proudly translating messages between field officers and the War Office.

To run these messages Nathaniel had recruited a corps of small boys, children still too young to be drafted by the desperate Confederacy. It gave these idle children something to do and made them feel they were doing their part in the great conflict. Some of the runners were girls and some were colored; all were welcome.

His favorite runner was a little colored girl named Isabel. She was always at the office early in the morning, her clothes were always immaculate, and she took her work very seriously. Nathaniel liked giving her messages for the President, first because he knew they would be delivered, but also because he was amused by the image of the tiny girl, her hair up in ribbons, sternly telling Davis' secretary that she could only place the message in the President's hand.

He himself ran several messages a week to the Presidential Mansion. The messages themselves were usually trivial but he always managed to catch the eye of Davis' maid and spend a minute or two with her. Although Mary Elizabeth seemed a simple woman she was anything but. She could read and write as well as any white person and had a quick grasp of all she beheld. She was able to glance at a map or document on Davis' desk and describe its contents in detail several days later.

Nathaniel didn't regret the good he was doing the Cause: the Union was certainly receiving the same information he was and was probably putting it to better use. Moreover, he reserved the best for himself. Several times a day he would copy a message, then tell one of the junior operators to take the key while he worked in his office.

These messages he decoded with the keyword Joshua, using the unbroken Union encryption method. Sometimes he made a reply himself. Other times he would run a message to someone else in the city. One of his regular recipients was an old free colored tailor who served the officer class; another was a white clergyman.

He gave Christian a briefing down by the docks one afternoon. He went through the usual things: Lee was in the city; food was expected from the south any day now; there was another typhus outbreak.

"Give me something to give the Rebs."

"I don't know much."

"Tell me what you do know."

He shrugged. "There's a new ironclad at Fort Monroe."

"Everybody knows that."

"A nigger army is coming in from Michigan."

"A whole nigger army?"

"I heard it three times now."

"I didn't know there were that many niggers in Michigan."

"There's lots of niggers everywhere."

"Tens of thousands of buck niggers of military age, all hankering to fight?"

Nathaniel shrugged. "That's the official rumor. They might have made it up for our benefit."

"What else?"

Nathaniel looked around the harbor. Most of the ships were battened down, their sails tightly furled, awaiting the increasingly distant day when their crews would march back and they would proudly sail down to the sea. Some ships were still manned, their crews drilling endlessly and keeping their vessels nicely trimmed, every man Jack preferring this futility to the futility of the battlefield.

And then there were the ironclads. Three of them lay in the harbor, black and organic looking. They looked ready to fight, though none ever had.

At some point Billy Yank would enter the city and their moment would come. Would they fight or surrender? The great beasts shimmered silently in the heat.

Nathaniel said, "Abraham Lincoln had a roll in the long grass with Red Sally last week. He's already gone blind from it."

Christian made a sound like he was suppressing a sneeze, then said, "I don't think they'd buy that." Then he turned away, laughing. It was the only time Nathaniel ever saw the son of a bitch laugh. He looked like he didn't like it very much.

As March progressed he found his communication with the Union command structure was deteriorating. Some of his messages went uncopied. When he demanded a reply later he found himself having to reconstruct the original message and encrypt it again, as he dared not save incriminating messages. Even at that he often got no reply.

Certainly everyone was very busy, but he had important things to say. He began to feel as frustrated by his espionage experience as he had been by his experience with the Balloon Corps.

A coded message was sent from General Lee to General Joseph Johnston in North Carolina. Nathaniel copied the message and decoded it in his office. The Army of Northern Virginia, it said, may have to evacuate the Richmond and Petersburg region. If this occurred it would need resupply. Johnston was ordered to bring food, fodder and matériel to Amelia Station, some thirty miles from Richmond.

Nathaniel looked at the decoded message on his desk. The message might have been copied by the Federals, but had it been decoded and brought to Grant's attention? He doubted it.

He wrote a new message and encrypted it. He then told Cartwright and Ness that he was going to get a few hours of sleep.

There were plenty of horses in Richmond but nearly all of them were lying dead on street corners or in alleys. Nathaniel found himself hiking instead of riding. He walked west of the city about two miles to a telegraph pole he had used for previous special messages. He donned spurs and climbed the pole, then removed the wire from one glass insulator and attached it to a lineman's key. The other end of the line was attached to a ground wire.

He could now send a message west without much danger of it being copied in Richmond or Petersburg. He pulled a message blank from his pocket and transmitted its contents. The message ordered Johnston to send the supplies not to Amelia Station but to another location farther west.

Then he returned to his tent for three hours of much-needed sleep.

The Union blow fell at Five Forks, and in the best tradition of Union attacks it fell clumsily. Warren, in charge of half of the Union force, was deployed half a mile farther east than intended, leaving the rest of the force unsupported. The result was a weak attack upon the Rebel forces.

The Confederate commanders were so lulled by the tepid attack that two of them, Fitzhugh Lee and George Pickett, actually left for a shad bake. It wasn't until late afternoon that Warren came into action, and it was to devastating effect. His corps swung around the Confederate left, forming a pincer with the two other Union corps. The Confederates were surrounded, outmanned and leaderless; by nightfall they had been decimated. The entire force was routed, with the survivors fleeing back toward Petersburg.

So utter was the collapse that word failed to reach Richmond by telegraph before fleeing men began straggling through the streets. Ness manned the silent key as Nathaniel, Cartwright and Isabel stood in the door of the telegraph hut, watching the soldiers stream by.

"It won't be long now," Nathaniel muttered.

"Until what?" Cartwright asked.

Nathaniel turned away without answering. Like most in Richmond, Cartwright had been lulled by years of close calls into thinking that the city would never actually fall.

The next morning Nathaniel was asleep in his office when Cartwright woke him. "I just got a really funny message in, Sergeant," he said. "Can you make heads or tails of this? I sure can't."

Nathaniel read the message, then read it again. At first it was nonsense but it took on more import each time he read it.

TO AP HILL RMOND
FROM LT MACCABEE PBURG
GEN AMBROSE HILL WAS KILLED BY A CHRISTIAN THIS MORNING STOP DOES THAT ANSWER YOUR QUESTION 73

"Oh my God."

"I received that myself. I swear I got every character right, the sender was transmitting real slow like. Then I decoded it."

"Decoded it?"

Cartwright smiled sheepishly. "I've seen you starting a square with 'Joshua,' Will. I hope I wasn't being forward."

It gave him a thrill of fear to hear Cartwright speak the name. "You done good, Enoch."

"It don't make sense, Will. It's a message for General Hill saying that General Hill was killed?"

"Yeah."

"And it says a Christian did it. Are there a lot of Jews on the Union side?"

"What do you mean?"

"Well, I figure this Lieutenant Maccabee has to be a Jew. Judas Maccabee was a Jewish fighter against the Romans in the Bible."

"He was?"

"Yes. His boys were like the Moseby's Raiders of their day."

"I—I thought Maccabee was a Scottish name."

Cartwright shook his head. "What do we do about this, Sergeant?"

"Nothing." Nathaniel crumpled the message and threw it in the stove. "One thing, though: don't do nothing to any more Joshua messages. Just copy them. You like to get both of us shot doing that."

"Yes, sir."

"Have you heard anything else saying that General Hill was killed?"

"No, sir. Ness is working the key right now and nothing's coming in at all."

Nathaniel nodded, then said, "Thank you, Enoch. That's all."

He stood in thought by the door. Was that message really from Manchester? Had he actually witnessed Alphonsus Christian shoot General Hill? That would answer every question he had as to Christian's loyalty. "Christ Jesus," he murmured.

Did he have to kill Cartwright now? He would hate to do that. Even thinking this, though, made it clear to him that he could kill him if he thought it needed doing. He would just hate doing it.

He recalled standing and looking at another street in this same city. Had that only been three and a half years ago? Then he had imagined the city rising to demand his life. Now he stood ready to destroy the place himself, and it felt no better.

The next moment he pricked up his ears as a message came over the wire in clear. When it finished he demanded, "Did that say what I thought it said?"

Ness stared at the key with a pencil in his trembling hand. He hadn't written a single character. "I think so," he said. "Lee is going to skip."

"Never say such a thing about Robert E. Lee!" he shouted, then sat heavily down on the other side of the table. "Listen," he said, "we have to do our duty. Write that message down and I'll deliver it to the President myself."

"I d-d-don't remember what it said."

Nathaniel took the pencil from him and wrote:

TO J DAVIS RMOND
FROM RE LEE PBURG
I ADVISE THAT ALL PREPARATION BE MADE FOR LEAVING

RICHMOND TONIGHT

He looked at Ness. His face was ashen and tears were running down his cheeks. "Your home is on the north side, isn't it, Phineas?"

"Yeah."

"I suggest you find a new place south of here, for a little while, anyway."

"I wanted to stay to the end, Willie."

"This is the end." Nathaniel put the message in his pocket. "Boys, I have no authority to tell you to stay or to go. But the monkey's coming to town." Cartwright and Ness looked at each other.

He turned to Isabel. "You should go on home, too. And thank you."

She came to attention. "Sergeant, I'll stay and tell the other runners they are dismissed."

"Yes, good idea."

He ran to the Presidential Mansion where the sentry informed him that the President was at church.

"Church?"

"Yes, Sergeant. It's Sunday, you know."

"Oh. No, I didn't."

The sentry gave him directions to the church and he ran there. As he came in the minister was delivering his sermon. Nathaniel hesitated to intrude upon the service.

The minister spotted him and stopped speaking. All eyes turned to the intruder. Blushing, Nathaniel walked down the aisle and handed Davis the message. The President glanced at it and said, "Is this genuine?"

"I think so, sir."

Davis left his seat and went into the foyer of the church. Every military officer in the church gathered around him, as did the delivery boy. "The day we have long dreaded has arrived," he said, his voice trembling. "The Army and Navy must quit the city at once. The Army must form up under Lee to continue the defense."

"What shall the Navy do, sir?" a commander asked.

"Can you make a run down the James?"

"No, sir. We've put too many obstructions in the river. And the Yanks have it pretty well blocked farther down."

"Then destroy every piece of equipment you can."

Some of the men moaned at this, but all recovered quickly.

"Destroy all documents related to our government," Davis said. "Let whatever foodstuffs and supplies the Army cannot carry be distributed to the populace."

"What about the liquor, sir?"

"No, that should not be distributed, of course—"

"Sir, I mean that in other cities the Yankees have taken, if they got hold of liquor they behaved terribly."

"Yes. Have all liquor in the city destroyed." The men saluted and started away when Davis said, "Wait! We should wait until the service..."

He looked the length of the church to the pulpit, where the minister met his eye. This worthy held his hand out in sign of benediction. He spoke to the congregation and to the nation, but his eyes, and the eyes of every person present, were on their leader.

"The Lord bless thee and keep thee; the Lord make his face to shine upon thee and be gracious unto thee; the Lord lift up his countenance upon thee and give thee peace. Amen."

"Amen," everyone said.

Everyone fell to their tasks. Nathaniel started back to the telegraph hut. Around him were the cries of people responding to the news, for bad news always travels fast.

Soon there were piles of documents burning before every government building. He overheard an enlisted man tell his commander that their building had too many documents to bring out and the officer replied that the building itself should be burned. When the soldier hesitated, the officer screamed at him, "Burn it, God damn you! Let me show you how!" and ran into the building.

Horses had been scarce in Richmond; they were suddenly plentiful. Their owners loaded everything of value into every conceivable conveyance and drove like demons out of the city.

Word spread that food was being distributed. The loss of the war and the imminent destruction of the city suddenly became secondary in everyone's mind to getting something to eat.

Nathaniel, who was hungry himself, followed a crowd to a storehouse. As he stood with the others he felt a heat on his back that surpassed that of the midday sun. Soldiers opened the gates and began handing out food, but the starving throng pushed right past them and came out bearing a bounty. Smoked meats, dried fruits and other delicacies flowed out the doors. At first this largess was greeted with cheers, but the crowd soon became angry as they realized that while they starved mountains of food had existed in the city. Angry voices arose to denounce the speculators who had hoarded this treasure. Nathaniel glanced around at the crowd, noting in passing the flames that were starting to rise.

The crowd turned to the nearby shops and smashed them open, taking whatever they wanted. Suddenly they saw an astonishing sight: a stream of whiskey flowing through the street. The food was tossed aside as men and women got on their knees, picking the liquor up in their hats and even sucking it from between the cobblestones.

Nathaniel picked up a sausage and a wheel of cheese and started back to the telegraph hut. He turned back for a final look at the queer scene: men and women, now quite drunk, were splashing around in the puddles of whiskey while around them the city burned merrily.

As he ran to his post it seemed to him that the State Capitol was on fire. He soon saw that it was actually the great tobacco warehouses beyond the Capitol that were burning. A large explosion came from his right as the Tredegar Iron Works, a great shell factory, went up. Seconds later there were more explosions as shells fell back to earth.

As he got to the telegraph hut he was knocked flat on his back by an even greater explosion. The Navy was blowing up the ironclads in the harbor. Stunned, he lay on the ground and looked around. The African Baptist Church was right beside him. The church itself was still standing but its windows were blown out and some of the gravestones in the cemetery had been knocked over by the force of the blast. Not even the dead are safe, he thought. An iron rain began as he entered the hut.

The government, the Army and the Navy quit the city that night. Only the most loyal and the most treasonous remained. Nathaniel Curry slept beside his key.

The next day was one of anarchy. There was no civil authority left in the city at all, not even the fire department. Some of the citizens tried to put the fires out on their own but too much of the city was burning for them to have any effect.

Nathaniel left his post unmanned and went to his family's home. This required walking down several streets where the buildings on both sides were fully engulfed in flame.

The store was gone as were the living quarters above it. He had a glimpse of the two-story building lying in ruins before his clothing got so hot he feared it would ignite.

His next stop was the Swanson home. The handsome green and white Georgian house was gone; only the chimneys at each end remained. He could not get too close because the street was macadam and it had melted, but he could see that the outbuildings were also destroyed. The hitching post with its shiny brass ball was all that remained intact.

He turned away, more angry than ever at the Confederacy. It wasn't the Federals but the Confederate government itself that had destroyed the city by abandoning it. Some of the government and the military should have stayed behind to maintain order. Yes, they would have been captured, but that would have been a small sacrifice.

He had no idea where his mother was but he suspected that Amanda was at one of the hospitals. The first two he went to were burned out. The third was a stone structure a mile away from the fires. Its staff was still on duty, caring for its charges. No one noticed a three-striper with a bandaged arm moving through the wards.

She wasn't there. On a whim he returned to a ward he had passed by because there was no staff in the room.

All of the patients there were women. He stepped in and looked around the room, then went over and sat at a chair beside one of the beds.

The patient stirred at the sound but it took her another minute to wake up. "Who is it?" she croaked.

"Can't you see me?"

"No. I'm blind."

"It's Nathaniel, Sally."

"Nathaniel?" She opened her eyes but they rolled around without focusing on anything. Her lips were cracked and bleeding. Her orange curls stuck to her clammy skin.

"Nathaniel Curry."

She relaxed. "Oh. Nathaniel, give me a drink of water."

There was a pitcher at the front of the room. He held the cup as she drank. "Thank you, Nathaniel."

"You're welcome."

She needed to be cleaned up as well, by the smell of her, but he didn't offer to do that.

"You've come to see me?"

"How are you, Sally?"

She sighed. "Every beat of my heart feels like a knife in me."

"That's too bad."

"How is the war going?"

"It's almost over."

"That's good." Tears rolled across her fevered cheeks.

"Sally, what did Clarabel find out about you?"

"What?"

"I know what she meant when she said she'd dream about me. You couldn't have made that up. She never said she thought I shot her. It was you that done it."

She tried to push herself away from him. "No…no…"

"I ain't a-going to do nothing to you," he said.

"You're not?"

"No. Looks like God is just, after all."

She wept openly now. "I was doing my duty," she said. "Same as her. Same as you. Same as…all of us."

"Are you Cardinal?"

"What?"

"Did you send messages under the name Cardinal?"

"Do you think that could be me? A bird with red feathers? I may as well have hung a sign around my neck. But even if I had no one would have read it. People are fools."

"I don't get it, Sally. If you worked for the Rebs, why did you try so hard to recruit me?"

The blind eyes sought him out, did not find him. "We thought you'd fail," she said. "Thought we could use you."

"But you couldn't, could you?"

She shook her head. "You were stronger than we thought."

"So you sicced Carl on me. What did you say to get him to try and kill me?"

"It was easy. Niggers are fools…men are fools."

"What about Captain Thomas?"

"Cunt. Bitch. You haven't seen *her* around lately, have you?"

That was too bad, he had liked her.

"Sally, some folks still think I killed David Miller."

She began to sob. "David…"

"Did Christian do it?"

She shook her head. "No one killed him. He went to California."

"California?"

"He sent me a letter. Said he was going to strike it rich and come back." She squeezed her blind eyes shut. "But he's never coming back. Not to me, not never to me."

He thought of the Californians he had seen, wild men with long hair and beards. "Do you have this letter?"

She thought about it. "Why do you want it?"

"To prove I didn't kill him."

"I threw it away. I'm glad," she said, bitterly. "I'll kill one more Yankee after I die."

He turned away, was actually out the door of the ward before she called him back. He came back and said, "Yeah?"

"Do you have any food?"

The balls on this woman ... he sighed and said, "Yes."

He hadn't dared leave his food in the telegraph hut so he was able to pull from his tunic hardtack, dried meats, fruit, cheese and even a small bottle of cognac. She gobbled it down, then lay back.

"Oh, thank you. Why did you do this for me?"

"I'm a fool."

She fumbled at the small table beside the bed, opening the drawer and pulling out an envelope. "Here. Now get the Hell out of here, you Yankee-loving scalawag."

He went to the office of Major Norris. The officer was standing in the middle of the room, seemingly frozen in mid-stride, a pen in his hand. His hand trembled as if working a telegraph key. He was now a lieutenant colonel, Nathaniel saw.

"Are you all right, sir?"

Norris turned his head to him as if he didn't understand the question. "I – I have to destroy the records, but there are too many."

"Can I help you?"

"There are too many to carry to the street before ... in the remaining time. And I can't fire the building, the quarters are too tight here. It would take out half the city."

Nathaniel considered the matter. "What records do you want to burn, sir?"

"All of them. I have the payroll records of the army and navy here, plus the records of our group." He ran his fingers through his thick, wavy hair. "The payroll records take up a full room, there must be a ton of them."

"We can burn the records of our group, sir, and leave the others."

"The ... the victors will have records of everyone who served in the military of the Confederacy."

"And no man would deny that he served, sir, if the Yankees asked him. But our group should leave nothing behind."

"Yes, you're right. Men ... could hang for these things."

"Can I help you, then, sir?"

Norris shook himself as if waking up. "Yes. Yes, take all of this stack, to start with. No, these things here, take that first."

Norris was a commander again. Half an hour later there was a fire of broken furniture in the middle of the street with burning scraps of paper rising into the air. Norris ran up and down the stairs with stacks of paper with the energy of a man half his age; Nathaniel had to struggle to keep up.

At last there was nothing worth burning. The two of them gave a last look around the office, then Norris turned to him with a smile.

"We leave Lincoln only ashes, Curry. May he enjoy the taste."

"Yes, sir."

"Dismissed."

"Yes, sir. But I have nowhere to go."

Norris thought for a moment. "Nor do I. But I at least should avoid capture. I'm heading out."

"Will you join up with Lee?"

"I don't think so, because I think Lee will soon be captured. But I could yet end up standing with him. Yes, and if it comes to that, falling with him. There are a lot worse ways to go out."

"Yes, sir."

Norris held out his hand. "Curry, if my word is worth anything after this, your name is cleared."

"Thank you, sir."

"Walking out now?"

"I want to give one last look around here, sir."

"As you will." Both men came rather stiffly to attention and exchanged salutes.

The riot outside grew louder as Nathaniel looked the office over. In one corner there stood a large chiffonier. Poking through the drawers he found several uniforms in both blue and gray. He left Norris' office a first lieutenant of the First Massachusetts Cavalry and carrying a carpetbag.

He had never been tricked out like this before. He felt as if he was on his way to a fancy-dress ball. The uniform was complete right down to the saber at his side. It didn't even have the hole over the heart that he was now accustomed to in his attire. He wore his sidearm, still in its shoulder holster, on the outside of his tunic.

The sight of a Union officer in the streets drew glances but no comment. He picked his way through unburned and already-burned streets to the telegraph hut.

Isabel, one hand holding her hem, the other in the air, danced before him. She turned and saw him and came to attention.

"At ease."

She looked at his uniform: the dark blue cloth, the silver bars on the epaulets, the saber, the brass "chicken" buttons that every female coveted. She opened her mouth but did not speak.

"Cartwright and Ness gone?"

She nodded. "And I done sent the other runners home."

"Good." He knelt before her. "Isabel, the war's over, the Yankees won. You know that, don't you?"

She nodded.

He touched her arm. "That means you're free now. You and your mother."

Her eyes blazed. "We *already* free."

That was the only answer he was going to get. "Well, then … dismissed."

She snapped to, then ran out the door.

He looked around the empty hut. So Ness and Cartwright were gone. He pictured them high-stepping it down some southerly road, becoming more firmly civilians with every step.

He sent a message in clear to the Union forces at Petersburg, telling them the city had been evacuated. He received a testy reply that they already knew that and he should keep the line free if he had nothing useful to say.

He went out in search of more food just in time to see the Union troops arrive. Their first tasks were to distribute food to the civilian population and to put out the fires. They were in high spirits and they set about their tasks with relish.

A master sergeant approached him and saluted. He returned the salute. "You weren't in our party, sir. How long have you been in the city?"

"A little while, Sergeant."

"Do you know where there's a working telegraph line?"

"Yes, there's one three blocks away."

"Begging your pardon, sir, but we don't have any modern maps of the city. That over there is surely the Capitol, but where is Jeff Davis' house?"

"That's a few blocks away. It's just down that street over there, in fact, but you won't find him at home."

"You sure about that?"

"Quite sure. He left on the train last night. He was one of the last to leave."

"Did he tell you where he was going, sir?"

Nathaniel shook his head. "Sorry." He smiled and tossed a quick salute as another officer approached. "How are you, Manchester?"

"Curry!" He took his hand in a firm clasp. "Gotten a promotion, have you?"

"Yes. Give me a minute." He gave the sergeant directions to the telegraph hut and added, "Tell your operator the juice is fresh but there's more if he needs it plus another crow's foot."

"I...don't know what that means, Lieutenant."

"Well, he'll figure it out." He saluted the sergeant away, then turned back to Manchester. "Yes, I guess I was the first Union officer in the city."

"Did you get my message?"

"About Christian? Yes. Tell me more about that."

"The Union made its push through the Rebel lines at Petersburg yesterday before dawn. I was in a gray uniform in the back right near General Hill as the Rebs counterattacked. Christian stepped in front of us and turned and shot Hill in the chest."

"God Almighty! With a musket?"

Manchester shook his head. "It was a tiny pistol hidden in his hand. I never even saw it. It looked like he shot him with his finger. Hill went down and didn't get up. Everyone thought it was Union fire that did it."

"Lord!"

"I'll tell you, I thought he was a-going to shoot me next. But he just walked away."

"Where is he now?"

"Damned if I know."

Nathaniel pointed at the State Capitol. Both came to attention and saluted as the Virginia state flag came down and the Stars and Stripes rose in its place.

"Well, looks like Richmond is ours at last, hey?" he said.

"Looks that-a-way. Lincoln is chomping at the bit to come here."

"He is? Tell him to come on ahead."

"I would if I had a telegraph line."

"That sergeant is on his way to one now."

"Then let's catch up with him."

It was easy to follow the commotion the next day from half a mile away. As Abraham Lincoln made his way through the city he was greeted by throngs of cheering colored people. The white people were out in force as well for their first sullen look at their conqueror.

Nathaniel Curry waited with a small military delegation in the square in front of the Capitol. His arm hurt, his head hurt and his stomach hurt.

He had fallen in with a group of young officers who had been given the freedom of the city. They were curious as to who he was and how he had beaten them into the city. Hearing him speak answered most of their questions; hearing him mention Colonel Sharpe answered the rest.

He had led them to a restaurant. The colored staff gave them a most hearty welcome. Food and drink appeared as if by magic and the party began. Nathaniel ended the evening by losing consciousness in a chair about three o'clock in the morning.

He awoke when he fell out of said chair. It hurt to open his eyes, but he got a bleary look at the room. It looked like the aftermath of a battle: men were scattered on the floor in various arcane attitudes, groaning weakly or else utterly immobile. His mouth felt as if he had been eating cotton. He was on his hands and knees, looking for a good place to puke, when someone screamed, "Oh, shit! Look at the time! Reveille, God damn it!" Fifteen minutes later he was standing in this formation.

Lincoln came into sight, walking hand in hand with a small boy, surrounded by soldiers and sailors. As he approached, the officers and men were called to attention and the senior man saluted.

Lincoln approached the senior officer and shook his hand. After a moment of discussion the officer indicated Nathaniel. Lincoln came over and said, "Why, Nathaniel! A first lieutenant now? Well done!"

"Thank you, sir." Nathaniel was uncertain if he should salute, since the President was addressing him directly.

"Lieutenant Nathaniel Curry, may I present my son Tad." Nathaniel threw the boy a quick salute, then shook his hand. "Now, Lieutenant Curry, I understand you know the way to President Jefferson Davis' residence."

"I do, sir. Would you like to go there now?"

"I should like that very much."

Nathaniel led the way down Twelfth Street. Along the way many people watched from the sidewalks. Some of them wore Confederate uniforms. It occurred to Nathaniel that the war was still on and that the President was a legitimate military target, but no one molested him.

The sidewalks were also full of colored people of every station. They gave voice to the admiration and gratitude they felt for Lincoln, cheering and tossing their hats into the air. Nathaniel wished to converse with the President, whom he had always found most congenial, but had no chance.

The sentries at the Presidential Mansion wore blue uniforms now and gave smart rifle salutes as the party passed through the front doors. Nathaniel brought Lincoln into Davis' office. Lincoln was interested in everything he saw there and had many questions. "So this was President Davis' desk?" He sat down. "Did he take his correspondence here? Then you've met with him? What is he like as a man?"

Nathaniel answered every question as well as he could. It was passing strange to see Abraham Lincoln seated at Jefferson Davis' desk, with his old stovepipe hat sitting where Davis used to rest his teacup.

There was a knock at the open door. "Begging your pardon, sir."

"Yes, Captain, what is it?"

"We have some trophies, sir. We thought you might like to see them."

"Where are they?"

"Right here. We can bring them right in."

Lincoln came around the desk and stood as a squad of soldiers came in bearing furled Confederate battle standards and unit colors. They lay them on the floor at the President's feet.

Nathaniel had seen such flags flying above many a battlefield. The staffs were worn and notched by bullets, and the flags, though bound tightly around their staffs, were tattered and torn. He could see several Stars and Bars in the pile. He also recognized the colors of the Georgia National Guard and the North Carolina Militia. The smiling soldiers stepped back and stood at attention before their leader.

Lincoln was quite moved by this simple act. "Why, do you know," he said, "for the first time I really feel like a conqueror. This is how Caesar or Alexander of old must have felt."

"Yes, sir," the captain said.

"I have to leave the city now, but have these sent on to Washington, would you?"

"Yes, sir."

Nathaniel accompanied the President outside. A colonel approached and saluted, then asked Lincoln a question.

Nathaniel felt a tug at his sleeve. "Master Nathaniel?"

He turned. It was Rachel and several others of the Swanson slaves. "Rachel!"

"Master Nathaniel, is that President Lincoln?"

"Rachel, where is your mistress? Where is Miss Amanda? Can you tell me?"

"Master Nathaniel," she asked again, "is that Abraham Lincoln?"

"Yes, yes, it is, but you must tell me –"

Rachel and the others turned away from him, their faces lit with a light he had never seen on human faces before. There was another tug at his sleeve, this one more insistent.

He turned. It was Alphonsus Christian in the uniform of a Pennsylvania sergeant-major. "You!" he exclaimed involuntarily.

"Curry," he said, "you're back on your original task now. You and I have to find Lee."

"Lee?"

"He's lit out and Grant is after him. Grant doesn't want to lose contact with him."

"I know where Lee's going. He's—"

"Get up! Get up!"

Both men turned to Lincoln. The Swanson slaves – no, the former Swanson slaves – had knelt behind him and he had just turned and caught sight of them. It was the only time Nathaniel had ever seen Lincoln angry, and it was a terrible sight. He loomed above them, a towering figure in black, and shouted again, "Get up! For, by God, while I yet live, no one will ever make you kneel again!" He took Rachel's hand and pulled her to her feet. The others stood as well.

"Curry!"

He turned back to Christian. "Yes, sir?"

"Where is Lee going?"

"Oh. He's going to Amelia Station. He thinks he's going to get resupplied there, but –"

"Do you have a gray uniform?"

He held up the carpetbag he still bore in his hand. "I have that three-stripe one right here, sir."

"We're both going as buck privates."

"Oh. I have one of them, too."

"Good." He nodded at the Presidential Mansion. "We'll change right in here, then we head west. We'll be stragglers that pick him up."

"Yes, sir. I just have to—" He turned, but Rachel and the others were gone. Lincoln was gone as well, departed on other business; and a few days later he was gone for good, gone from this Earth and from the nation that he had saved and that would never see his like again.

Nathaniel followed Christian into the Presidential Mansion, leaving the street empty.

They rode all night and part of the next day. Their escort, a dozen Connecticut cavalrymen, stopped only to water their mounts and to change horses. They seemed indefatigable, so Nathaniel Curry pretended he was as well.

By eleven the next morning they overtook the Union forces shadowing the Confederates. The Fifth Cavalry, First Massachusetts had received detailed orders by wire and was waiting for them.

A colonel welcomed them to his tent. A quick bite to eat had been laid out for them and they refreshed themselves as the colonel outlined the situation.

"Lee brought his army to Amelia Station," he said. "It seems he was looking for relief there but didn't find any. We're not really sure what happened."

"I think I know, sir," Nathaniel said. "He was expecting a supply train from the south but it had been diverted."

"How sure are you of this, Captain?"

"Quite sure, sir. Uh, I'm not a captain."

The colonel smiled. "Don't you know? These orders include your promotion."

"They do? How did … I mean—"

"I won't tell you what name was on those orders, but—"

"Oh. Oh, I see."

"The next stop is field grade, young man, and I wish you well. Of course, this is only a brevet commission, so you may be demoted again after the war. But it's yours for now." The colonel's accent reminded Nathaniel of Thaddeus Lowe.

"Thank you, sir."

"Good. As I was saying, Lee set out from Amelia yesterday. He tried to head south but we've blocked that. He seems to be moving west, into Appomattox County. His forces are spread out and following as best they can."

"Sir, the supply train he was looking for was diverted to Appomattox Court House. He must be hoping to link up there."

"How do you know this, Curry?"

"I sent the message diverting the train, sir. I'm sure."

"All right." The colonel turned to an aide. "Send word to intercept that train." The aide saluted and left the tent.

The colonel turned back to the spies. "Now, our boys are keeping up with Lee and harassing him but there's still the danger he'll slip away. He's done it before.

"That's where you two come in. Your orders call for you to fall in with Lee. If he breaks contact you pick it up again. Set fire to the woods or something."

"Can you ask your men not to shoot us, Colonel?"

"You'll just have to duck, Curry."

"We'll have to do more than that, sir."

"Well, yes, it's likely you will. Go easy but do what you have to do."

They mounted up and rode past the infantry, down a road marked by the passage of bloody feet. As they drew close to the Confederates they left the road to flank them.

The cavalrymen dropped them off in a small wood, wished them luck and wheeled back toward Richmond. "How are you doing, Curry?" Christian asked.

"Fine, sir."

"How long since you slept?"

"I got a few hours night before last. How about you?"

"I think it was three nights ago that I slept."

Nathaniel shook his head.

"You look like shit."

"Thank you, sir. So do you."

"Well, we should fit right in. Here they come."

They looked out from the wood. The Rebel forces streamed past about a quarter of a mile away. Even at this distance and without his glasses Nathaniel could make out the figure of Robert E. Lee, bowed but unbeaten, riding at the head of his forces.

The forces did little to maintain military order. The men were not marching but walking at ease. The line was thin in places, bunched up in others. Many of the men were unarmed.

Nathaniel glanced at Christian. He was looking at Lee with an expression of pure hatred. No, he realized, it wasn't hatred. Christian looked at Lee like a predator looks at its prey. He wanted Lee, pure and simple. "Curry," he said, "don't call me sir."

"Okay."

"We're back to one stripe separating us." He pulled a bloody bandage from his kit and put it on his head. It was already knotted as if it had been worn before, though Nathaniel had never seen it.

"Why don't you go as yourself?" Nathaniel asked.

"Myself?"

"You're an officer."

"I don't want to ride herd on these fools, I want to blend in."

They stepped out of the woods, pretending they were buttoning their trousers.

"How's your wrist?"

Nathaniel flexed his hand. "All right. I can use it."

"Okay."

"How well can you see?"

Christian scowled by way of reply.

"I need to know what cards are in my hand."

"I can see well enough but I have trouble telling how far away things are when they're close to me."

"Can I call you by your real name?"

"You don't know it."

They fell in at the rear of the army, slouching wearily along with their muskets over their shoulders.

In addition to his musket Nathaniel carried his pistol beneath his tunic and a Bowie knife at his side. He had no idea what Christian had.

The bandage Christian now sported was the perfect disguise. It covered his empty eye socket, hiding the injury. On the side of his head was a bright patch of blood. Whose, Nathaniel wondered, and his reeling brain conjured ranks of bleeding men.

They fell in. The column made its way through an area of open farmland. Ahead of them a section of wood came into view.

Christian said, "Keep your eye on that patch of brush on the right."

"Yeah, the one about a hundred yards up?"

"Yes."

"Yes, I saw that. Come to the other side of the column."

They crossed the road. Christian looked behind them. "Shit."

"What?"

"We're in the thickest part of the column now."

"Something's wrong with my kit," Nathaniel said. "Straighten it out for me."

They halted and Christian moved the pack around on Nathaniel's back for a minute, letting the bulk of the Rebel force drift past them.

Their instincts were right: a minute later gunfire erupted from the bushes ahead of them. Both took cover on the other side of the road.

Some of the men who had come under fire stood still or kept walking; these were cut down. Others fled into the brush on the far side of the road. Still others counterattacked. With the use of their bayonets and a little precious ammunition and at the cost of a few dozen lives the Yankee skirmishers were driven off.

The column, such as it was, formed back up. A second force of Yankees immediately attacked from the rear. They ran up the road, firing and shouting like banshees. As he stumbled for cover, Nathaniel couldn't help thinking that their war cry was not as stirring as the Rebel yell.

These Yankees did not have repeaters. After their initial volley they made a bayonet charge. Nathaniel and Christian fell into the heavy brush at the side of the road. The Yankees, not wanting to scatter their forces, stuck to the road.

Two Union soldiers ventured into the brush after them. Both went after Nathaniel. He pulled his pistol out and pointed it into the air so they could see it. One of the men hung back; the other kept after him.

Nathaniel fired at the man from about ten feet away and missed. A knife flew past his ear and struck the man in the chest, killing him. Nathaniel pointed his pistol at the other man and he fled. Christian reclaimed his knife, wiping his blade on the dead man's sleeve.

They returned to the road. The Yankees were gone.

So was Lee. They were near the end of the column, walking with the wounded, the exhausted and the beaten. They had to hoof it hard to catch up with the front.

An hour later there was a larger engagement. A company of Union infantry attacked the column. The Rebels fired what ammunition they had, then charged into the firing bluecoats with bayonets.

Some men charged without bayonets, swinging their weapons like cavemen wielding clubs. When they lost their muskets they attacked their foe with their bare hands, punching and biting like madmen. Nathaniel saw more than one man reach into his ammunition bag and pull out a rock.

Nathaniel and Christian hung back and watched this. "Did you ever see the like?" Nathaniel murmured.

"No, I haven't. This is like the Spartans at Thermopylae or something. Fighting tooth and nail."

"You mean this could go down in history like them Spartans?"

Christian stepped back onto the road, staggered for a moment and got his feet under him. "This is history, Curry. And you know what? These men look like Hell, but they look damned good, too."

The Yankees were driven off again and the march resumed.

"So you and I are going down in history."

"They are. Not you and I."

"What … what do you mean?"

"Curry," Christian said through clenched teeth, "go into any city of any civilized place in the world. Search every piazza, every palace, every museum. You'll find no graven tablet, no painting, no statue raised to a God-damned spy."

The next attack involved men with repeaters. A number of the Rebels simply halted and turned their weapons upside down in token of surrender.

As the Yanks approached them, Confederates in the rear of the column fired, knocking several of the Federals down. The Federals responded by cutting down the men trying to surrender.

The spies fled from the road, ducking into the long grass on the other side. When things quieted down they went back to the column.

Nathaniel glanced at the men around them. The filthy, starving soldiers wore expressions of grim determination. He thought of the Yankees. They looked grim as well, but hesitant. They knew their cause was nearly won, and none wanted to be the last man to die in the war.

During the next attack Nathaniel repaid Christian by shooting a Union soldier who was running at his back with his bayonet fixed. The man fell against Christian, knocking him to the ground, and died. Christian kicked the corpse off of him, cut the man's canteen strap and took a drink, then threw Nathaniel the canteen.

Nathaniel drank, then said, "Listen, Christian, we're doing more harm than good here. Lee's never going to break contact. All you and I are doing is killing our friends. What say we drop out?"

Christian wavered for a few seconds, his weary head lolling back, then lowered his knife. "No, Curry," he said, "I won't kill you for that. Not this time. Don't say that again, you hear?"

"Okay."

They lifted the dead man's ammunition and rejoined the column.

Gunfire came from the rear. Two men in front of them slowly turned, then gasped in horror. One of them tried to turn his gun muzzle to the ground, dropped it and died picking it up.

Nathaniel turned and his blood ran cold. Fresh troops were pouring in on them. They were well armed and well fed. Their blue uniforms were spruce and there was hatred and death on their black faces.

A man bore straight in on Nathaniel and Christian. "Jesus!" Christian gasped, and both raised their weapons and fired. The Negro's head flew off like a hat in the wind and the man behind him ran over his back. He ran up to Nathaniel and made to stick him with his bayonet, but hesitated. Nathaniel recognized it: the man had never killed before, and as it turned out he never would.

The two ran through the other soldiers, some firing, some surrendering, others just wailing "Niggers! Niggers with guns!" The men in the rear covered their retreat.

Somehow the Army of Northern Virginia broke free again. Christian glanced behind them. "I don't think them niggers liked us too much."

"Can't reckon why."

"I know, I always been partial to niggers myself."

"Yeah, me too."

"What!" shouted the man beside them. "You like niggers? I hate 'em! How can you ... how ... you ..."

The soldier's voice trailed off and an expression, part puzzled, part sad, came over him. He fell on his face, dead. He may have been struck by one of the soft patterings coming from behind them, or been felled by an older wound; or maybe his soul simply decided it was time to skip.

Day's end eventually came. Some men sank to the ground in exhaustion. The rest, having received no order to halt, trudged around them. They had marched all night the night before and would do so again tonight. Let the Yankees take the men who had fallen out.

"I thought you were supposed to hold it with the point down."

"Yes, that's what you always see in stage plays, isn't it?"

"Yes."

"You can do that if you're coming up behind someone." The knife floated in the air and Carl was holding it point down. "With the element of surprise. It's nice because you can strike a lot harder."

"But not from the front?"

"A man would see it coming a mile away." He spun the knife with his finger and the point was up. "This way you can hold it low. Even if he sees it he can't block it."

"Okay, so like this?"

Carl's hand was on his. "Hold the blade turned horizontal like this or it'll get stuck between his ribs."

"That could be embarrassing."

"This way, it might hit a rib, but just try again and you'll be in the money."

"God damn it, nigger! I hate that look in your eye."

"You had just better hope it's not the last thing you—"

"Curry!" Christian shouted. "Wake up!"

Nathaniel stumbled and caught himself. "I'm awake. I wasn't asleep."

"I'm not your sergeant, I'm not going to shoot you. But I've had to pull you back on the path three times."

"Talk. Let's talk."

"Okay."

Nathaniel drew both hands down his face. "Did y'all ever figure out that letter?"

"The one you rubbed the pencil on?"

"Yeah."

"No. Couldn't get no sense out of it."

"Oh."

"Why did you do that with the pencil?"

"I wanted to see the scratches better."

"Scratches?"

"What, don't you know about that? I guess Sally never told you."

Christian frowned. "What the Hell are you talking about?"

"That letter had scratches on it and it made words in Morse code."

"It did? No, Sally never told no one about that."

"She was bad, you know."

"Yeah. I know. When she recruited you I thought you must be bad, too."

Nathaniel glanced at him. "I'm not."

"Ever find out what happened to David Miller?"

Nathaniel pulled the envelope Sally had given him from his tunic and handed it to him. Christian took the letter out and read it, then handed it to Nathaniel.

Nathaniel hadn't even looked at the letter yet. It was a single page, in a woman's hand, and it was only the last page of a longer letter. He looked at the signature, then stopped and read the rest:

> some place where David at least will be safe.
>
> I met with the household slaves last evening to discuss the situation. We agreed that we should stay a family for the moment and succor each other. We will wait for a better day to decide our next steps.
>
> We have a cook you have never met. She came as my mother's dowry and is ancient beyond reckoning. She is known to me only as Mrs. Norris. She is like most of her race unlettered and has in recent years grown utterly deaf. The question arose as to how we might inform her of what was transpiring. She never leaves the house and must know precious little of the world beyond our hitching-post.

Crassus, a boy of about ten, said that he would explain things to her. He went to the tack-house and returned with a piece of chain about two feet long. He wrapped the ends of the chain about his wrists and went to the kitchen. Rachel and I, curious, followed.

She was cleaning a pot as we came in. He approached her slowly, his hands before him. She watched him, utterly perplexed. Then he stopped and pulled his wrists apart. The chain fell to the floor, and she dropped the pot and sank to the floor, weeping.

At that moment, my love, the scales fell from my eyes. I can but tell you that you were right and I was wrong. There is more that must be said, much more, but it must wait until I can say it to your face.

They are here. I know not how this letter may reach you, or if we will ever meet again. Know, however, that

> I remain
> Your loving
> Amanda

"Christ Jesus!"

"You won't want to have that letter found on your person."

"You're right." He dropped it on the road.

"Where'd you get that?"

"Sally."

"How'd she get it?"

"I have no idea." He gave Christian a venomous glance. "What do you know of this?"

"Not a thing. Where you see her?"

"In the hospital in Richmond. She was blind and her heart was a-going."

"It caught up with her, huh?"

"Reckon."

"Christ. Give me a battlefield death any day."

"I know." A thousand questions roiled in his head but he pushed them aside for another day.

"Did you finish her?"

"No. I'm not sure there's a Hell beyond this."

Christian nodded. "Say, you know where Bobby is?"

"Up at the head, I guess. Want to catch him up?"

"That's our order."

They quickened their pace and made it to the head of the column. A light rain pattered around them.

About noontime Christian fell out. Nathaniel was surprised at how it happened. They were walking near the head of the column when he stumbled and fell to his hands and knees. Nathaniel paused, but Christian didn't rise. The column spread and slouched around the pair. Christian looked like he was praying, or else figuring out how to stand up again, or maybe he was asleep with his eye open. Nathaniel, his mind reeling, could only stare at him. The birds were making an immense racket. It was impossible to know if the enemy was nearby or not.

A strange clarity came to his mind. Christian appeared to him a human being suddenly bereft of humanity, reduced to the state of a beast, unable to stand, unable to speak. What would the Bible say of this development? What would Darwin?

A technical sergeant was minding the stragglers. "Get him on his feet," he barked at Nathaniel. "The Yanks'll shoot him if I don't."

Nathaniel poked him in the ribs with his shin. "Git up," he said, and Christian bestirred himself. He evolved back into a man, pulling himself to his feet on his musket, though he could not yet walk.

Nathaniel could hear no Yankees coming from behind, so they had a few minutes grace. Still, he would clearly have to get him moving. He was considering what to do when seven Yanks, one of them an officer, stumbled onto the road ahead of them. They had their backs to the stragglers and didn't know they were there until someone behind Nathaniel shot one of them in the back.

"Git 'em, boys!" the noncom shouted, and the ensuing volley roused Christian. Nathaniel looked around him. There were about fifteen Rebs there, and they gave the Federals a quick dose of lead.

The Federals were all scouts and probably had no interest in doing any actual fighting. Their captain made a quick decision and ordered them to stand their ground and return fire. Two more men fell, but the other three opened up with repeaters.

The Confederates swore at this unsportsmanlike conduct and reloaded. Nathaniel and Christian stayed low and kept moving. The Federal captain paid for his mistake by watching all of his men die. The Rebels didn't shoot him because he made no move to draw his pistol; he had no musket or saber. The Yanks for their part ignored the sergeant, who was unarmed. When the firing stopped the only Confederates left standing were Nathaniel, Christian and the sergeant. Even the birds fell silent as the four regarded each other.

The Yankee officer stood trembling, sure he was at the moment of death. The others ignored him.

The technical sergeant looked much like every "testicle sergeant" Nathaniel had ever known. He had close-cropped hair and a reddish walrus mustache that hung below his chin. His suspenders and baggy pants showed that in more prosperous times he had been beefy, but his clothes and his skin hung loose now. He glanced back down the trail, then at Christian, who stood right beside him.

Christian turned to the man and thrust his knife into his throat. He misjudged the distance and struck him hard enough to drive the knife out the back of his spine. The sergeant fell, taking Christian's knife with him.

"Christ in Jesus! What you do that for?"

Behind him two men rose from the dead. Nathaniel turned back to Christian. "Yeah!" he demanded. "What did you do that for?"

Nathaniel knew what had to happen next, and it sickened him. This would be worse, much worse, than looking a man in the face and shooting him. He closed his eyes for a second and steeled himself.

The two men advanced on the unarmed Christian. Nathaniel fell in lockstep behind one of them. He reached around his neck with his knife. He muttered, "Sorry, soldier," and pulled back hard. The knife cut both the blood vessels and the large muscle on the side of his neck. The man fell to the ground with a cry. The other man was already dead. Christian put his foot on the sergeant's chest and pulled his knife out. "Come on," he said.

Nathaniel hesitated. "I can't – I don't –"

Christian paused and looked at him. Time stopped for a few seconds; then Nathaniel found the words: "I hope that next time it's me that gets it."

"You won't think that when it's your turn."

He nodded.

As they passed the quaking Union captain, Christian said, "Tell them Christian and Curry are still in play." The officer gave a jerk and nodded his head.

Christian looked at Nathaniel. "If you really can't do it, go ahead and drop out. You can be this fellow's prisoner."

He shook his heavy head. "Let's go."

"It's because *he* asked you to do it, isn't it?"

"Reckon."

"You're really his nigger, aren't you?"

They started down the road again. There was no sound of fighting anywhere. A bird muttered something to its neighbor and a few seconds later the trees were as raucous as before the shooting started.

"Everyone is somebody's nigger, Curry. You could do worse."

In the early afternoon they arrived at Appomattox Court House. The army was ordered to halt and fall out. All eyes turned to their trusted leader.

Lee looked to be at a loss. It was the only time Nathaniel had seen him so. The tall man on the gray horse turned this way and that, looking for an army he could not find.

Scouts were sent out to find Johnston. The weary soldiers sat on the ground, placing their weapons in stacks. Those who had shoes removed them to rub their sore feet. Ever and again men looked around them, expecting an attack from any quarter. Many slept.

The scouts came back, riding their exhausted mounts hard. They pulled up in front of Lee and spoke to him, keeping their voices low. Lee looked from man to man until the last soldier had spoken and withdrawn.

Lee wept.

General Lee sat upon Traveller and wept. A great groan arose from the dusty soldiers on the ground. Christian turned to Nathaniel and whispered, "This could be it."

"You think so?"

"Yes. I don't think he –"

"*You!* Why, you God-damned Yankee pig!"

Nathaniel turned. "What?"

A soldier was struggling to his feet. "Give me a gun! This here son of a bitch is a nigger-loving Yankee!" He pulled a musket off of one of the stacks and pointed it at Nathaniel.

"What the Hell are you talking about?" Nathaniel demanded.

The soldier responded by pulling the hammer back to full cock, aiming it at Nathaniel's head from three feet away, and pulling the trigger. The hammer fell with a clack.

All the other soldiers nearby were looking at them now, though none got up. A captain made his way through the throng. "What's going on here? Soldier, why are you pointing a weapon at your friends?"

He snatched another musket from the stack. "These here ain't no friends of mine. This man's a Yankee spy and his friend probably is, too."

"How do you know that?"

"Why, he told me he was, don't'cha know. Then he shot me and left me for dead." The soldier pulled up his tunic and revealed the scar of a bullet wound three inches from his navel.

Nathaniel felt the blood drain from his head. If he had not been seated on the ground he would have fainted. "Parker!" he said, or tried to say, as he hadn't breath to speak.

"Let me shoot the son of a bitching bastard, Captain. Let me shoot them both."

"You'll do nothing of the kind, soldier, until we get to the bottom of this," said the captain, putting his hand on the musket and pointing it at the ground.

Other men around them, perhaps in frustration at being cheated out of another meal, started to take up the cry, denouncing Nathaniel and Christian as Yankees. Another officer, a colonel, came up and was briefed by the captain. A minute later all three soldiers were hauled before General Lee.

Lee had by this time recovered from his shock and coolly demanded to know what was going on. Silas Parker pointed a finger at Nathaniel and said, "This here man shot me in the guts and then he told me he was a Yankee spy. He did it up in Maryland just before the Sharpsville battle. Sir."

"You're nuts. General, sir, this man is crazy. I never shot him."

"Are you sure about this, soldier? For I know this man…" Lee's voice trailed off.

"Sure I'm sure! Look at this."

"Well, someone surely shot you, but what makes you so sure it was him?"

"Search him, General! See what he has on him."

Lee looked around. He had nowhere else to go. "Very well. Captain, please search these men."

The captain came up and thoroughly searched both of them, going through their pockets and kit bags. He even searched the linings of their tunics but found nothing.

This drove Parker nearly mad with rage. "They must have something! Keep looking!" he screamed at Lee.

"Soldier, you're addressing your commanding officer," the captain said. "Watch your tone."

"Look in their shoes! I know they have something!"

"Very well," the captain said wearily, "take off your shoes, boys."

The captain stuck his hand in Nathaniel's shoes and found nothing. He reached into Christian's shoe and looked puzzled.

"Did you find something?" Lee demanded.

"There's a bump in the sole of his shoe, sir. The bump is square."

He pulled the insole out of the shoe, then retrieved a square of paper about an inch on a side. "Look at this, sir. It's very thin, like cigarette paper."

"What is it?" Lee asked.

The captain carefully unfolded the paper. "It lists dates, sir, with a word after each one. March the first, phoenix. March the fifteenth, Gideon. April the first, centurion." He looked up at Lee.

Lee said, "Well, it sounds to me like that has something to do with codes. What do you have to say about that, soldier?"

An officer stepped up and yanked the bandage from Christian's head. There was a stir and gasps.

Christian said, "Well, sir, I am an agent, but on the Confederate side. Those are the current keywords for our codes. You can ask Colonel Norris about that and about me."

"You're a spy for our side? But a minute ago you weren't a spy at all. And as for you, young man, I've seen you come and go and each time you have a new name and a new story. What do you have to say for yourself?"

Nathaniel looked up at Lee. The tears had left dark tracks on the old man's dusty cheeks. He had nothing to say.

"Well, that settles it," Lee said sternly. "I guess you boys know what you're in for."

Christian came to attention and said, "Yes, sir, and you have every right to shoot us. But you might consider letting us live, sir. The war's almost over."

Nathaniel was surprised to hear Christian speak so. He thought that he would face death with defiance, not with a plea for mercy.

"Take them away," Lee said in disgust.

"Shall we –?" the captain began.

"Hold them until I decide what to do. I have to find out what happened to the supply train first."

"Yes, sir."

Nathaniel and Christian sat under guard against the wall of the

Appomattox Court House, their hands bound behind them. The April sun had come out and was drying the damp ground. In the surrounding forest birds were singing. Their guards were both about sixteen years old and it didn't occur to them to keep their prisoners from whispering to each other.

"How's your arm?" Christian asked.

Nathaniel flexed his fingers. "Still hurts. That's a good sign, I guess."

Christian nodded.

"Do you think he'll kill us?" Nathaniel asked.

"What would you do in his place? Would you kill us?"

"Hell, yeah!"

"Well, I'm glad you're not Lee."

"Well, I'm glad I'm not Lee, too. He has some really tough choices right now."

"Yes."

They sat in silence for a minute. Nathaniel said, "Quiet day."

"Yes. So far."

"How long do you think we'll hear these cannon in our ears?"

"You mean the ringing in our ears?"

"Yeah."

"It sounds more like bugles to me," Christian said. "Bugles playing one long note."

"Yeah, but it was the guns that done it."

"Well, yeah. The rest of our lives, I reckon."

"Reckon so."

He listened to the music in his ears for a minute until Christian said, "So we finally won the war."

"Yeah, and we'll die a-winning. These boys will lose but they'll live."

"Yeah, how's that?"

"That's a hard road for us."

"Yeah."

"I always thought I wouldn't live out the war," Christian said.

"That's a sad way to feel."

"Well, it left me free to do what I did."

Nathaniel glanced at him. "You think it was worth it?"

Christian thought it over. "I think we would have won anyway, but I think I did my part."

"Yes," Nathaniel said, "I feel that way too."

They fell silent again.

"How did you start in this business, Christian? Did they train you?"

"No, there's no training for this kind of thing. I just took to it."

"Oh."

Pause.

"How come you're doing it?"

"What do you mean?" Christian asked.

"Why'd you come in on this side? You sound like a Southern boy."

"I'm a nigger."

"Oh."

Pause.

"What about you?"

Nathaniel thought about it. "I guess it all started because I wanted to see the balloon."

"A balloon, was it?"

"Yeah. I read in the paper that –"

"Hush, now! Someone's coming."

Epilogue: A Coke and
a Bag of Chips

They were one of the last families to arrive. The Model T Fordor Sedan pulled into what had been until today Dave McCullough's west forty and was now an airfield.

The boy was the first out of the car. He ran around and opened the back door on the other side. He grasped his right wrist with his left hand, then clasped the hand of the old man in the back seat. "Come on, Grandpa," he said, and pulled. Grandpa's feet slid across the running board to the ground and he was up.

Grandpa needed help getting up, but once he was up he was okay.

The aerial troupe had flown over the town twice that morning, both times at treetop level. The first time they had landed at McCullough's and negotiated a price for the use of the field.

The second time they had thrown handbills from the planes. These offered a free flight to the first person who arrived at the show in possession of a handbill, thus guaranteeing the attendance of every boy in town. The handbills displayed a fanciful image of a pilot, his scarf trailing out of the cockpit, shooting Germans from the sky like so many clay pigeons.

The handbills also offered rides for a dollar a minute. As a further inducement the handbill contained legal language absolving Captain Spengler's Flying Cadets of any liability resulting from said plane flight.

The show was in full swing. Young David Dobbs was so excited that he alternated between making his way through the crowd, watching the planes overhead and urging his great-grandfather to hurry. The old man walked along as fast as he could, his left arm crooked before him, his eyes on the sky. David's mother and father were presumably somewhere in the rear.

A loudspeaker was playing Dixieland and above the music an announcer was describing the action: "And here's Debbie again. The Queen of the Wing-walkers is going to attempt to climb up to Lou's plane from the roof of a speeding Chevrolet! This would be a tough stunt for a man, folks, and I don't know if the little lady is up to it. She's got hold of the ladder now, and look!"

There was a sustained "Ohhh!" from the crowd as the announcer, his voice cracking with excitement, cried, "The Chevy is slamming on the brakes! He's run out of field! And look at Debbie! Will she make it to the plane?"

David's enthusiasm for the show abated temporarily as he induced his father to buy him a Coca-Cola and the new snack sensation of 1926, potato chips. He stuffed the greasy chips into his mouth as he and his great-grandfather watched the show.

"And here comes Charlie! That's Charlie Lindbergh on the wing of Captain Spengler's plane, and he's – why, folks, he's fallen off! Can this be it for Charlie? But wait! He's got a parachute and he managed to get it open. It looks like he's going to be – oh, no!"

Five hundred feet above them the tiny black figure fell from the parachute. Charlie plunged to the ground as the parachute fluttered overhead. The crowd screamed in horror.

"He's fallen from the parachute! He's plunging toward the earth! I can't look, folks!

"Wait a minute, ladies and gentlemen, Charlie has a second chute! He hit the silk a second time, just seconds from Mother Earth! Let's have a big hand for Charlie!"

The last plane came in for a landing as "Charleston" was playing. The plane danced down the field, bouncing from one wheel to the other in time to the music. As the pilot cut the switch he kicked the rudder to the left, making the plane ground loop to face the audience. The crowd went wild.

David waited impatiently for a chance to meet the flyers, his autograph book in hand. The pilots were over by McCullough's summer barn, talking to the crowd about flying and signing people up for brief flights.

As Captain Spengler signed his book David asked him, "Where did you learn to fly, mister?"

"I learned it in the war, sonny. That's where the whole world learned to fly."

"What war was that?"

"What war was that! How soon we forget. Why, I mean the Great War, of course. It only ended eight years ago."

"It was only the biggest war in history, my boy," another pilot said. "The captain here was in the Lafayette Escadrille. He made ace before the United States was even in the war."

"Did you fly those planes in the war?"

"No," Spengler said. "They're war-surplus Jennies and they're only training planes. We all learned to fly in them but they never carried guns."

"All right, folks," the other pilot said. "Who's next for a flight?"

The old man stepped forward, a crooked smile on his face. The pilots laughed. "Sorry, Pops," Spengler said. "You'd flunk the physical."

"I'm afraid you're never going to get to fly, old fellow," the other pilot said.

"My grandfather flew a plane in the Civil War," David's mother said proudly.

The pilots laughed again. "I'm afraid not, lady," Spengler said. "The airplane wasn't invented back then."

"Are you sure?" the woman said. "I remember my grandmother used to say that she saw him flying over Richmond during the war, and she knew it was him, too."

"No," Spengler laughed. "These old veterans are full of tall tales. Say, Pops, did you know Abraham Lincoln?"

"Grandpa can't talk," David said. "He had a stroke about five years ago. That's why his arm's like that." He ate the last of the chips and tossed the bag aside.

There were no more takers for flights so the fliers closed up shop, loaded the planes, spun the props and flew away. By this time most of the townspeople had already gone home.

David and his great-grandfather were the last to leave. The two stood watching until the planes had passed over the horizon. "Come on, Grandpa," the boy said at last, turning back to the car.

The old man started to turn but something caught his eye. David's wax paper bag was blowing against the barn in the late afternoon breeze. As he watched, it mounted the wall, then flew to the ground again, making its way toward the end of the barn. Once more it struggled upward, hung in the air for a moment, and then it was gone.

THE END

Notes on some of the historical characters in this story

After the War, Thaddeus Lowe developed new processes for producing hydrogen and ice, started a bank, and constructed a scenic railway, among other ventures. He made and lost several more fortunes along the way and died in reduced circumstances in 1913.

John Wise made more than 400 flights in his aviation career. In 1879 he and a passenger embarked on a flight over Lake Michigan. Days later the body of his companion was discovered floating in the lake. Wise and the balloon were never found.

Little is known of the life of John LaMountain either before or after the War. Some sources say he died in 1870, but a circus advertisement shows him flying in 1877.

General Fitz-John Porter spent most of the rest of his life fighting his unjust conviction at court martial, finally receiving full vindication in 1886.

After the War, James and Ezra Allen made military flights for the Brazilian Army, keeping alive the notion of military aviation.

Please let me know what you thought of this work. Write me at kris@krisjacksondesign.com.

Made in the USA
San Bernardino, CA
13 March 2013